Kanwaljit Deol joined the Indian Police Service (IPS) after a MSc in Physics from Punjab University. She has served in Goa, Delhi and Arunachal Pradesh, among other places. She was also on deputation with the National Human Rights Commission (NHRC). Her previous books include *101 Tips to Survive the City*.

I0646913

The YEAR of the HAWKS

a novel

Kanwaljit Deol

SPEAKING
TIGER

SPEAKING TIGER PUBLISHING PVT. LTD
4381/4 Ansari Road, Daryaganj,
New Delhi–110002, India

First published by Speaking Tiger 2017

ISBN: 978-93-86582-18-8
e-ISBN: 978-93-86582-17-1

10 9 8 7 6 5 4 3 2 1

Typeset in Minion Pro by SÜRYA, New Delhi
Printed at

PROLOGUE

That night he is drawn to his window by voices raised in excitement across the Bagh Wali Gali.

The house of the sardar with the white patka is bathed in the glare of jungle lights, and he watches mystified as soldiers sling ropes down its side. The babel of shouted directions and urgent commands from across the wall, the jarring scrape of metal against masonry, and a heavy piece of machinery lumbers upwards in heaves and starts. At dawn it squats on the roof like a huge toad with a tube stuck into its belly; its nature is revealed at first light when with a sudden rumble it emits a series of loud, angry bangs.

From the Bunga, a shower of rubble sprays the farthest corners of the parikarma. Another series of bangs and the fortifications atop the water tank, the sandbags, the bricks and mortar, disappear into oblivion.

Men fly through the air like rubber acrobats.

'Bhhenchod!' someone says.

The shout in his heart leaps like a hot white flame.

We are in it now! At last, the enemy! At last the clear, the justified response!

He is finished with the bitter after-taste that licks the heels of every action.

Gratitude flows out of him like a prayer.

A man must do what he has to do.

The sun, like a blister on his skin, stings in every pore, and he has a sudden desire to tear off his clothes. In a surge he lifts his turban, and whooping, holds it high above his head.

'Come, you bastards!' he roars at the invisible enemy.

A bullet snatches the turban out of his hands to send it spiralling up, up, through the air. In spite of himself, he whimpers.

As the sun makes its slow journey across the sky, splintering the dust, they wait, their rifles snug in the holes made for them. The roof of the Guru Nanak Niwas is untidy with bricks and jagged mortar, baking hot. A fly buzzes in his ear, pleading for blood. The day passes. Darkness descends in slow, agonizing steps.

At eleven o'clock the night explodes.

The fortifications on the North Clock Tower open up on the soldiers assembling in the square outside. A cheer rises on the roof, but dies an instant later when earth-shaking booms still the sound of rapid fire.

'Oi maan di… They're using tanks!'

And before they can stop him, he is running. Down the stairs, and across a ladder bridge, across the langar roof, then down another ladder, and on to the marble parikarma, hurtling towards the Clock Tower where the battle is…

1

In hottest summer, the long school break of 1982.

Under the shade of a Peepal tree, the boys, the children of Moranwale village in Central Punjab, gather at the village pond. New competitions are invented every hour: who can spit the furthest, whose legs and arms are longest, who can flick his tongue to the tip of his nose. This last has the tenth class boys stretching their lips in cadaverous grins and rolling their eyes, till Fareed, with his tongue sore and dry, gives up, and starts the collapse into laughter. Only Jeeta continues to show off, his pink tongue darting in and out to lick the insides of his nostrils again and again.

'*Kutte da nak*, dog-nose,' Fareed calls out. 'Parrot-beak. Buffalo-face.'

But it has no effect. Jeeta never wins at anything and no one's going to stop him from squeezing every drop out of this victory.

God has been generous with Fareed and stingy with Jeeta in almost every department. While Fareed is tall and fair with light brown eyes and a straight, sharp nose, Jeeta is small and dark, with a flat nose that flares widely below his slit eyes. Even after all these years, Jeeta can manage no more than a puppy paddle in the pond, a violent splashing that moves his body not an inch, and when they play at chasing each other in the branches of the tree, Jeeta, clinging for life to the lowest limbs, is always the first one out.

From year to year, the boys have measured their growth

against the girth of the Peepal. Scratched the span of their arms with their names in Gurmukhi into its milky bark. And no one yet has been able to match the two vertical lines that proclaim, like the ends of a ruler, the expanse of Dilsher Singh's arms.

Shera, as he is called, has taken a breathtakingly quick leap into manhood leaving them all behind. The densest patch of shade is reserved for him and his two friends, as they lounge among the roots talking lazily to each other about college, village events, and about girls. Even about Women. When the sun starts to lose its heat they enter the pond and swim, arrow-like, to race each other to its opposite end, where another Peepal tree trails its branches over the water and the village cremation ground. Later, when the yellow haze turns to orange, they return to climb into the tree, balancing on its longest branches to dive straight into its central depths.

Shera braves the highest branch. High enough to make him look small and intensely important against the sky as he lets go of all support, and inching closer to the edge, raises his arms so slowly that on the ground the muscles of every neck craned upwards is shot through with sweet agony Not looking below or about, but straight, always straight ahead, he springs off, jack-knifing through the air to cut the water with a modest splash as hoots of applause shake the community that peoples the pond.

Fareed's cheers sound hollow to his own ears. His chest will never flare out like Shera's, nor his upper arms swell like football bladders. Only two years behind Shera's eighteen, he is still a head shorter. His daily searches in the mirror reveal cheeks and upper lip still smooth as a baby's. The virility that promises to him in urgent whispers every night never seems to deliver.

'Bet you're dreaming you could do that, Cat-eyes,' says Jeeta, blundering in, as always, when he's least wanted. 'You'll break your neck and run hollering home to your mother.' And Jeeta is the closest friend he has.

'How will I run hollering home if my neck is broken, dog-nose? I will be dead, floating on that slimy bitch of a pond.'

'With your buttocks in the air!' And thrusting out his bottom Jeeta waddles about clutching his sides and rolling his eyes, pretending more than actual, that he is helpless against the waves of laughter that engulf him.

So it is the simplest thing to jump him. And, with a foot levered between his ankles, to wrestle him into the ooze at the water's edge. And then, to set the horse-play free, so that it teeters every second towards a serious fight. The coils of hair on their heads unwind, whipping their cheeks as they grapple, trailing in the mud like rats' tails

Shera, emerging after his dive, steps on Jeeta's head that has, at just that moment, been thrust under the water, and shouting, leans down to grab Fareed by his hair and lift him out.

'What has he done that you're out to kill him for, *hain*?' he asks, thrusting his face into Fareed's.

Struggling in his grip, Fareed whines, 'Nothing. We were just playing.'

But Jeeta, leaning on his hands, coughing and retching liquid mud into the water, gives the lie to that statement.

'Playing, *hain*? Come outside then, *bhhenchod*, and I'll play with you a little,' says Shera, shaking Fareed like he was a fish.

They wash in silence, each absorbed in digging out the grime from various orifices. Walking back in a cloud of dust behind a group of buffaloes ambling homewards, Fareed is sullen and mean-mouthed; Jeeta swollen-faced but placid.

'I'm going to jump off the highest branch. Tomorrow.'

Jeeta, stopped in his tracks by Fareed's eruption, hurries to catch up with his friend. 'You're not!' he says. But Fareed turns on him a look so drenched in scorn, that even Jeeta understands that his friend was speaking only to himself.

The road from the pond turns along an orchard of guava and

prickly ber after which Jeeta's path breaks off. Fareed, crossing a lane just wide enough for a tractor, arrives at a big blue door studded with iron nails black as old coins. There is a cement seat outside on which he sits, steeling himself to enter his house. His father's house.

It is never really good to come home.

*

The trepidation has started to build up, as it always does, at the turn along the orchard. He goes hurriedly over the events of his day, chalking up all that could possibly be counted against him, and weighs the chances of information about it having already reached home before him. Which involves detailed consideration of his father's daily circuit—the fields, the gurudwara, the booze-shop—and the opportunities it could have offered would-be sneaks. There were spies everywhere in the village; only he tended to forget about them till he took that turn at the orchard. Then they all lined up in his imagination with their vicious motives: some rudeness, someone who was jealous of his looks, some hurt pride. By the time he reached the blue door he was always in a state of high nervousness, eyes darting to left and right, nostrils flaring to the scent of danger.

Inside the door the outer courtyard is deserted, as is the veranda along its right, the room it leads to, his father's baithak, bolted from the outside. The old man isn't home yet. At the far end of the courtyard, the five buffaloes chew the cud of peace, the single white cow noses the stale fodder in its manger. When his father is sitting in his chair in the veranda, dominating man and beast, they chew faster, filling the courtyard with futile clicks of their blunt, broad teeth.

Apart from the baithak the outer courtyard contains the bathroom, the cattle-shed, the five outdoor mangers and the half of the well they share with the neighbours. As Fareed walks towards the arch that leads to the inner courtyard, a bucket crashes against the wall of the well from the other side, and he yells '*Hoi, hoi!*'—his stock challenge to the sound when he was a child.

The hum of the fodder machine fills the inner courtyard and, undetected, he approaches the kitchen, where his mother, pounding ginger and garlic in the stone mortar, is startled by his hands grabbing her suddenly from behind. She laughs a breathless, hurried laugh before her features resume their pinched mould that tells him everything is normal, unremarkable. It is safe to proceed to the fodder-shed and join the two boys who tend the cattle.

For a few minutes he gives himself up to the sweaty, male activity of feeding the greens into the jaws of the electric machine. Lifting huge sheaves of mustard and lucerne, he pushes as close to the blades as he can without slicing off his fingers. Faster and faster he goes, just to see the boys' shining faces laugh at his parody of a fast-motion-film. Then, patting each brown back, he puts on his shirt and walks lightly to where his sister, Dishan, sits under the naked bulb with a frown of concentration fixed on the lentils she is cleaning.

She looks up to smile at him with an air of conspiracy that affirms the day is surviving, could well survive till nightfall, and to bed-time beyond.

'There's enough light,' he says, switching off the bulb.

'Put it on, Veera,' she pleads. 'Don't blame me then, if you break your teeth on the stones in your dal.'

He switches on the light, then off, then on again, her squeals of protest goading him. Dishan, two years younger than him, already seems more of an insider to the world, and it is with vengeance at being so unfairly overtaken that he torments her.

'Faree*daa*,' his mother calls from the kitchen. She can be tormented too. He has only not to reply. He tiptoes up the stairs with her voice 'Freed*aa*! *Fareed! Son!*' trailing behind him.

From the parapet of the terrace he looks down the road which, right-angling outside their door, heads to the centre of the village, to the gurudwara and beyond. He can see the white dome of the gurudwara where his father's father, Babaji, the old, old man, will be sitting with the other white-beards by the long dry well of the gurudwara. Talking, no doubt, about what Sant Harchand Singh Longowal said at the World Sikh Convention and how Sant Jarnail Singh Bhindranwale reacted. Both Sants, but as different, Babaji would say, as water and fire. It is clear the two are rivals now, and Babaji fears that the hatred spread by Bhindranwale will win, especially with the youth and the people of the villages.

Babaji, retired from the army as an honorary captain, has opinions that are treated with respect by all. He reads the English *Tribune*.

Sometimes Fareed asks to hear his stories of the Great War where white men fought each other, only to marvel at the image of this old man, whose left eye waters continuously, as a youthful soldier fighting battles in strange, sandy deserts. He never doubts the truth of the tales but that the wasted, hairless legs he massages each night could have jumped in and out of trenches—that is too intriguing a possibility to imagine.

He will go down to the gurudwara soon to fetch his Babaji for he is notorious for falling when the light is low, especially now with the road being paved and broken bricks lying all around.

He sees his father turn the corner in front of the gurudwara and come to a lurching halt before its gate. Perhaps he is planning to bring his father home himself. No, he is merely stopping to have a word with Bhaiji, the priest. Doubtless, more about Bhindranwale, for no one talks of anything else these days, especially since after his arrest, young men out on motorcycles have opened fire in market-places killing and injuring dozens of Hindus in places like Jalandhar and Tarn Taran. It is a short conversation and Fareed watches his father turn towards the house and negotiate the half-bricked bit without a problem. He still has all his senses about him, his father, no matter how drunk he is.

Climbing off the parapet, Fareed goes inside—no sense in showing himself before he has to.

*

On the side away from the pond, the Peepal extends a long branch on which hangs a pair of rope swings. Here the girls sometimes gather, chattering and singing as they push their little brothers and sisters in the swings, for girls need a pretext to have fun. On the pond-side the boys carry on like nothing is different. Only their voices go gruffer, their breaststrokes acquire a measured grace and the space around the tree becomes a battlefield where furtive looks twang like random arrows, swiftly back and forth.

The prettiest of the girls is Khushwant—golden skin, long brown hair, big clear thick-lashed eyes, a waist like the neck of a sculpted pot. She has been in the same class at school with Fareed and Jeeta for ten years, but she might as well have been on another planet. Each class, from Class 1 onward, has been split down the centre by a three-foot aisle down which the teacher patrols, stick in hand. A stick that connects promptly with one's knuckles; as Fareed found out years ago when he leaned across to borrow a pencil from a girl.

At the gurudwara where the village gathers every Sunday to hear the Gurbani, the same pattern is followed. After making their obeisance before the holy Granth, families that eat and sleep together instinctively split up, each member going left or right according to their sex, for young or old, crippled or healthy, no one has ever violated the sacred aisle.

In a sense, then, the Peepal, with its pond-side and its swing-side, observes the laws sanctified by education and religion.

Khushwant, her legs outstretched, is on the upswing, her two long plaits trailing behind her as she soars. Her younger brother, abandoned on the ground, whines as Fareed and Jeeta pass, but in accordance with the rules, they pretend to neither see her nor hear his cries as they cross to the pond-side.

Seeing that Shera and his friends are already settled in their usual spot, Fareed makes straight for the tree trunk. Even the girls fall silent, as he climbs slowly, carefully, higher and higher up the tree.

At Shera's branch he stops and risks a quick look downwards: everyone, but everyone, is watching him. An expectant hush has fallen on royalty and subjects alike.

Below him the mosaic of the village spreads out. Pale mud, bright brick, square roofs, open terraces. A breeze that barely stirred the thick heat on the ground, here rustles the leaves, with a sound like the clapping of small hands. Out from the tree, on the swaying branches, he fancies it strong enough to dislodge him and clutches the trunk. The thin branch near the top that he had marked, looks green and tender. Foolhardy. He decides to tackle Shera's branch itself.

At his first step, the branch bows alarmingly under his weight and his hands shoot out to grab at stripling branches to the sides. Waiting to let his breathing steady, he feels the limb accommodate him with an elastic swing. His next step is surer. Ahead is a stretch, a few feet of solo branch, with nothing to hold on to. That is where he has seen Shera stop and then stare straight ahead of him for every step of the way to the point where he dives off.

From down below the white dots of faces stare up at him; he imagines their surprised expressions, incredulous, as he is, that he has survived so far. And then looking straight ahead, he steps out once again with measured steps, not slow, not fast. It is like walking the high wire in a circus. He closes his eyes now, readying for the jump. Then suddenly, impossibly, he turns, walking as he has come, back to the trunk again.

The hubbub of sounds from below comes from another world with which his connection has been broken. Broken and joined to the crown of this shivering tree, so that it is as if both he and the tree, with foot to foot-hold, hand to hand-hold, are specially designed for each other. He knows the branch he's marked will bear his weight as surely as if he has mathematically calculated stress and strain. The speed of his pulse is not from fear, it is a rush of power that fills his chest, makes him feel like a fast ship whose sails are swelling in the wind.

At the last moment, steeling himself for the jump, he finds he is above the forbidden Peepal on the opposite bank and can see beyond it to the cremation ground, where a single plume of smoke hangs unmoving. Old Peelu Chacha, he remembers with surprise, done in yesterday by his asthma.

He jumps then, sailing through the air with Peelu Chacha in his head, to cut a mass of floating green slime right through its heart.

*

So full is his pride in himself that when Dishan screams downstairs, he hardly hears her. Then she screams again and he hears her shout, 'Stop it, Papa. Stop it!'

Another scream, from his mother this time, sends him running out to the parapet from where he sees her on the floor, being dragged by her hair from the kitchen by his father. Her hands are up on her head and her feet are churning the earth in a sliding shuffle to push her body in the direction it is pulled. The two boys have come running out of the machine-shed, making appeasing noises, entreating him to let her go, and Fareed half-turns, then stops, hovering, a tumult in his mind.

Going downstairs means intervening; to be thrown off like

a fly by his father's big calloused hands, bigger than anybody's. Flung around heedlessly when he is drunk they slam into you like bricks in the dark. Best to say, 'He's at it again', and stuff your fingers into your ears. That's the way he has managed all these years. He is not in control here, has never been in control.

Yet that was a real force—that wind that swelled his chest in the tree. But he wasn't opposed there—not by a brute, bloodthirsty beast. He would never be...Never. Unless...

He takes the stairs two at a time and catches his father's arm on the upswing. Talking, talking all the time, through teeth clenched at the befuddled face turned to him. 'Stop it. Beast! Don't hit her. Mad man! Bastard. Stop.'

His father looks puzzled, as if he's been dragged from sleep. For a second, time pauses as their two faces explore each other, motionless. Then he feels the forearm in his grip enlarge, and his feet leave the ground. He is swinging in the air by his fingers now, but his nails are digging in, refusing to let go. Nothing matters now, not his mother's voice whining at him, not Dishan's urgent calling, not even his own voice, so different, so thick and guttural, meeting his father's, roar for roar.

The old man swings to hit him left-handed, getting his teeth at an awkward angle. Probably hurt himself. Not Fareed, who clings on still. For life now—the survival instinct. He will not let go. Cannot. It is the two boys who, grasping his waist and adding their strength to the old man's in gross betrayal, bring him down. So that he is now the prey, presented for the kill.

A part of him is running, out the door, on the road, already at the gurudwara, crying, 'Babaji! Babaji. You have to come home. I've come to fetch you. You must come home.' But the other part stumbles, backing off, bending slyly for the wood pestle—the thick, unholy club, dragged out of the kitchen with the body of his mother. Legs wide apart, he stands with the head-crusher in his hand, keeping the mad man at bay, silent, breathing like a horse, his eyes challenging, 'Hit me you bastard. Come on. Hit me.'

His father's red eyes bulge as if they'll burst, and like a shiver he knows the something that passes between them, something toothed and burning, but at its heart cold as ice, hard as steel.

And then the old man turns, and walking like he was sober, heads out of the arch to the outer courtyard.

2

The nineteenth of May, 1982. Fareed's life is changed forever.

A month before his sixteenth birthday, he has learnt that to win you must step out, ready to lose everything.

To his brother, Randhir, 'Randy' in San Jose, USA, he plays it as an outright victory.

'*You remember my jagged tooth?*' he writes. '*The one he broke with a single blow when I was twelve? The selfsame one it was that cut him. A great big gash across the soft part of his hand—it won't heal for many days. He bled like a chicken with its head lopped off. I thought I was done for, his eye was murderous. So I picked up the ghotna, which had been dragged out with Ma. I wish you had seen him then...*'

The neat revenge, the tooth and the ghotna, his father's weapons, turned on himself, that's what he embroiders on, preferring not to dwell on the times when, alone in his room in the heat of the afternoon, a hollow longing for something forever lost, buzzes fitfully inside him like a dying fly.

'*I didn't abuse him,*' he writes. '*At least not the really bad ones I've learnt since you left. All abuses in any case have to bring in his mother, sister, daughter or wife. All our good relatives. But I remember saying Mad Man—our secret term disclosed! I might even have said Bastard. Rest of the time I growled strange sounds*

*that even I did not understand. It made him really mad. You
would have been proud of your little brother then.'*

*

A Mahabharat, a war of wars, had been fought in the house
before Randhir finally went to the States. He has done nothing
to deserve it, the old man said. A third-class BA left you fit only
to clean utensils, and that could be better done in Ludhiana than
in Louisiana. That way it would be our own non-beef-eating
brethren's spit he'd be cleaning.

Babaji was more reasonable. It was far better to clean utensils
in America, he said, it paid more, and the people at home didn't
come to know about it. Who knows he may even pick up some
respect for the dignity of labour and not balk at farming his own
fields? One of Babaji's pet theories was the collapse of the green
revolution and the decline of Punjab because the Jat youth didn't
want to farm. 'What's there left to farm, anyway?' was Randhir's
rejoinder. 'The green revolution's at saturation point, the land
is yielding all it possibly can. On plots like handkerchiefs, you
need technology; the kind that comes with dollars.' And his
father would cut him off with a guffaw that made rubbish of
all his college talk.

It was Babaji eventually who made his father let Randhir go.

'Why did we educate him, Kartare, if we wanted him to do
the work of a seeri, a farm-boy?' he said. 'Even if he's ready for
agriculture, the seeris will do it better than him.'

'So *I'm* a seeri, then? You went away to soldiering and your
brothers did the farming. When it was my turn, did I balk? Say
I wouldn't get my knees dirty? But now I'm a seeri. Something
my son is too good to be.'

'Times were different then,' said Babaji, gently, almost like
an endearment, almost as if he'd called him billiya, little cub, a
term he used with his grandchildren still. 'He's never going to
work the land. Let him go.'

'Let him go, let him go, *let him go.* As if I am holding him like a woman. It needs money, Bauji, something I don't have. Something he, with his paid-for college education, and you, you too with all respect, can't seem to understand. Except in words. Words.' And then the *Huunh*! with which the old man ended every emphatic offering.

'Give him his share in the land. Let him do what he must,' said Babaji quietly.

This was blasphemy.

From the moment of their birth his father has feared his sons. Known they were up to no good; that they had taken birth simply to usurp his land. And his wife, a female serpent, had given birth to them, fed and nurtured them, solely so they could one day grow up and wreak vengeance on him, their own father. Their share in the land!

'Snakes nursed in my bosom!' he would mumble to the fading light as he sat on the veranda of his baithak, nursing his glass of flaming-orange country liquor. This was the way he began, the build-up. And after he had worked himself up into a frenzy and flung himself around like a whirlwind leaving a trail of devastation around the house, this is the way he would end.

'Snakes!' Muttering and mumbling; trailing off into the silent night.

Eventually no land was sold—there wasn't much to sell anyway, after the land ceilings had come. Returning from the sale of the harvest in Ludhiana with bloodshot eyes he had given Randhir the twenty thousand rupees for the ticket. To his attempt at thanks he had slurred, 'Go and make a hijra of yourself. Don't ever come back.'

'A hijra, a eunuch!' Randhir had exclaimed later, clutching at his manhood, as if he really believed in the old man's dark powers, the black spot on his tongue. Or whatever.

Irony that Randhir got his first job as an agricultural labourer in California; a fruit-picker in season.

'A bloody seeri,' his father said, 'on someone else's land. *Huunh!*'

But now that Randhir owns a Japanese car and a partnership in the gas-station where he works, the Mad Man acts like he never existed. As if the extra money that comes into the house and allows him to drink dark rum instead of the orange rot-gut, arrives from some magician in the skies.

*

He hasn't always been like this, his father.

Fareed remembers a time, being led to the fields. Randhir, six years older, kicking up the dust ahead, and his own small hand exploring the earthen crusted ridges of his father's. A hand that feels so homely, and yet, with its blunt and cracked squareness, seems to secure his world; to be the sentry against its fears. Or on his cycle, Fareed safe in the circle of his arms, perched on the bar in front; Randhir on the back and the cycle producing familiar creaks, as if it too were a part of the family. His father has to lean hard on the pedals on the rutted track, and each time his warm breath tickles the short hairs on Fareed's neck, the boy giggles in short breathless spurts.

It was towards Randhir that the old man first changed. As if he had woken up one morning and seen in the twelve-year-old boy with his long hair full of lice, a whispered threat. Not that he'd never hit them before, but there was a difference. Slaps became blows; scoldings, curses. The knot of hair on Randhir's head became a handle, convenient to pull and drag him with, to throw him on the ground and to hold him there, hard and steady, for the well-aimed kick. Although Fareed was left alone, there came a change in him too, and with that his father too, changed towards him.

In the dark little kothri room under the stairs, the mice scampered over a growing mound of empty bottles, sometimes shattering the fermented gloom with a startling avalanche of tinkling glass. His mother, a prisoner, walled in by silence and tears, and Dishan a bewildered toddler. Babaji, growing suddenly limp and tired so that you said, 'By God, he's an old, old man' to yourself.

And Randhir, a prisoner too, but cunning, watchful, skittish as a colt.

Fareed himself smouldering, uselessly fuming away his anger. For years.

Yet today, at the beginning of freedom, needing to poke about in the embers of his victory for a lukewarm elation.

His face in the mirror is new: he feels shy, ashamed almost, to meet the stranger in its eyes. He has put it there, this stranger, and now is unsure how he can measure up to its demands. In short, how is he to live from now on?

And, although in the letter to Randhir he makes it sound as if his father has been cured of wife-beating for ever, he knows already that things could never change that much.

For his mother they'll probably be worse.

*

In 1849 the Sikhs thought they had lost the Second Anglo-Sikh War. The British, who thought *they* were losing, arrived at dawn to find the battlefield deserted and, to their astonishment, snatched victory out of certain defeat. For Fareed the process is reversed. Out of his victory he has snatched defeat, and his father, in his defeat, has won.

Sitting at his typewriter three hundred miles away in Delhi, Sikand muses that it is often like this with the Sikhs. Victory and defeat are like two faces of a coin at the end of a chain, twirling this way or that at the whim of the breeze. From a ragtag band of warriors on horseback snapping at the tails of the armies that raided the land of the Indus each year for plunder, the

Sikhs had risen to a formidable power that spanned in 1839 the entire basin of the Indus—from Afghanistan to the Sutlej, from Kashmir down to Sind. Yet, within ten years, they had lost it all. Their infant Maharajah had been separated from his mother, and consigned, along with the Kohinoor diamond he wore in his turban, to the charge of British nannies.

Sikand is a journalist, a gaunt forty-year-old. Not a journalist alone, but one often referred to as a man of a myriad talents. His photographs—not those of his leathery yet rather wistful face, but those taken by him—win prizes. Hang in galleries and museums. He thinks of himself as an analyst: history, politics, sociology, geography, even biology and literature, are merely tools for the musings of his mind. Time has marked his face, not with laughter or worry, but with muse-lines, varied and changeable as those the sea makes on the seashore.

As an analyst, what Sikand hates are concepts. Pre-digested knowledge is anathema, like someone else's food regurgitated: he will not go within a sniff of it. That is why the history of the Sikhs that he has just typed out, from the birth of the Khalsa to the advent of Bhindranwale, is only a paragraph—all that he needs to launch off from.

*

'The Khalsa was born on the Baisakhi of 1699, a culmination of a movement started by Guru Nanak in the 1500s as a monotheistic gathering of the strings from the Hindu pantheon. Guru Gobind Singh, the tenth and last Sikh Guru, gave it it's distinct outward identity—the long hair, the comb to dress it, the long underwear to replace the dhoti, and the weapons of the iron kara and the kirpan. These 5 K's of Sikhism characterised them as the militant arm of Hinduism, a virulent gene they had picked up along the way and have not been able to shed till today. Guru Arjan Dev, the fifth Guru, who built the Golden

Temple in Amritsar, was martyred in the cause, as was Guru Teg Bahadur, the ninth Guru, who presented himself before the Moghul court of Aurangzeb as the protector of the Hindus of North India. Guru Gobind Singh, the tenth and last Guru, lost each of his four sons in the course of the struggle. These martyrdoms form a moving part of the Sikh scriptures, the Guru Granth Sahib, and even today, all prayers end with a lingering tribute to the martyrs. After the Moghuls, the Sikhs, under the formidable leadership of Ranjit Singh, the one-eyed Maharajah of a prosperous Punjab that spanned the Indus, found a new enemy in the British. It took countless skirmishes and two major wars for the British to subdue the Khalsa, the battle of Chillianwala in the Second Sikh War bringing the British the closest, by their own admission, to losing the Indian Empire. But the British were generous in victory and within eight years had the Sikhs on their side when the Mutiny of 1857 threatened the empire. Independence came, and with it the partition of Punjab: half a million dead in a mass move across a border that no one claimed later to have agreed upon. Hindus, Muslims, Sikhs, all were deprived, but the loss of the land was a loss that hit the farmer worst, and the farmers of Punjab were the Sikhs. That is where a moot point was to arise: alienated from acres, they invested what was left with Godliness; and their tools— water, fertiliser, seed and soil—with the status of reliquaries. The Akali Dal, a farmers' political party, took on its mantle of quasi-religiosity. To agitate for the distribution of river water for irrigation was on par with demanding holy status for the city of Amritsar. Yet the party's attempts to mean all things for all Sikhs were frustrated. Although it gained control of the Sikh temples, the gurudwaras in Punjab, the Akali party could not gain control of the minds of all the Sikhs, especially of those who were not farmers. And anyway, the Sikhs constituted only 48% of the population of post-Independence Punjab. The Akali struggle then, was to carve out a Sikh majority state and to extend their hold to gurudwaras outside Punjab. All the while, trying to forge a fusion of interests in their fractured electorate, so that the 48% would vote en bloc. For the Congress Party, the party of Freedom, which counted its voters over a broader spectrum that included Sikhs, it was suicidal to let these efforts succeed. Its particular dilemma was how not to seem to oppose the legitimate demands of the Sikhs, and yet to undermine those who articulated these demands. Enter Bhindranwale.'

It is a long paragraph, but then Sikand is a practical man.

*

Enter Bhindranwale. In springtime. When each seed in its snug hole-bed clenches its energies for the last great push.

Prime Minister Indira Gandhi says Bhindranwale is not a good man, and the Akali party are wrong to support him. The Akalis reply that her Congress has supported him for two years and they only for twenty days. The talks between the Akalis and Indira Gandhi's government break down, are resumed, break down. And all this time Punjab is in optimum ferment, warm with expectation of the incubus.

After she returned to power in 1980, the prime minister was wary of all those who had opposed her during the Emergency and thereafter, including the Akalis. To add to her woes, her years in the wilderness gave an opportunity to the Hindu right to organize itself, raising the spectre of the Congress being deserted by its majority Hindu voters. The Anandpur Sahib Resolution, a document articulating Sikh demands first drafted by the Akalis in 1973 and redrafted over and over again till 1978, was projected by the Congress government as communal in tone and theocratic in intent. So confusing has the document become that Sikand has to re-read it to verify his earlier impression: that it asks for a genuine federal structure and more powers for Punjab under the constitutional framework. Except for the religious overtones that the Akalis can hardly avoid, he sees it is innocuous. Besides creating apprehension about the Sikh demands, the Congress also seems to have overplayed its hand by promoting fringe organisations like the Dal Khalsa and individuals such as Bhindranwale. The Akalis have been destabilised no doubt, but so he fears, has Punjab.

Sikand has contacts from the old days, his heady years with the Press Information Bureau when, freshly returned from England, he still believed that working with the Government was the best way to make a difference, when Indira Gandhi was still acquiring her warrior-goddess image, riding the tiger. When the nation paused with bated breath as she audaciously carved Bangladesh out of Pakistan, and then, in tumultuous applause, voted her into absolute power. Her fledgling days, as they had been his own.

'Why should she give in to the Akalis?' his contact from the Congress party asks. 'We have twelve of the thirteen parliamentary seats from Punjab. For the state assembly too, we polled many more votes than the Akalis. Why should Indiraji make them look good to the Sikhs, you tell me?'

'But their demands,' Sikand protests. 'Many of them are genuine grievances of the people of Punjab. This distribution of river waters. And Chandigarh, which we all know was built as their capital to compensate Punjab for the loss of Lahore.'

'Genuine demands, yes. It's not like Indiraji isn't concerned about the grievances of the people of Punjab.'

'But if something isn't done soon on the genuine demands, they'll lose faith in the talking process. That can't be good.'

'But why should she concede anything to the Akalis? Across a table? If she has to make concessions it will be unilaterally. To the Sikhs.'

Sikand wearies. 'So the talks won't be resumed?' he says.

'Oh no, they will. Then they'll break down. Then they'll be resumed again. And so on. The Government will be ever ready to talk.'

He pays scant regard to Sikand's prediction that the humiliation of the Akalis will rally the Sikhs behind them. 'The only man who gains is Bhindranwale,' he says sadly. 'I predict that everyone, politician, farmer or youth will court only him.'

'Why look so tragic, then?' Sikand asks. 'That should make the Congress happy. After all he is their man.'

The man raises both hands into the air. 'Who can harness the wind, Sikandji?' he sighs.

'True enough,' says Sikand, 'Especially when it threatens to become a hurricane.'

In his years at the PIB Sikand had handled media and information, then railways, then parliament, finally ending up in the photography unit, for by then photography had become more than just a hobby. Two years later, tired of the bureaucratic functioning of the organization, he had left to join the *Statesman* in Delhi. His photographs now hung in galleries across the country and abroad, and as he rose steadily in the newspaper, his was a name to follow in the media world.

It took the Emergency to make him lose his faith in newspaper journalism.

Now, once again, Indira Gandhi was displaying the same arrogance that had cost her so dear.

It is not Sikand's job to predict, but how can he resist? To every Indian, worth his Indian salt, prediction is a democratic calling. Even the corner paanwala, who sells him his cigarettes, prophesies freely on subjects ranging from the weather to the national budget.

Sikand forecasts that the treatment meted out to the Akalis by the government will rally all the Sikhs behind them. The Akalis do not agree: unless the government gives them something, anything, a face-saver, they fear they will lose prestige with the Sikh masses, and prestige is pre-eminent if you're a Sikh. At their third meeting with Indira Gandhi they are not offered even a glass of water, and Sant Harchand Singh Longowal, the Akali President, is so insulted, that he vows never to talk to the lady again. There is nothing for the Akali leaders but to return to Punjab, hauling the burden of their injured pride.

*

Fareed does not need the daily lessons he gets from Babaji on reading the *Tribune,* to learn about the murders, bank-robberies, the extortions and dacoities that seem to be occurring almost every day somewhere in Punjab. Ever since Sant Bhindranwale has moved into the Guru Nanak Niwas attached to the Golden Temple, the Harmandar Sahib, young men have flocked to it in droves. The illiterate old men who sit outside the gurudwara in their village know more about it than any newspaper ever reports, and at the booze-shop the uncles, the chachas and the tayas, sit with half-closed eyes enumerating yesterday's toll of people killed by the uggarwadis, as these extremists are called.

Even schoolkids know the score. 'No longer swords and spears. The boys carry automatic weapons now. Fifteen twenty bullets in one burst.' He hears one of them do an imitation of the quick fire. Just a few days before, the Sant has thundered across the state with truckloads of armed men and no one has challenged him. He rails against the Sikhs who have cut their hair and calls them 'patits'—the fallen. The Nirankaris, he says, have no reason to exist.

He pours so much scorn on the Hindus that Babaji is sure he is trying to provoke Hindu-Sikh riots. 'That is the way politicians do it,' he says. 'Make two communities kill each other and it is sure that one will flock to you like bees to honey. They even desecrate their own places of worship to provoke their qaum.'

The paper reports that the police are investigating cases of the Granth Sahib having been found burnt in some gurudwaras. 'No one will ever be found responsible,' he says sadly. 'This is how they play with us.'

The other Sant, Sant Longowal, has finally decided to join forces with Bhindranwale, which Babaji says is a big mistake. 'Longowal is giving legitimacy to someone who says every Sikh boy should keep 200 grenades with him. How can the panth be one with him? Is this what our faith is reduced to? What is going to become of Punjab?'

No one can answer Babaji.

*

Predictions are so popular because sooner or later they all come true, muses Sikand a month afterwards. Frustrated, the Akalis announce they will disrupt the Asian Games to be held in the winter of 1982. 'Over my dead body!' says Bhajan Lal, the chief minister of Haryana, the state that was carved from Punjab in 1966 and lies between it and the citadel of Delhi. Most of the Akali demands, if conceded, will hurt Haryana, and hurt its chief minister where he's most tender. It is not difficult to predict that Bhajan Lal will block all roads to Delhi for the Asiad.

A spectacular opening witnessed by the nation on television, unmarred by so much as a grey flag. Everyone is vindicated. But all Sikhs: Members of Parliament, Judges or Generals, serving or retired, commoners or peasants, are pulled out of trains, buses, cars, at Sonepat, Bahadurgarh, Faridabad.

A sea of turbans washes up at the borders of Delhi.

Shivi, Sikand's Sikh friend and colleague in the magazine, after being stopped at four borders, worms his way through dusty villages to enter the city by a little known route, but feels no pride at his achievement. At the impressive new stadium, a Muslim friend leans across and whispers under the beat of the drums, 'Now you know how we Muslims feel.'

And Sikand is surprised to see Shivi's eyes fill suddenly with tears. While entering the stadium he has been the only one of the group who has been thoroughly searched and frisked. Even now his turban attracts wandering policemen in the stands to hover around their seats.

It is no longer the Akalis alone, an entire community has been banished and sent searching for the comfort of its numbers into the wilderness.

3

In the evening, Shivi is reduced to bathos by a mix of alcohol and humiliation. 'The Akalis represent all Sikhs, that's what they've been trying to say all these years. Bhajan Lal has said all Sikhs are Akalis. And proved it in a day.'

Sikand's antennae are out—testing predictions, hazarding new ones. It's clear he was wrong; it isn't the humiliation of the Akalis that will rally the Sikhs, it is their own. He has to make corrections. 'Have another drink, my friend,' he says. The soda siphon and the clockwork of his mind whir in unison.

'How come you have a name like a surname?' Shivi asks suddenly after all these years.

'It's a short form. It stuck.'

'Short for what?' His eyes have locked on to Sikand's so that he cannot look away.

'Sikandar,' says Sikand, his nonchalant voice ringing false to his ears.

'Oh. Sounds too much like a Muslim name, *hnnh*?'

Sikand has known Shivi to be the most amiable of men. It has to be the alcohol that makes him look so hostile.

'Not at all,' he replies. 'Only too heroic for a man like me.' Sikandar being the Indian name for Alexander. The Great.

Only late at night in bed, when Sikand uneasily projects his knowingness on the evening, does he feel Shivi withdrawing from him and realizes it's more than the alcohol; it's the process by which his prediction is coming true.

His knowingness is alien to Sikand, an impostor set to do him out of his rightful inheritance of knowledge. All his degrees—from St. Stephens, from Cambridge, his History, Political Science and Philosophy, his English, the cold logic of his thinking—all these make him contemptuous of his knowingness. It is a nether consciousness informed by cliché, modified subliminally by the strident cries for attention, the counterfeit currency that the world utters to devalue and to drown the truth. In the guise of emotion, it can even masquerade as the truth.

As he lies awake thinking, Shivi is asleep in the guest room, in the room that used to belong to Sikand's mother before she left him to go and live with her daughter. Damn Shivi for having invoked his knowingness and her voice calling 'Sikandar'. For with that name he is conscious of a reduction, and against that voice, affirming, even from her pale frailness, the claims she holds, he is helpless.

His mother is a Sikh. Left to himself, Sikand's father would probably have called him something innocuous like Ramesh. He had named his daughter Nina, after all. But it was his mother who had to pick a name with its tawdry sheen of History, its odour of the deeds of men.

'When he was hungry, he would bawl like a General,' she would say, justifying herself and sickening him. So much unfinished business there, the weight of her expectations; the strength of her certainties. Even in her absence they hovered—her shadowy representatives.

What his mother had really wanted was for Sikandar to be a Sikh.

The first major fight he remembers his parents having was

over cutting his hair. He was not meant to be listening, but he heard, and his memory dredges it up now. 'Let him decide when he's old enough to understand, Nimmi. Don't burden him with long hair so that he feels like an apostate if he wants to cut it later,' his father had said.

And his mother, as strong about her beliefs as ever, responded, 'Children have to be led, Subhash—that's what parents are for. You can't postpone your responsibility as a parent, delegate it to the future.' Or words to that effect.

Sikand feels sure his mother would have been happier if the young Sikandar had been taken to the temple and had his mundan done like a Hindu, or even if she and her husband had fought over whether to make the boy a Sikh or a Hindu, but this postponement of the decision altogether must have smacked to her of weakness, something that made her blood boil. 'Don't be a weakling, Sikandar!' her voice echoes to him over the chasm of years.

Over toast and tea in the morning, he is short and surly, prompting Shivi to apologise for drinking too much the night before.

'Don't let it worry you,' Sikand shrugs him off. But as mild revenge, he asks, 'Would you agree that to scratch a Sikh is to find an Akali?'

'No.' Shivi is quite definite.

'Think about it for a bit, Shivi. A responsible journalist and writer, a Sikh, said that last year.'

'It isn't true,' Shivi shakes his head with emphasis. 'Not to my mind.'

Shivi is young—well, younger than Sikand—but although he defers to Sikand as his mentor, he is unwilling to be led, to simplify into a stream. He will insist on remaining a wretched droplet. And despite his urbanity, his carefully trimmed beard, his matching turban and tie, he will insist on referring to Sikand's mother as Auntyji.

'I wasn't happy to occupy Auntyji's room last night,' he says. 'I'd rather sleep on the divan like always, if you don't mind.'

'Why make yourself uncomfortable? It isn't her room any more, it's the guest-room. She'll sleep in it as and when she comes. If she comes.'

'It's her bed,' says Shivi. 'She brought it in her dowry. That's what she told me.'

It's a ridiculous, huge India Gate of a bed, its carved legs solid, like the thighs of some voluptuous female wrestler. And a great big headboard that casts a Taj Mahal shadow on the wall, dwarfing all else in the room.

'Thanks for reminding me. I must get a carpenter in to do something with that bed. Do you think it'd make a sofa?'

Shivi looks horrified.

'Yes that's it, I think a nice sofa would be more comfortable than a divan. Although it might look like a sparrow perched on a Greek temple, with those legs. He'll have to shave them down.'

'You wouldn't do that,' Shivi protests. 'It's a beautiful bed. And it belongs to Auntyji.'

'Let me ease your mind on that score. Before she left she, quite cheerfully, mind you, advised me to chop it up for firewood.'

Does Shivi feel this irrational loyalty to his mother because they share a religion? Sikand likes to believes that his own interest in Sikhism, and in the situation in Punjab, is purely intellectual and journalistic. His mother, it is true, would have liked him to be a Sikh, but he doesn't remember her ever having said so to him. That was not her way. Perhaps she thought— rather was certain as always—that he would choose Sikhism of his own accord.

His father couldn't have cared either way. A botanist by profession and interest, he always wondered why human beings needed religion at all. 'We forget we are the children of Nature like animals, plants and everything else. We think we are outside it, observers and exploiters, not part of it. That is why we need gods to keep away our fears, and religion to identify us. What a pity!'

The fight over young Sikandar's hair had resolved itself when he fell out of a guava tree, hurting his head, which had to be shaved and stitched. But as he grew, all religions eventually revealed themselves as man-made instruments that only muddied thinking. Sikand, as he called himself now, found that his reading of the philosophers gave him more to think about than any religious text, so that was that.

*

The carpenter tucks his pencil under the dirtiest turban that either Shivi or Sikand has ever seen, and stares at the bed with an air of mesmerized tragedy. Then he takes the pencil out and taps the headboard.

'Wood's good,' he says.

He speaks a strange language that makes itself understood by associations which sound like tricks, devious little conjurings that pick niftily at every Northern tongue. A Sikh who can't speak straight Punjabi is too much for Shivi and he insists on engaging him in a long-winded conversation to determine what sort of vegetable he is.

Quite unfazed, the carpenter states he is Kirat Singh, from Rajasthan, a Labhana Sikh. 'Originally we come from Sind,' he says, and goes down on his haunches to peer at the bed from its underside.

'Termites,' he announces, bobbing up.

'Show me,' demands Shivi and both the Sikhs, Jat and Labhana, crawl under the bed. 'Those are not termites,' comes Shivi's voice. 'That's just sawdust.'

'And why would there be sawdust on old wood, Sardarji?'

It is a question to which Shivi seems to have several answers, all of which he encapsulates in a single, knowing smirk.

There is a point in all this, Sikand muses. For reasons inherent in themselves, the Sikhs can never simplify into a stream. They will ever remain solitary, seething droplets. No matter how bad things get in Punjab, he cannot see them club into a mob, to loot and murder Hindus.

And now he makes a new prediction: there will never be a communal conflagration in Punjab as many people fear; no matter how many individuals may die at individual hands.

*

But individuals are beginning to die at individual hands with alarming frequency.

The djinn of terror released from its bottle back in September 1981 with the shooting of Lala Jagat Narain, is running amok. Jagat Narain, a prominent Hindu social leader, had been owner editor of the *Hind Samachar*, a group of papers that fearlessly vented the Hindu voice in Punjab, denouncing as Janus-faced the Akalis who claimed they spoke for Punjab, but in the name of the Sikhs alone. The Punjabi Hindu considered himself no less than a Sikh, and post-Independence his aim had been to sabotage at every step the Akali campaign for a Sikh majority state. To the extent of a solemn orchestration, led by Jagat Narain among others, that had made every Hindu in Punjab falsely declare Hindi and not Punjabi as his mother tongue in the census of 1961, creating thereby an insurmountable barrier in the linguistic definition of a Sikh majority state. 'What do you expect from those who will disown their own mother?' Bhindranwale was to lash out against the Hindus on many an occasion.

Mourners in Jagat Narain's funeral procession torched the offices of a pro-Akali newspaper, and attacked Sikh passers-by.

A wave of killings had followed, of Hindus and of Nirankaris, a faction exiled from Sikhism. Even of Sikhs who protested against the violence.

The media now routinely attributes all murders in Punjab to Bhindranwale as he goes around the countryside holding up the deeds of the victims for post-mortem justice before congregations that grow ever larger.

It is the turn of the prediction ventured by Sikand's Congress contact to make its bid for truth.

The press in Punjab is fully polarized on communal lines. Sikand hears that at the Press Club in Amritsar, Hindu and Sikh journalists gather in separate bar rooms.

'How bad are things really?' he asks Shivi over the phone. It is a question from one journalist, familiar with the mechanisms of hype, to another.

'There is a lot of fear,' Shivi's voice crackles long distance from Amritsar. 'Although the Chief Minister says everything is normal. I have a press release of crime figures that shows murder to be no higher than the annual average in Punjab. Between five to six hundred, much lower than in some other states.'

'Comparing Punjab with Uttar Pradesh, no doubt. Thirteen districts against sixty-two.'

There is a static-riddled silence. Shivi is surely nodding vehemently in emphatic agreement.

'What did you say?' Sikand raises his voice.

'Yes, yes. I said Yes, Sikand. But it's...unnerving. Seriously unnerving. The Government is in terminal paralysis. They're not just playing political games like before.'

Unnerving. Paralysis. The snake that spits its poison over sixteen feet to immobilize its victim; the cornered rabbit that turns to stone in the hound's gaze; somewhere in these images is Bhindranwale abstracted, the essence of his meaning and his influence. Supposed holy-men, Sants and Mahants, are everywhere—but this man has caught the imagination of Punjab, touched a nerve that ticks somewhere, and *that* is unnerving.

'Write up a good story, Shivi,' Sikand says in farewell. 'Try to get the atmosphere.'

'I will,' says Shivi gloomily.

'Don't be scared of Bhindranwale.'

'I won't,' says Shivi, sounding even worse.

They have watched the government after Jagat Narain's murder.

Bhindranwale, named in the First Information Report of the crime as conspirator, is in Haryana. Instead of arresting him, Chief Minister Bhajan Lal has him escorted out of the state, minutes before the Punjab police arrives. Back at his own headquarters at Chowk Mehta in Punjab, surrounded by his supporters, Bhindranwale receives the emissaries of the Congress government of Punjab who plead with him to fix a date and time for his arrest. He obliges, and collects more supporters about him.

On 20 September 1981, at the time of his choosing, a senior police official's car is arranged for him to travel in, but as he is driven away, violence breaks out and eleven people are killed in the street battle that follows.

The Dal Khalsa, an organisation believed to have been funded by the Congress government of Punjab to counter the faith-based appeal of the Akalis, hijacks an Indian Airlines plane to Pakistan to negotiate for his release, and the Akalis hurriedly redraft their charter to include, besides the river waters and Chandigarh, a demand that Bhindranwale be freed.

In twenty-four days the Home Minister of the Government of India informs Parliament that there is no evidence to show Bhindranwale's complicity in the conspiracy, and he is freed to drive in triumph through Delhi with hundreds of his supporters perched atop the roofs of buses bristling with unlicensed guns. A massive reception is arranged for him by Santokh Singh, a Congress stooge set up to manage the gurudwaras in Delhi. Two months later, Santokh Singh is shot dead and Bhindranwale attends the funeral along with the son of the Prime minister and the Home Minister of the Union.

And yet, 'Don't be scared of Bhindranwale,' is what Sikand says to Shivi.

*

'I read somewhere about a man who's writing this book called *Understanding Hitler* or something to that effect. And he talks about it to a Jew who says it absolutely won't do, because any attempt to understand would be necessarily to justify. And that, dear Sikand, is what is wrong with this project of yours. People like Bhindranwale are to be classed as vile and dangerous...'

'And left pickled on the shelf in formaldehyde like some poisonous snake?'

'Exactly.'

To think that he had been waiting for this meeting with Ambika for a whole week. 'But my dear Ambika,' he says, 'we study those poisonous snakes, do we not? Their habitats and habits? To define safety regimes for ourselves, perhaps? Even their venoms we research for antidotes and, yes, for medicines even. It would be little use to let valuable specimens moulder on the shelves because they're evil.'

'And have you noticed how people who study those snakes hate them less?' she says with an air of having clinched her point.

He laughs out loud. The light of battle is in her eyes, and he knows nothing will infuriate her more than a laugh.

'Just like a lawyer,' he says. 'You change the premise of your argument in mid-breath. Are we not to study him because he's evil, or because we're in danger of hating him less? Which would mean, incidentally, that he's really not evil and we're simply hating him because we don't understand him. And also, not willing to understand him for fear the ground may shift from under our hatred.'

'You know what I think Sikand?' she exclaims. 'I think you're fascinated by evil, like some scatological kid! And I wouldn't be surprised if your fascination stems from a specious, absolutely specious, connection you're drawing between evil and courage. Horrified, yes. But surprised, no.'

He has really got her mad and is reaping the fruit. There is a barb intended, it gets through. And although he laughs again, the barb is unfairly crooked and perilously close to some obscure bone. He is going to have to work very hard to make himself genial to her for the rest of the evening.

'Well I must confess that the actual reason for this visit was to call on the Brigadier. But I'm glad you've put me in my place at the outset. How is he doing?'

Her face softens. The Brigadier, Ambika's father, has been ailing for several weeks, and will, Sikand knows, be happy to see him.

He has known the Sahnis since the time it was possible for a child to know another family outside his own. Lahore, where they came from, had also been his mother's home before she moved to Delhi to marry, so the association with the Sahnis went back to before Sikand was born. When they were forced to move to Delhi after the Partition, it was his mother who did everything to help them settle down. 'More than even our closest relatives, I tell you,' the Brigadier often said with his eyes misting over.

*

'What do you think, Sikand, about all the Sikhs being kept out of Delhi? Generals. Judges, even?'

'Appalling.' Sikand can't help noticing how much weight the old man has lost.

'They've equated everyone with that brigand Bhindranwale. I fear for this nation.'

They are in the Brigadier's bedroom, Sikand has helped him into his favourite chair by the window and is hoping Ambika will join them soon.

'I'm trying to work out what makes that man tick. He's not a politician. The Congress Party's quite at a loss about how to handle him.'

'Classic Frankenstein story, if you ask me. They thought they could use him, but he seems to have figured them out better than they've him. And now he's becoming quite a hero for the rural Sikhs. That's what drives him, I think.' The Brigadier takes a keen interest in national affairs and Sikand enjoys their discussions.

'The attack on the Nirankaris that started it all. Three or four years ago, was it? That's when his fame as a protector of Sikhism started to grow.'

'1978.' Sikand confirms. 'But his role in it wasn't that sterling. He left mid-way, when he saw things were getting too hot. He wasn't even there when the actual clash occurred. Most of the thirteen Sikhs killed were Fauja Singh's men, the Akhand Kirtani Jatha their organisation was called, if I recall correctly. Fauja Singh was also killed. His widow calls Bhindranwale a coward to this day.'

'So then there is some opposition to him still? In the Golden Temple?'

'Oh, yes,' says Sikand. 'This jatha too has a sword arm, the Babbars. Led by Fauja Singh's widow. And from the Golden Temple too. So there's bound to be trouble. She holds him squarely responsible for her husband's death.'

The Brigadier couldn't be older than seventy-four, seventy-five, Sikand thinks, but he's suddenly looking much older. He isn't actually a brigadier, but a few years of military service at some stage of his chequered life have left in him a certain smartness of bearing, a touch of vehemence in his voice. Not to mention the stoic manner that has seen him through his tragedies: the loss of his wife, the return of his only daughter from a badly botched marriage.

When Ambika was born prematurely, Sikand's mother, Nimmi, had sailed like a battleship into the maternity ward to ensure that the best of the scarce medical resources were devoted to the baby, so that Ambika's mother would often say, 'She's really your daughter, Nimmi.' Later, when Ambika's mother had succumbed to cancer, Nimmi had become a permanent support for Ambika. 'What a fine woman, what a beauty, what a smart and intelligent human being!' he hears his mother saying, and thinks of all that he has had to bear for this devotion!

At last, Ambika. She sits on the settee close to him and Sikand feels the familiar frisson at her nearness. But his mind is still picking at her words.

She is wrong. On so many counts. It isn't even a project, as she's said. After so many years, he has his claims, he doesn't do projects like some journalist. Analysis is a continuous study—no moral issues there but the pearls of truth, and the beading of them into a necklace. The pearl and the necklace, both genuine; not some Mikimoto creation.

And the courage she implies he doesn't have, the lack that he needs to compensate for with Bhindranwale? He is aware that in all these years of knowing her he hasn't given her any evidence of courage, at least not her bold-faced Joan of Arc kind of courage that she's limited enough to think is the only kind.

He wants to sit her down and tell her about his mother's bed. How swiftly, in a single karate chop of courage he has decided its fate.

At times he asks himself if it isn't his mother's love for Ambika that he's mistaking for his own. His inability to pop the question back in the day was just another way of disappointing his mother—as if he did everything just for that sole, nefarious purpose.

Ambika, sensible and clever as she was, had moved on.

'I feel like I've lost a daughter!' his mother had wailed to his sister Nina, after the wedding.

'She really felt that marrying Ambika would have saved you, Sikki,' Nina told him solemnly.

'And why do I need to be saved?' he'd asked, but all she'd done was smile.

Of course, he knew the answer. Every time he was doing well he'd wanted to quit and do something else. Leaving the Government, and then the *Statesman* to start a magazine. He didn't have Ambika's quick judgement or her confidence in herself. How she'd chosen to study law without once prevaricating or considering another option. But when her marriage fell apart, had any one questioned her rock-solid judgement? No, all they'd thought was: True, she'd made a mistake but she was setting it right, wasn't she?

He'd like nothing more than to sit her down, he thinks, and talk. Really talk. But then, there's nothing he'd like less.

*

Inevitably the talk has followed his thoughts, and they're asking after his mother.

'I hope Nimmi will be back soon. I spoke to her on the phone the other day. I said we oldies should stick together. Who knows when…'

'You know I don't like you to talk like that, Daddy,' Ambika interrupts. 'He really misses her though, Sikand. Hasn't she had her fill of Nina yet?'

'Well I don't want to be the one to hustle her. She makes her own decisions, as you know.'

Always making clean breaks, his mother, leaving no ragged edges that could snag at her clothes, fool her into thinking someone was trying to keep her.

Like with his father, who, turned out by her pride, had gone helplessly and steadily downhill, to the day he lay covered with a shroud on a slab. It was Sikand even then, who had gone to identify him in the cool white room; to fill the interminable sheaf of forms.

His parents had never really separated officially. Sikand remembers his father just going away to a professorship at the Forest Research Institute in Dehradun. When he took time off from the paper to visit him in Dehradun, his father had simply said, 'Nimmi and I have decided to live our separate lives.' His mother never alluded to it, never visited him or even spoke about his father again, not even when he died a year and a half later so suddenly in a car crash. That was her way.

'Nimmi is quite concerned where all this is going, let me tell you. Punjab won't recover for ten years, she said to me.' The Brigadier, like everyone else, invests his mother's remarks with the sanctity of absolute truth. She never says anything casually.

She wanted something else for them, his mother, for his father and himself. Her standards were just too high. Only Nina with her too-earnest forehead ever made her happy. In despair she had withdrawn from them, like one pushes cowering children into the deep end at last, sink or swim. His father, the man who she'd once said went in one breath from his mother to his wife, had sunk. And he himself is floundering.

*

Ambika fetches a blanket from her father's bed, wrapping it over his legs. As she opens the window Sikand's eyes follow the economy of her movements. 'Not too cold?' she asks, and the Brigadier smiles and shakes his head.

His mother, of course, couldn't look beyond Ambika. Although it had to be said that he too was always comparing the girls he took out in those days to her and finding them wanting. When he was finally seeing Ambika, it seemed so right. But every time his mother suggested they marry Sikand had said, 'Not yet, not yet.' Until it was too late and Ambika had chosen to give herself away to a man who looked like he'd walked off a magazine cover.

Afterwards, when she was back, he had another chance, a definite chance. Everyone had been ready for it—his mother, the Brigadier. Even Sikand himself. Until he suddenly sheered off in fright one evening when Ambika referred to what she called her ecstatic revelling in singleness. He didn't want it said he'd gone straight from his mother to his wife, was the reason he'd given. Mocking his mother with words she knew so well.

Now that she's not here he regrets his words, and wonders how to start afresh with Ambika.

'If only she'll give me an opening,' he rues.

4

The short cut to Samnaula follows the irrigation canal for a couple of miles. On this track Fareed and Jeeta, on their way to college, are arrested by something in the water. A waving mass of black floats towards them as they stand perched on their bicycles. Closer, it becomes long, human hair. Rooted to the spot, they watch as a body floats face-down on the canal, the water lapping and making strange sucking sounds at its sides.

'Is it a man or a woman?' Jeeta's voice trails into the air.

Stark naked, hands knotted behind its back with a red cloth, the body glides past at a fair speed to quickly become a smudge in the distance.

'A man!' Jeeta says. 'It was a man. Murdered by extremists! Uggarwadis!'

'What are you croaking about?' Fareed glares. 'Man, Uggarwadi! How do you know?'

'Didn't you see? The hands—they were tied behind his back.'

'And he was naked. So what?'

'The red cloth! Only uggarwadis use red.'

'And I shit green when I've eaten sarson da saag! Sometimes I think your head is full of hay.'

They stand arguing till the possibility of overtaking the body has passed. When it is sure to have floated past the turn to Samnaula, they push down on their pedals and make it just in time for the second class of the day.

During the eleven o'clock break Fareed sits fuming silently as Jeeta flutters like a butterfly from group to group, and after classes are over for the day, he finds himself surrounded by senior boys from the first and second year.

'I don't know anything about uggarwadis,' he disclaims.

'But Baba Fareed, Baba Shaikh Fareed, your bosom pal Jeeta knows everything. He's shooting his stomach out of his mouth.'

Fareed shrugs off a hand from his shoulder. 'You know he's just showing off.'

'No, no, sir. He's even identifying the group who's done it.'

'Like a whore screaming rape…'

'What d'you mean?' Fareed turns, 'Why talk about whores?'

'Well if you don't know why, I'm not going to tell you. I'm only warning you, you understand?'

'What we mean is clear. Shut up your friend. And keep shut yourself, if you know what's good for you.'

Pushing him away, they leave, one of them throwing another warning over his shoulder: 'Stay away from your friend. I would if I valued my pretty backside.'

'Why did you have to be such a hero?' Fareed asks the moment Jeeta and he are on their cycles heading for home.

'What? Who? Me?'

'Yes, you. Telling the whole world and its granduncle. Now we'll have to go to the police. That's what you get for your dysentery.'

'What did I do? I'm not going to any police.'

'Can't you see, idiot? You've left us no choice. The police are going to hear we saw that body. If we don't report it now, they're going to think we're involved in some way.'

Jeeta digests this in silence.

'You go to the police if you want,' he says finally. 'I'm going home.'

'Fine, fine.' That's Jeeta. Gets them into trouble and then backs out when it comes to facing the music. Suddenly Fareed is furious. 'Where did the uggarwadis come into it, you mother—'

'Leave my mother out of it,' Jeeta bristles.

'Even they're going to hear of it, your uggarwadis. Why couldn't you have kept your stupid mouth shut, you sister—'

'I said leave my mother and sister out of it, didn't I? You watch out for your own mother, your own sister…'

Fareed lunges for him and they hit the ground in a clatter of cycles. Jeeta has grown almost as big as him in the preceding year, but the blaze of Fareed's anger has its own momentum. His arms move like pistons, landing blow after blow in a furious cloud. As they roll on the ground, the dust layers their bodies, stuffing their mouths, their noses. Boys are running up to them shouting, 'Fight! Fight!' and Jeeta is trying to roll out from under him. Fareed, only dimly aware of the sounds about him, is spurred on till he is sure he will kill Jeeta today, with this next blow, this one.

A dozen hands are pulling at their limbs, trying to prise them apart. Separated at last, they sit a foot from each other, breathing hard and painfully, not looking at one another. The boys, seeing it really is over, drift away.

Wiping his face, Fareed rises and mounts his cycle without a word. After a few wobbly yards he has to dismount to straighten its handlebar, but then he cycles steadily onwards. At the canal he hears Jeeta huffing up the incline behind. For a while, Jeeta wheezes and sniffles, then in a voice that is half a sob says, 'You really hit me hard, you bastard.'

Remembering his feverish anger, Fareed is instantly sorry. But Jeeta has really got them into a dangerous situation. An ordinary pair of eyes and ears can figure that no one is immune these days, everything has mounted so rapidly to a head. In the college fear and bravado stalk the corridors arm in arm, it is time either to cower or strut, and only the wisest know which to do when.

When they joined the degree college in summer, Fareed had outlined their strategy: lie low, do nothing to attract attention. 'Do you remember malign-benign?' he had asked Jeeta.

'Is that Hindi?'

'Not Hindi, you fool. They're the opposites we learnt in English in school. Like good and bad. Harmful and Helpful. Get it? Right now one can't tell the difference, see? One doesn't know what's going to harm, what's going to help. So one has to avoid everything.'

And Jeeta had nodded like he was smart, like he understood. But today, he had blabbered away at the very first chance he'd got, so that now neither of them was safe.

Fareed stops suddenly and wheels his bike around. 'I'm going to the police,' he says. He isn't bothered what Jeeta will do, but hears him hesitate, and then trundle his bicycle around too, coughing loudly to show he is following.

Outside the police station Jeeta hangs back. 'I better not show my face to the black thanedar,' he says.

'We haven't done anything, Jeete,' Fareed reasons. 'We've only come to report…'

'No, no, you don't know. You won't understand.'

And Fareed, in a hurry to get it over with, not wanting to know, doesn't wait to find out what it is he doesn't understand and enters through the arch alone. A sentry with a rifle moves behind him as Fareed approaches the single desk in the reporting room. The policeman at the desk looks no older than him, so Fareed is angry with himself at having to swallow and mumble, 'I've come to report a dead body in the canal.'

A slow, silent look measures him. Perhaps he's been too direct. He starts to juggle fresh words in his mind, but before he can speak, and before he is prepared for it, he feels two arms wrap swiftly around him from behind, and hears the sentry's rifle clatter to the floor a moment after. He struggles. Wildly at first, then growing sluggish, he stops altogether when the cop behind the desk jumps up and holds a gun to his chest.

A rough, quick search of his body and he is walked into an office. Behind the desk, scowling at him, is an enormous dark Sardar. The black thanedar.

'Who's it?' the man says in a friendly voice, indicating a chair. Fareed squeezes himself into it, saying, ' I'm—a student from the SD College.'

'First Year?'

'No, Prep.'

The man's round eyes widen as if Fareed has said something very significant. Fareed stares at his own feet, noting how grimy his toes look in his dusty sandals.

'Village?' comes the next question.

'Moranwala.'

'The pond with the two Peepals?'

'Yes. Yes the same.'

The thanedar looks so black because of the hairy mask of his beard. From his eyebrows to the collar of his khaki shirt, the thick strands are gathered and tucked tightly into a thread.

Under his chin it goes and along two puffy cheeks to disappear up his turban.

'You been in a fight?' he asks as if he were talking to his favourite son.

'Yes. No. The reason I came was because there was a dead body in the canal. It was naked and we saw the hands were tied at the back. With a red cloth.'

The man's whole face quivers, pulled by invisible strings as he raises his eyebrows. 'Who's we?' he asks.

'My friend and I. We were cycling down the canal to...'

'Who's this friend? Where is he?'

'He's—outside.'

The bell on the table jingles and a minute later Jeeta is brought in. Under cover of a humble look so fake, that Fareed has a mad urge to laugh, he darts an eye-ball full of accusation at his friend.

'So it's you—the friend?' the thanedar says. 'This bastard has told me everything about you.'

Fareed, shell-shocked, has just opened his mouth, when Jeeta, the stupidest son of a bitch in the world, turns around to look at him openly, with frank accusation. There could be no better way of confirming the thanedar's shot in the dark!

And then, to top it all, the moron son of an owl, suddenly drops to the ground, grabs the Inspector's feet and starts to babble, 'I swear on the Gurus, on my mother, my father...I'm not involved. I know nothing. On the Guru Granth Sahib, on the Satvin Patshahi...' till he is silenced by a well-aimed kick in the teeth.

Fareed, who has already risen, sees Jeeta clap his hands to his mouth and the blood fall in quick large drops from under his fingers. The thanedar gets up too and leans across the desk to hit Fareed hard on both shoulders so that he collapses back into his chair. Four uniformed men run in and start without preliminaries to hit and kick at Jeeta on the floor.

What is happening? The room is suddenly crowded, khaki arms and legs, sticks and boots. 'Didn't I tell you I'd get you? *Didn't I*?' Curses, mother, sister, mingle with a thin wailing litany, 'On the tenth Guru, on the Book...' to form a horrifying duet, while Jeeta's hair is being pulled out of its roots and slaps and blows and kicks are being aimed at his head, his sides, his groin.

'Leave him, leave him,' Fareed begs, folding his hands, but every time he tries to get up the thanedar hits him on the shoulders and plasters him to the chair. Finally, he is screaming too, unintelligible groans and squeaks and muttered 'Wahegurus'.

A sudden silence. Jeeta no longer whimpers and the policemen seem all at once to lose interest. One of them has a red welt across the side of his face, which he nurses with a hand; in the tight space the cops have been hitting at each other too. Fareed, his face in his hands, is silently intoning, 'Waheguru, Waheguru...' and a smell, a nauseating, inhuman smell is permeating through his tight, taut fingers to his nostrils.

The Inspector, his nose wrinkled in disgust, orders, 'Take him out,' and two of the policemen drag Jeeta out by his arms.

'What were you saying about the dead body? Who was it?' the thanedar leans back in his chair and folds his hands on the table.

Fareed can only shake his head.

'Don't hide anything boy,' the man advises. 'You saw what happened to your friend. He's related to a big terrorist, but that doesn't mean we're scared of him.'

Fareed tries to speak but his voice is an unrecognizable croak. When he stands up his legs give way and they have to half carry him too.

In a corner of the lock-up Jeeta is folded over like his spring has broken. Fareed huddles in the opposite corner trying not to look at him, trying not to think about what has happened.

If he can numb his senses, let hot white flashes burn out all connection with time and space, he can still be fine. He is on this threshold when his eye catches a movement in the corner. Jeeta isn't dead.

'He's still alive and I am unharmed,' he thinks. 'That's the important thing.'

After an hour he crosses the cell to sit in Jeeta's corner. Hears him groan, softly at first, then louder. He gets a rough blanket from the cement bunk along the wall and spreads it over his legs without touching him. Smells the strong, sickening smell again. Sits on the ground with his arms out, his head upon his chest. Every time Jeeta makes a sound he takes one more step towards sleep.

When he wakes, Jeeta is sitting up. The blood cakes the hair on his upper lip. Fareed rises and lifts his face in his hands.

'How do you feel?' he asks.

'All right.'

He asks the guard outside the bars for some water. Jeeta drinks, but when Fareed tries to wipe his face with it, he leans away.

They sit and wait for something to happen.

The bulb in its wire mesh cage on the ceiling is too bright, and Fareed closes his aching eyes.

*

His father is at the bars.

He keeps his eyes closed listening only to his voice.

Someone, a cop, talking loudly back. A swear word. He feels his father's humiliation like a knife and thinks, 'I am to blame.'

They open the barred door and take him out.

'What about Jeeta?' He looks not at his father but at the man behind the desk. It isn't the same boy as yesterday. A night has passed.

'He stays. He's mixed up. We'll deal with him.'

'No! He's just a college student. My friend.'

The man looks at Fareed's father, who says '*Sat Sri Akal*, Sahab,' hustling Fareed out into the sunshine. Stepping back to the door he shouts, 'I'll be seeing the Thanedar Sahab tomorrow.' Under the table, as they move, Fareed catches sight of four bottles of his father's booze, wrapped in newspaper and string.

Their cycles lie, one on top of the other, in the station compound. Jeeta's on top.

'Papa, Jeeta has done nothing. It was all my fault.'

The words catch the old man in a side-swipe—his face, his mouth, everything, goes fractionally crazy. 'Shut your stupid face!' he shouts, but not before Fareed has seen the eddy of surprise and fear. His father can only be scared of one thing: that Fareed will go the way the others are going, swelling the numbers of the uggarwadis. Knowing his father is scared makes him suddenly not afraid.

When they near the Peepal by the pond, he breaks the silence. 'There was a body in the canal.'

'Yes, it was fished out in Madhok,' says his father.

'Who was it?'

'What do I know? Some uggarwadi. Or his victim. With a bullet through his forehead.'

'But we just saw it. We only went to report...

'Why? Was it your sister's husband? Your wife's brother? You go to college and you come back that's your job.'

They cycle along to the orchard, words brewing and bubbling in Fareed's mind.

'But what right did the police have? To beat up Jeeta; to lock us up? Jeeta's badly beaten, Papa. And he's still locked up.'

His father stops, dismounts. 'You forget about Jeeta, you hear me? He's no good, he means trouble. For you and for us. You hear me?'

'Yes. But...'

'What d'you talk, you yesterday's boy? Right this, right that. You can't blow your nose, and your words are big as mountains? You're lucky they didn't put a bullet up your backside,' he thunders. Quite out of control. 'Your backside, Shaikh Sahab! Up your tight little backside, you Mister Right!'

His breath hits Fareed full in the face. The bastard's drunk, he thinks. Early in the morning, the bastard. A stab of guilt catches him quite by surprise.

'Don't such things happen?' the bastard turning back into the old man, complete with voice thick with conspiracy. 'Don't they? How many men, boys, are being shot as terrorists. Boys who don't know the backside of a gun?'

The ring of truth catches Fareed in a sudden spasm. This is not just drunken bawling. This is the malign-benign. Anything can happen.

'Are the police to answer to you, Sardar Fareed Bahadur Singhji? What they can do, what they cannot do? Are you some Maharaja?'

And while he rants, Fareed is thinking: Why ever did he go to the cops—the Mamas, the Spatas? They were the enemy! He is certain that Jeeta will never get out of that cell alive.

'Clean the dirt from your ears, Sardarji, and hear me,' his father is intoning. 'This is absolutely the last time I come to get my beard dragged in the dirt for you. Never again, you hear me?' But Fareed is already cycling away, up and down and up the potholes, riding with the wind behind him. What his father will do when he sees him turn into Jeeta's courtyard matters not at all.

*

His heart is knocking solid inside his chest so he sits on the string cot saying nothing. Jeeta's mother, whom he's never really

seen before, brings a glass of milk and his fingers wrap around it
for the heat. When he starts haltingly to tell what has happened,
Jeeta's old father begins to nod his head even before he's really
begun. His mother sits on the ground with her head covered,
almost at his feet. And Jeeta's sister, home from her in-laws',
busies herself with the animals at the far end of the yard. Yet
with face averted, she's always within earshot—the only one
who stiffens in reaction to his story. The mother simply clucks
her tongue as if he was talking about a far-off mishap, a train
accident on the Howrah Bridge or somewhere, and the father
nods away, either knowing everything beforehand or incapable
of knowing anything at all.

Although they are practically neighbours, he can hardly
remember having visited Jeeta at home. Their friendship was of
the street and of the school ground, of the Peepal by the pond.
The courtyard, the animals—a buffalo, a cow and a scrawny
goat—surprise him with their sparseness. If he had stopped to
think he would probably never have come, is already wishing
he had not. The strangeness of all that has happened is starting
to wear off, and in the hard new task of recovering himself he
no longer wants to be in this strange place.

'I'll go and see the vakil in Madhok tomorrow,' Jeeta's old
man says to himself a whole minute after Fareed has trailed off.
'Produce him before a magistrate. Get bail.'

'But, Chacha, you have to go now. Instantly. To the thanedar.
Get Jeeta out, take him to a doctor.'

Yet even as he speaks Fareed sees it is useless. The buffalo,
the sleepy rhythm of its tail swishing at flies, is more real than
his words. The old man shakes his head: 'That man? He will
make me sit also. Money there is not.' Defeated even before he's
begun, he continues to talk to himself, 'As it is, I don't know
how I will manage the vakil and the bail.'

'Bail for what?' Fareed's voice rises. 'There was no crime.

Haven't I said that?' Checking himself, he mumbles, 'I'm sorry, all the fault is mine.'

'Not yours. It is mine. All mine.' It is Jeeta's sister who speaks from right behind him. Startled, Fareed turns to see her eyes blaze with momentary defiance: 'Let me speak, Father. What is the use of always keeping things in the heart? You must know, Fareed, who I'm married to?'

Through his embarrassment at being spoken to so directly, Fareed recalls something strange about her marriage last year. No singing and dancing; no drunken groom's party; just four quick turns around the Granth, a langar meal at the gurudwara itself, the whole thing over in half a day.

'I met my husband in Amritsar, at my cousin's, my maasi's daughter's wedding…'

'Daughter, keep your talk to yourself,' her father warns, using the formal not the affectionate form.

'But I spoke maybe ten words to him! Why won't you people believe me? I have sworn on everything…'

'Of what use is it now?' These are the first words from Jeeta's mother, and as if she has delivered the moral to a story, she rises with a clicking of her knees and shuffles towards the dark. Her daughter hesitates, then snatching up Fareed's empty glass from the ground, follows, leaving behind a heavy silence that becomes heavier still when they hear her banging about the pots and pans in the kitchen.

*

At home his father has arrived and gone out, so that they are emotional without shame, his mother and Dishan, acting like he was a soldier-boy home from the front. And he, lapping up the warmth till it creeps inside his bones and carries him upstairs, rocking him in his bed.

He wakes with the words Likeawhorescreamingrape.

Rapescreamingwhore, shredding his mind. What had Jeeta done? What did it all mean: his sister with her face like an angry widow's, and his mother and his father so ready, so eager, to accept defeat?

'Is there something wrong with Jeeta's sister? With her marriage?' He says it quickly to surprise his mother into the truth, but she has the ladle to the pot and plenty of time to reply.

Wreathed in smoke and steam, secured by the bubbling from her pot, she chooses precisely the words he's tried to sidestep. 'It isn't good to talk about our neighbours. Otherwise what's there to stop them talking about us?'

'So there is something wrong. Dishan!' he calls, and when she is there he asks again his question and knows from her face that she knows. 'How is it I'm always the last to find out anything? Tell me,' he demands.

'Well she went to a wedding, her maasi's daughter's, and they say she met a boy there...

'I know it was in Amritsar, so there's no use not telling me,' and he worms it out of them in low conspiratorial tones that makes them feel he wouldn't tell. The boy to whom Jeeta's sister says she spoke only a few words turns out to be from the Student Federation, one of Bhindranwale's boys. One night they arrive with guns and press her father to give her to him in marriage. It is impossible to believe. That the Federation boys came here—to their sleepy little village.

'It was all very quiet. We didn't hear about it till after she was married and gone with them. She didn't want to, she wept and wailed, the poor thing, but what could the old people have done?' his mother asks, turning to her pot.

'They could have made a noise. We could have all gone to their aid—there are guns in the village...'

'Hush. Hush, Fareeda,' she says. Only the walls have ears. They have literally lifted a girl from their village without a single son of a Jat giving them so much as a "Who's it?"

'Who can make a noise? Her old people? Perhaps they thought that she was, you know, compromised, involved in some way...Why would they have come otherwise?'

He watches his mother's face in silence. The steam has left little beads, like perspiration, on her forehead; one is fattening on the tip of her nose, preparing to drop. 'With guns?' he asks. 'To take a bride who has already been compromised?'

She wipes the drop off before it can return to the pot where it has risen. 'You know as well as me, Ma,' he says. 'Because they didn't have the guts to save her, Jeeta's old parents, the whole village, can only say it was all her own fault. It is for the best any way: who else will marry the poor, polluted thing?'

The police could arrest and beat anyone. The uggarwadis could shoot and rape anyone. Anyone at all...

Suddenly he turns on Dishan. 'Don't you so much as talk to a boy, you hear me? No one. Not even Jeeta, nobody. I'll cut off your legs if I see you.' Cornered by his growling presence, for he has taken a threatening step towards her, her eyes widen with fear. 'Those poems, don't think I haven't seen what you scribble in your notebooks, hearts and doves and roses. You better hear me, it won't be good. I'll slash your throat, you hear me?' Her eyes plead, as if for silence alone. Without reproach. And shame washes over him. With a slight stumble over the doorway, he leaves them. There is an animal trapped inside of him.

A mule. That kicks and brays but can't beget.

It is back. The fear, the powerlessness. Anything can happen. He starts to write but his fear is too deep to explain. All he can say again and again in a rambling letter to his brother is, '*Take me away, Randhir. Get me out of here. Call me to you. Please.*'

A small voice mocks inside him—how can you get out? Your wavering kismet will take you where it wills. No one is ever spared his fate.

He has always been unsure about wanting to leave the village, but now he feels the certainties of his life being overtaken by a murky darkness. With this letter to his brother he has made a sincere attempt to break out. He has been decisive.

He will be in control.

5

Fareed thinks that the old old men, the dadas and the babas, are far better company than the middle-aged, the chachas and the tayas, who will be thick as flies at the booze shop by now. By the old dry well at the gurudwara he listens to their mellow voices under the tamarind trees. When one speaks the others are still and rapt, as if the speaker were performing a complicated feat with symbols, rather than uttering the first words that have entered his head. In the pondering silence that follows the words hang like a message written in the air with Diwali sparklers, so that he can close his eyes and see it still, being slowly absorbed into meaning. Then someone else, how did they know who or when, breaks the silence with another feat and the whole cycle begins over again.

A delicious calm comes over Fareed and he doesn't know when he leans his head on his Babaji's shoulder.

They have spun a web of peace around him, the old, old men. They are at peace with everyone. With their wives, their children, their children's children. No fears, he thinks, no need to pretend. No shame at sounding soft. He is wishing he was old; already over with what is to come. Dreaming that he has leapt in one quick bound over this terrible business of having to become…

A voice rises suddenly in excitement rousing Fareed.

'The Golden Temple,' it says, '*the Holiest of the Holies!*'

It becomes a broken shriek: 'To kill a police officer, a DIG of police, in its very doorway? What more is there left to say, what greater crime?'

It seems the old old men are not at peace with the world after all for a babble of voices, all mellowness gone, is triggered at the words.

'Blood in the Harmandar.'

'Sacrilege!'

'But where did the bullet come from? From Dilli, I say.'

'What has Dilli got to do with it?'

'It is the Dilli Sarkar. What did their police do? There is police...'

'Everywhere. I heard...'

'But where is Dilli, where is the government...'

'You listen...'

'No, *you* listen...'

Peace comes in slow, coughing stages.

Dasaunda Singh, a retired Akali with a white beard that curls down to his navel, holds the floor. 'Longowal is the man for us now. A true saint, not like Bhindranwale, not a dacoit in sant's clothes.' He holds up his hand and chews on his handful of surviving teeth till the interruptions cease. 'Longowal is born to the tradition. He knows the Gurbani, and he understands the Sikhs. The Miri, and the Piri.'

Fareed has heard these words before. The Piri, the spiritual, and the Miri, the temporal. The Sikhs are not a religion alone, they are a political force.

'But first, the Piri,' says Dasaunda Singh. 'That is our Kohinoor—the diamond in the crown.' Everyone is silent. Fareed listens carefully because he has never understood what asking for votes has to do with God. 'The diamond in the crown,' says Dasaunda Singh.

'Serve God,' he thunders all at once. 'Serve God first. And you serve the people.'

The cycle resumes. 'That is what you always say, Dasaunda,

and I agree with you with my whole heart,' says Lalkar Singh, a man whom Fareed has taken for senile ever since the day he came out to find Lalkar Singh, without his dentures, fast asleep in the sunlight on the cement seat outside their house. But this is a different man. 'Only remember Dasaunda,' he says, 'that you have also always said that the Akali plan to raise a lakh of volunteers for the Sikh cause was fool-proof.'

'What is one lakh? The Sikhs would give ten.'

'Yes, but only if it wouldn't end like this, in adding to Bhindranwale's strength. He gives speeches at the Golden Temple, in the Teja Singh Samundari hall. They say he tells the volunteers they must fight, that they must kill for their rights. And Sant Longowalji, for whom all the volunteers have gathered, comes only second to Bhindranwale's fire. A poor second, I'm sorry to say.'

Baba Dasaunda Singh falls into a deep silence at these words. He taps his stick in the mud, swings and turns it to make a swirl of patterns in the dust.

'The Akalis are putting themselves into a corner, let me warn you,' Fareed's Babaji speaks, raising a finger. 'Leadership has to be earned by trust; you can't do one thing and say another. And a leader has to sense the direction of the wind. He has to take stock of his followers, he has to count them first of all. Choose his objective according to his numbers. Not go attacking a target that needs a company with just a platoon! You don't rattle empty scabbards, that's the first principle.'

'So what you mean is that these lakhs of volunteers are empty scabbards?' asks Dasaunda with some spirit.

'If you must see it like that, that is also a valid meaning. They come to the Harmandar for Longowal who has raised the spark, and they go out to court arrest for Bhindranwale who knows how to blow the spark into a fire. Longowal should never have agreed to share a platform with that man. He has undercut himself,' says Babaji.

'I am sorry, Dasaunda, but I have to agree with Captain Sahib,' says Lalkar Singh. 'Your Akalis have no control over Bhindranwale. Instead they're losing control over themselves. They shout themselves hoarse, but still can't sound like him. Because he's the real thing. Desi Ghee. He believes in what he says, while all they're doing is playing dog to his wolf.'

Fareed has always dismissed this man as just one of Babaji's old cronies. For the first time he is listening to his words. The history that was dosed to him in school, the current-affairs magazines he crammed for the college interview, the daily newspaper headlines that Babaji makes him read—for the first time he is consciously trying to blend it all with the talk in the college corridors and the words he is hearing now. All the dry stuff, the words on pages, have gathered together, pushing at the crowded entrance and he doesn't know which to let in first. He only knows that all are vital. They will impact on his bones and his flesh; they will determine his days and his nights, the chasm of life that he cannot leap.

The Akalis, the blue turbans who have been filling the jails from the time of the British. For control of the gurudwaras, for a free India, for a language-based state, and now for river water for the Punjab, for a capital for the state. And arrayed against them the mighty Congress Party. Mahatma Gandhi's party, the party of freedom, the one that threw the British out. All the big names—Jawaharlal Nehru, Sardar Patel, Netaji Subhash. And now Indira Gandhi.

In school they had made rhymes about her:

Pandran Agust phullan naal marhi hoyi hai,
Indra Gandhi scooter te charhi hoyi hai,
Ohdee saree ik halke kutte ney pharhi hoyi hai,
Jee karda hai bacha daan, par oh mere naal ladhi hoyi hai,
Mussalmanan dee bhabhi bani hoyi hai...

Independence Day, and Indira Gandhi riding a scooter, her flying sari caught in the jaws of a mad dog. I wish I could save her, went the rhyme, but I'm afraid she and I have fought. The Muslims are her husband's brothers now. A woman driving a scooter? An image enough in itself to raise a hoot. How has something so laughable acquired such weight? Rushed across time and space to seed and grow till it threatens his very future? He must listen intently to these old old men; perhaps they have the answer.

'The Congress created Bhindranwale. Everybody knows it. What was he before they started sharing platforms with him? Supporting his candidates in the gurudwara elections, seeking his support for their Congress candidates in state elections? What was he? I will tell you, a minor religious figure. Just another sant or mahant. It was Sanjay Gandhi, the woman's son, and Giani Zail Singh, her lieutenant, who made him. Only to help them steal the Akali support.'

'What you say is hundred per cent correct, Dasaunda. But now it is the Akalis who are sharing platforms with him. It is too late in the day to say he's a Congress creation,' says Lalkar Singh.

'How is it late? The Akalis are not in power. The Congress is. They can arrest him, not the Akalis. What has their government done? Even now when a police officer is killed at the door of the Harmandar. Did they enter, did the police search the premises, find the killers hidden inside?'

What a son of an owl I am! thinks Fareed. A senior police officer is killed and *I* go like a bloody goat's kid into the slaughterhouse? No wonder the Mamas were so jumpy. I never paid any attention to all this, that was a grievous fault. And now Jeeta…it is all my fault. A fatal fault.

'But who is Atwal? This DIG who was killed? What was he doing at the Golden Temple, I ask you?' This comes from Umrao Singh, a comparative newcomer to the gathering, a Chacha-Taya in the process of becoming a Baba-Dada.

'What was he doing? Why, what any Sikh does at the Golden Temple.'

'He was washing his feet in the doorway.'

'Preparing to meet his Guru.'

'No, no, he was coming out, not going in.'

'He was a Sikh!'

'Yes, but, don't forget, a Sikh policeman. They say he killed many of our boys in staged encounters. Caught them, let them off, then shot them in the back of the head and said they were trying to escape. That was Atwal. There was some other purpose for him to go to the Harmandar, this much I know,' Umrao Singh says.

'If a policeman has to go with a purpose, as a spy, as a decoy, to gather intelligence, into the Harmandar Sahib, then what does it say about the Harmandar Sahib? Policemen have to spy not in temples, but in places frequented by pimps and murderers. In addas...' Babaji has started in a reasonable tone of voice and obviously has more to say, but his choice of words, 'pimps and murderers' spoken in the same breath as the Harmandar, electrifies the gathering. These people, these silver mellow men, are suddenly quick with raw, burning energy. The points of sticks gouge at the soil around the string cots. Voices shred into hoarseness. Language that they ought to have forgotten, bubbles out unbidden. Coughs and curses blend into mayhem.

It is left to Babaji to rise to his feet with a painful 'Waheguru' and shuffle for his stick; to Fareed to draw it gently from the clench of Dasaunda Singh's hands; and as the two walk away, Babaji leaning heavily on Fareed's shoulder, it is left to the words of the *Rehras Sahib*, the evening prayer, that wafts out like a signal over the loudspeaker from the gurudwara to break up the gathering.

'Did they hurt you at the police station, son?' Babaji asks, stepping carefully, watching for the jagged ends of broken brick.

'No. But they hurt Jeeta. Badly.'

The old old man sighs and Fareed feels the heat rise inside him. The unacceptable is acceptable. Has to be accepted. This is the knowledge that has been kept from him all these years. He yearns with bitter longing for his days of sweet fatal ignorance.

'I can't understand,' he says, 'how normal people will take it. Every injustice; every crime. Not raise a voice, no murmur.'

They drift to their doorway in silence, while the Gurbani rises behind them:

'They are liberated who remember the Lord…For them the noose of death is cut away…'

On the doorstep the old, old man stops. 'Son,' he says, 'the sparrows are millions, it's true, the hawks are few. But it is not in the nature of the millions to stand up to the few.'

'But why? Why? The hawks too have risen from the sparrows, have they not?'

'Yes. But don't you see, my boy, the moment a sparrow stands, it changes its nature. It too becomes a hawk.'

*

The tenth Sikh Guru, Guru Gobind Singh, is whom the old, old man alludes to. In his Gurbani it is said that he set out to make sparrows fit to fight hawks, founding the Khalsa along a martial ethic to confront the mighty Mughal Empire. Today the sparrows are the hawks.

Sikand has to work out the contradictions though. Technically he notes that baaz should translate as falcon instead of the commonly used hawk, but that is not his concern. The history and the politics is easy, journalism and reporting is easy. The difficulty is in the interpretation. For this, all experience is grist, to be tumbled into the mill lock and stock and wholesale barrel, and ground somehow. The power will be found, never mind, he says. Look at the fineness; the end result.

'But that means we'll never have the article, Sikand. No use writing it for our grandchildren to read. We're a current affairs magazine, you know,' says Bibs at what he calls their Editorial Board meeting.

'Come on, Bibs, I'll give you those any day. You know I've been hacking away at it before, twenty, fifty, thousand words a week.'

'Yes, but so long ago that was, ages. If I'm not mistaken the last thing we carried by you was a piece on the Indian Airlines hijacking and that was when? Years ago.'

'You've forgotten the piece, allow me my modesty, the masterly analysis of the Elections? And of the predictions before? You remember how accurate the results of the Elections were? Be kind to me, Bibs. Be fair.'

'Those two pieces were great; they were marvellous, absolutely. But Sikand, correct me if I'm wrong, weren't they even before the hijacking piece? 1980 I think.' Bibs never gives up.

'I'm anxious you may have forgotten how to write,' he says. 'And great things, earth-shattering things, are happening every single day. Take the killing of this DIG, the Golden Temple's blazing hot.'

'But Livleen did that, didn't she? And rather well, I thought.'

'True, true. She's shaping up well, Livleen. Credit's due to you for that. No doubt. Absolutely. But Sikand you can't simply head a department, not just administer and train, however competently. However lovingly.'

'That's a nasty cut Bibs.'

'I meant it as a compliment, you goose. But you're an editor too, you see. You have to help with policy, and most important, you have to keep your pen in.'

Bibs is the chief, Sikand says. 'Right you are Bibs. Absolutely.'

Suspicious of the too easy capitulation, Bibs is cautious. 'The other thing is Shivi.'

'Person you mean, Bibs. He's not a thing.'

'True, true…where was I? Yes, Shivi. Now Sikand, this piece that Livleen's done, it's much better than anything Shivi's given us. And he's our man in Punjab, in Amritsar, in fact. We must ask ourselves how a young girl who joined us yesterday is capable of better stuff than our veteran in the hotspot? I have asked myself that. Have you?'

'No,' says Sikand, totally absorbed in the paperweight on Bibs's table in which three big brilliant fish are swimming, swimming, around a drab little boat. 'But I'm sure your answer will be good enough for the both of us.'

'Exactly. He's not being supervised. That's it. His last few pieces were newspaper stuff gummed together. I don't see your touch in him anymore, Sikand,' he says sadly.

I could chuck this job today, Sikand is thinking, I should ask him to shove it up. Call him Birbal Nath, so he'll never forgive me. But he nods slowly, sharing the burden of Bibs's sadness. The fish are moved by magnets, he sees, that's why they have to be so big. And the boat is plastic, unresponsive to magnetism.

He is weary with the interview but Bibs hasn't had his say yet. Not all of it.

'Did you think when we both started *In Sight* that it would be such a big success? Did you, Sikand?'

Of course I did, you oaf, why else did you think I started it? But when it got moving you suddenly wanted the lion's share, wanted to be chief. See Sikand, you said. You're the thinker, the man of vision, blah blah blah. I'm the practical man, the money guy. And we both can't be chief, it doesn't work for the corporate image, yak yak yak.

'No I didn't, Bibs. I really didn't. Truly.'

He watches the satisfied smirk hover *uno momento* around Bibs's thin lips and then leap like a frog into his eyes. 'Exactly. I said, didn't I, that a magazine has to be handled like a commercial venture? It is a commercial venture, a professional business. Advertising, the corporate image, personnel policy, but you know all that.'

'Yes, Bibs, I do.'

'So. So we're there. Congratulations, Sikand.'

They both rise, exchange solemn handshakes, and resume their seats. 'So,' Bibs says. 'I won't bore you with figures, turnover, expenses. We're not just friends, we're partners. I'm sorry, that should be the other way around. What I mean is, I know that as your friend I'm expected to deal with all that. Absolutely. And I think it is possible, not only possible, but plausible. Entirely. Anyway, I'm taking the privilege of adding to what we take home. In fact, I'm doubling our salaries.' He looks so pleased, even the hair in his eyebrows quiver.

So that is why you are hustling me, you creep. Value for money. The holiest of corporate commandments. You louse. Sikand looks him straight in the eyes waiting for expectation to develop, replace the glee. It comes.

'Great,' Sikand says. 'Absolutely great, Bibs.'

Sikand has known Bibs since college. I have only myself to blame for him, he thinks, for before they had started *In Sight* together he had intuited that Bibs would do everything, right or wrong, down to the absolute criminal, if he had to, to make their venture a success; and he had thought that a good enough reason to go along with Bibs.

*

Time is inexorable. Sikand thinks provisional thoughts. So much is outside his control, the march of time with every second a discrete tick, perversely picking at emotion, character, circumstance—the baggage, to shape only itself. Utter disregard of purpose; of pattern. He would that time stepped with the movements of a symphony, like waves on long beaches.

Sweeping in its large-hearted billow the fragmented moments, the insignificant detritus, to deposit them like broken seashells on the shore. Returned to sand.

'This Giani Zail Singh!' his mother used to say. 'He couldn't win an election without the support of the Jat Sikh farmers and now he's out to sabotage them.' For every complex situation, find someone to blame and presto! the situation simplifies itself. Sikand agreed that the Congress was throwing oil on fire, but he also knew that the Akalis were stoking the fire for their own political purposes.

She had strong issues with his article on the Indian Airlines hijacking. The Dal Khalsa, which was responsible, was widely believed to be a Congress creation, something his mother believed absolutely of course, but to conclude that the Congress was behind the hijacking was certainly imprudent. Which is why his brilliant article did not conclude so.

'Just because that woman is in power again, a magazine of your stature shouldn't be shying away from telling the truth,' was his mother's admonishment. He had started staying out late to evade her analysis of what the magazine had written instead of what it should have.

Bibs, it seemed, cares even less than her for the travails of those who aspired to the Holy Grail of truth. All he wants is that *In Sight* should be the first to break the news, as if it were not a magazine but a wretched daily.

Time did step with the movements of a symphony, like waves on long beaches.

And he would that he were an observer apart on that shore, seeing the wave break, able within a reasonable margin to predict the advent, the shape, of the next, the next. Only then would he have the right to put pen to paper.

Sometimes, he was willing to grant, there would arise the need to get his feet wet.

He would have to go to Amritsar. An obligation that has been pressing on his mind long before Bibs said anything.

The only problem is the bed.

*

Kirat Singh, the carpenter from across the river, has finally reappeared after a long exile with a permanent solution for termites—a foul-smelling liquid that will perish them and their forthcoming offspring forever. The seven pieces of the bed, pasted with the magic liquid, are disposed individually inside the house, for Sikand to skin his shins upon. The carpenter has promised to return in ten days when the process will be completed to his satisfaction. Locking up the house for the days that Amritsar will take will mar Kirat Singh's plans. Nor can he trust the open rooms to the care of Raja Ram, his anti-Jeeves, who has a healthy Eastern contempt for the Northern realities of burglars and robbers. Despatched to various haunts, he declares them all devoid of Kirat Singh's presence, 'Not even a whiff of him, Sahib,' he says.

Meanwhile a number of banks and armouries are looted in Punjab and his sister Nina calls from the Dooars, where her husband is in Tea, to inform him that Mother is as tiresome as ever, refusing to be medicated by a doctor who doesn't look right, for a bronchial inflammation that could well be pneumonia.

'Does she want to come here?' he asks, and doesn't know if he's relieved to learn she will definitely not change her mind on that.

Mother is definite about everything, that is her saving grace. Someone so sure is predictable.

'Why don't you come here, Sikki? The weather is lovely, unbelievable drama of clouds and rain…'

Nina can be trusted too. To make it sound like the poetry

of rainclouds is sufficient reason for him to fly across the subcontinent.

'Has she asked for me?'

A silence, long enough to grant him a leisurely tour of her emotional landscape. 'Well,' she murmurs, exactly when he expects her to. 'She doesn't say so. Not in so many words...'

'In a few words then?'

She is irritated, as she has a right to be. 'No,' she says abruptly. 'But it wouldn't do you any harm to come and see her, on your own, without an invitation. After all she is...'

He knows this conversation must end, like so many before— 'I know, I know. All that is genetic knowledge, punched without permission into the double helixes of my cells'—in inanities.

6

Raja Sansi Airport, Amritsar. Shivi is there to receive him, with an extra umbrella. The long-awaited monsoon has arrived, and as the taxi swishes through a bank of water, Shivi's account of shootings and killings has no relevance to the scene outside. Washed of all stain of fear and terrorism, the landscape is innocent. It is the song on the driver's radio querying an almond-hued maiden where she is off to dressed as a mustard flower, that holds the moment.

In three rooms above a ready-made garments store, Shivi has fashioned an uninviting home.

'What to do?' he asks, clearing a chair of its clutter. 'I have forgotten how to live as a bachelor and the wife and kids had to go to my in-laws in Chandigarh.'

'Nothing wrong, I hope?'

'What is right here, Sikand? I have to live here. It's a question of a living. They don't. She said she couldn't breathe, that she felt the three of them were hostages to fear. Hostages to fear, imagine that.'

As if a tap had been opened Shivi's words continue to spill. 'And not long ago she used to go to the Golden Temple every day. Isn't it nice to be in Amritsar, so close to the Harmandar Sahib, she would say. She's very religious and all that, not like me. But in the end she was saying hostages to fear, in the dark shadow of the Golden Temple, things like that. She would hear shots being fired in the night. They're better off in Chandigarh, I can say.'

Fear. Shakespeare wrote imaginings are worse. Reality is only a dismal second for there can be no greater terror than an imagined fear. Sikand knows that well, although it is knowledge that he prefers to ignore.

'I went to listen to Bhindranwale one day,' says Shivi. 'The people, all villagers from the countryside, come to court arrest for the Akali morcha. Open-mouthed in awe of the Harmandar; the city. In the Teja Singh Samundari Hall, wonder-struck by all its pillars. Longowal spoke first, his usual speech on how Punjab had been tricked out of land and water, how the Dilli Sarkar was unhearing, blinkered. He was heard quietly. Respectfully. And then came Bhindranwale. I told you all before, he said, to buy motorcycles and guns instead of TV sets. Now when they come for you, the Hindu Sarkar, the Hindu mobs, point your TV antennae at them. And he sent those rural people, innocent when they came in, out into the city with murder in their hearts. Acting like the city was captive to their new-born strength.'

'Why can't you write like that, Shivi? That would have old Bibs curling his toes.'

'Write? I can't even afford to talk like that…only because it's you.'

Shivi is convinced this is an inspection tour and vacillates between what he thinks are thumb-nail sketches of his life and atmosphere, and an inadequately damped pride in the contacts he's built up, the information he's privy to. He knows the killers of the DIG of police, for instance. They've been pointed out to him in the Golden Temple by a source. Of course he can't identify them in print, Sikand would understand that. Even the police know, but don't dare do a thing. He insists that Sikand must meet all these people the Superintendent of Police, his Akali contact, his Student Federation mole, his Bhindranwale friend.

*

The Akali contact is invited to dinner. He is a small, angular man whose normal method of communicating is a hoarse whisper. Drinking is taboo, though when Sikand insists he almost gives in, but Shivi pre-empts by refusing himself. Pouring just the single drink for Sikand, he offers one word: 'Boss' as a lame absolution. Under the circumstances, the conversation hovers interminably in the formal frame.

Sikand is congratulatory on the Akali morcha, over two lakh volunteers have courted arrest. The contact is modest, two lakhs is not a large number for the village folk, who it appears are ever ready to give themselves in large numbers to whatever cause. Allowing nothing to be lost, Sikand is able to get him to admit that the cause is irrelevant for the volunteers, it is swelling the numbers that counts. A question of prestige. The Golden Temple counts too, is Shivi's contribution. Earlier the attempt to prevent the distribution of river water, the nahar-roko agitation, petered out because of its venue, the remote rural site of the Sutlej-Yamuna link canal. Every successful agitation in Akali history has proceeded from the Golden Temple.

With an air of revealing some terrible secret, the man confides that the river-water cause did not fire the farmers' imagination. He is contradicting what he has admitted a moment ago, that causes were irrelevant, and in confusion sinks into a glum silence. Sikand has long ago lost the cub-reporter's delight in persecuting politicians, but Shivi is still keen and sniffs around for a bit, uselessly scoring points off his own contact.

Some excellent brain curry from a dhaba across the street revives everybody's spirits. Breaking bread with companions can have the same effect as drinking together, and Sikand thinks there is hope for the world yet. The contact becomes Jagtar Singh and then Jagtar for him. He even toys with Jagga as they press curry and parathas on each other.

'See, we jumped into a well. That is nothing, it can be forgiven to Sardars, they are known to jump into wells because they're there. But can you, you, stand outside and refuse to help me? Just because I jumped in myself? That is not good, no gentleman— that is not human.' Jagtar's voice has lost some of its hoarseness. 'So the Dilli Sarkar is wrong, criminal. And don't forget they dug the well themselves, left it in our midst, knowing we would jump in, given the chance.'

'Only History will decide whose creation he was, your well,' Shivi says and enjoys his joke so exuberantly Sikand suspects his frequent trips to the bathroom point to a bottle of booze among his shampoos.

After dinner Sikand is out alone on the terrace smoking his cigarette. The city is dark, and he is amazed at how the bustle of the day has snuffed itself out so completely, so early. He sends his cigarette butt travelling over the parapet in an arc of sparks, and it is then that he hears them: two clear shots, *thha! thha!* pierce the night. An abrupt silence. No echo. Sounds lost to the irretrievable past. A clutch of fear to his heart passes too.

*

Sikand has not been inside a place of worship since he was ten. Even this morning, the Golden Temple does not bear a solemn air—crowds, the jostle and pull of a fair-ground, these are his abiding impressions. And the posters on the walls. As if written in blood. Knowing it is red paint makes no difference.

One hails the killers of the DIG. Shivi reads aloud the lurid prose ending with a Lal Salaam, a red salute. In his last article he has mentioned the infiltration of the leftist Naxalites into the militant movement, and now is keen to validate his credentials before Sikand. Albeit in a muted, looking-over-his-shoulder way; as if too much emphasis itself is a crime in these environs.

Bhindranwale is in the Guru Nanak Niwas, a guest-house attached to the Temple, a stone's throw away. But his presence broods over the complex. Even the little Sardarjis, fair faces aglow under the saffron of their turbans, seem to acknowledge it, weaving through the jungle of legs on the marble parikarma with the ratatat of machineguns tilting off their tongues in a parody of guerrilla warfare. The marble slabs under their bare feet, paid for by devotees, bear legends in Gurmukhi, in Urdu, in Hindi: testimony that in the past, the temple has been a place of pilgrimage not for Sikhs alone. In the sheen of gold reflected in the sacred pool that gives the city its name, Sikand traces the influence of a secular architecture, reflecting on the journey of the dome from Saracen mosque to Sikh temple.

A voice rises from the sanctum, drowning all awareness but of the moment. It draws the mass towards it, the children too, with faces gone suddenly solemn, the picnic becoming at last a pilgrimage. He must wet his feet, he decides, and is funnelled down the stairs where the water in the doorway is cool and cleansing. The voice of the kirtan beckons from the shrine.

He is of the faithful, feeling the strange peace of return: his mother's faith shares with her its strangeness and its familiarity. Before the Holy Book, he is a lost child, bedazzled by the silks and satins, bowing, touching his forehead to the ground in imitation of the other children. The congregation shifts, accommodating him, and something which was merely pleasant before is turning into the gentleness of comfort, mounting in a breathless rush, as of revelation, so that the words of the song, simple, even banal: a sister waiting, wailing, for her brother Nanak to return from his wanderings are, he knows not how, the yearning ache of a soul.

The voice is joined by another and together the voices rise, above the silken canopy, above the golden dome, and something within him, light as gossamer, rises too.

He is slowly aware of being spoken to.

'Pardon me?' he says.

The man he is pressed against in the congregation repeats softly: 'Nowadays we are not finding converted models such as yourself. Not many.'

There has been a terrible mistake Sikand wants to say, I'm not a convert, I'm an impostor.

'Though convertible, those we still find. A few.'

'Pardon?' he says again. This is something else, the man is not talking about faith at all.

'In fact,' he divulges, leaning closer. 'I'm one of those myself. You know, mechanised.'

He begins to understand. Converted means a Sikh who has shaved his beard and cut his hair, there aren't many of those left now. Not in Punjab. And convertible, Shivi confirms, is a Sardarji with a beard and a haircut; at will he dons a turban to be a khalsa, at will he joins the eccentric bearded of the cities. He is convertible. Mechanised means the same thing, although Shivi is quite at a loss to explain why.

'Our men are cutting their hair, taking the scissors to their beards, our women shaving, shaving!—arms, legs, underarms. With pincers they are pulling out their eyebrows from their roots! What is this? Is it not terrible for Sikhs?' Shivi's Bhindranwale friend is storming.

Terrible, Shivi nods. Terrible, Sikand nods. He is still dis-anchored after the unexpected depth of the experience in the sanctum. The man is tall and long-bearded and, although properly introduced by Shivi, for Sikand he is 'Clone Singh'. That has to do for the moment, but he agrees it is terrible.

Satisfied with all the nodding, the tone turns forgiving, it is not their fault after all. 'See the problems that Santji has? People have to be brought back to the faith, otherwise what is the difference between Sikhs and Hindus? In five, ten years there will be no Sikh. Finished.' He makes the appropriate gesture slitting his own throat and Sikand nods eagerly.

'Two things Santji says.' Clone Singh raises two fingers to count them off. 'One, the Sikhs must come together, be united. And two, they must realize that they are discriminated against, unequal. In Delhi, Bombay, Calcutta, everywhere.'

The two things are of course one, thinks Sikand, his balance returning. Problem, solution, strategy, encapsulated.

Clone Singh sits across the table in a dank office room of the Guru Nanak Niwas. The concrete building of offices and dormitories for pilgrims is almost part of the shrine. You have to take off your shoes and cover your head, as if in the presence of the Granth.

'Is this a part of the Golden Temple?' Sikand asks. It is mild interest, to cover his reluctance over the coagulated tea that has been brought to them as Clone Singh's guests, but it has an impact quite out of proportion.

'Let them say it is not. Just say it, utter the words. Our blood will flow to mingle with theirs!' Clone Singh thunders. 'For Santji, thousands will lay down their lives. You must write this—thousands!'

Shivi is no help at all, he just nods vigorously at everything the man says.

And then promptly does the same thing in the office of

Amreek Singh Gill, the Superintendent of Police, when that gentleman expresses a contrary, totally opposite, opinion.

'The Guru Nanak Niwas is a sarai, a rest-house for pilgrims. That is all. We go there every day. The SGPC, the administrative part that manages the gurudwaras, they have their offices there, administrative offices, you understand?'

Sikand, who has decided to distance himself from Shivi's nodding, says, 'So what's the problem then? Why can't you get at the killers of your DIG?'

'But they are not there—they are in the Golden Temple itself.'

The SP is different—for one thing he does not seem interested in striking a pose. But he is cajoling, dangerously so. 'Your own sources will tell you. I know Shivinder Singh well. He is a contact man, a deep contact man.' Shivi looks bashful, but nods all the same.

'Wait a minute. So what you're saying is that you, the police, know the identity of the killers but are powerless to arrest them because they're hiding in the Temple?' Sikand asks.

'Not hiding, Sikand Saab, strutting. With guns better than any we've got. The power you talk about is theory. We have closed the book on that power. And arresting is worse than useless. Do you know, these boys have laddus brought to the court in advance when we produce them before the magistrate?'

'Laddus? You mean sweets? For what?'

'No magistrate has the guts to refuse bail. So the laddus are for distributing to the court staff afterwards. After the bail order.'

Sikand slowly digests this.

'But why are you asking me? Ask your own man. Ask Shivinder Singh.'

And Shivi is spot-lit in the hard expectant glare that the SP fixes on him. Sikand watches with horrified interest as Shivi's features—nose, chin, mouth, all except the eyes, which are hooded—do a sort of three-sixty degree turn through what composes them. Spilling their insides. A rainbow of indecisive expressions, fear and cunning, and also something else in the quick sideways dart of his eyes; a plea for reprieve, for understanding. Nodding will not do now.

'SP Sahib, you know better than me, everything,' he begins, with admirable composure. 'I just try to do my job. In difficult times. That is all, a job. It takes me to dangerous places and I find out dangerous things. And I try to keep my mouth shut. That is all.'

'That is not all, Shivinderji. At least my information says there is more. But let us leave that for now. As a journalist I think you're doing only half your job. I have said as much before to you, have I not? You have not only to find out the truth—you have to tell it too. But don't worry; I will not persecute you. When it is time, you will come yourself. You will tell us, you will want to tell us.'

Sikand feels the atmosphere sing. He doesn't want to know what this is all about. He'd really rather give Shivi the understanding he craved in that one unguarded moment. He will not persecute him either.

After a long silence has underlined his purport, the SP too is true to his word, inviting them for dinner, saying, 'These are times to be generous...'

They arrive in a flurry of revolving lights and screaming sirens at a restaurant which bears above its crumbling plaster facade the legend 'Sweet Dreams Chiken House. Prop. Sohan Singh'. The dark interior, where they are the only guests, is dank and musty, although the proprietor's effusive welcome brings with it an appetising aroma of butter-chicken.

Both are acknowledged by the SP with benevolence. 'These are guests from the Dilli press, used to the very best. That is why I bring them here.' In the dim lighting, Proprietor Sohan Singh's babyish face swells and gleams with obligation. A posse of policemen, part of their convoy, fans into the interstices of the restaurant to invisibly lift the atmosphere of stagnation into a creditable imitation of spit and polish.

It seems hardly the best way to ensure one's security, announcing oneself with flags and lights and sirens, but the SP is convinced that the day he has to travel incognito, he will be a sitting duck. It is not just the common man who must be impressed with his authority, it is the extremist, the fundamentalist killer too. The DIG was helpless, without his shoes in the temple; these people do not respect helplessness.

Only authority is bulletproof.

'The common man, your Nehla and Dehla Singh, expects two things from authority: benevolence and summary, vicious despotism. Authority in Punjab has always been a mix of these two—moulded by public opinion—the essence of democracy,' and he laughs *Ho! Ho! Ho!* The place has no licence, but Scotch and soda is being served in liberal, if not elegant, style. 'The extremist is not far removed from the common man. Only, he sees himself as a soldier, and as a good soldier he does not expect benevolence. But the other thing that he expects, *that* he respects. Without that, I may as well take off my uniform and start collecting sticks for my funeral pyre.'

Shivi, silently chafing since the exchange in the SP's office, breaks out in words that stumble over each other: 'Where was it then? This summary despotism, vicious, retributive? Where was it when they shot Atwal down?'

The SP acts like the napkin he has been absently folding and unfolding has suddenly uncoiled itself and bitten him. It is to Sikand that he raises his eyes in reply.

'That is a tragedy,' he says and Sikand is almost sorry for him. 'One Inspector, the local SHO, was enough. With ten, fifteen men, no more. To rush in after the killer, Golden Temple or no—the law doesn't recognize any temple. Nothing would have happened, nothing. Everyone, the pilgrim, priest, extremist, everyone would have recognized our right to do so and would have parted like wheat before the wind. They might even have caught the killer and presented him before us. Without a single shot being fired. But there had to be no delay, no more than the minute required to take off one's shoes. And that is the tragedy. You see it? One Inspector; one stitch on time. Not a thousand stitches, clearing it from headquarters, advice from Chandigarh, instructions from Delhi—what do they know about it? And so nothing was done. We gave away the initiative, squandered away authority. And they? I tell you it was with amazement they realized that the Golden Temple was mightier than the law. Than the will of the Sarkar. A dangerous revelation it was. For them, and for us. The greatest tragedy.' And he leads them in long, silent drinking—a wake over the slain body of authority.

It's a fragile symbol, Sikand thinks, authority. A glass sceptre; a soap-bubble orb. He nods, and continues to nod as the SP delivers the obituary:

'Today, when even an Inspector's transfer is ordered from Delhi, they know it for what it is. A gust of wind has blown from the capital. It has blown away our garments, and they have seen our nakedness underneath. Now it will take bombs, aeroplanes, tanks, where our one Inspector, the three stars on his shoulder, would have done it.'

*

In the short flight to Delhi the clouds are dispelled, the plane landing at Palam under a bracing blue sky. Amritsar is a dream, an island adrift in the black fumes of a heavy night. Sikand wants to let it permeate and sink into the depths of the unremembered, the never felt.

Yet his behaviour is strange, even to himself. Almost the first thing he does on reaching home is to call the Dooars. His mother is asleep.

'She sleeps two-thirds of the day and is wide awake at night,' Nina says, 'I'll wake her up.'

'No, no. Don't. Tell her I called. No. No, don't.'

He replaces the receiver and is relieved and dejected in turn. Stares at the apparition against the wall that resolves itself into the severed headboard of her monstrous bed, and drives to another island of the night, the land across the Yamuna.

Trilokpuri. In the jumble of streets—narrow, dirty, oppressive to lung function—he tries to find the house of Kirat Singh, the carpenter. The block, the street, the house. A milk-booth in a corner. It is not the sameness that makes it difficult, for everywhere he looks he sees a new sort of squalor, yet in the end it all coalesces into a grey ugliness, geometric, laid out, but numbing to his navigational brain. Again he feels the cycle of relief and dejection. Returning over the jammed bridge livid with horns, to the avenues of Lutyens' Delhi, again relief.

*

Bibs is locking up, but is glad to see him. Things have been such a rush, his head has been in a whirl, and it has rained all the time Sikand has been away, the city flooded, impossible to breathe. First clear day today.

The cup has the familiar indeterminate liquid, hovering between tea and coffee, and his fingers cling to it.

'Bibs, I would say Shivi should be recalled from Amritsar.'

'Why? Do you want to take that over then?' Bibs asks brightly, as if he expects to be answered yes, yes, I do, I do.

'No.' You clown. 'It's just that Amritsar is not…well… conducive to writing. You said yourself he's not doing well. After having been there, I agree with you. You're right, Bibs. He'd be better off elsewhere.'

'Where?' Bibs is starting to whine. If you mention anything that's better for people, not for the magazine, that's what he always does.

'How about Chandigarh? I think we need someone there. It's the capital, we'd get a sort of overview on everything, the whole Punjab situation.'

'I agree, let's send Lola there…

'Livleen, Bibs. No she wouldn't do. She's still learning, feeling her way around. Besides she's a woman. She wouldn't do at all.' Wipe that smirk off your face, you numbskull, you nincompoop. He always arrives at healthy swear words for Bibs through strenuous mental gymnastics, merciless editing, an effort he's incapable of making today. Ninny, numbskull, idiot, clown, is all he can think of.

'Something's wrong with you, Sikand. It's the weather. Dulls one's brain. Makes things fuzzy. You were supposed to put the guy right, slap him into shape. Instead you come back pleading for his reprieve. Bad thing, emotional bias. One mustn't get involved with personalities, it just doesn't do. He's the only Sikh we've got, you know that. Him and Lola but she's a Sikhni, as you say. A woman.'

'Amritsar doesn't necessarily need a Sikh.' It does, in fact. No, it doesn't. Too much pressure for a Sikh. Too much trammelling of the rootlets into the giant all-encompassing root. Shivi is lost and found and lost again.

'Who else, but? It's hardly safe for the others you know that,' says Bibs.

'I don't. You think there aren't any Hindus walking around there? In broad daylight?'

'Broad daylight is right. But did you see any at night?'

That's Bibs's way of closing a topic, a puny witticism dribbling off his tongue, a sparkle like a snake's quick tongue darting, on then off, in his eyes. And he rattles the keys in applause: it's time to go home, and he always locks up after himself.

Sikand hangs around after he's gone. His desk is full of paper: letters, journals, news, all of which he pushes away from him into one big pile. His trusty fountain pen. He squeezes out all the ink, cleans the nib on something from the pile, and refills it with his nice black ink, opaque and hard.

Shivi has not asked to be moved. But Sikand cannot forget the moment of silent pleading in the SP's office, which he has decided to interpret as a plea for reprieve. On the other hand, there is merit in Bibs's stand—the profession demands equanimity in troubled times and places. He has said as much to Shivi in parting. Advising a cultivated distance from events. Paint them like an artist who stands well back and views his canvas through narrowed eyes.

But Shivi's reply: 'To me, Sikand, you seem like a man looking back on life even while it's happening,' has a tragic ring, like last words.

As a sop, for Bibs and for himself, he decides to write a piece on turbans; he will ambulate on the periphery, he thinks, drawing links as they come.

'*There are fifty-one types of turbans*,' he begins, '*but I shall draw your attention to the half a dozen I admired on my recent trip to Amritsar…*'

7

A smart turban makes the greatest contribution to a Sikh's good looks, and Fareed aspires to tie the smartest turban, not just in Moranwale, but in Madhok, Samnaula, Jaito, the entire region. In Ludhiana, the urban capital of the villages, he will lean right out of the bus window and screw up his eyes to examine every fold of any smart turban he spots in the street. The colours have to be right for a start: lemon yellow, sky blue, a pink the colour of onions. Of course everyone wears saffron nowadays, as dictated by the militants, but saffron is really a colour for ceremonies. It looks good at weddings and festivals, but otherwise it is a little loud, a little vain. Babaji says it is the colour of battle, but even the Sikh Light Infantry, whose regimental colour it is, wears only the drab army green for daily duties. Ceremony will allow even a full-blown rose pink or the dignified maroon—old-fashioned it's true, but he is a traditionalist in such matters. The sprinkling of turquoise blues and flame oranges, the rich purple of ripe brinjals—these he discounts, no matter how well they're tied.

Colour is a fragile thing.

For the past two years he has been buying off-white turbans, and getting them dyed in Samnaula from Maluk, his father's man. Although Maluk's hand is a trifle heavy on the old man's turbans, he knows Fareed's must be treated like eggshells. In that respect he is no different from the other tradesmen in Samnaula—all of them handle the youth with utmost care these days.

'One of them came up and said, "Malukay, your blood is the colour I want on my turban," and then laughed right in my face,' he complains.

'Look at the bright side,' Fareed consoles. 'All the Sikh boys who were cutting their hair, becoming like the Hindus, they're all growing long beards and hair now. The turban business is booming.'

'Of what use is business, Sardar Sahab, when my head may be lying in the gutter tomorrow?' is Maluk's bleak response.

After a good colour, a turban must be starched just right, and here the amount of cloth used is critical. You can save on best quality muslin and starch it heavily, so that the turban is almost solid like the queer hats of the Phapa businessmen in the towns, whose time, being money, can't be squandered on tying fresh turbans every day. But if you want a proud turban, you'll be generous with the cloth and stingy with the starch. And if you really care, you will stitch two turbans along their lengths and hardly starch at all, so that the fold upon fold of soft cloth is a royal dome on the head, a Patiala Shahi turban.

'The Jat boys want no more starch than this.' Maluk, who wears no turban himself, just a piece of oily cloth that matches his rusty beard, will touch his forefinger to his thumb and roll his big eyes heavenward at the impossibility of meeting such fatwas. 'How I wish this terrorism would end.'

'If it does they'll all start cutting their hair again, and where will your business go?'

'Into the well. I will happily dye turbans for the frogs I tell you. But let it end. Boys strutting around with guns in the open marketplace! Boys not old enough to pee standing up. They have scared you too, I see. That's why you're getting this saffron.'

'I'm not scared,' Fareed protests, 'There's a wedding in our village.'

'Good, very good. It's a wonder people are still getting married, having babies, dying in their beds. But this colour is good on you. You will be a Shah at the wedding. Maybe a beautiful girl there will not be able to resist your brown eyes. Then you can wear this same saffron on your own wedding, sit like a prince on a white horse...'

'Stop it, Malukay—that will be many years hence. But don't worry, only you shall dye my wedding turban.'

'If I am alive...'

'And I too.'

With the neatly packaged turban in his basket, Fareed has wheeled his cycle round to cross the crowded market, when he is hailed from behind. Across the square stands Jeeta, pale and thin, with what appears to be a smile on his face. Fareed drops his cycle. Hemmed in by other cycles, scooters, handcarts, he sees Jeeta joined by two men, one of whom he recognizes as Jeeta's father. The other, younger, carrying a suitcase, turns when Fareed calls. Then placing an arm around Jeeta's shoulder he leads him up an alley to the side of the store they were standing outside. Just before he is lost to view, Jeeta turns his head and looks back once at Fareed.

Retrieving his fallen cycle, Fareed weaves through the mindless crowd, furiously ringing his bell. Shoppers, sellers, carts, and all manner of fruits and vegetables, toys and farm implements hold their ground. Forced to dismount, he pushes his way with shoulders down to emerge out of the crush, breathless and disoriented. Cycling up the alley reveals a fork at the end with no sign of Jeeta or the shiny blue suitcase.

Overcome by the strangeness of the encounter, the sudden disappearance, he slowly wheels his cycle back. All the way to the village he can think of nothing else. Jeeta is alive and free. He flushes hotly when he remembers his stupidity in walking them both into the police station that day. But Jeeta can't possibly blame him, he can't still be angry—why else would he have called out? And then he realizes who the third man with the suitcase was. Jeeta's brother-in-law, his sister's gunpoint husband, the uggarwadi.

He stops with one foot on an anthill by the side of the road. Why was a known and marked extremist walking around the Samnaula market place in broad daylight like he owned it? Big ants scurry out of their holes holding their thin eggs above their heads. It hits him in a flash—the cops are scared of the uggarwadis. Every day there's some policeman shot dead. The papers still haven't forgotten the DIG at the Golden Temple. They're even targeting policemen's relatives. Just yesterday somebody's old mother was shot dead in a rickshaw in Batala or some place. Right in the market-place.

He is suddenly sure that Jeeta is free because of his brother-in-law. He imagines the black thanedar shivering, opening the barred door and standing aside to let Jeeta pass. The black face in which the thick lips gleam wet and pink swims before him. And the vice-grip of his own fear in the police station returns. All is avenged, he tells himself. He no longer has to feel shame. Yet the memory of his fear cycles with him through the darkening fields over which the lonely *kook kook kook* of a flourmill floats from somewhere across the broad, flat stretch.

Back at the village he finds a big lock on Jeeta's door. A seeri passing by with a head load of fodder says they left for Amritsar in the morning, the whole family.

No one ever did that in the village—leave a home, the whole family. What will become of their animals, he wonders, of their fields and crops?

*

For days the sound of singing has spilled over the mud walls of the house of the wedding. In the late afternoons when the women gather in their numbers, it rises to a continuous drone that travels beyond the school and the pond to the far highway. Snatches of softer song burst out at any time of the day, for the house is full of relatives—strangers who laugh and call to each other so gaily in the street that the natives themselves are reduced to bashful strangers.

Yet all their songs are somehow sad, saturated with the sorrow of parting. Of fathers, brothers, mothers, sisters crying in blighted gardens from where the nightingale has flown.

'Isn't it supposed to be a happy occasion?' he calls to the women as they enter one evening, looking amiable and content after their afternoon's moaning. 'Why all this wailing, as if it were a funeral?'

'Trust this boy to always spout the most inauspicious word,' his mother says through gritted teeth, and with a muttered 'Waheguru', is transformed into her everyday self, burdened with her hundred neglected tasks.

'It's a happy occasion only for the boy,' Dishan says. 'He gets a wife. But for the girl it's a tragedy.'

'Why? Isn't she getting a husband too? Someone who will care for her, buy her nail-polish and things?'

'And make her slave from morning till night, looking after his home and his parents and his buffaloes and his children and his...'

'Stop, stop. Isn't that what you do here, anyway? How would it be any worse?' he laughs.

'Here I do it in my own home, for my own people,' Dishan starts hotly and then, for some strange reason, bursts into tears.

They are a mystery to him, these two.

Early each morning, much before first light, the 'Japji Sahib' prayer comes over the gurudwara loudspeaker like a signal for Dishan to rise and go to the aid of her mother, who has been up for an hour already.

Fareed has never been able to tell when exactly his mother wakes. As a child he would feel for her in the pitch-dark of night to find her gone.

'How do you know it's time to get up?' he had asked and remembers her reply. 'I just know the things that have to be done and the hours there are to do them in. So I know by myself when it's time to wake up and begin.'

Once, sleepless with a burning fever in severest winter, he had risen too and followed, snivelling, in her wake, as she bustled from hearth to hearth. Hollow notes floated from her blow-pipe and the flames leapt to grab her hair as her shadow loomed huge and threatening behind her on the wall. When dawn glanced off the brass buckets ready for the milking, he snuggled in right between the buffalo's legs as she washed the purple udders. The first warm spray had hit him straight in the eye. The next hissed against the metal of the bucket in a pure singing sound that had often punctured his dreams. In those nascent moments all the secrets of the daytime were explained. The earthenware pot of milk that purred and rumbled by itself till mid-day, turning thick and pink in the clay oven, the mounds of rotis he had imagined growing overnight on their own. Spellbound in those hours of discovery, if he could have stopped the dawn from ripening into day, he would have done it then.

But his father was already stirring, the old old man was coughing his morning cough. And Randhir was hollering for something or the other.

The clanging of chain and tool and bucket, the bustle and call of men had claimed the world.

*

At the wedding, Fareed's eyes are riveted on the red velvet bag that lies in Khushwant's lap. Seated next to the bride, she is keeping account of the presents of money that neighbours and relatives offer as they bless the bride. All he sees is the hurrying of her hands as they draw open the string, slip in a currency note and pull the bag tight again with a busy, prim action. How fair and delicate are her hands in contrast to those of the bride, with nails painted with the reddest nail-polish like smears of blood, frightening to behold.

The memory of their last meeting is a painful embarrassment:

He had walked up to her on the flimsy strength of one of those dares he sometimes set himself, her friends moving apart as he purposefully planted himself squarely in front of her.

'Fareed! How tall you've grown!' she'd said.

And he: 'Yes. It's my age to grow tall.' Then all the girls had tittered in unison and he had beamed back like a stalwart.

'So. What have you been up to?' he'd said, acting like one of those people he found so stupid, but not being able to help himself. Through her account of the teacher's training she was undergoing, the six months left, the hoping to get a job later at a good school in Samnaula, he had kept his hands in his pockets and rocked, actually rocked, on his heels and toes.

'Very nice place, Samnaula,' he'd said. 'Lots of things to see there.'

'What things?' she'd laughed. 'Just dirt and dust and crowded streets!'

And her friends had melted away, quickly, as if they had to run somewhere at once to laugh.

'There are parks and gardens, full of flowers,' he'd insisted, thinking there surely must be some, and she had laughed again. But, for some reason that meeting, disastrous as it was, had made him settle on her as his chosen one.

A clapping and singing rises from the inner courtyard of the wedding house. For the men outside it is a discharge of high voltage in their midst and Fareed is carried like a twig on the rush up the stairs, to be deposited onto a flat roof. There is no parapet and he has to dig in with all his strength to stop being thrust over the edge by the throng of male eagerness, into the arms of the women below.

In the courtyard a young girl and a fat middle-aged woman are dancing inside a circle of women. Fareed's hands find the rhythm of the clapping and his body starts to sway. The men are supposed to watch the dancing from hidden corners, but here on the open roof, no pretence is possible, and the young girl, after a faltering circle or two drops out, running to hide in the veranda. The older woman carries on regardless, sometimes looking up brazenly, straight into their faces, to ensure she is observed.

'Climb on to my rickshaw, young maiden,' she sings, thrusting out her stomach obscenely before her, imploring with open arms her failed partner, the young girl now swallowed by the shadows. At Fareed's elbow, a little lad lets out a piercing wolf-whistle.

There is an understanding that he disturbs, and someone cuffs his ear from behind. The life suddenly ebbs out of the scene, the dancing becoming mechanical, like P.T., and it is several minutes before they are forgiven. The idiot really deserved that blow, Fareed thinks.

But now things are getting merrier and merrier as several women rise to swirl on their heels, their arms spread out before them. The drum ups its rhythm and the frenetic clapping conjoins them upstairs and downstairs, the women making diamond shapes with their fingers, the men heaving, shifting, pressing. Breathless with excitement, Fareed looks for escape. It is unbearable, the heat of the sun on the bare roof, the sweat, the jostling.

He pushes his way blindly out of the jungle of bodies, his eyes already searching the groups in the outside courtyard, in the doorway, on the road. In the bridal room he joins the queue again, searching in his pockets for the fifty rupee note, finding and clutching it, inching forward, noting that people are simply waving the notes over the bride's head and pressing them into the hands of the bride's friend. Her.

When their hands touch he whispers: 'Meet me at the outside door. Five minutes,' words running into each other, but as he reels around he thinks: it is done, it is there.

Boys he knows lounge around the door to the street. He wouldn't blame her, if she didn't come. She would be faultless. Forever.

But she comes.

Overwhelmed by the sunlight outside, hesitating, narrowing her eyes.

He turns and walks down the street, not hurrying but still as if with a purpose. Down the road, away from the wedding, not looking, not caring almost, whether she follows.

In his saffron turban his father cycles leisurely up the street at him. Oblivious. Heading for the wedding, like a buffalo. Fareed slides into an open doorway, deep into the dark before he breathes. The smell of toori, dry fodder, piled up high to the roof. Little husks of it beginning to tickle his nostrils, his throat, so that he has to hold on, not burst, till the wheels of his father's cycle putter through the dust by the door. He sneezes. Then, cautious, giving the old man time to dismount, to wheel his cycle in, he peers at last around the door and finds her face an inch away from his. Full of a suppressed something. Ready to burst. With laughter.

He shoots out a hand and pulls her inside with a violence he didn't intend.

'You must take this seriously,' he hisses.

Her surprised cry of pain brings him quickly to his senses, and letting go of her hand, he says, quieter now, 'You must take me seriously.'

The distance is collapsed. Although she tries, weakly, saying, 'Why have you brought me here?' rubbing her wrist where his fingers have been.

'You followed me…'

'You called me.'

That is the truth. Although to tell the full truth, he has not intended this. What did he intend? To walk out with her to the fields, to say something under the sky, to be taken seriously… not where he's ended up, in this dark room where the chaff goes up his nose and makes him sneeze! It makes her laugh again, and again he feels the need to make her suffer. She has come, she has followed him and that can only mean one thing…he drags her by the arm, into the darkness, onto the pile of chaff that slips and slithers, takes the shapes of their bodies, her body and his body and then her body, deeply her body, for he is on top of her, slipping deeper into the pile, grappling, groping, his lips landing anywhere they can in the melee, brushing and kissing, licking and bruising, while she makes soft sounds that have no meaning and the chaff squeaks with protest.

His hand is on a soft breast…

All of a sudden she is up, quick and lashing, 'You mustn't do that!' And before anything, she is writhing away, clumsy, trying to rise, sinking into the impossible shifting chaff, then leaping right off to stand, chest heaving, body blazing in a shaft of light from the door. With savage, futile gestures she strikes at herself, at the thousand slivers of chaff that cling to her clothes, her hair, everywhere. She flinches when his hand comes up, but it is only to help her and she stands stock still, her arms by her side, trembling ever so slightly, as he tries, flake by flake to remove every grain he can see, thinking all the while, 'I just squeezed too hard.'

When he has finished, he stares at the floor and says: 'I'm sorry, I think I lost my head,' and she nods, steps to the door, leans cautiously out once and then quickly over the doorstep, is gone.

Back at the wedding, the ceremony has begun under an awning in the outer courtyard. After making his obeisance before the Granth, Fareed squeezes in next to Lala so called because of his quivering stomach and his narrow shifty eyes. They dart sideways at him now, as he says, 'You look like you've been having a roll in the hay,' in what is meant to be a whisper. Fareed looks down at his clothes, trying to shake off the chaff, a piece here, a mote there, as innocently as he can. He should have gone home and changed, now it is too late.

'No use removing the evidence. I'm going to tell everybody anyway.'

'Tell them what?' Fareed tries a long hard stare, but it doesn't work.

'Unless you tell me who it was with.'

He tries the casual brush-off. 'Nobody, yaar. Just had to dump a stupid sack of toori into the store before I came.'

'In your best clothes?'

'Shhh.' He puts a finger to his lips. His eyes gesture to the Granth, its glowing hangings. He shuts his eyes to underline his meaning.

A stir outside announces the bride and all eyes are now on the slow procession. Not on the bride herself, for she is just a shape in red garments, but on the faces of the friends who accompany her. Solemn and self-conscious, with downcast eyes, they lead her down the aisle to where her future glitters in the person of the groom before the Granth. Khushwant, in the lead, never once raises her eyes although she must, she has to, feel his gaze bore holes into her.

'Which one?' Lala's ridiculous stage whisper makes him wildly divert his glance. To the velvet folds around the Granth, the rainbow ripple of its canopy in the breeze. To the bride now seated beside the groom in front of it, and to her friends, their backs to the congregation, arrayed about her, so decorous and subdued.

Across the arch of Khushwant's back, the thin fabric is stretched tight, translucent with promise. And on the nape of her neck, the short hairs curl, golden in the light. And in them, shining for him like a diamond, stranded for all the world to see, a thin, almost non-existent, fragment of chaff.

'What makes you fidget like a frog, then?' asks Lala, clearing his throat.

'The toori, you bastard!' he says, ignoring Lala's look of pained astonishment at this blasphemy in the presence of the Granth.

8

If the old man were to give up drinking and beating his mother, if Babaji were to recover the full use of his eyes and knees, and if he himself were to marry Khushwant and have children with her, there will be nothing left for Fareed to want of life. Although there has to be—where will he feed Khushwant and the babies from, for instance? He can't see himself in the fields, the joy he took as a child in watching things grow has deadened along the way. And his one attempt to join the army ended in him running away from the ground to see a film when the boys, in their underwear, had to line up at the measuring post to the sound of whistles and drums. Then there is the curtain of fog through which it is impossible to see the road ahead. It is perfectly logical, he considers, that there isn't even a road beyond the fog, just an abrupt drop into space.

A month after the DIG is killed, they shoot dead the Dean of the Agriculture University in Ludhiana. He was a hockey player of repute, not just some unknown professor, and the crime is talked about for days all over Punjab.

'They've started on Sikhs now,' says Babaji shaking his head. 'The machine is going mad.'

The machine, as everybody knows, is Bhindranwale. When Fareed had not bothered his head with it all, the machine had been disposing of Nirankaris and Hindus. There was the murder in Delhi of the head of the Nirankari sect—their Guru, whom you weren't supposed to call that—that is the only significant thing he remembers of it now. Delhi was so far away. Later, closer to home, they had shot the Hindu Lala of a big group of newspapers in Jalandhar. This killing the newspapers still have not forgotten, even after all this time when every day there are more and more murders to report. Sant Jarnail Singh Bhindranwale, a strange sort of Sant with a revolver in a holster and a belt full of bullets instead of the traditional kirpan, is ever present in the papers too. Even the naked kids at the pond jump in holding their noses and shouting *Bhindranwale!* where Fareed and his friends used to shout *Sat Sri Akal!*

From village to village, Bhindranwale has travelled, raising dust and excitement like in an election. Railing at Sikhs to give up drinking and cutting their hair like the Hindus and making them sip sweet holy water Amrit to seal their promises. He came to their village too, but they did not go to sip the Amrit because the old, old man said it was all politics. Bhindranwale was being used by the Congress to wrest the gurudwaras out of Akali hands. And the old man was sore about the no-drinking clause.

'Someone should tell the Congress what a dangerous man he is,' he muttered, and Babaji said, 'Well it won't be the Akalis. They're breaking their backs trying to look more dangerous than him.'

This was the Anandpur Sahib Resolution, a lot of confusion generated by the Akalis. They don't know themselves what species of bird or animal it is, says Babaji. Some call it the Khalistan Resolution, a demand for a separate nation, while others say it is simply a document claiming more independent powers for Punjab. And also, for good measure, for the other twenty-five states of the Indian union.

It is all politics, as Babaji says.

But what is politics?

Sometimes Fareed is sure it means a service, like running the railways. Making sure that trains are not derailed and a man reaches his home not too late. The people are supposed to be the rajas and maharajas, the rulers. Not the Congress or the Akalis. That's what the text-book says—government by the people. Making asses and sons of owls of the people. Bribing them. 'We'll let you decide every five years who's to rule you. The Congress or the Akalis.' And now it seems that politics is a race. Who will discredit the other the most and fastest? Bhindranwale comes in here. One only has to wait and see who he will discredit the most, the Congress or the Akalis.

Fareed, labouring through the *Tribune* under the watery eye of Babaji, doesn't know if what is reported there is fact.

Printed words can lie, just like in his textbook. 'It says here that Bhindranwale proclaims he is protecting the Sikh faith,' he says, looking suspiciously up at Babaji.

'That he does. The Nirankaris are Enemy No. 1 for him. Let them start afresh, build their own religion, write their own scriptures, he says, not take ours and corrupt it.'

'So why don't they?' The Nirankaris have a living guru. Yet they revere the Granth, which says that there is no guru after Gobind Singh. That the only guru is the Granth.

'They have. But their Amrit Baani starts off after the Granth and refers to it in many places. Just as the Granth quotes the Hindu scriptures, and refers to Ram, Krishan and Allah, all the time.'

So being a Nirankari is not such a crime. Every religion dives off the bank of another.

'Can anything be new,' Babaji asks, 'except by being imposed on the old?'

And you can kill people but not what they think. That is the meaning of the Sikh prayer, the Ardaas, that ends every prayer with the list of sacrifices. The bricking up into walls, the boiling in hot oil, all that Sikhism has survived. Remembering the martyrs, Guru Teg Bahadur and Arjun Dev, and the sons of Guru Gobind Singh, and all the Sikhs who died saying, 'I give my head but not my faith.' Remembering atrocities ensures survival.

At other times politics, religion, violence, everything confuses Fareed, presses down on him saying, 'Decide, decide or you are gone.' And he can't decide, can't for the life of him understand what it is he must decide and why. He isn't ready, he thinks; it isn't fair to press him so. Suppose under all the goading he decides in haste...?

He asks simple questions and gets answers that are other questions. When innocent Hindus are pulled off a bus and shot

Babaji asks, 'Suppose the eighty per cent Hindus start to murder Sikhs all over the country in revenge, where will be our two per cent Sikhs then?' Killing Hindus is political—so Punjab will have only Sikhs left. When the Hindus react in other parts of the country, the Sikhs will all run back. It will be like Partition again, a Hindu movement out of Punjab, a Sikh movement in.

But why kill Sikhs then? The answer, a question, is the hawks and the sparrows over again. 'If a sparrow raises its voice, you think the hawk will leave it?'

*

'There is more hell to go through, Sikand. None of us want it, and I want to ask what the politicians, the Congress and the Akalis, and you, the media, will take to stop creating it?'

Ambika is on the warpath once again. Sometimes Sikand sees the striking resemblance between her and his mother, even though they look so different. And he has to admit that, in some dimly lit recess of his mind, he admires them both.

Fixing a pleasant look on his face he moves away, making listening movements with his head to the kind of conversation that is the staple of Ambika's parties. But he is still watching her flounce around the room, her slimness proclaiming a youth, a spurious youth she is well past. She leans over to fill a glass, exposing her gums in a hostess smile, so frank and so false.

'How thin you've gone,' he says the moment she drifts towards him with her plate of soggy biscuits dotted with their virulent sauce. 'I begin to fear that some day you'll be blown away by a puff of breeze and I shall lose my best friend and critic.'

She abandons the plate to sit really close to him, thigh pressing thigh, and says into his ear: 'Don't you wish I was plump and fair, instead of dark and thin? That way your eyes could finally believe your heart that tells you, you love me...'

Suddenly she is delicious and he laughs out loud. His arm is around her waist, gently fitting in, there is an island in the party with just the two inhabitants. Briefly. She slips out, planting a chaste kiss on his cheek, and is receiving with exuberance the young woman who has just walked in.

'Ah young Livleen,' he says his eyes lighting up as the plump and fair woman makes straight for his corner. Every eye is on her as she wraps her arms around his weather-beaten neck, and says in her breathless, melting voice, 'Did you expect me, Sikand?'

'Not at all. A pleasant, a delightful surprise,' with his nose in her hair. Beneath the flowery perfume she smells like a freshly-bathed baby.

'Neither did Ambika,' she giggles into his ear, 'I'm afraid I gate-crashed.'

It doesn't matter. His self-confidence totally restored, Sikand watches over her as she arranges a flame-coloured netted thing about her front. 'Now I'm too embarrassed to go looking for a glass of wine,' she laughs.

It doesn't matter, he thinks, going to the bar for her drink, that she is dressed in the boots and baubles she follows like a faith, nor that with this single glass of wine she will begin to talk too shrill and too loud. Right now she is youthful; a heady elixir. Her audacity at being where she isn't invited bubbles forth in inane epigrams. She has a tendency to cling like one of those delicate vines, the pink passionflower, to his accommodating side. It doesn't matter that as the evening wears on she will unloose her hair and swing it with increasing life and vigour while the energy starts to leak out of those about her. He will stretch his eyelids open and wearily pretend to be there beside her, draped over a ridiculous bar stool, amused by her jejune wide-awake chatter. But it doesn't matter.

They talk inevitably about the magazine and about Bibs. Wedged in beside him, Livleen talks to the room, pouting her lips and wrinkling her forehead, calling him 'Great Master'. Indulging her unashamedly, he plays the sage to her nymphet.

'You may know, Young Livleen, that I have saved you from a fate worse than death,' he says. 'Bibs wanted to send you to Amritsar.'

'Did he?' she squeals.

'Yes. But I put my foot down.'

She goes down on her knees before him. Frank, drinking stares reach out from all sides to the little tableau they make. He is not usually this showy but he takes a willing break now from good taste. Offering his hand to be kissed, he thinks: They don't have to know it's not like that, let them entertain their filthy imaginations!

His one regret is the hostess's bad timing. No doubt she will enter a moment too late with another plate of lukewarm snacks, puffed with pride at being a successful career woman *and* a good housekeeper.

He suffers eventually, as he must. Just when the party is thinning out, becoming intimate and quiet, just when the hostess is preparing to relax on the sofa and put her feet up, Livleen wants an ice-cream at India Gate. Anticipating quietness and intimacy he would rather remain, but feels payment is due to Livleen. Besides he can't let her sweet plumpness go solitary into the dangerous night.

'Come back later if you can,' Ambika says as he takes leave of her, 'Daddy has been asking about you.'

In the car Livleen slides over to rest her head on his shoulder, and he finds he doesn't like himself any more. Just two people in need of each other, he thinks, but can't remove the traces, clandestine like lipstick smears, that sully the question. True, she needs him, but does she know? And he knowing, does he have the right to fit need with need? Now he is glad Ambika was out of the room. In hindsight, his moment of glory is a moment of fatuous stupidity. Yet he tells Livleen again about how Bibs suggested she should go as their correspondent to Punjab. Bibs hadn't been totally serious, but what the heck, sometimes his self-imposed webs of hesitation irk him. He inhales the free air of being like other people, cruising the wide directionless streets of night.

'What does Bibs think, that I'd be scared?' she asks.

'No, that I'd be. And I was.'

'Oh you are *tooo* sweet,' and she cuddles up. His discomfort with himself grows into fascinating distaste. Taking his eyes from the road he plants a brief kiss on her forehead, but she turns her lips to his and the kiss is a bruised accident of intention. He pulls up and she is in his arms. 'Old enough to be her father,' he thinks and surrenders to himself.

'Honey child,' he mumbles between kisses, and the words echo in his mind, honey child, honey child. At last they strike him as incongruous, accelerator and brake collocated. With the return of reason, he puts her gently away from him, and wiping the taste of her from his lips, turns on the ignition to drive her home.

*

Returning to Ambika's he finds her alone, having difficulty emptying a brass ash-tray into a dustbin. 'Always couldn't stand people who stuff paper napkins into ash-trays,' she says.

The room is a mess. He tries to help but ends up in the kitchen with a stack of glasses he can't get unstuck. Laying them gently on their side in the sink as they are, hoping she wouldn't think it was him, he returns to the sitting room. 'How's the Brigadier?' he asks.

'Come,' she says abandoning her bowls and plates.

The room is dark.

Sikand whispers a protest. 'He's sleeping, Ambika.'

'No, he's not,' she says, switching on the light with a loud click.

Her father is sitting up in bed blinking his eyes in a rapid, unseeing manner.

'Stand here, Sikand,' Ambika says. 'He can't see much to his right.'

'Sikand?' the old man says tentatively.

'Yes. Sir.' Sikand takes his hand, cool and dry like paper. 'I'm sorry to disturb you so late.'

'A long time. I wanted to talk to you. I've been meaning to tell you.' His speech is slow. Sikand sees the effort needed to form the words.

'I've been out on work. Amritsar, Chandigarh, Delhi. Up and down. But I've been wanting to see you too.' There is a little sigh from the bed, as if his words have consoled. 'What is it you've been meaning to tell me. Something about Punjab?' he prompts.

For a moment the old man opens his eyes wide, startled. Then he shuts them and seems to fall asleep. Sikand stands stiffly, his hand held. When he tries to withdraw it, the eyes open wide again.

'And Nimmi?' the old man says very clearly.

Taken aback at this mention of his mother, Sikand doesn't know quite what to reply. And when Ambika, fiddling with medicine bottles at the writing desk, calls across the room, 'Daddy you're forgetting that Nimmi Aunty's not here any more,' and when the old man asks involuntarily 'Dead hain?' he is more tongue-tied still.

Ambika comes over to the bed and pours the medicine into his obedient mouth. 'She's gone to the Dooars, to stay with Nina. You remember she came and saw you before she left? You spoke to her on the phone a month ago.'

Her father swallows again and again as if the liquid refuses to go down his throat.

On the way back from dropping Livleen, Sikand has imagined a gentle rambling talk. Gathering the old man's insights as he's done so many times before. Now it's just a call on a sick man.

'I had no idea he had gone down so rapidly,' he says when they have closed the door behind them and are in the dishevelled sitting room again.

'I'm sorry for—for what he said. He hardly knows sometimes where he is.'

'I had no idea,' he says again. 'He was more than okay the last time.'

'Sometimes, strangely, he's back. As if a ray of sunlight has pierced the fog.'

'I wish I'd come sooner. There was so much I had to say, to ask him about.'

'You know how with children you see them grow in sudden spurts? With the old, it's like the process is reversed—you see them fall vast distances in a single day.'

She is tired, flakes of makeup muddy her eyelids. He should go, but loath to leave unless she asks him to, follows her to the balcony and sinks into the roomy armchair, its cushions moulding around him into the ready built space of other days.

'Till last week,' Ambika says, 'he was managing his meals on his own. I could even trust him in the bathroom by himself. Then five days ago he just walks out of the house. All alone. In five minutes he's at the taxi-stand, looking for a cab to the railway station. To go to Benaras, he said, when we found him. With not a naya paisa, no money at all, in his pocket. And then every second day after that he was asking about trains. *Does the Kashi Express still run? Do you board it from Old Delhi?*'

'I won't be able to call him the Brigadier anymore,' Sikand says, almost to himself.

'No? But Sikand believe me, there are times when he's like he was before. The other day he remembered Nimmi Aunty so clearly. He said when she was a girl she could run faster than all the guys and no one wanted to race with her. I'm sure he knew then that she was in the Dooars with Nina.'

'Don't let it bother you, Ambika,' he murmurs.

A jasmine bush in the garden below perfumes the silent night. His weariness starts to flow from him, thick and slow as honey. There seems no need for more words and they sit, their silent worlds gently lapping against each other in the darkness, till daybreak.

*

A month later a series of armouries are looted. And banks all over Punjab. Arms, and money for arms. This time even the villages are not spared. On the midnight of 18 July, 1983, the old village, a mile from Moranwale, is struck for two shotguns and a rifle with a split barrel, one for which the ammunition is no longer manufactured.

Fareed waits at the canal to cycle to college with Tara from the old village.

'I think they were almost happy to hand over the arms,' says Tara. 'Our retired Subedar for sure had no license for his crippled rifle. Must have been worrying himself mad the police would find out about it. He threw in milk for all four of the uggarwadis, and got his daughter to serve them.'

'What did your Subedar learn in the army? Cowardice?' asks Fareed.

'I don't criticize him. I don't know what I would have done in his place.'

'I would certainly have left out the milk. But seriously, doesn't anyone think what they'll want next if no one resists? They probably know the arms are useless. They just want to frighten people. So tomorrow...'

'They'll want our sisters. Like with Jeeta?' Some things are to be thought and not spoken out, but Tara is an imbecile.

He shows as much by almost cycling Fareed into the canal, leaning across to whisper, 'Jeeta was one of them, one of the four!'

'Not possible,' Fareed responds immediately, irritated with his air of distributing pearls.

'Why? The Subedar's daughter recognized him. His head was wrapped in a shawl but she held the lamp up to his face when she brought him the glass of milk. He pushed it away angrily, is what she said.'

'To you?'

'No, not to me. But he was the only one who didn't open his mouth, she said. For fear his voice would be recognized, see?'

Fareed stops his cycle. 'You fool,' he says, then moves in to grab Tara's throat, squeezing hard: 'You watch out your crowing doesn't get your head lopped off for chicken curry. How would this Subedar's daughter even know what Jeeta's voice sounds like, *hnnh*? Or what his face looks like, *hnnh*? In the old village?' He doesn't know whether it is Tara's face going purple, or the sudden thought that his quick anger may decide his destiny that makes him give up. He releases his hold, recovers his cycle and carries on in a white, unthinking silence.

'What about yourself?' Tara says after a while, understanding that nothing is supposed to have happened, but not to be silenced still. 'Do you think you would be recognized in our village?'

'Never.'

'See? See how wrong you are. All the young girls recognize you. They ask about you. What do you think they do at weddings, except look at boys? Their faces, their voices, even their turbans, they memorize them like arithmetic tables.'

'Then they should all become police informers, there's money in young men's faces. Nowadays,' Fareed says, the laughter bubbling out of him like a fountain.

Later, Tara's story sounds entirely possible. He has always known this about Jeeta. It is inevitable, even somehow, right.

This placid judgement is soon to crumble however. At the

end of the month the countryside erupts in numerous fires that, with no one doing anything to put them out, threaten to become an all-consuming blaze. Immediately after come killings, explosions, shoot-outs. Bank and shop robberies. Strikes and bandhs and a series of Akali-sponsored Rasta-rokos, Rail-rokos, Kaam-rokos. Violence and legitimate political protest roll together in an explosive mix that leaves no doubt the Akalis and the militants are working hand in hand towards a common goal.

Every day it seems that someone Fareed knows has been seen with the militants, is involved in robbery or murder, and every day it seems another gaping hole has appeared in the wall between our side and the other. Twice there are rumours concerning Jeeta. He was seen holding a gun outside a bank, and another time riding a motorcycle away from a scene of a shooting with the killer of a newspaper vendor on his pillion. Soon these things are not discussed anymore. People read the papers, pick up whispered clues, but talk only of the weather and the crops, of marriage and sickness and death. And while they speak, Fareed sees the sense of doom that writhes like smoke inside him reflected in their faces and in their hooded eyes.

In August the murderer of Lala Jagat Narain is convicted and sentenced to life imprisonment. Bhindranwale reacts with a listing of atrocities committed on the Sikhs documented in harsh vernacular on audio-tapes that spread everywhere. Blood frenzy flows with his words, entering institutions and individual mud-walled homes and a sea of saffron flows out into the streets. In three days the state government is forced to close all schools and colleges and then there is nothing to stem the flow.

*

Fareed starts a frenetic round of travel agents from Ludhiana to Nawashehr, his desperation fuelled by a chilling certainty of his fate if he stays. Students, propelled by the words of Bhindranwale, are lining up to join the Federation. Those who are reluctant are beginning to look weak and gutless. It is going to suck him in, this madness, what is so special about him that he will survive? He must escape before it gets him, this is all he thinks about. Randhir must find the money and he must find a passport.

'No passports,' the travel agent who had helped Randhir says. 'The boom is over, police have no time for verifications, there are no clerks in the passport offices, nothing. We may as well close up shop.' 'Forget it!' says another, but as Fareed refuses to go away, the man suggests a fake passport, very confidential, very good, true-blue like the real thing—watermarks, stamps, everything. Only fifteen thousand rupees for risking prison and his life.

'How much does a real one cost?' Fareed asks.

'A pot full of diamonds. Get it?'

A third has the forms but advises him not to even risk applying. 'Who knows who's got a bead on you, hain?' he says. That's the advice he would give to his own son. Nowadays.

In a darkened studio Fareed twirls his sparse moustache with a cream the cameraman gives him and has his picture taken. Then he sits on a bench at the bus-station and fills out the forms while his moustache attacks him with the sweet smell of roses. For attesting the photographs and testifying that he has known him for the last five years, a bored official takes two hundred and fifty rupees, which requires the pawning of his watch. It is evening by the time he is at the travel agent's again asking, 'Now what?'

'Now you wait. Maybe they'll send a policeman to verify you.'

'In how much time?'

'Who can say? Fifteen days, a month, a year.'

'And after that?'

'After that, if the report is okay, and if it goes to the passport office, they'll issue you a passport.'

'In how much time?'

'How do I know? You talk like I'm an astrologer. Three months, a year. Maybe never.'

As he is walking out, the man calls, 'And after that, you'll have to apply for a visa. At the embassy in Delhi.'

'How much time?' Fareed returns, but is already in the street and cannot hear the man's reply.

9

Intoxicated with too much sun, a fly buzzes maddeningly in Fareed's ear. Trapped in a thicket of thorn trees, he can risk a swipe at it only at the cost of scratching himself and giving away his hiding place. He shies at it feebly but the fly is no quitter. When it lands on his upper lip, Fareed snorts and it whizzes its tickling straight back to his ear.

But here is Khushwant at last. About time. Their bus is late, otherwise she and her two giggling friends would certainly have missed it. The fly scolds in his ear. There is to be no compensation today—no hearing her say, 'Isn't it a day made for mischief?' or laugh her breathless laugh.

Honking its horn, the bus comes down the road. They board in a hurry, which makes her drop a book. Having to climb down, panic in her eyes at seeing the bus already start to move. Fareed curses the stone-hearted son-of-a donkey driver, till in a cloud of dust they are gone. He makes a vicious swipe at the fly and scratches himself from elbow to wrist.

In a black mood he waits for the police constable to arrive for the verification, curses the government, his little sleepy village, man and woman. God. In the afternoon, himself. For not being capable of going right up to Khushwant, damn the scandal, not being able to fix a chance meeting, nothing but hiding and drinking in like a thirsty man these glimpses of her each morning.

As it had begun, the day ends badly. His mother, bringing him a glass of milk, finds him lying on his cot in the open staring up at the stars that crowd the sky. She is good at such times, treating him like a son who has gone away on a long journey and returned wounded and several years younger. They talk about how the mosquitoes have not subsided with the cold, but he is thinking how dark it is beyond the stars. She knows this winter will be the coldest one, for the water already numbs the fingers in the mornings, and he is thinking where he will be this winter, of the indescribable loneliness beyond the stars.

'After the partition, people said life would never be the same again. But it was, see? We have buffaloes and fields and a house just like before.' Yes, but what about the children, the boys? Were they the same inside, afterwards? Did they grow up as if nothing had happened? As if they had not seen, not done, things too horrible to condone? Did they not wish sometimes that they had died on some train from Lahore?

'Our fears are always more dreadful than reality.' How can he make her understand? That time can take his life and twist it like a wire, willy-nilly, without his leave? Can't she see how dark it is getting, as if all the clouds have gathered into a vast mushroom of darkness, stifling their world? It is pointless to try to make her see. For her life is like a river from cradle to pyre. The immense rocks that tear the flow, make it go where it was never meant to, the vast tumults, what is the use of explaining these to her? All she will do is banish the thoughts with a single, shuddering 'Waheguru.'

*

It is seven o'clock and growing dark when Fareed approaches the Peepal by the pond. In the wide circle he takes around it he spots no one in the shadows under its branches. It is a trick. He should have grabbed the little scamp who sidled up to him outside the gurudwara, but he had run before Fareed even understood that the piece of paper that had been thrust into his hand was a note.

'Meet me at the Peepal at seven tonight,' was all it said. And it was signed 'K'.

His heart had leapt and sunk quickly, like a hand-pump. It was not the handwriting of the classmate he had known for so many years, but she was older, after all. He ran his fingers over the shapes of the letters but that had told him nothing. Seven o'clock. With the whole village at dinner, already battening down for the night. She couldn't possibly get out at that time. But he had believed, in the end, for he had wanted to.

Now he thinks of Lala. His beady eyes never missed a thing; he could spot a quarter of a rupee, a chavanni, in the dust. That tell-tale stick of chaff in Khushwant's hair at the wedding. That had to be it. Or perhaps he'd seen Fareed go to his hiding place in the thorn thicket. Lala was so smart, he would have put two and two—but for what?

He decides to wait. If she has written the note, and if she comes he will hold her so gently she won't feel his touch.

The minutes pass slowly, marked by hollow plops as he chucks mud balls into the water. Each plop silences the frogs, freezing them in mid-croak. But then forgetting too soon, they sound off again till the next plop hits them with its bullet-like surprise.

Slowly it becomes evident that he's been duped, and when he hears the sound of cycles on the track he is sure it is Lala with friends, come to gloat. He rises, determined to stop the merriment before it begins. As quickly, he sits down again, for dismounting from the bikes are four men. And the dark shapes that grow out of their shoulders are unmistakably guns.

One is pointed in a flash in his direction, for he has been seen.

'Come out, you little son of a bitch.'

He walks slowly out of the shadows with his arms in the air.

'What are you doing here?' says the pointed gun. White handkerchiefs hide the faces of all the men.

'Nothing,' Fareed says, his voice sounding low and calm. 'Just sitting.'

'Waiting for somebody, *hain*? For a girl?' the man says coming forward.

Fareed starts to shake his head, then feels it wrenched right off his neck by a tremendous blow. The sound in his ear is like a thunderclap. Before the singing ceases, another blow hammers into his chin, lifting and dropping him to the ground. The sour taste of blood is on his tongue. He feels himself gag and turns over on his elbow. A kick gets him in the ribs and his face falls into the dirt. He does not move again.

'Don't kick him any more,' a different voice says, 'unless you want to kill him.'

'I'll shoot him dead, the bastard.' The first voice again. On the ground, Fareed recognizes it and lifting his face, says to the mud, 'What have I done to deserve this, Shera?'

'Shut up, maan chodeya! I'll give you a bullet down your throat.' And he moves his shoe into Fareed's nose, and places the cold point of the barrel against his forehead. The others move back to the road, keeping watch. No one is going to come this way, Fareed thinks, not till dawn. And then the thought—even if they do, who'll say anything to them?—brings a weight of water to his eyes.

'The girls of this village, of your own village are sacred. Your sisters, understand?' Shera thrusts the muzzle deeper into his forehead with each word. It has the effect of shouting.

So stupid of him to think this was revenge for that childish cheek on the Peepal tree. This is adult. This is Khushwant.

'Then they are sisters to you too. You are of this village.'

'Maaan chod!' The barrel cracks the skin on his forehead for he feels the blood at once, running down his nose. 'I am not from this village, understand? My grandfather came from Jaito, just to till his sister's lands. Ask anyone.'

'My great-grandfather came from Rajasthan then,' Fareed speaks to the mud. 'A hundred years ago. And her grandfather must have come from somewhere too.'

He sees the shoe pull back, knows where it will come, and rolls out from it. What he is not expecting is the gunshot and the ear-blast of its sound. He waits for the pain, can't understand where the bullet has gone, waits for it to ricochet off something and strike. His hands cradle his head against its coming.

From the road comes a curse, and the rattling of cycles. But Shera is in no hurry. Fareed hears his step and waits, coils himself to grasp the foot when it kicks, to drop him to the ground, to seize the gun. But there is an urgent shout from the road. Shera hesitates, then turns and runs, yelling, 'I'll get you, you bastard. Make no mistake. I am with the boys. The Sandhawalias. Don't forget it.' The cycles creak, swish, and are swallowed steadily by the darkness, faster with each moment.

He turns over on his back and through the branches of the Peepal he thinks he sees more stars than ever before in his life.

*

As he slinks into the darkened house through the cattle-shed, the buffaloes raise their snouts at him but are silent. Upstairs in his room he lights the kerosene lamp rather than the bulb and raises the mirror to his face. It looks pitiful, and all hope of keeping everything to himself is fled. His tongue is like a toad inside his mouth. In bed, on his back, he opens his mouth wide so it will not touch his palate.

For some reason his life is already the past. Even today morning is history, a flashback in a film—connected, relevant, but with no link to the forward movement of the story.

Khushwant is history. Never again will he hide in the thorns to watch her float by him in the morning. Her laugh, her inane chatter gone. He should have known Shera was interested there. But then, so was everyone. She had been made just too pretty. With a sudden drying of his throat he thinks of what could make Shera claim her as his own. Did he have something more than kisses in a toori shed? Some commitment?

After he left for college in Chandigarh, Shera has not been seen in the village, not even on holidays. Yet it is possible he has been coming in the night, like a wolf. Like Jeeta's brother-in-law. Suddenly, in a village that has held no secrets for a hundred years, there is a mystery behind every brick.

If he is with the Sandhawalia boys like he claimed, he could well be in Amritsar, where blood is said to flow out of the drains of the Golden Temple. Men disappear inside and are never heard of again. Even the police are scared to enter. A senior police-officer is gunned down on the doorstep and they cannot do a thing. The sarkar too, it does not do a thing. Except arrest Bhindranwale and release him with fanfare, when everyone knows he is involved in the newspaper-owner's murder. And their courts are too scared to hang the killers when they're caught. Yet he is looking to this sarkar to give him a chance to get out.

His innocence mocks him. The whole night, while his body lies on the cot, his spirit roams, haunted, unable to rest, kicking at the rubble in the stark wasteland of his thoughts.

In the morning his father says '*Hnnh! Hnnh!*' and '*Hnnh.*' As if he has done this to his face himself. As if he is inventing it all, not just the boyhood rivalry he dwells on as the reason for it. Which isn't an invention either, just an elaboration, with the hard stone of truth inside all the pulp. His mother says Waheguru, Waheguru, Waheguru. And Babaji stares at Fareed's ruined face for a long time with his bad eye streaming. In the end he makes sucking sounds, as if he were swallowing his teeth, and mumbles, 'It had to happen, it has happened. The uggarwadis have our boys with them now. We shall never be at peace again.'

It is time to send Fareed away, he says, to America, to Randhir. And what had been the only answer till then, now reeks to Fareed of the rank, dry smell of cowardice, of running away.

The old man sits in the veranda of his baithak the entire day, not stirring, not even when the call of the liquor shop is usually answered each evening. At dusk the giant bolts on the big blue door occupy him and for the first time in his life, Fareed sees the fly-bitten plank door of the cattle-shed locked and barred for the night.

*

In the raw morning, the old man wheels his scooter out of the hessian in the grain-store and says to his wife, 'I'm off to see about the boy's passport.' Weary, he sounds.

The whole day people come to see Fareed, or rather his mother. Lala's old woman says they thought they'd heard a shot, they live just across from the pond. But it is nowadays. Nowadays, when you hear things and cover your head with your blanket.

Was it your son, Mother, who betrayed me? My brother? The whole village, this village in which he was born, in which he grew up, this village is in the grip of doubt and fear. That is the change, nowadays.

Shera's mother comes and Fareed is produced for inspection. 'Oh, my God!' her hands go up to her cheeks, cover her eyes, cross her forehead. As she breaks into a flood of tears, Fareed's mother sits pressing her arm, consoling her. He climbs the stairs to his room one by one. There is nothing he has to say to her.

The surprise of the day is Khushwant's mother. Behind her shuffles her son, a young boy who seems embarrassed of the space his body occupies. And behind him comes Khushwant. Not willing to be paraded any more, he does not come down but is at the window with a corner of his turban between his teeth, hiding his face in case she looks up. Her left profile is presented. He tries to see her beauty as a fault, resisting to the last the sort of flowing thing that happens to him at sight of her. Concealed and watching, that is the nature that suits him best, the atmosphere secret and promising, as in a cinema hall. The snatches of conversation that drift up are meaningless, pricking at his absorption like thorns.

Dishan comes out of the kitchen and beckons her in and for him the movie is over. As he turns away his mother's voice rises in amazement, 'How could they ask for Khushwant's hand? A girl from the same village!' and his attention is riveted. Just as hard as his ears had tried to shut out the earlier words, they strain to hear these new ones. But now his mother, as if ashamed of her one outburst, leans right into the other woman's ear.

'So glad we refused them, sister. Waheguru. So glad. He's seen her open-faced since childhood. Waheguru,' he hears Khushwant's mother say, as he creeps down the stairs and presses his body to a pillar. 'You don't know how difficult it was. So insistent, they were. Shera's chachi came from Jaito with jaggery and dried coconuts. And I had to return everything in double. She's too young, I said. And Khushwant's father so angry. Waheguru. And so glad I am now.' His mother raised her folded hands to her forehead to say her own 'Waheguru' and then they were whispering again. Arched eyebrows, rounded lips, eyes as big as patashas. The mime on their faces could mean so many things.

'What did you give him?' he explodes at the threshold of the kitchen, catching Khushwant and Dishan in mid-secret. They are shocked into motion, but searching in their sudden coming apart for guilt and finding nothing, it is he who is paralysed at the doorstep.

Awareness of his disfigured face begins to dawn as she turns on him a look as of metal out of a furnace.

He turns as abruptly as he had come, stumbling out and up the stairs, in a fume with himself. There is nothing else to do.

*

His father returns at dusk with one more story, things are happening that fast. A kilometre from the Jaito turn, on his way back, right in his headlight was a man wrapped in a blanket. Out of which poked a gun. He thought this is it, it's time to meet my Guru, and pressed his brake so hard his finger caught in it. The man got on behind him without a word.

'I drove on, saying nothing myself, trying not to think about the gun and everything,' he says. 'After a while he leans forward "Drive, till I tell you to stop," he says, as if I had planned to do anything else. "Faster, faster," he says.' And the old man, who never drove over forty because of his drinking and all, says he touched sixty. But his finger was bleeding from the injury with the brake and soon it was too slippery to hold the wheel straight. He had to stop, regardless.

He holds up his hand to the lamplight, for there is no power that night, and they see the bloody piece of turban—old-fashioned stripe—that binds it. 'That's his turban, there,' he says.

'Where was his gun when he was bandaging you?' asks Fareed, not able to help himself.

'Stupid. He could have put it into my hand for all I could have done with it!'

The story is disrupted and it's a black mark against Fareed.

His father says it was one of those modern things, automatic fire. 'You would have known a lot, Sardarji. I would have liked to see you in my place,' he challenges.

'So then what happened?' asks Babaji.

'We went on and I asked him about the gun,' the old man finally resumes. 'It was a 9mm carbine, he said, fires fifteen shots at a go. We had quite a conversation then.'

And all this time his father expected to be killed. Not wanting to know too much; not wanting to sound unfriendly. A fine balance. But his passenger wanted to talk. The boys were fighting among themselves. The old man named several factions as if he were already on first-name basis with them. The Bopagarh group to which the man belonged had several blood feuds; the Babbars were opposed to the Dal Khalsa, and so on. A string of details exciting in their uselessness. A conference had been arranged to sort out the fighting inside the thorn forest near Jaito, and that's where Fareed's father was carrying his passenger.

'He started out on a cycle but had a puncture on the way, and that's why he stood in my path. I said to him, you've left your cycle on the roadside, someone's going to steal it. But he wasn't bothered. The man I took it from will find it, he said. Once he took a tractor, and the owner found it the next day, not twenty kilometres away. It's just to get there, see, not to take.

'So then I knew that he wasn't about to cut my thread, and I told him, you're like my son. Why have you chosen this life? He said, every Sikh has to struggle. What's wrong with the Sikhs, I said. We have fertile land, we have rich farmers amongst us. But he would have none of it. In fact, he got quite angry with me. What you villagers do not understand is that seventy per cent of our money goes out, he said. In Punjab there's nothing to invest it in, no mills, no industry, no real progress. Why don't farmers grow cotton, or even sugarcane anymore? Because all the sugar and textile mills are outside, fattening on our money.

Our power and water is given away to other states to run their industry and we have tube-wells but no power to run them. He had a long list of injustices, I can tell you.'

'And you fell for it? For his ideas or for his gun?' asked Babaji.

'Don't laugh at me, Bauji. I was thinking all the time, what if we're stopped at a check-post? Bullets were whizzing over my head in my imagination. I thought, I am his accomplice...'

'But not a willing one...' Fareed began.

'Who would have stopped to ask me that, boy? A bullet in my head before I could say Waheguru. I was so relieved when he asked me to stop near the forest. And before he disappeared into the bushes he turned and said, you are like my father. So let me give you a piece of advice, don't trim your beard. It's not Gur Sikh.'

Babaji is amused. He has been telling his son not to trim his beard since he was a boy. 'It seems fashion has come a full circle,' he says slyly, and everyone laughs, even Dishan. It is possible to laugh at the old man only when Babaji cracks the joke.

On the next day they hear of cycles, scooters and tractors being taken away all over the region. In the old village someone has even lost a bullock-cart. They will be found by the morrow, his father declares, all around the Jaito jungle. And they are.

10

Nobody can say what urgent summons could have come during the night for a family to clear the village by dawn, taking with them just their most rudimentary belongings. Fareed has only what he can prise out of Dishan to build shaky theories about why Khushwant, her brother, her mother, and her father, whom he remembers as so much younger looking than the wife, melted into the night just like that.

They have gone into hiding. Now that they know Shera is a militant, it is the wisest thing to do. With the boys and their guns to back him, Shera may not accept the refusal of a second proposal. He could even be expected to take Khushwant like they had taken Jeeta's sister. And on the other hand, there is the police. A hint that Shera is interested in the girl would be enough to make the whole family suspect. Even their sudden disappearance would look shady.

The policeman who finally comes to verify Fareed for the passport says people are disappearing all over like that, in a snap of the fingers. No use going into hiding, he says, there is nothing to hide from if you have done nothing wrong. And nowhere to hide. Unless you go to America, Canada. 'That is why we run a comb through your hair, pick up the smallest nit,' he says. 'If you're trying to go into hiding, we will know from what.'

And Fareed, answering the unending questions, wonders how they would know if you just needed to hide from yourself?

Afterwards, the policeman, in civvies, but wearing khaki socks over his pointed Punjabi shoes, makes the round of the neighbours, and returns to have a drink with the old man in the baithak veranda. Dishan is quickly frying cauliflower pakoras and the air smokes with the fumes of mustard oil. Fareed offers to carry them out to the guest and her eyes flash gratitude up at him.

'Here, boy!' the policeman says. 'Come here.' The rum on the table is already half gone. 'Open your mouth, boy,' he says. 'Show me your tongue.' Then peering into his mouth, he asks, 'What are these blue marks on your tongue?'

'What blue marks?' The old man jumps up. 'Fetch the torch, boy.'

But the batteries are dead and the old man flings the feeble torch to the ground. 'Turn your head this way. Not that way, you donkey. Don't you see where the light is coming from?'

The policeman seems to lose interest, but Fareed turns his face this way and that for his father who keeps asking for his mouth to be opened wider and wider till his jaw aches. 'What blue marks, *hain*? Can't you push your tongue out a little, you owl.'

Back in his room Fareed shines a lamp into his mouth and sees the blue marks on his tongue, glistening like the scales on a fish's back. They are all that are left of his injuries, and he feels suddenly cold to think that the policeman had somehow known they would be there.

And he knows now that he will never get that passport. He was a fool to think that all this could be left behind by just getting into an aeroplane and flying off into the blue. The pain of Khushwant. What can he do for her, his chosen one? He had some crazy plan in his wooden brain that he would get a job in a foreign land where he could finally carry her away to. Why did the cop ask him to open his mouth? Did he know how he'd got those injuries? It was impossible to know who was hiding what, and how much he knew and whose side he was on. A complicated world in which he was worse than the village idiot. He could not get out of this net, that was sure. And he couldn't do it, live like…like a hijra, with someone with a gun telling him what to do. Who to love, who to marry. Soon they'd come for his own sister—what would he do then? Be relieved that it wasn't his own backside they were after? That they weren't going to cut his thread? No. He couldn't do it. And now he knows there's no option. The fog is suddenly gone: he too has to have a gun.

*

When the ring of the phone wakes him and he hears Nina's voice, 'Sikand, it's awful news,' he knows what she's going to say. Their mother has passed softly into the night. They couldn't wake her. Nina thought it was the first good sleep she was having in days.

'Will you come?' It is already time to talk about arrangements.

The bed, he thinks. It is the bed in which he had been born, arriving 'like an express train', too quick for her to be taken to the hospital, the bed she'd said should be sold for firewood when she'd left, deserting him for Nina.

'Call that carpenter, that Kirat Singh. Tell him the bed must be put together again. Today itself.' She would lie in it, for as long as she was in the house.

He knows now that he should never have let her go.

'A magazine of your stature,' she'd said; somewhere inside she was proud of what he'd achieved! Why couldn't he just have stayed with that thought, and ignored all else thereafter?

'You should call a spade a spade', she'd said.

'Calling it a digging instrument gives me much more latitude.'

'Latitude for what?'

'To get at the truth, Ma.'

'You wouldn't recognize the truth, Sikki, if it woke you up at night and tweaked your nose!'

But—'A magazine of your stature,' he'd remembered.

'You must keep some distance, Ma. That's the only way to get the right perspective.'

'I see Punjab being devastated, and you want me to keep distance? You are so good at distance, you need a telescope to see what's in plain sight!'

And that night he'd snapped. After all those years of silence, he had blurted out: 'You had a lot of distance with Dad. So much distance you didn't even know he'd died!'

He remembers her response—a silence so profound that it had continued into the next day and the next. It was like she had dropped a sound-proof curtain between them. He could sense the clamour that was going on behind the curtain but couldn't hear a thing.

After three days, he'd come home to find her packing.

'I'm going to be with Nina,' she said.

'For how long?'

'That I can't say. As you said, I need some distance.'

He had winced. He could see she was packing for a permanent shift.

'This is your home, Ma. You cannot leave it for long.'

'You are there to look after it. And Raja Ram is there to look after you.'

'What am I to do with this huge place? This bedroom? This colossal bed? You brought it in your dowry!'

'Oh, it's an old bed, too old,' she'd said, quite cheerfully. 'Sell it for firewood, is all I can say. Get something modern.'

*

Shivi arrives in the night to find him on the floor beside the reassembled bed, his head on the crook of his elbow, the single shaded lamp casting an unhealthy glow across Auntyji's pale features.

Ambika's father is at the funeral, supported on both sides. Big tears flow down a groove in his cheek when the Granthi reads from the Gurbani. And as Sikand carries the flame around the pyre, their eyes meet in a brief flicker and he sees a ray of sunlight has pierced the fog.

When they have all gone the house is emptier than it's ever been before. He can have no regret for her, she wouldn't have stood for it, but for himself the sunlight that he'd once hungered for, is sharp as acid on his skin. He feels the weight of his years, and knows it's too late to begin again.

In wretchedness he calls Ambika, she is picking up the phone, saying 'Hello? Hello?' to the silence. She will be kind, he knows, but she will not have him back.

Several days he wallows in his thoughts, shunning his emotion, then giving into it, repeatedly. He could never come up to her expectations, and now it was too late to even try. Perhaps it was time now to forgive himself and her, but that is easy to think about, difficult to do.

Again, and yet again, he is floundering.

*

Bibs will not allow it.

'Communal carnage in Dilwan, bus hijacked at night, eight Hindu passengers segregated and shot,' he says speaking in headlines. 'They're declaring Punjab a Disturbed Area, damn you. The army is to be deployed. Get your backside here.'

Bibs sees him as a pushover; impractical but useful, someone not really there, like the sun behind a perpetual cloud. Not missed so long as it gives enough heat and light. Of course he brings the burden of himself to his Sikand-view and it isn't authentic, is what Sikand wants to tell him. Ask Shivi about his Sikand-view. Or Livleen. Shivi doesn't think Sikand is a pushover. And Livleen thinks he's a mix of Aristotle and Burt Reynolds. With fizz.

What is he then? His own Sikand-view couldn't be that authentic after all, for he must bring himself into his perceptions and that must mean that he brings Bibs's and Shivi's Sikand-view, and Livleen's and Ambika's too. Not to mention his mother's and Nina's, the Brigadier's, all of them. Even Kirat Singh's and Raja Ram's. There he is, looking at Sikand through their eyes. Like a man holding a mirror looking into another mirror, seeing his reflections, clone after clone, receding into endlessness.

'Why do you think so much, Sikand? It's only going to depress you,' says Shivi, coming into the office and running his finger over the dusty typewriter keys.

'Hey. You're still here? I thought Bibs would have got you back to Amritsar post-haste. Disturbed Area, President's Rule, and all.'

'I don't think I'm going back,' says Shivi, tapping a single key and printing a long line of *i*'s across the page. 'In fact, I've come in today to resign.'

'That won't do, my boy. It won't do at all. Where are you staying, by the way? Giving up the guestroom. Convincing me you'd left.'

'I'm sorry, Sikand. I thought you'd want to be alone—sorrow is such a personal thing. All the same, I'm sure you shouldn't think so much. It's pessimistic.

'On the contrary, dear man. Why would I bother to think if I didn't hope to solve the problem? It takes deep thinking to realize there is cause for optimism. Believe me. I prescribe a strong dose of thinking for you too, and no more talk of resignation.'

'No, boss.' Shivi's body language says it all. 'You say yourself that analysis is the key. But what can I analyse about death and useless destruction? They're such full stops. And in Amritsar, I can't find the distance to analyse. I'm right in the thick of events.'

'So who asked you to analyse? What'll I do if you start to analyse? You're supposed to report the facts as they happen. For me to analyse. You're the eyes and ears, dammit. Our man at the frontlines. How can you quit?'

Sikand is well aware of having said something quite the opposite to Shivi the last time in Amritsar, but feels what the heck, the expedient thing is to bring the man's confidence back. He picks out of his memory all the good stories that Shivi has ever done, holding up his article on the Akali campaign to ban cigarettes in Amritsar as the best thing the magazine has ever run. And more and more of the same, till Shivi's morale is back. According to the Brigadier, soldiers are given a double ration of rum just before the big battle, so that they can run up to the objective shouting, 'Jai Bajrang Bali', giving not a fig for their lives. When Shivi leaves Sikand's office he may as well be shouting, 'Bole Sonihal, Sat Sri Akal!'

Bibs is unappreciative, of course. He wants nothing less than that big article from Sikand, and he wants it now. Bibs has no empathy with the pangs of birth. Why can't he see that every word on paper is critical? That so much has to happen yet?

'Why don't you not bother with it until it happens?' says Bibs. 'Leave astrology and prophecy to the pandits, Sikand.'

How ordinary, how painless, how obscure. To be a slave of that damned moving finger, the ticking moment.

'Astrology's to do with the stars, Bibs, prophecy with cards. Or tea-leaves. Analysis, on the other hand, is quite down to earth. The deeds of humans, your facts, seen against their backgrounds, where they come from, again facts. Then projected ahead. On future backdrops. A slow, a ruminative process. You have no patience, Bibs, it's your one human failing,' says Sikand, raising a mild finger in injured reproof. 'What use would it be, simple reportage of the past? A calling for a cub reporter!'

'It's not the past, it's what's happening now.' Bibs's mouth is set hard.

'Right now there are people being shot in Punjab by boys on motorcycles, with automatic rifles, fifteen bullets to the second.' But he is a little confused, and seeing he's going to let him off the hook, Sikand twists the knife. 'That is the irony, my dear. When we report it, it's already the past.'

'Right. So you analyse the past. As an aid to understanding, a warning.' Tenacious Bibs.

'Warning! You said it, I didn't. How do you warn unless you can present a future impact?'

Ultimately it's compromised with Sikand's undertaking another visit to Punjab.

In any case, he tells himself, he wants to see how Shivi fares after his shot of adrenaline. And he wants, if possible, to talk to Bhindranwale himself.

*

The Harmandar is at its best at break of dawn, so everybody says. The golden dome rises dark as copper in the rosy light and the white of the marble path around the sacred tank glows strangely blue. The water is so still you feel a glance will crack it. And when above the quietness, rises the morning prayer, it is as if God and all the world care only for you.

While the rest of the boys go to the sanctum for prayers, Jeeta walks on the parikarma, the path around the tank, and thinks neither of God nor man. The marble is cool against the soles of his bare feet and the sound of the prayer is not balm but opium to his soul. It makes the bubble of sky, water, marble vibrate with it, like the gourd vibrates to the strings of a sitar.

He is special for Lal Guru, their leader, who often tells him not to waste his strength on thinking. For some people it needs too much expenditure, he says. It is best for them only to act and leave the thinking to others. Which suits Jeeta just fine. When he tries to think, he always ends up confused. About being trained to aim for the head, for instance, mixed with the compulsory prayers, morning and evening. Soldier-saints, Sant Bhindranwale says, holding up the lives of the Gurus, but it's a sort of double-roti, like the one about religion and politics. Too complex for a simple rural brain like his.

Lal Guru will not be really angry with him for having missed the prayers. The boys will say, 'You did it again, Karnail, now you're in for it!' and he will act suitably scared for Lal Guru's military voice can make the strings of your calves vibrate. But all the while he will know that Lal Guru's knitted brows are only pretence.

For Lal Guru has hugged him to his chest, one terrifying night. 'You have saved my life, Karnaila,' he said. 'Now it is forfeit to you forever.' And then he had laughed his laugh, those explosions of breath so impossible to imitate. It always made them fear that he was choking to death.

That night, of course, Jeeta had been more worried that the cops would hear it. And they had; for the next second a string of bullets took off the plumes of the sarkanda grass in which they lay. He remembered Lal Guru on his stomach, like a huge fish. Gasping for the breath he had wasted on the wind a moment before.

In the scant light, worshippers pass him by. Shapes bundled up against the morning chill, bending low in greeting. The shared hour, pure as ice, makes comradeship flow. He cannot bend in return, because of what he refers to as 'the old wound'. Besides the Mauser under his cotton blanket would give him a nasty kick in the ribs. He tries to compensate with a loud 'Sat Sri Akal', but his voice is such an intrusion, that in the end he bows his head as low as it will go.

It is the greatest shock, when one shape breaks from the group and lunges straight at him, grabbing his arm in its automatic swing for the Mauser.

'Jeetay' a voice says urgently in his ear, leaving him in such confusion that all instinct deserts, freezing him rigid on the parikarma. 'It's me, Fareed, you fool.'

'Don't say fool!' and his hand is free, triggered by that word. As the Mauser breaks out of the blanket, Fareed leaps and hits the marble floor with a splat.

The pilgrim shapes scurry apart at the action, bringing Jeeta to awareness. Overcome, he bends, feeling the old pain like a dagger in his thigh, and raises Fareed from the ground.

'Don't worry, old friend,' he says. 'How you shiver. I wasn't going to shoot. Not really.'

*

The room in the Guru Ram Das Serai which Jeeta stays is meant to sleep four pilgrims. Already they are five and Fareed will make a sixth.

'No one will mind,' Jeeta says, 'so long as you take the place nearest the door. Of course everyone will step on you going to the bathroom at night.'

It is a small bare room, sparse as an army barrack. There are no cots, for everyone sleeps on the floor, rolling up their bedding during the day under a low planking that runs along three walls. On it are combs, torches, bottles of red and yellow hair-oil, lined up as if ready for inspection. A big poster of Guru Gobind Singh on his horse, with his white hawk perched on his fist, is stuck high up on one wall. One edge is curling stubbornly.

'You don't know how many times I've tried to fix this,' Jeeta says. 'Come on, give me a hand.'

Fareed is on all fours with Jeeta standing on his back when Lal Guru's voice booms from the door. '*Oi*, Karnail. I see you're busy entertaining guests, when your monkey face should be in the Darbar Sahib at prayers.'

Fareed stands up straight as a lathi. Of course Jeeta falls off.

'Who is this?' says Lal Guru, measuring Fareed with a frank stare.

'A brother from my village,' Jeeta says rising from the floor. 'He wants to join us, Lal Guru. He's my brother.'

Fareed keeps a steady eye on the big man.

'Why are you staring at my face, boy? As if I was Yam Doot? Do you recognize it from somewhere?'

Instantly Fareed lowers his eyes.

'What's your name?' the gruff voice demands.

Question after question follows. Village, family, education, fired straight at his face in bursts. If Fareed overruns his space he is cut short by the next, and if he takes a moment before speaking, the broad face darkens so ominously the words leapfrog out of him in a stream.

'Ever used a gun?'

'I have. In the fields. My father...'

'Birds and animals! Have you ever shot at a man?'

'No.'

'All right, we'll have to teach you then. It takes more than matching hand to eye.' Short, sharp bursts of breath follow like those of some great animal in pain. Fareed turns in confusion to Jeeta and is relieved to see him smile. It is supposed to be a joke and that unearthly sound is supposed to be a laugh.

'Show him what we've got,' Lal Guru tells Jeeta. 'Safety, loading, unloading, taking apart, cleaning. Tell the rest there's nothing for them today. And I must see you at prayers this evening. Hundred per cent. With your friend, Shaikh Fareed.' Another burst of sound and he's gone.

'What does he find so funny?' Fareed grumbles.

'Don't go taking offence, he's a Shah among men. Saw how he sized you up in a second?'

Now what is that supposed to mean?

Jeeta is called 'Karnail'. Two of the others are 'Major' and 'Kaptan'. Major, tall and thin and fair as a girl, and Kaptan dark, pockmarked and stocky. When Fareed wonders why Jeeta has the senior-most rank and Jeeta announces he was given it by Lal Guru, Kaptan has objections.

'Not true,' he says. 'We came later, so we got what he left. "Brigadier's" reserved. For Lal Guru. He can't be "Jarnail" because of the Sant. You can be "Leftand".'

'He's already "Shaikh". Lal Guru gave it to him,' Jeeta says.

'What's wrong with "Subedar" or "Havaldar"?' Fareed wonders.

'Why not be officers if we can?'

'But we're all equals, see?' Kaptan insists through the laughter. 'We all have our uses.'

'Equals, yes,' says Jeeta. 'But some of us are more useful than the others.'

'Go on, Karnail. It's you who should have been called Shaikh. The way you boast.'

'No boast-toast. Pride is courage. Didn't Lal Guru say so?'

'Big, big word. Courage,' says Ameer, the third of the group.

'So? I use big words. Big words bring big deeds.'

'Sure. But the words should come later,' says Ameer quietly. He unrolls his bedding in a corner, lies on it, and turns to Fareed. 'You're going to hear this word again and again. Courage. Everybody's rated according to it. Groups, squads, men, boys. I don't let it go to my head.'

Jagat, the last of the lot, is a serious-faced boy with no beard to speak of. In the first few days when they're always together, he follows Fareed and Jeeta everywhere reminding Fareed of an abandoned calf.

'The fellow has no parents,' Jeeta says. 'So I keep him with me sometimes. I'm going to take him for a recce tomorrow. We're planning to rob a bank.'

11

At the bank, Fareed's job is to shoot off three quick rounds as a warning and a general scare-them-up if anyone tries to enter while the operation is on. His place is on a string cot outside a shop, next but one from the bank, with the liquid dirt of the street riding up his bare legs. The pistol, its safety off, is an uncomfortable bulge under his long shirt. Otherwise he has no problems. Anyone who passes him is to be judged before a foot is set on the first of the three steps that raise the bank above the muck in the street. An interesting mental game. He knows he won't panic and pull out the pistol unless it's needed. Minimum expenditure, maximum gain, is how Lal Guru puts it.

Across the road at the tea-shack, Lal Guru is impressive. Every inch the prosperous truck-driver in tahmat and saafa, obviously enjoying himself. The first part of the plan has worked beautifully. Fareed had doubted it could be done, but with a loud hospitality towards the world in general, Lal Guru has lured the bank guard to the teashop. The man has loosened his crisscross of 12 bore ammunition belts and is leaning back on his hands on the charpoy, engrossed in Lal Guru's booming chatter about towns and roads and women. His gun, removed from its chain, lies behind him. On the middle step of the bank stands his abandoned stool.

The boys, Jeeta, Jagat and Major, have entered the bank one by one. Fareed tries to imagine what is happening inside. There are only six employees. Pigeons in rickety cages, Jeeta had called them after his recce, incapable of resistance. Any moment now they should be coming out Fareed thinks, and checks quickly on Lal Guru, who is trying to force a second glass of tea on the guard.

For a brief second Lal Guru's gaze shifts to the bank steps and Fareed is surprised by a feeling that a thin snake has darted through the short hairs on the back of his neck. Immediately after, two shots ring out, and for some stupid reason he is hurtling towards the sound. Colliding teeth to forehead with one of the boys rushing out, he continues to run straight down the road, realizing in a confused way that the crash has dropped the boy in the dust behind him. He stops, looks to the teashop where Lal Guru seems to be embracing the guard, and turns back towards the steps where Jeeta and Jagat are tumbling out of the bank. Major, whom he has felled, is trying to rise, and he grabs him under the shoulders, muttering apologies under his breath.

They run, following the others to the tempo parked under the trees. Lal Guru is clambering into the driver's seat and miraculously the engine is sparking on the first hit. In a cloud of dust they are off, Fareed expecting any moment to hear a shot tear through their tyres, or petrol tank or something, forgetting his earlier contempt for the guard's ancient belts of orange ammunition. Squeezed between Lal Guru and Jagat in the driver's cabin, he urges the speedometer needle to climb, faster and faster, fifty, sixty, seventy. On the open highway the old crate, pushed to its limits, touches eighty.

'Did you get the money?' Lal Guru asks through teeth clenched on a snatch of turban.

Jagat is silent, shrugs, says 'No. They rang an alarm. Didn't you hear it?' he asks Fareed, who remembers the snake at the nape of his neck. Perhaps he had felt the alarm, but hadn't heard a thing.

'Did you shoot anybody?' Lal Guru asks.

'No. Yes.'

Lal Guru takes his eyes off the road. 'I told you before, Jagat, when in doubt, tell the truth.'

'Yes. Karnail shot the chap who pressed the alarm. Through the forehead.'

'There's a jeep behind us,' says Lal Guru. 'Ask them to check.'

Fareed opens the panel in the back and confirms it is a police jeep. With a curse Lal Guru presses his foot to the floor. His teeth gleam a vicious white.

The needle is stuck at eighty. Before them the road glitters in patches, as if washed with mercury.

'Do you know Kairon?' Lal Guru asks suddenly.

'Who? Pratap Singh?' Fareed says, surprised.

'Yes, yes. The same. Know him?'

'I know of him. Or rather, I heard of…'

'The first Chief Minister of Punjab?'

'Not the first, I think.'

'It doesn't matter. He built this road. Smooth as glass. The bastard.'

Fareed turns again to the back. Jeeta and Major are stuck to the floorboards. The jeep is closer. Why don't the cops shoot, he thinks, and immediately a shot rings out. He ducks jerking Lal Guru who shouts above the drone of the engine, 'Small arm,' spitting out the edge of his turban.

Up ahead the road curves in a wide banking turn. 'Turn, turn,' Fareed yells. 'To the left.'

Lal Guru doesn't hesitate, wheeling blindly in obedience, and they clatter around a clump of thorn jungle down a dirt track. Lal Guru cuts the engine and they come to an abrupt halt at the base of the slope. They turn in their seats to see the jeep take the curve on shrieking wheels and shoot above them, straight down the glass road.

'Out, out, everybody out,' Lal Guru hollers, and in a cloud of dust they are scampering, all in different directions. Fareed goes backwards up the track, streaks across the road and down the steep bank on its other side, leaping across a flowing irrigation ditch that suddenly appears at the bottom. There is a splash behind him, someone in the ditch, but he does not break his stride and stops only when he makes the cover of a field of sugarcane high as a man. On his knees, gasping for breath, he hears the jeep return and turn down the track they had taken. 'Too fast,' he thinks, and hears them crash into the tempo that Lal Guru has abandoned smack at the bottom of the slope.

The sugarcane groans and creaks as he runs deeper into the field. At its far edge, he drops down again, for there are other sounds to the right of him, ceasing a moment after his. Someone else is in the sugarcane field! He holds his breath till his chest burns. Then he remembers the splash. It has to be one of them, he realizes, but lies motionless, listening to his heart pump against the earth.

Then he hears the shots, one, two, three, followed by an echoing silence. Then two more. The sugarcane whips, and he hears Lal Guru's hoarse voice shout No, No, as he crashes through the field back towards the road. He cannot understand the shots, nor Lal Guru's strange behaviour, but follows, stumbling over a brood of wild hens that flutter up, squawking in his path. He breaks through just as Lal Guru lands again in the ditch. And is helping him out when two more shots ring out. Lal Guru leaps dripping and cursing up the bank. 'They're shooting at the cops, the bloody idiots,' he huffs. They approach the track through the jungle from the left and see the police jeep through the trees, crushed against the back of their tempo as if in a hurry to climb in. Behind it with their guns trained into it stand Jeeta and Jagat.

'Don't shoot, don't shoot!' Lal Guru emerges from the jungle, wet and muddy, waving his arms. Sheaths of sugarcane wave about his ears and fly out of him as he runs at them. The two turn in slow motion, as if hypnotized.

The whole operation is a disaster.

'We have no money for guns, and we killed four men. Too much expenditure, no gain.' Lal Guru doesn't explode like they said he would, his voice is quieter if anything. They sit as if in mourning, even Ameer and Kaptan who are not involved at all.

'The cops would have got us if we hadn't finished them,' Jeeta says, repeating himself like a multiplication table.

'No, Karnail. They were injured. Their driver was probably dead.

'Not the two in the back. One of them was moving, I tell you. He tried to climb out of the back. Real fast. Didn't he?' he asks Jagat who continues to stare at his toes.

'So instead of running in fear that he will get you, you run straight towards him. Is that it?'

Jeeta shakes his head like a bull. 'We ruined the first job, it's true, but not the second. The second was good. We really gave it to them. Like partridges they were sitting there.' He looks all around but no one meets his eye. 'Even the first,' he says obstinately. 'We had no clue about the alarm. It gave us such a start.'

'So who was to tell you? You went for the recce yourself, didn't you?' says Lal Guru.

'What's a recce? It wasn't out front for us to see. I couldn't have asked could I? Have you people fixed an alarm?'

'What's the use of an alarm, Karnail, if no one can hear it outside?' Lal Guru's voice is raised now. 'We never did. It was probably a puny bell. To call the guard, or peon, or something. You simply panicked. No, hear me now. Even if the man had rung an alarm, killing him was useless—you could wipe him out, but not what he'd already done.'

'But I warned him,' says Jeeta. 'I warned them all as we entered.'

'Killing is easy, Karnail. *Tha!* And a man is dead. But it can become a disease. A disease that shortens your life. It's that much cheaper, your life. That much more useless. Do you understand?'

Jeeta obviously doesn't, but there is a pressure now on him to be silent, the air is heavy with it.

'I have not insisted that you attend the morning and evening prayers, Karnail. It is my mistake. From tomorrow it will be serious disobedience if you don't,' and so saying Lal Guru rises wearily to his feet and leaves the room.

'Serious disobedience,' says Jeeta, the moment he is out of hearing, 'As if we were in the bloody army or something. What army? Where's the war? Where's the enemy? *Hnnh?* If the cops aren't the enemy, who is?'

Ameer is the only one who responds, turning to the wall and raising up the volume on his transistor. It is a song of the road—the weary truck driver wishing he was home. 'No one makes rotis like you, my tinsel wire,' he sings along in his tuneless voice.

Against the background of the morning prayers, Fareed's thoughts are suddenly cool and clear, as if spun out of air. His chosen corner is uncarpeted, the marble against his thighs cold and hard. 'There is one God. Truth is his name,' the words of the Japji Sahib prayer soar through the open arch to the spotless sky, and a sense of profound relief wraps around him after the heat and stale breath of nights in the overpopulated dormitory.

'Soldier saints,' Jeeta mumbles beside him. '*Hnnh!*'

Afterwards at the langar, blowing into his tea, he will suddenly remember:

'Attend morning prayers, evening prayers, grow your beards, become Babajis. *Hnnh.* Then pick up your gun and shoot people dead. Not cops. Only Hindus on buses. Do you remember the cops? In Samnaula?' And he will raise the leg of his pyjama to show his horrible scars. 'Why don't you say anything you bastard? Got blisters on your tongue?'

*

Majestic with steel arrow in hand, crisply focused in royal blue, Sant Jarnail Singh Bhindranwale glares at the viewer from the cover of *In Sight*.

Bibs holds up the fresh issue, still smelling of ink. As it passes from hand to hand he presides over the table glowing pink with post-natal satisfaction. Each of them, Livleen, Sidharth, the two sub-eds, Goswami, the assistant editor, are given one expectant moment for reaction. And as the superlatives make the rounds, he bestows on Sikand such a generous look of self-congratulation that it almost includes Sikand in its embrace.

In spite of himself, Sikand is pleased. The technique and the aesthetics of the picture are perfect. But there is more. The colours: the Akali cobalt blue, the rich saffron, the pure white, seem to be telling a story. Threading Bhindranwale into the Sikh tradition so completely that his arrow and the belt of bullets across his chest are ornaments of that tradition. The sharp stare splitting the eye of the lens, the young gunman soft-focused in the background, every element of the picture in fact, appears to define the Sikhs as a people.

But that is also the source of his unease. As the day progresses with more hosannas and every copy of the magazine sold out, the feeling grows to one of oppression. He is almost glad when the phone rings and he hears Ambika's voice say, 'Execrable. Disgusting.'

'Ambika. Listen. I must see you. Now.'

'Frankly Sikand, there's nothing I'd like less.'

'You didn't call me up to say that.'

*

He waits with his coffee in his usual corner of the restaurant. It is early for the evening rush, a good time and place to think. The last fortnight has been like driving through one of those endless European tunnels where you have to maintain a minimum speed of a hundred or have a pileup on your conscience for the rest of your life. Your headlights pick up signs, an arrow here, a number there, they may be terribly significant but you can't read them as you hurtle by towards that O of light at the end of the tunnel.

He has careened through Punjab, Amritsar, the Golden Temple, Punjab, Delhi. Then through the hectic rush of transcribing the article, selecting the photographs, this cover. Of all the photographs he has taken the Bhindranwale is the best, yet he had resisted to the last Bibs's attempts to put it on the cover. There were options. The soldier's face half-hardening above a field in which his unexposed film must be lying even now, unravelled outside an olive green tent.

'State-of-the-art,' he had explained to a soldier awed by his bag full of Nikons and accessories, at one of the numerous check posts manned no longer by police, but by the army in no-nonsense olive green. 'Like your weapons.' The jawan's smile had disappeared the moment Sikand lifted and clicked the camera in one quick motion. All of a sudden a sea of olive-green had bristled about him.

By some miracle he'd managed to save both his life and his film. His Press card, though instantly confiscated, had got him before an officer, and outside a tent pitched below the road, he had been made to extract and expose his film. In Amritsar he was to discover he'd saved the shot—his two cameras had changed places in the pushing around. 'That is Punjab, Bibs,' he'd said holding up the photograph he had saved. But Bibs had not agreed.

Closer to Amritsar, when banter was no longer an option, if he had been surprised by the urgent arrogance of the soldiers, he had been struck by the docility of the Sikhs who passed through their hands nose to tail. He had risked several shots and all of these he had spread before Bibs. A disciplined line of burly-beards with their turbans held aloft; a close-up of a splendid looking Sikh bending to let a Madrasi soldier inspect his knot of hair. 'This is Punjab, Bibs,' he'd insisted, but Bibs was fixated on Bhindranwale. And then they'd made up, with him seeing Bibs's point of view, but it had pricked him throughout.

He sees Ambika enter, looking vaguely about her in the gloom of the restaurant. He has always suspected that concealed under her lawyer's coat and bold, level stare lurks a vulnerability. And as she stands confused, eyes widening in the sudden darkness off the street, a warmth rushes out of him tumbling over the empty chairs and tables. Not connecting, for at the n'th moment she's found her familiar face again, and is marching across to his table.

Immediately she is at it: 'You're making a hero out of the man, do you know it? Just to sell your magazine, you're making him respectable. A dangerous bigot! Scores of Sikh kids are going to think he's okay, he's big, he's powerful. He's legitimate, damn you. Can't you see? Or has the greed to sell that rag of yours totally blinded you?'

He lets her lash at him. In fact he wants more and more.

'Listen,' he says. 'You're right. I didn't want to do it. I thought we were making him look like he represented the Sikhs. To the others. Laying the blame for him on the entire community. But what you say is right too. We were doubly wrong.'

'You will have blood on your hands, Sikand,' she says sullenly sipping her coffee.

*

Ambika drives her battered blue 1972 Fiat each day between the district and the High courts. On Mondays and Fridays besides, she rides the evening rush hour to 'People's Power', a voluntary organisation, of which she is a founder member. And all the way, from New Delhi to Old Delhi to South Delhi and back, no one ever overtakes her. 'Oh, me?' she says of herself, 'I'm always in such a rush.'

To her career as a lawyer she brings a different passion, for she is a champion of causes, not cases. Her current cause is two Sikh boys who have been refused passports, and she is in writ, sans remittance on behalf of 'People's Power', in the High Court. She hopes to prove violation of Article Fourteen without rational criteria, but knows that she is more likely to hammer justice out of Milord's heart with a healthy sense of outrage than to pick it out with legal tweezers.

'These are boys who want to escape Bhindranwale, but can't. The police won't verify them. Forget visas, they don't even have a right to a passport any more,' she says.

Sikand, contrite, ministering to her, removing her used cup, holding out the sandwiches, is no doubt thinking it was an excellent image, though. Every magazine will have him on the cover. What a high for Bibs!

'Don't deny it, Sikand!' she says, 'Otherwise why wouldn't you stand up to him?'

'I've tried, Ambika. It's never any use,' he says, hanging his head.

'Well then, I am going to give him a piece of my mind. Tell him what I think of his magazine and its cover.'

And she does.

'I was in the area,' she says, 'So I thought I'd drop in.'

'Good thing you did,' says Bibs rising. 'We're in celebratory mode today. What will you have, Ambika? Sikand, see if you can manage some coffee that tastes like coffee, please.'

'No I don't want anything. Sikand, stay! I want you here to listen. Sit down, Bibs.'

'It's always a pleasure,' Bibs begins, folding his hands and pointing his tapered fingers at her.

'Now, Bibs, I am not going to let you bully me. I know exactly how to deal with a bully.'

Bibs smiles innocently back at her. 'What is this about? Surely not your party. I did send flowers, didn't I?'

'No, this is about your magazine. And putting Bhindranwale on its cover.' Bibs is just starting to curl up like a cat before a warm fire, when she spits 'Moral suicide!' at him. 'I am fighting cases for Sikh boys who want to escape him and can't. Those are the boys who're going to give in. It's much easier toting guns and being macho. A straight fit. An umbilical link.'

It begins to dawn on Bibs that this is criticism, and a small frown crinkles his broad forehead. 'Putting a man on a cover can hardly do that, Ambika. People are hardly that fickle.'

'Oh. So you know about people, then? You mean you can actually see them through the froth of your sales figures? And you,' she says, taking in Sikand who is smiling, 'through the scum of your pseudo-highbrow interest in specimen.'

'Where did you pick up such language, Ambika?' Bibs shakes his head. 'Not at that convent school you went to, surely?'

'Look, let's not fight,' says Sikand. 'We're fighting like children.'

'I'm not fighting with you, Sikand,' she says, undaunted. 'You're hardly worth it. It's Birbal Nath here. Mister Supercilious who needs taking down a peg or two, or even ten!'

There she's done it. All this way she has come specifically to say it. Birbal Nath.

Sikand, horrified, turns in trepidation to see Bibs deflate like the proverbial balloon.

What thoughtless harm parents will do when they name their children, he rues.

1 2

It wasn't like the old days, they both know it.

'Why did you bloody pick up your face and land here? *Hnnh?* Why did you come? *Hnnh? Hnnh?*'

'I told you, Jeete. I can't say myself.'

'To look for Khushwant, your milky-white bitch. That's what for.'

'I only wondered what had happened to her. That's all.'

'So you thought I'm CID? Or a magic man, some Gogia Pasha?' He twirls his hands in the air, grabs a fistful and waves it under Fareed's nose. 'Ah, here she is. The Mallika of Beauty. Mumtaz Mahal. In my palm. Saved from the villain, vile Dilsher Singh of Jaito. But imprisoned, alas. Transformed by my spell into a butterfly. A fairy. Entangled. Doomed. Get her out if you can. Come on. Try it.'

'I shouldn't have come. I shouldn't have come.'

'Come on, try it. Try it. Prise open my fingers.'

'To hell with you, you bastard,' Fareed says, and striking his stupid fist out of the way, he rises and stumbles out of the courtyard with tears like hot needles pricking at his eyelids.

The sense of impending tragedy had hit him not that night, although he remembers the plaintive lowing of the buffaloes turning their snouts to the darkness and the return of pain in swollen tongue and jaw. It was with the *gutter-goo* of pigeons in the ventilator at dawn. A sound so comforting changed overnight into the loneliest sound on earth. And he had seen sorrows stretch out like dunes on a sandy plain, dune after wretched dune, endlessly into the distance. For a second his heart had hammered like the hooves of some wild-eyed animal in his chest. As he stared at the ceiling, the pigeons made little pelting sounds on the sill, and he knew that never again would this room on the terrace, this house of courtyards, never again this village, the pond and the Peepal, never again his mother or his father, Babaji, no one, nothing, would enfold him, hold him to its chest, make it go away.

How can he say to Jeeta that this is what had made him come? The *gutter-goo* of pigeons?

*

It was as if the ordinance that had given special powers to the armed forces had changed their entire attitude. Like they were holding an occupied territory, the soldiers of the Madras Regiment, small peaceable people, herded the hulking rural Sikhs with barks and scowls. It had seemed such a parody to Sikand, like they were children hurling stones at a stray dog in the street, half expecting, every moment, the animal to turn. But the comic aspect had not held him long. For the good nature with which the villagers allowed themselves to be pushed and frisked and searched seemed much more of a parody.

'Even the most un-heroic of people would show some sullenness at being herded like that,' he'd said to Shivi in Amritsar. 'Do you think the Sikhs respect authority *per se*? More than others? Or could it be because it's the army? A traditional obedience?'

'It isn't going to last too long, if that's what it is,' Shivi had felt. 'The army's loss. In wartime, the border villages have always turned out at the bunkers with milk and lassi and parathas fried in butter. The more the army has to do this bullying and herding, the less help it's going to get in the next war.'

'I noticed that they take the pushing around from the police too. And the police have never enjoyed the kind of general approval that the army has.'

'I haven't thought about it too deeply, Sikand. I guess they just obey because they're scared of getting hurt. Like anywhere else in the world.'

'But surely they can look aggrieved. Remember what that SP, your police contact, said the last time? The Sikhs respect authority. Not that they're scared of it. They respect it.'

'Why do you always have to be researching some thesis, Boss? And that SP has become such a thorn in my side, I can't even begin to tell you.'

But Sikand had not let go and finally got Shivi reminiscing about his Sainik School days. 'One kind of boy everyone admired was the giving-sauce-to-the-housemaster kind. Who gave a damn if it involved a caning. But I was a different sort. The kind who didn't care about being caned; or being admired. I stood in line because I felt things got done better and faster that way. I think I believed in something like the usefulness of authority. I got caned all right but never for talking back or wilful disobedience. I guess I obeyed because I understood the mechanics of power, its nuts and bolts.'

A single Sikh in a crowded train compartment could organize everyone's luggage so that there was room to move. Sikand had seen it done, and realized with a lick of shame that he could have done it too, if he hadn't been so embarrassed at taking charge. No one would have listened to him anyway if he'd tried, which, coming to think of it, was the same thing.

They would have known he was faking, that he had no true understanding of power *per se*.

He had asked a crucial question then, 'So, then the general lot of Sikhs will follow Bhindranwale? His power as a justification in itself?'

And Shivi had studied his palm as if some all-encompassing answer lay concealed in the pattern of its lines. 'When will you stop researching, Boss?' he'd said.

If, years from now, the man were to be found to have irredeemably changed the Sikhs and the nation and the way the two viewed each other, then it was indefensible to suppress that image. He should have said that to Ambika when she was scorching him with, 'Bhindranwale as a study of power. Of evil. *Chahh!*' On one of her social occasions, with everyone else trying to build professional contacts over non-professional drinking, she had broken up the party with a scathing attack on the moral standing of her opponent in court. She simply has no distance, Ambika.

But that image. The kernel is that image. The magazine lies on the coffee table in his sitting room. He remembers Livleen gush, 'It looks like the *Time* magazine, Sikand!' and thinks: so it does. With his photographer's eye he matches stare for stare with Bhindranwale. And realizes with a cold dismay that putting those eyes on that cover was a choice that could itself decide the course of history. He should have been able to explain his reluctance at the very outset to write a single word for publication when Bibs was hustling him. He should have been able to hold out.

Bibs and his pragmatizing. 'Free solicitous access, Sikand. That's what Bhindranwale offers to any penny journalist. Putting him on the cover will give our currency more value. Preferential access. The dollar among the dinars.'

Despite his choice of metaphor, Sikand had listened,

swallowed his words: exclusive access, authentic information…
and—had thought, a shy at the truth! He had ignored the hardly
unsaid more circulation, more sales.

A fine glimmer at the end of the tunnel he had created for
some confused youth. *And* he had invited the nation to paste
that face on the Sikhs as a community.

His journalism was not a mirror; it was a lens.

*

The interview with Bhindranwale had not gone well. ('Don't
worry, the next one will. Now that he's on our cover,' goes Bibs.)

Sikand was given a chair in a corner of a nondescript room.
In the centre, on a cot draped with a garish bedspread, sat
Bhindranwale leaning back on his arms. Men with stens cradled
against their chests stood about. Open, proud young faces, sure
of themselves and their cause. Sikand lifted his camera but
was stayed by an absently raised hand from the cot. A slightly
cadaverous hand, gaunt and veined. But firm and confident. It
could dig a ditch, that hand. It could fire a carbine.

On the floor a woman, young, white dupatta draped over
her head, recounted a harrowing tale. A husband suddenly dead
of snakebite; his parents out to get rid of her without parting
with a single rupee. A corner of her dupatta came away so
limp from her eyes that Sikand was at last convinced it wasn't
a spectacle arranged for him, the press. The Sant asked a few
questions and repeated the woman's answers, details of names
and places, to a man who stood at the foot of the cot noting
everything in an exercise-book. He did little else to comfort
her, and she hesitated, reluctant to leave, when Bhindranwale
said, 'Go. We shall see you get your share in your husband's
property.' The secretary shut his exercise-book with a snap and
stepped up. As she leaned over to touch the Sant's feet, Sikand
in his corner raised his camera and again was stayed by the

Sant's hand. A wild looking Sikh who stood at the pillow end holding an automatic rifle reinforced the gesture with a glare.

'Are there any more?' the Sant asked when she had left, and when informed she was the last, he beckoned to Sikand. Everyone filed out of the room except the man with the automatic.

'I don't speak English,' said the Sant, 'but you understand Punjabi?'

'Only a little, I'm afraid. I have a tape-recorder, but the man outside said I couldn't bring it in.'

'No tape-recorder,' the Sant agreed, lifting his legs and crossing them on the cot.

The spare body was without a superfluous touch. A dark chest-length beard flecked sparingly with white. Hooded eyes nested in a fine mesh of wrinkles above a hawk nose. The overall effect was of some bird of prey and Sikand was nervous meeting the interrogating gaze. In addition, small movements from the man with the gun disconcerted him.

He decided to tackle the insecurity aspect first. Why the guns? Why the hiding in the Guru Nanak Niwas? Was it true what they said about warring factions among the militant groups?

Bhindranwale didn't like the questions. 'For a man of religion, there is no better place than at the feet of the Harmandar Sahib,' he said.

'You think of yourself as a man of religion?' Sikand asked.

'Without doubt.'

'But you never go out now. To the villages, the countryside. Perhaps outside you could be arrested?'

'Who is going to arrest me? For what?' Bhindranwale's eyes penetrated Sikand's. The gunman's finger twitched on the trigger. Sikand forgot about Lala Jagat Narain, the Nirankari Baba and a host of other questions, and busied himself with writing notes in his diary.

'I was arrested once, you know,' Bhindranwale said. 'For no reason. Then, for no reason, they let me go. Who can understand the Sarkar? If they want to act out the same drama, what is there? I can go out and be arrested. What is there to be scared about?'

'Is your war against the government or against the nation? Against the people?' Sikand asked suddenly.

He expected the counter 'What war?' but got instead a slow, formulated answer. 'My war is to unite the Sikhs. To keep our religion safe. To preserve it. Sikhs should not become Hindus.'

'What do you have against the Hindus?'

'The Hindus? What can I have against them? You are a Hindu, are you not? Who has molested you? The lady who was here when you came, she is a Hindu. Yet she came for help to me. If I am against anyone, it is Sikhs. Those who have forgotten the teachings of their religion. Those who cut their hair, become like Hindus, drink and smoke. They are the true enemies of the Panth.'

'So does that mean they are to be killed?'

'We have asked them to mend their ways. They are listening. Why should they be killed if they listen?'

Sikand had not expected a deep discussion, but had hoped at least to draw the man into revealing what moved him. Feeling he wasn't succeeding, he tried another line. 'Do you feel the Sikhs cannot be Sikhs within the Indian Nation?' he asked.

'You are asking about Khalistan. I have given my views on it a dozen times. Why should you people, the papers, be interested only in that? Have I ever said we want a separate nation?'

'But the Anandpur Sahib Resolution…'

'It is not my resolution-shezolution. Don't ask me about it. Go to Sant Longowal. In Gandhi Niwas.'

The gunman flinched, breaking into Sikand's thoughts. 'Why do you call the Akali office Gandhi Niwas?' he asked in a rush. 'Is it to make fun of Sant Longowalji or of Gandhiji? Or of peace and peaceful means in general?'

The Sant's long fingers played with his beard. Then he laughed softly. Appreciatively. Sikand waited, but got no other reply.

'Is it proper that guns should be carried in places of religion?' he asked.

'What is wrong with it? The Gurus themselves told the Sikhs to arm themselves. Earlier it was kirpans and swords. Now it is guns. Times change. Arms have changed.'

'But with changing times, the teachings of the Gurus would also change, would they not? Today there are no Mughal armies to fight, like when the Khalsa was formed.'

'But the need to defend the faith is still there. Do you see how our boys are shot down, killed in fake encounters by the police? How our Guru Granth Sahibs are burned, our gurudwaras attacked? How is it you don't write about it? The attempts to crush the Khalsa, the war against our faith?'

The gunman quite lost control at this and began to shake and swivel as if an electric current was passing through him. Sikand was stupefied. Bhindranwale turned on the man and shouted a single word that sent him into a blundering run, first into the cot, then into the wall, and finally out of the room. The secretary and another gunman rushed in, their faces contorted with fear. 'How many times have I asked you to keep that boy out? All he does is stuff himself with opium day and night,' Bhindranwale lashed at them.

It was the end of the interview.

*

'But I didn't get any pictures,' Sikand complained to the Secretary as he was led outside into the corridor. The man was apologetic, patting him on the arm, promising an exclusive photo-session on the morrow, 'You can see Santji is tired, can't you?' and Sikand had to nod, though the last thing the Sant looked was tired.

Reclaiming his tape-recorder, Sikand started to descend a flight of stairs to the first floor. On the bottom-most step with his face buried in his hands, sat the gunman who had just been thrown out of the room. Sikand had no choice but to pass him and he stepped warily down the stairs, noting with some relief that the man no longer had his gun. Reaching the bottom step, he had almost slithered past, when a hand shot out and grasped his ankle in a grip of steel. As he almost toppled over, his hair-raising cry of alarm rang through the building. As suddenly as he had been gripped, he was set free, and regaining his balance in a headlong rush down a second flight of steps, he emerged with racing pulse into the sunlight.

Disoriented, he ran towards the Golden Temple and reaching the tank at its centre, collapsed on the steps.

Quite out of breath, he sat panting, staring sightlessly before him at the water. Slowly he became aware that a woman preparing to take a dip was regarding him with some alarm. Swallowing her lower lip in pained self-consciousness, she had stooped to wrap her dupatta over her ample hips, when he came to and looked sharply away.

'Aren't you going to wait to see if she comes out all young and beautiful?' said a voice beside him and Sikand turned to look into the laughing eyes of a young Sikh.

'Is that why you hang around then,' he said, recovering fast, 'in the hope of such miracles?'

'Well, one hears tales all the time you know, about the holy water of the Sarovar turning crows into swans. Who knows when we could get lucky, *hnnh*?'

Sikand laughed, but wondered if he was armed or dangerous. His experience in the Guru Nanak Niwas had left him with no desire to be a journalist however, and soon he found it easy to talk to the pleasant-looking youth about everything but Punjab and politics, simply enjoying the company of one who so obviously was enjoying his. They talked about big-city life, about Sikand's profession and his barren marital status, about what it felt like to ride in an aeroplane. Then about the connection between earthquakes and tidal waves. The USA. All this in a happily jumbled sequence, while waiting half-seriously for the ugly duckling, or was it the crow, to turn into a swan.

'My name is Shaikh,' the boy said in leave-taking. 'You can usually find me around here, waiting, as you say, for miracles.'

*

Jeeta is now more often seen with Beera and Jeera, two brothers from Gurdaspur district, both wrestlers. In the training area behind the bathroom block they spread the sandbags on the floor and wrestle in their underwear. Boys who have money lay bets. It often gets rowdy with the cheering and the sandbags bursting and spraying everything with sand. Lal Guru and another man they call Ustaad have to physically break it up more than once.

On one such occasion Ameer, who has bet on Beera, is delighted. 'He was obviously losing it,' he says. 'Thighs like palm trees, but no technique. No planning.' The only one of them who's not a villager, Ameer knows everything under the sun and moon and stars better than everyone else, and is sometimes unbearable.

'I'd like to see you take on Beera. Show him the tricks,' Kaptan says.

'They're both smugglers, our wrestlers,' Ameer says. 'First it was opium and silver. Now it's guns.'

'Really? And how do you know?'

'Because smuggling is what their village does. Like other villages on the border. My father's trucks go everywhere. Bhatinda, Ferozepur, Gurdas...'

'So your father's a smuggler too?' asks Kaptan.

'No. He's a transporter,' Ameer says patiently, quite undisturbed by the insult. 'Smugglers and murderers, communists and boys too poor to do anything else…They're all here. You just have to look and you can recognize them by their faces.'

'There are also boys who are soldiers. For the faith,' Major breaks in, his eyes moist and aggrieved.

'Yes, yes, Major. There are those. The poor fools. Anyway there's not much difference between smugglers and bank robbers, if you think of it.'

'Nothing's black or white, *hain*?' says Fareed.

'Never was. Never can be.'

But Fareed cannot agree. There was a time, he remembers, when everything had been clear.

Jeeta is often out with his new friends. On trips he calls 'Operations' that involve motorcycles and long distances. Once he returns with a stengun and folds it into his mattress in front of them all. His eyes are daring them to tell and no one does.

He stays out nights and claims he has three girlfriends, all of whom he beds one after the other in a single night.

They go to prayers, offer sewa in the langar, sweep the parikarma. When the place is full with volunteers going out to court arrest for the Akali morcha, they hand out tokens for the devotees' shoes and listen to lectures. On many an occasion they hear Sant Bhindranwale, now spoken of only as Santji, rail against drink and loose morals and Sikhs who betray the path by cutting their hair, drinking whisky-shisky. But when Jeeta talks to them at night about women's breasts and the dark paradise between their legs, they still push at each other on his mattress to be closest to his whispered words.

And at every step, as he does the contrary, they wait for the legendary explosion that never comes.

*

Lal Guru is weighted high on courage. After the killing of the policemen he has a host of recruits. The rooms around them fill up.

'And who is responsible for all this?' says Jeeta. 'Me. He was angry with me for having shot the cops. Remember how he shouted at you, Jagat? And now when General Shahbeg himself drops in to see him training he says, Sir this, Sir that, and tries to hold his stomach in.'

General Shahbeg is Santji's right-hand. The man who is said to have created Bangladesh by training the Mukti Bahini. After that, the rest of the Generals got jealous of him and threw him out of the army.

Now that Jeeta is no longer special for Lal Guru, it is Fareed whom Lal Guru picks to show his progress to the General.

Fareed can shoot a man between the eyes from twenty yards. Not that great a feat when you see the very small eyes, and the space between them wider than a football field. They have to find a better artist to draw the targets, Lal Guru says. The General, a small man, old, with a white pointed beard, is concerned that the sound of the firing can be heard outside the walls.

'It might be better to use blanks. Live ammunition's too expensive for training, Sir.'

'It would help, yes. You also wouldn't have to worry about them killing each other that way. And A 4 targets.'

'Yes, Sir. That should not be too difficult. They're standard issue in the army. And the police.'

'Then find them. Try not to have your men practise on these parodies of Gurkhas again.'

When he has gone, Lal Guru takes the cardboard figures off the wall, and stands there himself.

'Try to miss me if you can,' he says.

He is weighted really high on courage.

Lal Guru believes in soldiering. That is how men like him fit in. He's fought the Chinese once and the Pakistanis twice, and cliff or desert, he's always gone into battle shouting Bole Sonihal. 'It curdles the enemy's blood,' he says. 'Or at least ensures I die with honour. It is the way of the Punjab Regiment.'

Life and death, he tells them, are two sides of a coin. 'You try your best to come out heads each time, but death is a part of a soldier's life and sometimes it is tails for the best. When you accept that, it makes each time you come out heads that much more valuable.' He breaks up all arguments about soldier-saints in the training area with, 'Black and white make grey. Soldiering is a way of life, just like religion. It has its rules and rituals. What matters is to site your target accurately, plan well, act boldly. Be generous in victory, thoughtful in defeat. And above all aim for economy: minimum cost, maximum gain.'

And Jeeta, who has problems with everything he says now, snorts and says under his breath, 'What is cost and gain to a Jat? He talks like we are bloody Phapas!'

13

The plan has Lal Guru's touch.

Selected for the recce, Fareed is at the gate of the Punjab Armed Police training centre before the sun. The grass, spiked with December frost, crunches under his feet. Fumbling with his suitcase and bedding roll and blanket he approaches the sandbagged guard post, thinking of what he is to say. He has filled in his recruitment form, Lal Guru managing the verification signatures from somewhere, but he is still nervous and shivering with the cold. Before he can open his mouth, the guard, so bundled up behind his bags that he can barely raise his arm, points down the road to the Recruitment Centre. Fareed creaks open the iron gate and lets himself in. 'May Waheguru bless you,' he shouts back through the bars.

On a large bald ground about thirty boys are running in a circle with their rifles held high above their heads. He sits down to watch and to wait. The sun whitens the eucalyptus trunks along the wall and he can see their faces, each accompanied by its puff of steam. With the vapour lifting off the ground like smoke, it seems they are running in endless space. More space than he has ever seen. He feels his own muscles spring and imagines the rush of wind against his face.

They come off the ground like skittish calves, jumping each other, running zigzag across the road, their khaki shorts ballooning about their legs. 'You're going the wrong way for the recruitment centre,' one of them says and points his rifle towards the shed with the asbestos roof.

'I came early.' Fareed falls in beside him. 'To pick up some tips. It must be tough for village boys.'

'Not too tough. Most of us are village boys. The physical is easy. You only have to know how to expand your chest properly,' the boy says, and before they have reached the armoury, Fareed is holding his rifle and the boy, Dharam Singh, is showing him how it's done.

In the veranda of the armoury the boys mill around a counter, thrusting their rifles at the man in charge. He is overwhelmed with having to identify each one and check it off against its number in a register, and Fareed has plenty of time to observe what he came for. There are two doors, two guards, and a barred inner door with an old-fashioned iron lock. Inside, the rifles are lined up in wooden racks but he notes, like Lal Guru has asked him, that they are not chained and locked in.

Fareed's work is already done, but he is reluctant to leave. In a mess hall that smells of burnt milk he shares Dharam Singh's breakfast of milk and parathas, and is given advice on how to impress the recruiting Inspector.

'The moment you see him, raise your right leg high and bring it down on the ground. Make a noise, like this. And salute. Try it.'

In the barracks, the cots are pushed four metres apart and he is shown how to clear the span by jumping off and landing forward on his toes. Then, as Dharam Singh joins a queue of boys outside the baths, he wanders around and is interested to find behind the bathroom block, a breach in the campus wall. As he is investigating, a man comes through it, surprising him. 'Looking around,' Fareed offers lamely, recognizing the cook who has given them breakfast.

'You'll be in trouble if someone sees you. Recruits aren't allowed in the servants' quarters,' the man says.

'That's where it leads to? I was wondering how the wall got broken.'

'It's a shortcut. Nobody goes all the way to the main gate. They keep repairing it, but someone removes a few bricks every time. But recruits can only use the main gate,' the man warns.

Fareed watches Dharam Singh dress. 'Let me tie that turban,' he says and impresses them all with his speed. There are more turbans to be tied. And more tips about the mile race, the push-ups, the high jump. Walking with Dharam Singh to the recruitment shed, his head is full of them and he is warm at the thought of competing, of testing and proving himself. At the door, as Dharam wishes him luck, he has quite forgotten what he had come for, and is brought up short by a policeman saying, 'Where's your call letter then?'

'You must have left it in your suitcase,' Dharam says, so real is Fareed's confusion at the question. 'I'll run back and get it for you.'

Fareed nods but says, 'No.' And then, 'The guard, at the gate.'

'He shouldn't have taken it from you,' the policeman says. 'They're always doing these things.'

'Maybe I can just run back and get it then?' Fareed asks.

'Go ahead. But if you're late the Inspector won't listen. He's like that.'

He pushes through the line behind him, leaving Dharam Singh looking quite anxious. As he is jolted along on the bus back to Amritsar, that look comes back to him many a time.

*

After all this planning, the actual raid on the armoury is touch and go. Fareed leads them through the gap in the wall at night. When he jumps the armoury guard and overpowers him in silence, Lal Guru whispers 'Shabash!' into his ear. But Jagat, although briefed about it in advance, is surprised by the second guard coming round the corner, and shoots him in the face. After that, all is confusion. Lal Guru fires repeatedly at the iron lock on the armoury door before it gives way, and as they hurriedly gather the rifles, from all over the campus there are shouts, and lights and whistles converging on them. As they start to run, Fareed grabs at the targets propped against the bars. Stumbling over each other at the break in the wall, they have to abandon some of the boxes of ammunition.

The targets are enough to wipe out the loss. Lal Guru has them nailed to wooden frames and lined up along the pockmarked wall.

'Let me explain,' he says with relish, 'the points for hitting the head, the chest and the trunk.'

*

The volunteers gather in their thousands. Sant Longowal has called for a hundred thousand, but already twice that number has courted arrest for the Akali morcha. The crowds pour out of the Clock Tower gate of the Golden Temple to pack the waiting police buses and the air is alive with *'Bole Sonihal. Sat Sri Akal.'* It is a great show of Sikh unity.

Inside the temple complex the story is different. Several factions have emerged among the militants in the guest-houses and hostels surrounding the temple, and under the surface there are silent but often fierce struggles for power. One night firing breaks out, the bullets digging into the walls to send chips of masonry whizzing through the darkness. They are surprised by Lal Guru who lumbers along through the racket and stands in their doorway to shine a torch over each of their faces in their beds. The beam lingers on Jeeta's mattress, then catches him standing wary guard in a corner in his underwear with his unauthorised stengun clutched to his bare chest. The beam plays along him from head to foot and then goes out.

Another night there are shouts and abuses, men being hit, a clattering and a thumping in the corridors, and in the morning several rooms have new occupants. Like a wild toothed animal the rumour creeps—Santji's men have been thrown out by the Babbars. Lal Guru growls at them not to gossip, but he can do nothing to stop them when Santji himself shifts out of the Guru Nanak Niwas into the Akal Takht, within the Golden Temple, soon after. The Babbars have been against Santji since the Nirankari days, when they say he led them to picket a Nirankari meeting and ran away when it came to the confrontation. Fauja Singh, their leader, was shot. It is his widow who they acknowledge as their leader now, and she has been in Guru Nanak Niwas long before Santji ran in there to hide, they claim. For so long, to speak against Santji was to draw capital punishment and they have smouldered in silence.

But now, such is the power of the gun, every group has gained confidence.

After prayers, the boys go into huddles on the parikarma. Guru Gobind Singh's hawk is said to have hovered over Santji's head, but there are some who whisper it was only a sparrow.

'Do you believe in the hawk?' asks Fareed.

Jagat does. And Major waits to see what Kaptan will say before nodding.

Ameer behaves like he hasn't heard the question. But when they're alone he says, 'I don't believe in any messenger from the skies. I believe in Lal Guru, that's all.'

'Do you think Lal Guru believes?'

'You can ask him. But don't think you'll get a straight answer. He's sharp, Lal Guru.'

He finds Lal Guru on the steps that evening and asks his question as soon as he can. In the Sarovar a few people are braving the cold water, bobbing their heads in and out. Under his turban, always slightly askew and untidy in its folds, Lal Guru's smooth forehead creases.

'Stories of faith,' says Lal Guru. 'We always had stories of faith. In the bunkers. On the march. Once I fired a single shot at a tree, just for practice. And I missed and hit a goat that jumped out from behind it. This happened in '71 in the Chhamb area. We took it as a message. The goat. And that night with one platoon we took a hill, three bunkers, guns, ammunition, all.'

'The goat. It jumped out just like that?'

'When you ask a serious question boy, you must behave serious. How do I care if the goat had stuffed itself with elephant laxative?' Lal Guru glowers at him.

'But you're talking about battle, Lal Guru. That's different.'

'What's the difference? Everything in life is a battle. Don't think otherwise, boy, don't make that mistake.'

That night the ache of home is in Fareed's heart. He will never be able to go back, no matter how hard he tries.

Why this battle? Some such battle. But why this one? Because he didn't even have the address of another battlefield, he thinks. What strikes him then is that he can feel, and not have to do anything about it. Feeling and acting are two different fields. You can dance with the heart swollen with pain. And you are still whole, still alive.

He imagines his hands on a woman. He mounts her in a

heat. She is ugly, repulsive. But he feels his response and is intrigued—the ripples go on and on. She is unwashed, she smells of sickness. She has running sores on her face. Hairy moles on her breasts.

He tears the limits of his imagination, and feels the bile rise in his throat, but still his body pumps on like an engine, a machine. In amazement he watches it turn on itself in clashing signals of bile and semen.

*

The man they have come to free refuses to be freed. When Fareed runs into the lockup and shouts 'Let's go!' he thinks the fellow has turned to stone. From outside comes the sound of rapid shots. It echoes off the walls in the narrow cell, and the man, whose name Fareed has forgotten, stares as if his eyelids are frozen in death.

Fareed jerks his gun to point to the door, but it is the wrong action. The glazed eyes register fear—something for which there isn't time. Starting to withdraw with his back towards the door, Fareed remembers the name, and shouts, 'Come on you bastard, Chhinda,' jumpstarting the man. He lands in one motion at Fareed's side, but already there are feet running on concrete, and as they turn, at the door there is a gun, a shoulder, a face. He fires. Just the single shot, and the man topples like a tree across the doorway. They run over his body, their feet massaging the flesh. In the corridor he fires again, the shot hits the ceiling and screams at his feet, even as he senses that behind him, Chhinda has come to a dead-stop. Why are we out here to free such a brainless son of a bitch, he thinks.

Six people die in the rescue from the court lockup. Including Chhinda, whom they had come to rescue. Including Jagat, whose bed unrolled that night by Jeeta, lies between them so that it is impossible to cover your face or turn your back.

When the light is put out they see each other's pale faces still turned towards the vacant mattress, white and unforgiving, in their centre.

Jeeta sits up all of a sudden in the dark. 'We're idiots,' he exclaims. 'We didn't expect them to shoot back!'

The silence in the room disagrees with him. Only Jeeta has been fatally lulled. That is why they mourn Jagat so deeply; he amongst them had followed Jeeta's faith, and he had genuinely not expected them to shoot back.

'Carelessness is not courage,' Lal Guru says in the grey morning. 'That is what I see as Jagat's fault. It will be best if we learn from it.' And although he looks at everyone, his words are meant for Jeeta.

But Jeeta is even wilder after that. One night he and his wrestlers march in four policemen, captured from their post complete with weapons. Their wireless set crackles: 'Alpha twosix. Alpha twosix,' as Lal Guru mounts guard, two boys at a time, before he goes across to the Akal Takht to talk.

'They don't need a guard,' says Jeeta, 'you think they will run?' He is right too; they look incapable of twitching a finger. If someone breathes too loud, they tremble.

'I want no harm to come to them while I'm gone,' Lal Guru says. Their eyes lock then, and Jeeta's do not give way.

One of the policemen dies in the night, bleeding to death because no one knows what to do for him. There are meetings and talks in the Akal Takht and they release the body to the police for cremation. The other three remain, and are eventually moved to the basement of the Akal Takht, with Jeeta arranging the movement on his own. Lal Guru acts like he has no interest in the whole thing.

'Whose side are you on?' asks Jeeta.

It is important to take sides, but Fareed wavers. On Lal Guru's side lies what he knows to be right, but he wavers. To abandon their shared childhood is disloyalty to his blood.

'What was the sense in kidnapping the policemen?'

Jeeta reacts like he's been bitten. His skin is so thin, the slightest jolt can make his insides wobble.

'You think I'm stupid?' he says. 'Those policemen are the biggest thing we've got. We don't have to go about getting killed in stupid rescues when we can barter them off for seven, ten boys in jail. And you know who thinks that? Santji. Sant Jarnail Singh Bhindranwale doesn't think I'm stupid.'

'I don't think you're stupid,' says Fareed.

'Don't deny it. You always will, no matter what I do to show I'm not.'

'It's just that you don't see ahead. You get lost in the moment.'

'And what's wrong with that? It is the moment that is life, the moment that is courage. Not thinking endlessly. I could do this. I could have done that.'

'I don't do that.'

'Of course you do. Brooding over women, sobbing into your pillow. *Hai,* my lost youth, *hai* my precious Khushwant. What use is such sense? Bold you are, but that is not courage. Courage is giving everything to the moment.'

'Who's been saying all this to you?'

'See? You can't even believe I could have thought it all myself. You think I'm stupid. And you still think you can wrestle me to the ground. Try it, then. Come on, see what happens. Come on, just try it.'

And in a moment they are fighting, their feet scrabbling at the ground in an effort to lock, to scissor, and to trip. Out on the grass behind the hostel buildings there is no one to witness their desperate heaving; only each hears the other's breath and feels the push and jerk of the other's guarded will. Suddenly Fareed is down and Jeeta astride his chest, his hand raised high like a dagger. His little eyes are narrowed, his nostrils flare, he bares his sharp teeth like a rat. A thrill runs through Fareed. He really wants to kill me! he thinks, and, electrified, he arches off the ground and rolls, his elbows and knees splayed for maximum damage. On top, he gazes into Jeeta's red eyes, gazes long and hard, till the animal spirit that splutters there begins to weaken. Then he springs up and starts to brush off the grass clinging to his kurta. He is careful not to look at Jeeta now, as if he doesn't care to look.

'I saw your Khushwant. In Mallapurana,' Jeeta says from the ground. 'She is no longer beautiful. You see, Shera found her too. Much before me. He doesn't want to marry her. Not now.'

He is lying, lies is his bloody mother. Fareed is determined to give him no satisfaction. No scraps of meat for the fallen dog. He shrugs, it is all the same to him. As he walks away he hears Jeeta, 'You don't believe me? Come with me then. Tonight. I'll show you…'

There is no doubt on whose side Fareed is now.

*

After this, two incidents happen in such quick succession there is no doubt in anyone's mind that they're connected. A man, known to be very close to Santji, is murdered in a teashop near the Temple. Minutes after the murder, a woman rushes from the teashop to fall at Santji's feet in the Akal Takht. His man had lusted after her, she cries, and her lover had stabbed him in a fit of jealousy.

'It's a ruse,' murmurs Ameer. 'She lures him to the teashop, her lover finishes him off, and Santji's hands are stayed because of the pretext.'

Furious rumours abound. Some whisper the Akalis are behind it. Others are sure it's the Babbars hitting back at last. Everyone agrees that a hand raised so close to Santji has to be a very powerful hand. The atmosphere thickens with fear and suspicion. The woman's tortured body is found miles away, on the GT Road, by the police. It is whispered she confessed before she died. Numerous plots are hinted at as bodies begin to appear everywhere. Ameer actually sees the cops fishing one out of a drain behind the Temple library.

The second incident is the sudden move of a large number of boys into the Akal Takht. Jeeta is gone too, along with his friends, the wrestlers. They stop talking of him the moment he's gone—he's a different level of person now, part of an elite squad. Santji's need for so much protection is talked about, and everyone is insecure. Groups break off, the boys wandering around uneasily looking for trust, and coming together in knots of village and caste loyalties.

Kaptan and Major are inseparable. Each morning even before the loudspeaker's whistle and the vigorous clearing of the granthi's throat announce the first words of the morning prayers, they roll up their bedding in the darkness and head for the Harmandar. Fareed and Ameer sleep on. Lal Guru hasn't changed his orders, but he has stopped taking notice of absences like before. It is difficult to be strict about attending prayers when anyone who cares to listen can hear the tortured screams from the basements.

So it is that Ameer and Fareed are alone, swaddled in their bedclothes, when three men burst in and, with noise and vigour, start to throw out their belongings into the corridor. Barely awake, Fareed grabs on to his blanket by instinct, sticking like a leech to his mattress when they try to prise him off it. Six hands grip and pull, at his arms, his hair, but he manages to roll over and cling even harder. As he grunts and snorts his eye falls on Ameer, lying absolutely still in his blankets, blinking his lashes like a doll.

'Get Lal Guru,' Fareed shouts at him, and bites hard into a hand that has fallen across his teeth. The sour blood brushes his lips as the hand is snatched away with a curse. A paralysing kick lands in his ribs but it's not enough to make him let go. He is living in the moment, the way Jeeta had said. And they, heaving and pulling at him, sometimes in opposing directions, they too are living in the moment. It is only when it dawns on them to lift the mattress itself off the floor, and Fareed remembering the gun under it, quickly sweeps his hand across the floor to lift and hold the muzzle in their faces, that the moment collapses around them all.

Ameer, who has not heeded his command to fetch Lal Guru, cheers from his bed across the room. Their faces, spotlit by the early light were such a surprise ending to the film he'd been watching, he says after they have fallen over each other in rushing out the door to the sound of his hoots.

A fractured calf-bone is one of the consequences of the drama at dawn. Another is their move to a house across the street from the Guru Nanak Niwas. After Fareed's defence of the room this is an anti-climax, but Lal Guru is firm about it. 'This is not some college hostel,' he says, 'where boys can go fighting over rooms.'

The three groups, Santji's, the Babbars', and a third confused force of the Akali SGPC combine, come to an agreement. A kind of border commission sits to demarcate the boundaries of each. The infighting is suppressed but all three groups now resort to large-scale taking of hostages, as a prisoner means undisputed ownership of the space required to confine him in.

Jeeta's feat with the policemen remains unmatched, but still, there are important pilgrims who can just be picked off the parikarma like mangoes. There are gun-runners and smugglers to be held as security against delivery. Bhaijis and mahants, priests of gurudwaras who have been reluctant to offer havens for the boys. Ransom, security, setting a gentle example, changing incorrect mindsets—there are so many good reasons. The common objective is to lock up space, to extend the borders.

'That's the trouble with Sikhs—they can never co-operate,' laments Lal Guru. 'Everyone is a leader. What sort of a leader are you if no one wants to be a follower, *hain*?'

In the night, retired soldiers and the like, friends of Lal Guru representing different groups, are assembled on the kitchen roof. Reduce areas of friction, increase areas of cooperation, is Lal Guru's recipe. Infighting brings zero gain.

Major, who has a voice inherited from a father who once sang on All India Radio, is asked to set the tone for the meeting with a song. He begins with a hymn from the Gurbani, but no one wants that kind of tone. When he starts to sing the Heer he creates a different person before your eyes. A person made up of home and Punjab and love and sadness that you want to clutch to your breast and weep over. On the flat roof everyone moves closer, and when his song is over the tone is just right to talk of cooperation.

'Training,' says Lal Guru picking his favourite topic. 'General Shahbeg agrees that the boys must train together. There are hardly enough trainers. Why should each of us waste resources separately? Let us each select two or three boys for training in explosives. I can have a training camp set up in the Mand in a week's time.' The Mand, a riverine area of tall grass and mosquitoes as big as birds, is unhealthy and deserted—the ideal choice.

The man from the Babbars shakes his head. 'Not many boys would be ready for the Mand.'

'It is our job to make them. I am volunteering Ameer,' says Lal Guru. 'Even Shaikh will go if I say it, but his leg is broken.'

Ameer is taken aback, but makes no protest and Lal Guru's face glows. 'And Shaikh I will volunteer for guard duty,' he says happily. 'Let's mount common guard, whoever has the hostages. Why waste good boys?' He leans back on his arms beaming with satisfaction. Common guard would finish off infighting.

The others are still digesting this suggestion when there is a commotion at the dark end of the terrace and Karnail walks up carrying his sten. Two men with guns follow close behind him.

'What are you doing here?' he asks the Babbar man directly.

'The same thing you are,' says the Babbar, but holds up his hand to restrain his two boys who have risen.

Lal Guru rises too. 'I called them here, Karnail.'

Karnail reaches out his free hand and pushes Lal Guru back onto the cot. Only Ameer has a gun but they all jump up at this: Major, Kaptan, even Fareed who has to rise stiffly from the floor.

'Leave it,' Lal Guru shouts at them. The Babbars, all of whom have guns, are standing and the other group is also up, but confused, not sure whether to leave or stay.

'Jeete!' Fareed calls but Karnail doesn't look at him. His eyes are for Lal Guru alone.

'I have called them,' Lal Guru says softly, 'because I have the authority of Shahbeg Singh.'

'And I,' says Karnail, drawing himself up, 'Of Bhindranwale Sant. These people, whom you have called, are not trusted here.' He waves his sten to take in everyone, even the Akalis, who look really anxious now to leave.

'Fine,' says Lal Guru, after a heavy silence. 'Allow them then to leave unmolested.' The Akalis are already walking towards the edge where the ladder is, and the Babbars too start to move, but reluctantly, turning and glaring at every step.

'You should think, Karnail...' Lal Guru begins, but is interrupted

'You forget it was you who told me not to think, old man,' says Karnail. And with impressive ceremony, he turns his back on them all.

14

Fareed shares guard-duty with a reformed opium addict, who has seen better days as a bodyguard to Santji himself.

'When you give it up after ten years, your body aches and shivers so much, you look more drugged than when you were on it,' he says bitterly. 'People think you're still gobbling it in secret. When I was on five golis a day, no one could have guessed, but when I gave it up, they all started to call me Amal Singh, and once when my bones began to do the Bhangra by themselves, Bhindranwale threw me out.'

Guard-duty involves long periods with the hostage, sitting in the same room as him with your gun across your knees and watching his every movement so carefully, you feel you know him better than yourself. Their wards are always docile, unnerved simply by being in the Temple. Sometimes Amal Singh's involuntary Bhangra has them so terrified Fareed has to step in to soothe their broken spirits.

Once Fareed comes in to find Amal Singh with his sten in pieces before him on the floor. With a blindfold across his eyes he is fumbling to put the pieces together while their prisoner, a granthi named Beant Singh, times him on his wristwatch.

'He was just helping me get my courage back,' he says afterwards. 'He won't run away—he's too nice a man to cause more trouble for me.'

Fareed hasn't heard of any prisoner trying to escape. One, a sarpanch from Gurdaspur district, reportedly fasted to death in the basement, but it could well be a rumour. Fareed's job takes him all over the complex, from the ramshackle house they occupy across the street to the Guru Nanak Niwas, to the Ram Das Serai, to the basements, once even to the Akal Takht.

Beant Singh has a sparse golden beard that together with

his smooth skin makes him look too young for a granthi. He belongs to Mallapurana.

The name of the village buzzes hotly in Fareed's brain—it is where Jeeta claims to have seen Khushwant. He is in a constant fever of indecision. Wanting to ask, but not wanting to know.

At dawn Beant Singh sits cross-legged on his cot with his eyes closed listening to the Gurbani that is a soft drone in the basement. His lips move, at moments his face glows happily like he is greeting something or someone familiar that he has just recognized. After prayers he lingers over the langar food that Fareed brings for him, chewing slowly, swallowing, taking a sip of water, clearing his throat and speaking a sentence or two before he takes the next bite. 'I don't mind it here,' he says often. 'It is a pilgrimage for me.' He has a good appetite and the meal takes hours.

Waheguru has brought him here and Waheguru will take care of the rest also. In his gurudwara in Mallapurana, he had too much trouble with the boys. 'If you don't resist, how do you live after they have gone?' he says. Sometimes he veils his eyes with his long eyelashes and talks of brutal acts. 'Worse than animals,' he says. 'And the villagers stand like statues of mud before them because of their guns.'

Fareed can never ask the details. What brutal acts? Who are the boys that visit Mallapurana? Is there a girl there from Moranwale? And if there is, do her eyes still blaze with shafts of steel?

But a certainty chills his insides. She is soiled. I am soiled. We are all soiled, he thinks.

No matter whose fault it is—we are all soiled.

*

The second interview is going well. The Sant is still not rid of his irritating tendency to answer a question with a question but his eyes twinkle in a way that says he really likes Sikand and is only teasing him.

'Why have you moved into the Akal Takht?' Sikand asks.

'Why not? All Sikhs have a place in the Harmandar. Why not this humble man?'

'But the Guru Nanak Niwas, where you were before, was almost a part of the Harmandir. I saw people take their shoes off and cover their heads there the last time.'

'Then I have only moved from one part of the Harmandar to another,' says Bhindranwale. 'Why should any one worry?'

'But you never leave the premises?'

'Why should I? Everything is available here. My needs are very few,' Bhindranwale positively beams. He takes off his turban, tightens the knot of hair on his head, and carefully reties his turban. With a corner of it held between his teeth as an anchor, he says, 'You are a good photographer. So I have had to get this mirror for tying my turban.'

Obediently, Sikand raises his camera, but Bhindranwale says, 'Wait. Let me finish.'

From outside the din of construction enters the room. Coming into the temple Sikand has been surprised to find the place a beehive of activity with workmen buzzing about several gaping wounds in the marble facade. He has had to step warily around ladders and misshapen tins and the piles of rubble that dot the parikarma. The air is stifling with dust.

'Do you fear for your safety?' he asks. 'There is a lot of talk about factions among the militants.'

'Government agents,' says Bhindranwale at once, spitting out the end of his turban. 'Some are caught now and then. They pose as our boys and try to start fights among them. Young blood is hot. If the government's agents succeed in killing me, there is bound to be fierce fighting. A war. That we don't want in the Temple. That is what we're trying to avoid. Otherwise, what is my life? For the Panth, we are ready to lay down a thousand lives.'

'How does the Panth gain?' Sikand said. 'All these killings. The security forces harassing the common villagers. So much blood and hate?'

'It tests the mettle of the Faith,' is the immediate reply. 'Whenever injustice is done to the Sikhs, they emerge stronger. With fine sharp blades, like swords out of a furnace.' He quotes from the Guru Granth Sahib a fluent history of persecutions of the Sikhs and concludes with a satisfied gleam, 'The Sikhs are not ordinary people, Sikand Sahab.'

'What about the nation? What is the sense if the strength of the Sikhs is gained at the cost of the nation?'

'We have no fight with the nation. Our land is our mother, as much as it is of the Hindus. But every mother will want that all her sons be treated equally, will she not? Not humiliated by drawing a line around the capital of the nation and saying one with a Singh attached to his name cannot cross it. Or singled out for cruel torture and fake encounters by the police and military forces. It is not the nation who wants to weaken the Sikhs, it is she, that daughter of a pandit. Indira Gandhi. She is not the nation. She is concerned only with her own power, her will to rule. What else can we do but fight?'

Sikand recalls the notorious Bhindranwale tapes in which he vituperates against Indira Gandhi calling her 'panditani' and other derogatory terms. The tapes are briskly inflaming the countryside with the informed details that Bhindranwale supplies so liberally. 'A Sikh girl was stripped naked and her father was forced to rape her...village Kahlkhurd, Moga tehsil. The name of the father was Jagmir Singh, he was a scheduled caste...They caught a Sikh Granthi and a Hindu policeman sat on him, smoked bidis and spat in his mouth, put tobacco in it. His name was Jasbir Singh, village Chupkiti, tehsil Moga...

Another Sikh, without finding anything on him, they cut his thigh, tore the flesh out and poured salt into the cut. Name: Jagir Singh, village Ittanwali, Moga…An Amritdhari Sikh was caught by Bichchu Ram, thanedar, Sadar thana, Fazilka tehsil. They shaved his beard and sent him back to me, "Go and tell Bhindranwale," they said…'

The most convincing propaganda comes from one who totally believes his own lies. Sikand understands the method and wonders if Bichchu Ram, thanedar, Sadar thana, Fazilka Tehsil, still survives.

A dark sardar with strangely Mongoloid features enters the room and touches the Sant lightly on his knees.

'Is it something urgent, Karnail?' Bhindranwale asks. There is a low conversation in Punjabi, which Sikand makes no effort to overhear, but when the boy in leaving appraises him with a single straight look, Sikand is vaguely ill at ease. He stares at his notebook and picks up a prepared question: 'Do you, even now, see yourself as a man of religion?'

'You tell me, what do you see me as?' Bhindranwale leans forward and regards him with amused interest. Sikand smiles, but now what he had taken as good-humoured teasing seems thinly laced with the sinister. He feels like a mouse being playfully pawed at by a cat.

'The atmosphere outside, everything, is so different,' he says avoiding the Sant's eyes and his question. 'It is as if the temple is being rapidly converted into a fortress.'

Bhindranwale looks out of the window at the placid reflection of the golden dome in the still waters of the Sarovar. 'It is still a place of religion,' he says.

'But the devotees,' Sikand points out. 'They are so hurried. So purposeful. As if they can't wait to finish with their task and be off. I'm sure I would be scared off by all this pounding and hammering.'

'But you are not a Sikh,' says Bhindranwale, silencing him.

A citadel is also a prison, Sikand thinks, remembering the tight, closed looks on the faces of the devotees. 'Does it not feel like a prison?' he asks, and for a second as Bhindranwale's gaze flickers, it seems like he has hit something between bone and muscle. He raises his camera quickly to catch the sudden hunted look, but it is fleeting.

There is a gap, after which Bhindranwale says, 'The Harmandar is the prime seat of the Sikh religion. In history it has been razed to the ground. Ahmad Shah Abdalli, the Afghanis...But you know all that. You are a learned man, not just a reporter or a photographer. People like you are valuable to us. To our cause.'

'Do you expect an attack on the Golden Temple?' Sikand asks, meeting his eye at last.

For a moment the link that has been broken between them is re-established. 'The prime seat of the Sikh religion cannot be left defenceless,' says Bhindranwale. 'You see us as soldiers? You must be right. The free press of India can never be wrong. We are soldiers. The meaning of Sikhism is soldiering.' He starts to quote from the Granth again, but this time it is not an illustration. It is an invocation. To Shiva for strength to fight the good fight. *'De Shiva war mohe, shubh karman ton kabhun na daro...'*

Sikand jumps in. 'Is stockpiling of arms in a place of religion approved by the scriptures?'

'Where are these stocks? Have you seen them?' Bhindranwale's gaze is piercing. 'Sikand Saab, have you seen the police check-posts at every entrance? Sometimes they shoot in the air for practice, you can hear them at night. How can arms be stocked here then? They cannot come by air.'

'I don't know,' Sikand shrugs. 'But everywhere I see guns. And bunkers and pill-boxes. If there are no weapons to arm them with, what's the use of them?'

'Look Sikand Saab, I will do this. I will have you taken around the complex. You can search the basements, everywhere, and see for yourself if I am lying. What do you think?'

Sikand is still considering the offer when the stocky youth called Karnail appears again carrying an automatic.

'This is Karnail Singh,' says Bhindranwale. The boy raises his gun by way of greeting. 'He will show you around. Go. Please see for yourself.'

Their footprints follow them down dingy corridors that thread rooms with dusty floors. Here and there filaments of light manage to pierce the clogged trellises to play like dim ghosts on the walls. In the innards of the building Sikand can still hear the muffled sounds of construction and the dust-choked air gets a stranglehold on his imagination, so that thoughts of freedom well as intense and sudden currents in his mind. Yet he follows the bullish back of Karnail down stairs and holes, numbed by their sameness, down, down, down, while the sunshine gleams off a golden dome in another world above.

He seeks equanimity in looking around, stooping to examine a hole that has been gouged into a wall, but his guide marches purposefully on and he has to hurry to catch up. At one point he says, 'Stop. Halt. Stay. Please,' but Karnail Singh turns and meets his hesitant smile with a stolid look of incomprehension and walks on. Sikand lags behind, slows, stops at the head of a flight of stairs.

'I am not going anywhere,' he says.

'Everywhere. You are going everywhere,' Karnail turns to say amiably. 'I will show you everything. Come.'

Sikand starts slowly forward, trips, and slams into the back of the figure two steps below.

'*Maan di...*' the boy says, turning like a whiplash with his gun, and the next instant they are tumbling down the steps together. In a moment, they are at the bottom, brushing themselves off, and Karnail is laughing. Sikand, who has expected every second the sound of a bullet to end his fall, cannot even manage a smile.

They are in a small ante-chamber leading to a bigger room from which a boy holding a pistol limps furiously out at them, clicking a plastered leg. 'It is you,' he says to Sikand's escort. 'Why all the noise?'

Sikand smiles then—he knows this boy; he met him on the Sarovar steps the last time he was here, but his mind can't come up with a something strange and Islamic that was his name.

'I've brought you another prisoner,' says Karnail, and the smile, the name Shaikh! that he's just recalled, quite withers on Sikand's lips.

*

'Why am I here?'

The boy Shaikh has no answer.

The granthi, Beant Singh, his fellow prisoner, is more comfortable. 'You are here for the same reason as I am.'

'And that is?'

'Well, you will call it fate…'

'I certainly will not,' Sikand says, quite vehemently for him, 'I have always hated the word.'

'I agree. It is a word worth hating,' says Beant Singh, placating him. 'But what I meant to say is that we are both here because we willed it. It is our desire.'

'I came here as a journalist,' says Sikand. 'To write and to understand. To report about a situation that everyone, the whole world, wants to know about. And I am held here. It is against my will. Against all my desires.'

'You think desires are so easily satisfied? You want and it will come? What would be the need then to desire? Where would come the force for the desire?'

Another day Sikand asks of the boy, 'Why are you here?' The boy has no answer.

Again it is the granthi who replies, 'He is here for the same reason as you and me.'

'His desire?'

The granthi takes a large slurping sip of his lassi, swirls it in his mouth, swallows, and says, 'Something like that.'

Another day the boy attempts an answer.

'A girl? She brought you here?' Sikand is surprised.

'Yes. No.'

Desire and will take them through many days. Both the granthi and the boy have a limited vocabulary, which makes Sikand feel that every word they use could have an ocean of meaning behind it, and his inability to understand them completely troubles him far more than the daily problems of baths, the vegetarian food, the lack of sunshine. He has a toothbrush and a comb, his clothes are the same as the boy's now, a kurta and a pyjama, a mud brown cotton blanket they call a khes, and a thinly striped tehmat, under which he is as adept at changing his underwear or his pyjamas as they are. He is of them and yet not quite there.

At night when they are alone, the Bhaiji leans across and whispers, 'Your desire is to communicate with the outside world. You can do it even from here.'

The guard sleeping outside their door is Amal Singh, whom Sikand remembers from his terrifying grip on the steps of the Guru Nanak Niwas; anything the man tries to do to ingratiate himself is not enough to still the panic that attacks him when Amal Singh comes within three yards of him. The man is always doing little favours for the granthi Beant Singh, getting him parshad from the gurudwara, or a glass of lassi covered with a crumpled piece of paper. 'He is from my mother's village,' says the granthi smiling enigmatically. 'Poor man, he too has his desires.'

Sikand doesn't know how it is done but five days later, the Bhaiji hands him the paper cover from his glass of lassi.

'*Do nothing. Just write,*' it says in English. '*We'll find a way to get your words to the world.*' The handwriting is Bibs's.

The bastard knows! Fifteen times a day Sikand has imagined he has been taken for dead, or at least missing. That could be the only explanation for the fact that twenty-three days of captivity have passed with not a finger lifted to free him. And now this. He pores over Bibs's words, the individual letters, the potbellied g's, the luxurious w's. The interminable day grows wings. There is a world outside these dank, underground walls.

It is only when his heavy lids are falling upon his eyeballs to the pleasant drone of Beant Singh's snores that he realizes Bibs hasn't said: we will find a way to get *you* out.

Only your words.

*

'I need more paper,' he wakes Beant to say.

They watch in amazement, the granthi and his relative, the furious pace of Sikand's first sentence.

'Religious eminence was Bhindranwale's original motivation,' he writes. Beant's suggestion, 'desire', has other connotations he tries to explain. 'Eminence' generates another discussion that carries on through the night. For Sikand it has the right ring, Bhindranwale didn't just want to be a religious leader, he wanted to be a Guru, up there, an Eminence. Witness the steel arrow.

'And the baaj,' says Shaikh, their jailor, bursting in abruptly at dawn and setting to naught all their efforts to conceal the papers that Sikand is writing on.

The falcon of Guru Gobind Singh, the baaj. Sikand listens as they dispute the myth. 'A baaj hovered over me too,' Amal Singh says. 'I was a child then, and it snatched my piece of roti right out of my fingers.' With a deep indrawn breath Sikand feels the intoxication of freedom course through his veins. I wouldn't be talking like this in the Amritsar Press Club, he thinks.

Bhindranwale dominates their discourse. When they drift to other things, Sikand gently leads them back.

'Deep religious study can be an education as valid as that of your public schools,' Beant Singh says, when Sikand wants to know how many classes Bhindranwale has passed, and Sikand acknowledges that the Sant certainly has intelligence far above the rustic cunning commonly attributed to him. But education and intelligence breed sensitivity, he thinks. How can he talk like that on the tapes, how can he accept the murders, the outrages committed in his name? How can he bear, every minute, every second, the suffocation of his prison?

'Simple,' says the granthi. 'Because he chose it.'

'Catapulted into the limelight by the singular nature of Punjab politics, Bhindranwale saw himself as a creature of Destiny,' he writes. 'Marked for a far greater role than he had ever envisaged in his early baptizing tours of the countryside. The Sikh gurus had given form to a faith and to a community, to Sikhism and to the Khalsa. That was the reality that glowed with the seductive lustre of myth; he was clever enough to see its grasp on the imagination, and egotistic enough to feel he could fit the role.'

Lying on their string cots, their eyes on the strange shapes that generations of peeling plaster and seeping water have etched on the ceiling: horses and soldiers, flying manes and waving flags, they unravel the relationship between politics and religion, the 'miri' and the 'piri'. Shaikh, with his chin cupped in both hands looks from Sikand to Beant Singh, silent and solemn, weighing the words of each. Twice he turns away Amal Singh, his relief. Twice he rises to tend the lantern as it burns quietly in its niche in the wall.

'Our religion is only a way of life,' says the granthi. 'It enjoins no fasts, no abstinence from the things of this world. It says simply what a man should do to be good. Whatever line you choose—journalist, politician or granthi—the Gurus tell us how to live as men. Be honest and fearless, they say, be generous and impartial.'

'If you put it like that,' Sikand says, 'then religion has a definite role to play in politics.'

'Exactly. The faith must show the way to ruler, and to the ruled.'

It is the world of ideals—anything can be made to happen with their words. The maps and oceans on the ceiling are innocent worlds in the warm lamp light.

'Yes, that is what miri and piri mean,' the granthi says, and turns over on his cot with a deep sigh. 'That is where the Akalis missed the point. Now they'll never realize their dream of catching every Sikh, no matter on what numbers or percentages they work.'

*

Bibs's response to the first of the despatches that is smuggled out is terse: 'Not analysis, Sikand. Please. Write about what it's really like in there,' he says.

Here Sikand is, paradoxically delivered to freedom in his imprisonment, insulated from the clamour of news and views, able to think so deeply and so finely in his isolation, and all Bibs wants is a chronicle of the shots that ring out in the night, the screams and shouts that torment his sleep. Or perhaps of his struggle for toothpaste, his broken comb, the pitiful toilet facility.

I am sorry to tell you Bibs, that I have not been tortured. All my nails are intact, and my hair. My genitals still work. I have nothing to tell them, you see. If you will not print my analysis under some name or the other, if you will only print the details of my horrors in a basement of the Golden Temple, the scoop that only our privileged magazine can scoop, what will become of me then, Bibs? And of my nails and my hair and genitalia?

Nevertheless, his mind now scouts the human-interest story that he can safely tell without identification. The granthi tells him about the boy. Shaikh hasn't come to the Golden Temple because of a girl.

'She is just a symbol, something he says to represent his desire. Like A for apple, B for bat.'

Desires are not simple. They hide. They reveal themselves bit by bit, in hints, in innuendo. In silent sprouting, like wheat beneath the darkness of the soil.

'The girl in any case is no more,' says Beant Singh. 'Last week she drowned herself in a well.'

'Why?' Sikand cries.

'I do not know. Maybe because she was raped. Repeatedly. By boys who are like brothers of our jailors. But there are too many such stories.'

'And does he know?' Sikand asks at last.

'Do you think it would be wise for me to tell him?'

Sikand watches the boy in unguarded moments. When Karnail Singh comes for his nightly round before the change of shift, he notes Shaikh's straight gaze, untainted by caution, and the downward tilt of the mouth with which he replies to Karnail Singh's queries. At night when the words twang back and forth between Beant's and Sikand's cots, the boy digs his fingers into his lips; his eyes cloud over, troubled with thought as he listens. Sometimes Sikand pretends to be asleep and watches him through his lashes. A third expression—the cheeks sucked in, the eyes withdrawing warily—surprises Sikand once with a sudden stab of compassion. 'I reject this world,' it seems to say. 'It does not make sense to me.'

Something that Sikand evades lies in wait, threatening to jump out at him from the dark corners of his own confused youth.

*

Lal Guru is ushered in one evening.

'I have heard much about you. Shaikh says Lal Guru this, Lal Guru that,' Sikand says.

'And I've heard about you. An educated man who makes his bread by kneading words.' His laughter sets his belly bouncing under his kurta. 'I wonder what you will write about us when you get out of here.'

'Not much, I think. It would be difficult to find readers for a description of hours of lying on a cot in a basement looking at the ceiling. I don't even know why I'm here.'

'That would help you to make it more interesting. You could invent all sorts of reasons.'

'No, no,' Beant Singh laughs. 'He is a different sort of journalist, Lal Guru. He writes only the truth.'

'Here is Karnail Singh,' Lal Guru says, as Karnail enters the room, as usual clutching his automatic to his chest. 'He will tell you, why you are held here. Tell him, Karnail.'

'Who allowed visitors?' Karnail says instead. His narrowed eyes rake the room.

'I am no visitor,' says Lal Guru. 'Is this the Taj Mahal of Agra that I should visit it?'

'Then what has brought you here?' Karnail says bluntly. 'Why are you talking to the prisoners, teaching them…'

'I am here to check on Shaikh,' says Lal Guru. 'In the army the commander will visit every outpost, in mountain or jungle, just to check on his men.'

'Who told you this was the army?' says Karnail Singh. 'Or that you are a commander?'

Sikand is mute with embarrassment. By his side, Beant Singh makes a crooning sound in his throat as if trying to soothe a baby. They are unprepared for what happens next. Lal Guru, whose manner so far has been of tolerant amusement, rises quickly to his feet, and seems to grow bigger with rage.

'You little puppy!' he thunders. 'You wretched puppy, kicked off your bitch mother's teats.' He advances at a furious pace, and Karnail Singh takes a quick step back and raises his gun.

'Shoot, you bastard. Shoot,' says Lal Guru, stopping and swelling out his chest. 'Let me see if you have blood or your mother's urine in your veins.'

Sikand, who so far has only been a little less scared of Karnail than he is of Amal Singh, is sure the bastard is going to shoot. How many bullets can that thing send out in a second, he wonders in a crazed, last-minute rationality. But Karnail Singh wavers, the muzzle of his rifle sinks an inch. Beant Singh breathes with a shuddering sigh.

'Where is the spunk in your marbles now, boy?' Lal Guru shouts, instantly raising the temperature again.

And then, inexplicably, he holds his arms wide and says, 'Come, you little cub.'

And Karnail drops his gun and is enfolded, sobbing like a boy, in his embrace.

15

Sikand can only make sense of it all when he writes. The all-powerful have freedom snatched away from them. Bhindranwale can never go back. The storm that he has aroused has closed that way forever, so that any settlement, any compromise, will be a betrayal.

The image of the gurus, complete in every detail of appearance and speech, can only reach its crowning glory in martyrdom.

But what of Shaikh? Every time he works on Bhindranwale, he sees Shaikh lurking somewhere. In the gaze that refuses even caution to taint it, he sees mirrored the defiance of

Bhindranwale. Do your worst, it says, it matters little to one who has thrown his survival into the ring.

Karnail Singh has provided the reason for his imprisonment. Sikand is a counter-hostage for their man, whom the police have picked up.

'We have not harmed a hair on your head, have we? That is Santji's greatness,' says Karnail. 'The Police have not been so kind to our man. But they will not shoot him and recover an automatic off his dead body, you are here to insure that.'

'Why me? I am not that important. They may shoot him still.'

'We think not. You see, he is a reporter too. From your own magazine.'

Shivi. I have failed you at a crucial time. And now it's too late for both of us.

'May I see Santji?' Sikand asks.

'He will see you soon. He is very keen to meet you. In the meantime he has asked me to see that you are comfortable. We are shifting you upstairs to the Guru Nanak Niwas. Santji is concerned that you should not be kept in a basement.'

'What about my—the granthi Beant Singh?'

'He is being set free. We have no use for him now.'

Beant Singh has nowhere to go. His gurudwara at Mallapurana has a new granthi installed by the boys.

'Surely there are other gurudwaras in Punjab who could do with a fine granthi like you?' Sikand says.

'It will be the same story everywhere, my friend. Where can you run in Punjab?'

'Then go to Delhi. I can give you names, Bangla Sahib, Rakabganj, so many gurudwaras. I know people who can help you.'

'How can he run away like that? He will not be happy,' says Shaikh.

'Happiness has nothing to do with it, my boy,' the Bhaiji says,

'I am not running away. Tomorrow, or the day after, I will come back to my home. Waheguru will see to that.'

*

Sikand pushes hard but nothing happens. At last when he leans his shoulder against the window it opens suddenly, with such a loud creak that he whips around in horror expecting the guard to burst in through the door. Then he leans gingerly out of the window and surveys the wall beneath. The dusty ledge will just take his feet. He can shift along it till he finds a way to the second floor, there must be pipes, open windows, something. He scissors his leg over the edge and pauses, considering if it wouldn't be better done at night. But he needs to see where to place his feet. And at night the guard will probably be inside with him. Below is the bustle of the street, vendors and shopkeepers, a police check-post. If he walks along the ledge and makes a noise someone will look up. The policemen will hear him. They must have ladders; they would call the fire-brigade. Surely. It was like getting out of a burning building—ordinary people did it all the time, women and old men, in Delhi or Hong Kong or New York.

He sees the policeman spot him, and wants to wave, but he is stuck fast, a spider against a brick wall, and cannot free his hand. There is the dot of the upturned face and the minuscule stick of the policeman's rifle. When the shot hits the moulding, missing his finger by an inch, he tumbles back into the room he has left, confused and out of breath. All he feels is indignation at the betrayal.

The door crashes open and Shaikh limps in like a whirlwind with his pistol out. Without ado he empties his magazine into the street, covering himself to bang the window shut, and turning viciously. 'I told you to stay away from the window, didn't I?'

'I'm sorry. I was just…Some fresh air.'

'If you'd been killed, do you know what would have happened to me?'

Sikand doesn't want to think of it. 'I'm sorry,' he says again.

'They would have shot your friend Shivi too, you know. In return for having shot you themselves. Just think of it.' And the boy is laughing. 'What a joke it would have been!' he chuckles to himself, infecting Sikand with his frank delight, so that both of them are convulsed with helpless laughter and Sikand falls weakly on his bed.

'I can't believe that a shot really means death—it is still a toy "bang" to my mind,' Sikand says, wiping at the tears in his eyes.

'Your body certainly knows better than your mind. You should have seen yourself crouched like a wild rabbit with your whiskers twitching,' says Shaikh, and again a mad wave of laughter lifts and shakes them.

Sikand's moods flip between twilit despair and serene indifference. He is often taken out to eat at the langar, escorted by Shaikh, whose limp, he notices, is severely exaggerated in company.

They hear Bhindranwale deliver a sermon from the roof of the langar building. It is time, he says, for every Sikh to ask himself if he is ready for the supreme sacrifice. Those who aren't can leave now, no one will harm them. The Panth will be purer without them; they will do it a favour. When no one leaves, he says they have passed the highest test manhood can demand of them—the test to defend their faith.

'Should we abandon the Harmandar to desecration?' he asks, and is almost knocked off the brick roof with the resounding, 'Never!' that shakes the congregation.

*

The next morning Karnail Singh comes to see Sikand. 'I saw you at the langar yesterday,' he says. 'If you have to report what you saw and heard, we will ensure that your words reach the world press.' It is his words alone that everyone shows such solicitude for.

'But I am a prisoner,' Sikand demurs. 'What credibility will I have? I do not even have access to Santji.'

Bhindranwale looking preoccupied, shoulders weighed down, creases on his forehead, complains as Sikand enters: 'You have not understood us.'

'On the contrary. My stay here, most congenial, every comfort.'

Sikand is surprised to see that this time he has more energy for the sparring than the Sant has. But when an aberrant ray of the morning sun angles in setting afire the tired face and Bhindranwale, as if drawing sustenance from it, sparkles suddenly with zeal, Sikand is left thinking what an unfair advantage it is that all these Sikhs are so goddamned good-looking.

'Fear is a weapon, a tool,' the Sant is saying. 'And it is being used against us. You see how we are being hemmed in here? Our boys who go out are searched, picked up on frivolous grounds, disposed off in cruel, hideous ways as examples to us. This is the fate of a Sikh. But a weapon can be made useless. You have seen every Sikh is prepared to die. Without fear of death, their weapon is blunted. The Sarkar is lost.'

'You have used the weapon too,' Sikand says. 'You mention names and addresses of people in your lectures, on your tapes. You denounce the Sikh political leadership. And yet you never clarify your own position. You answer question with question. And dub all those who try to break out of this impasse by negotiating, as weaklings, fools, betrayers of the faith.' He quite loses his head; he has been waiting so long to say all this. 'Systematically all escape routes have been shut off, for your followers and for yourself. This can end only in disaster!'

Young men like Shaikh will die, the words bubble like a cancer in his brain.

He waits for the outburst to come, but in the silence Bhindranwale studies his fingernails, which the stray light has chosen now to glorify. 'We know your spirit has sagged because of your imprisonment,' he says softly. For a second their gazes meet and hold, and Sikand is looking at the man Bhindranwale must have been before all this happened to him. 'Ours is a young religion,' he says. 'In no time it will slide back into the old, the mother religion. Yes, the Hindu religion stands like a mother with open arms. If mothers are allowed to have their way, none of their sons would ever grow up, is it not?' He smiles and Sikand too, has to smile. 'We have to strive to prevent the slide. That is our task. A very difficult task. Will you help us?'

*

That is how three articles appear under Sikand's name in different national dailies. In each he writes about the worst course of action for the Government: that of trying to enter the Golden Temple by force. 'I believe such a step would damage irreversibly the relationship between the Sikhs as a people and the nation of which they are proud citizens.'

Writing to order. Why does he have to do it when there is no gun at his forehead? To the seeds of scorn sprouting in Shaikh's eyes, he can only say, 'I wouldn't do it if I didn't believe in the truth of what I'm writing.'

Yet in his notes on Bhindranwale he is writing: 'It is not what such people are in themselves, but how they are viewed, how they are used by the people around them. B has been a tool. The Congress, the small-time Sikh theocracy, all have seen in him only an opportunity. But they have ended up in helping B along his way. Of course it is perfectly possible to be used and be using at the same time. Symbiosis. Like putting B on our magazine cover.'

And it is perfectly possible to know that one is being used and still serve one's own purpose. Fine shades, impossible to explain to a boy of twenty, who wants all the answers before he's even learnt to ask the right questions. 'Yes, I wouldn't do it if I didn't believe in the truth of what I'm writing,' he says.

Shaikh sits on the sagging office chair, and slides off his plaster cast. His leg emerges, white and hairless. Vigorously he kneads it with mustard oil and propping it on the table compares it with his other leg.

'Seems quite healed to me,' Sikand says.

'Not healed. See how much thinner it is than the other leg? And pale and sick-looking?'

'It will be okay if you will not put the cast back on again. Fresh air and sunshine will fix that.' Sikand knows that after his unguent ministrations the boy will slide the cast on again like a grotesque sock and limp out of the room. It will take a doctor and an 'Exra', as Shaikh calls it, to remove the cast, and as the doctor who put it on has been picked up by the police, there is nothing for it but to let it waste away in the dark gloom of the cast. It has been merely amusing till today, but now that Shaikh is accusing him of cowardice, Sikand is ready for revenge. He knows why the cast is slid on before the boy leaves the room: it ensures a perpetual guard duty.

'Soldiers at least shoot themselves in the foot to get evacuated from the battlefield,' he says. 'This is fine courage, for someone who can accuse me of writing to order.'

Shaikh turns violently, upsetting the bottle of oil. 'What do you know of courage, *hnnh*?' he says through his teeth. 'Even with my leg in plaster, I could show you.'

Sikand shrinks back. 'Of course you could. I never doubted you. Not physically. You are strong and you are brave. Undoubtedly.' He lets his guard down by degrees as he sees the boy regain control. There is a silence. The room reeks with the pungency of mustard.

'What do you mean "physically"?' the boy asks.

'Well, courage is of different sorts, isn't it?' He has acquired the habit too, of answering questions with questions. 'Sometimes one sort may require action that is contrary to another sort. That is when the difficult decisions have to be made.'

'You have found that? In your own life?'

'I have found that life is difficult, yes. And at many points, I have not had the courage to make the right decision.'

'But you have known what the right decision is? Or is courage involved even in the knowing?'

'Both,' Sikand says. 'Sometimes this, and sometimes that. On occasion I have found the courage to do the right thing when it is no longer right.'

'And how do you live with your lack of courage? Isn't that difficult?' Shaikh asks. He waits intently for the answer, with his troubled eyes on the older man's face.

'It is difficult, yes,' Sikand says. 'Sometimes it needs the greatest courage to face the sorriest bits of yourself, I think.'

'Back in the village, my greatest friend was Jee...Karnail Singh,' says Shaikh. 'Now we don't see courage in the same way, I think.'

*

On the first night of June, thirty-four days into his captivity, Sikand is transfixed at the window by the sight of Russian tanks trundling down the city streets. An adventurous torch beam angles downwards from the cluster of ramshackle roofs that surround the temple. It bounces off a turret and plays along the barrel of a long gun. A hoarse threat from below, a couple of curses, and the gun wheels in a slow arc, coming to rest with its muzzle pointing upwards. Men, women and and children stampede off the roofs, followed by shouts of laughter from the soldiers below.

Several of the two and three-storey houses that dominate the approaches to the temple are occupied by the boys, their roofs and balconies fitted out with machine guns covering the maze of streets below. Sikand waits to see them react, but they are silent on the dark rooftops, watching as he is. A face leans timidly out of a lit window across the Bagh wali Gali, the lane that exits at the rear of the Guru Nanak Niwas. Fear, as palpable as a heartbeat, arcs across the space from window to window with the speed of an electric discharge. He waits till the man, a middle-aged Sikh with a white cloth tied over his top-knot, steps back to shut and bolt the window on the night, before turning away himself.

'It is the army, Shaikh. With tanks and guns on wheels. Cannon and mortars. Howitzers, bazookas. Like they're going to war.'

'So? Let us see what they will do with their bazookas. The police have been looking up our noses all these days. Now it's the military. Get away from that window. Go to sleep.'

He carries his fear to bed with him and wakes unrested, tossed like a stick on its ebb and flow. In the evening Amal Singh finds him crouched below the table, too scared to raise his head.

'*Oi*, what are you plotting there?' he asks, bringing him speedily to his senses.

The next day is holy—the anniversary of the martyrdom of Arjan Dev, the fifth Sikh Guru. Karnail Singh, taking him to Santji, strides ahead of him parting the sea of devotees on the parikrama. Sikand, overcome by the crowds, wants to cry at them: *Go away. Run. This is not a holy place. It's a fiction. Run while you can.*

*

In the Akal Takht, Bhindranwale is holding court for the international press. Taken by surprise, Sikand stares speechlessly about him. He recognizes several faces in the group, but their world seems divided from his by a chasm of years.

'See,' Bhindranwale says, displaying Sikand. 'Ask him if he is comfortable.'

No one asks. Bhindranwale's eyes in their bed of wrinkles suggest he hasn't slept for nights, but he sparkles before the press as usual. 'Have you read his learned articles?' he asks them. 'He understands the situation better than me. Much, much better. I am only a villager. Ask *him*. Ask him anything you want to ask,' he urges.

'Is he free to leave?' a single voice says from the back.

'Why not ask him?' Bhindranwale says, gazing directly at Sikand. Sikand waits politely to be asked. The journalists he recognizes avert their eyes when he casts a vague look about the room.

Bhindranwale is the sun that makes the little stars disappear in the daytime sky.

'It is the sarkar that has imprisoned the press, not me,' he says. 'Let them release Shivinder Singh. Or at least show him to you. Dead or alive. We have clean hearts. Sikand Sahab is our honoured guest. It is our kismet that he is here to see what is happening with his own eyes.'

That, for all purposes, closes the file on Sikand. No one favours him with so much as a glance thereafter.

'Last evening Indira Gandhi made a broadcast to the nation on TV. Did you see it?' asks one journalist.

'Of course,' Bhindranwale smiles about the room. 'How could we disappoint the Pandit's daughter? A broadcast to the nation it was, but her words were only for us.'

'She said the government can no longer remain a spectator. And the army is outside the walls. Doesn't it show she's serious?'

'You are right,' Bhindranwale says. 'More troops are coming every second. Hundreds and thousands. Madrasis, Kumaonis.

Guards and Commandos. Even Sikhs. As if the Sikhs will fight us! The roads are jammed from Ambala to Jallandhar.'

He waits as his audience scribbles furiously in their notebooks. 'But one lion can take a thousand sheep, and still be hungry,' he says slyly.

There is a general hubbub as Sikand's tribe confer amongst themselves. 'What did he say?' 'What have you got?' 'Did he say a hundred or a thousand?' 'He said a million.'

'So blood will flow,' a voice is raised. 'Hundreds will die, Santji.'

'If one is afraid to die, one is not a Sikh.'

The next day's papers will splash his defiant eyes above his words: 'No Sikh will fight us. The military will not dare to enter. If they do, we will teach them the lesson of their lives!'

Back on the parikrama, being led like a goat to its manger, Sikand wants desperately to believe Bhindranwale. The army will not enter. How can they start a war with all these innocent devotees inside? They will hang around outside. Like the police: the Punjab police, the central forces, the border security. Now and then a flurry of bullets will be exchanged; a few will die. That was it. The tanks and bazookas are a bluff. Sabre-rattling, meant only to frighten.

But inside him a little voice asks, 'All this to frighten a single man?' A man who gazes far into the distance as he says, 'A Sikh is not afraid of death. If he is, he is not a Sikh.'

*

Bhindranwale has had his last chance to communicate with the outside world.

That night the power is switched off all over the city, and army vehicles patrol the street, announcing curfew. 'Shoot at sight,' Sikand hears at his post by the window. In darkness the city explores its silence. No power, no television, no newspapers, no telephones. In the sweltering, fan-less June night Sikand looks for the man with the white patka, but the window across the Bagh wali Gali remains barred and shut.

16

Ameer, back from the Mand, is welding pieces of metal into star shaped mines.

'Take off that cast and make yourself useful,' he says, pushing up his goggles to throw Fareed a round metal ball.

Barely catching it, Fareed holds it gingerly away from him. 'What is this? What if it blows up in my face?'

'It's a pomegranate. It'll only blow up if you don't screw this nail in properly,' says Ameer throwing him a nail slashed with an untidy handmade thread. His goggles are back in place and the whoosh from the cylinder finishes off further debate.

Fareed quickly hands pomegranate and nail to Major, who sits looking bewildered with it in his lap. Kaptan would certainly have told him what to do but from the langar roof they can see his red turban against the sky, high up on the swollen-bellied water tank with Lal Guru. All morning he and Lal Guru have been running up and down rickety ladders in the wake of General Shahbeg, surveying the twin towers of the Ramgarhia Bunga and the water tank, while an endless line of boys relays sacks of sand up the ladders to stack beside the old ones.

Small and sprightly, the General climbs down with short, impatient steps, followed by Lal Guru, who is ponderous as a pregnant buffalo going up, and round and rolling coming down.

'Here give me that,' Fareed says, retrieving the pomegranate from Major. 'You can go and join them on the water tank.'

'Lal Guru asked me to wait here,' Major says. 'We have work to do at the Clock Tower gate when he's finished at the tank.'

Basically, he doesn't like heights, but this is not the time to talk of it. 'He's going to be a long while yet,' Fareed says, holding the pomegranate to his ear and listening carefully. The relay is sending up bricks and sacks of mortar now to bolster the sandbags and make niches for the guns.

'Lal Guru isn't going to be much use when he's finished with that,' says Ameer from the floor. 'He must be sweating up a tube-well.' Every time the nimble General goes up and down the ladders, Lal Guru valiantly follows rolling from side to side.

'But he asked me to wait,' says Major.

'Wait all you want. Only do it where Shaikh won't blow you up with that pomegranate.' Fareed has started to ease the nail into the hole. 'I told you, Sardar Sahab, to take off your cast and sit down. Hold it in your lap otherwise you'll never get it right.'

'I'd rather get my head blown off, Sardar Sahab, than say Sat Sri Akal to my groin.'

'How can he take off his cast just like that? Without an ex-ra?' Major says in defence, keeping, nevertheless, a good distance from Fareed.

'Maybe the Army doctors will give him his ex-ra. As a special favour, along with his post-mortem.'

'Unless this bitch thing of yours gets me first,' Fareed says, finally managing to slide the nail into its snug hole.

At the end of the day every possible niche will become a bunker under Shahbeg's eye. Every arch will be bricked up. Rat-tat-tat the drills go like machine-guns, piercing ancient marble walls. *Chooker chooker chooker* go the generators. In a daze they watch as before their eyes the Temple becomes a homemade wonder of a fortress.

'It will be time soon to put it to the test, my boys,' Lal Guru says in the evening, to the two boys massaging his calves with mustard oil. He wipes at the flecks of lassi on his moustache with the gestures of a prince, while outside in the streets the tanks churn up a dust storm.

*

'Fear is no stranger though, with Bhindranwale a neighbour. A bullet fired from the temple can search out the very innards of these houses. And the boys evacuate at whim any place they find strategic. Never knowing when your house is next. Or when you'll have new neighbours in the morning to inject daily doses of terror in exchange for cups of sugar and milk. Fear is the younger brother of uncertainty.'

Sikand has a refill that will not fit his ballpoint, and writes with the plastic tube held between his calloused fingers. It is supple as a quill.

'An opaque shroud has descended upon the city. Intermittent sniping since midday up to seven p.m. How many dead? The media must have been bundled out with barely time to pack their toothbrushes. There's no one to see and tell, but me.

The soldiers thread the labyrinth of streets around the Temple, the residents crowd their roofs, grim and curious. Bhindranwale's bees will sting the hand that dares to touch the hive, sting it badly, and the air will swarm with angry buzzing clusters ever after.

For two whole days and nights the might of the nation is only a cautious shadow. Biharis and Kumaonis, creeping stealthily about in military fatigues. Do they need this long to familiarize themselves with streets that have existed so since the beginning of time? And why all the fuss with walkie-talkies and telephone wires when, despite the curfew, there are boys strolling in those streets with automatics under their shirts? One group comes around a corner and busies itself with its wires and poles while the other glowers and gawks as they do at strangers in Punjab. At one moment I know the army will enter, and the next moment

I'm equally certain that it will not. Sometimes the two beliefs coexist at the same very moment!'

In the afternoon he feels a bubbling in his brain and wonders if it is the heat or the onset of madness.

Like the sudden snap of a high-tension wire from high up on a Ramgarhia Bunga comes a barrage of machinegun fire that makes everyone, soldiers and boys, in the streets below dive for safety.

*

The consensus on the langar rooftop is that the Bunga towers and the water tank will get it first.

'Not a chance' says Kaptan. 'The army cannot blink with the guns we've put in.'

'That is precisely why you'll get it first,' says Ameer. 'You'll have to.'

Lal Guru scowls. 'How do you think the soldiers will get up there, you bag of wind? Climb single-file up ladders? With guns up every tower ready to make them remember their grandmothers? You don't know General Shahbeg. The beauty of his ideas.'

The beauty of General Shahbeg's ideas is indeed breathtaking. At the main Clock Tower entrance to the north where the enemy will have to enter, he has hung huge birdcages of wire on both sides of the steps. If the soldiers escape the guns atop the entrance, Major and the boys hidden in these cages will open up with everything they've got. It will be like the very walls are firing at them.

The brains behind the beauty is that the army cannot really afford to enter the Golden Temple. Their artillery and their tanks is psychology—a battle of stares, the fierce but empty snarls of a bitch with suckling pups. In Moranwale it is called *Budki Marna*.

'He has rolled up kabaddi with the tactics of warfare,' says Lal

Guru. 'When the enemy has a narrow approach, make him pass through the eye of a needle. Try to understand the enemy, but side by side, make up for not understanding him thoroughly. If we can't scare them enough and they enter, scare them double at the entrance and see them run. I wish there was time for me to explain,' he sighs, 'The beauty of the whole idea.'

But Kaptan has understood. 'The man who threatens the loudest wins,' he says, 'And up on the water tank we're in a position to deliver the loudest threats.'

That night Sikand is drawn to his window by voices raised in excitement across the Bagh wali gali. The house of the sardar with the white patka is bathed in the glare of jungle lights, and he watches mystified as soldiers sling ropes down its side. A babel of shouted directions from the ground, the jarring scrape of metal against masonry, and a piece of machinery sways upwards in fits and starts. Till dawn it sits on the roof like a huge toad with a tube stuck into its belly, and at first light its nature is revealed when with a sudden rumble it emits a series of loud, angry bangs.

From the Bunga a shower of rubble sprays the farthest corners of the parikarma. Another series of bangs and the fortifications atop the water tank, the sandbags, the bricks and mortar, disappear into oblivion. Men fly through the air like rubber acrobats.

'Bhhenchod !' Ameer says.

We are in it now, is the shout in Fareed's heart, leaping like a hot white flame. At last the enemy. At last the clear, the justified response. He is finished with the bitter aftertaste that licks the heels of every action. Gratitude flows out of him like a prayer. A man must do what he has to.

The sun like a blister on his skin, stings in every pore, and he has a sudden desire to tear off his clothes. He lifts his turban, and whooping, holds it high above his head.

'Come, you bastards!' he roars at the invisible enemy.

A bullet snatches the turban out of his hands to send it spiralling up, up, through the air. In spite of himself, he whimpers.

*

As the sun makes its slow journey across the sky, splintering the dust, they wait, their rifles snug in the holes made for them. The roof of the Guru Nanak Niwas is untidy with bricks and jagged mortar, baking hot. A fly buzzes in his ear, pleading for blood. Darkness descends in slow, agonising steps, and at eleven o'clock, the night explodes.

'That's one of my air-borne mines. Did you hear it?' Ameer shouts. The fortifications on the North Clock Tower open up on the soldiers assembling in the square outside. A cheer rises on the roof, but dies a minute later when loud booms still the sound of rapid fire.

'*Oi maan di*...they're using their tanks!' Fareed shouts, and before Ameer can stop him, he is running. Down the stairs and across a ladder bridge, across the langar roof, then down another ladder and onto the marble parikarma, hurtling towards the clock tower where the battle is.

He collides with Amal Singh, who grabs him in a stranglehold to say that he has come to the DukhBhajni Beri, the ancient miracle tree on the banks of the sacred Sarovar, to cure himself.

'But Bhindranwale's finished the power of the miracle,' he cries. 'He's put a curse on it. A toona.'

'Come back tomorrow morning when we've removed the curse,' Fareed shouts, and is miraculously freed.

Now the cages on both sides of the entrance staircase open up with machine guns. Fareed is suddenly entangled with a dozen soldiers who have survived the nasty surprise, and leaps with them to hit the marble floor. Bullets fly at them from all sides of the rectangle. He dashes for cover into the northern veranda and turns to see Amal Singh go down with his arm around a soldier he has accosted.

In the veranda there is little time for relief. Each of the heavily barricaded rooms along its length explodes with gunfire. As he tries vainly to burrow his way into room after room, the ground opens beneath his feet and he is clasped by the heels and dragged in.

'What are you doing here?' says Lal Guru, shining a torch into his face, 'And where's your cast?'

They are in an underground passage below the veranda and in the darkness above them the soldiers are attacking room after room to silence the barrage of bullets. He follows Lal Guru down the passage to another manhole and spews an abrupt burst of fire into the melee. They run up and down the passage, now rising suddenly at the feet of the enemy, now sinking quickly back into the subterranean darkness. In the confused grappling that follows, it is impossible for the soldiers to know their own men from the enemy. They fire randomly at each other, or stand paralysed with indecision.

From across the Sarovar, a light machine gun mounted a foot above the ground by Shahbeg opens up from the southern veranda. The low, sweeping fire makes it dangerous to stand and fatal to crawl.

Soldiers under attack from right, left and below, flee the northern veranda, but the moment they're on the open parikarma they come under observed fire from all four directions and crawl right back.

Lal Guru's face shines at him. 'See?' the glow says, 'the beauty of Shahbeg's ideas?'

Colonies of rats, disturbed from their hideouts under the veranda, join in the confusion. Big rats, crazed by blood and fury, stumble into running legs and fling themselves into faces creeping along the floor. Or attack bellies, buttocks, legs, anything that follows. A soldier falls dead across Fareed's face with a rat clinging like a hideous goitre to his throat, its rope of a tail wriggling madly.

Still, more soldiers keep on coming. There must be a hundred thousand of them out on the square, being pushed in blindly to their deaths. The resistance at the gateway, the Clock Tower and the cages where Major was, has long been silenced. In the veranda there is hardly any progress, but Lal Guru spots a group of soldiers in dungarees stranded at the corner of the parikarma burrowing into the shadows of the western wall.

'Commandos,' he shouts bobbing up to throw one of Ameer's grenades at them. 'They're heading for the Akal Takht.' Fareed climbs out, weaving and lurching, and throws two grenades, one with each arm, at the wall.

'Did I get them?' he asks, tumbling back.

'Shabash, mundia,' says Lal Guru, speaking funny.

'You're injured!' Fareed grabs him by the shoulders, and at once feels the blood flow in thick spurts down his hand.

He half carries half drags him and then props him up with his back against the underground wall. Don't die, Lal Guru, he mutters, but it's already too late.

*

And now the battle takes on the colour of Lal Guru's blood. The Akal Takht is where the enemy must not get to. The commandos cannot proceed till their rear is secured, and in desperation the soldiers in the veranda are throwing aluminium ladders to shin up and cut off the fire from the first and second floors. At some stage they will have to link up with the troops on the ground and Fareed is there in a hole bored into the well of the staircase to open up with close carbine fire when they do. Then he is on the first floor, and then the second, following his nose and the shifting sound of battle. 'When you can't think what next to do, carry on what you're doing,' is what Lal Guru would have said.

With the north wing still not taken the commandos start to inch forward, and all five sandbagged and bricked tiers of the Akal Takht burst out at them with bottled-up fury. The open quadrangle becomes a killing ground. Thirty or forty commandos dash across to still the firing from the Darshan Deori that faces the Akal Takht but only a handful make it. A second dash kills another dozen. They shoot some sort of gas up at the Akal Takht, but the canisters bounce up and off and choke them in the quadrangle below.

In the darkness everything is amazingly real. The screams of wounded men, the whine of bullets, the bombs. But then a sudden flare lights up the parikarma and in the lingering white light it becomes a scene from a bad film, impossible to believe.

*

A large rat, the biggest Sikand had ever seen, pushes open the door and pauses, its button eyes transfixed in the quick flash of his torchlight. Then with a lumbering shuffle it crosses the floor to the corner where Shaikh's plaster leg lies, abandoned as he's left it. To Sikand's great surprise, for it looks impossible that it will fit, it climbs into the plaster tunnel and scurries forward out of reach of the beam of his torch. The leg sways, and as if alive, scrapes the floor.

Crouched under the office table with Punjabi numbers painted down its leg, Sikand tries to place the firing. The bulk of the fighting is distant, but every once in a while a bullet slices the night with an irritated whine to shear the masonry outside. A quarrelsome bullet divorced from its source, but capable still of communicating its urgent query—who am I for? Or the next moment an insidious antenna waving in the darkness—who's for me?

The Langar side eastern entry, surrounded by the buildings of the Hostel complex—the Nanak Niwas, the Serai, the rest-houses, and halls—is a melange of guest rooms and offices flowing into each other with hardly an open space in between. Tanks manoeuvre for hours in the confined space, striking at the steel gate near the langar but cannot break it down. Above the groaning and churning rise flashes of sullen static and hoarse frustrated shouting.

A grey morning is just starting to leak into the room when Sikand hears a tremendous clatter and realizes that the gate has fallen at last. Almost immediately the roof above him, and of the buildings around, open up with everything the boys have been saving and all his inchoate fears freeze into hard reality.

*

With the sky steadily lightening behind it, an armoured carrier mounts the parikarma in the east. A lull falls in the firing as it makes its slow trundling journey to the corner and turns clumsily down the south parikarma towards the Akal Takht. All eyes are fixed on it. Fareed sees the battle changing.

In the Akal Takht, Karnail and all his boys, Shahbeg, even Bhindranwale, can have nothing in their arsenal to prevent that droning metal monster from landing at their doorstep. While all attention is fixed on the southern wing he creeps down stairs slippery with blood to head back towards the hostel complex. But when the armoured carrier is a few hundred yards from its goal a single rocket whistles out of the Akal Takht. In the flicker of an eye the carrier explodes in a whoosh of flames.

In a moment of pure silence the words of the Asa di War rise suddenly from the Harmandar, drowned a second later by a hoarse cheer of Bole Sonihal that sets the cordite laden air ringing with echoes of 'Sat Sri Akal'.

The battle now rises to a pitch of desperation on both sides.

A suicidal dash at the Akal Takht by more than a hundred men is beaten back inches from its steps. A handful of commandos clings precariously to a toehold gained at great cost by the side of the Akal Takht, but marked now by the merciless dawn are ruthlessly mowed down. One's dungarees are on fire and as he writhes on the ground two others start to crawl towards him when the grenades on his belt explode and blow all three into the air.

With the advantage of darkness lost, the soldiers are picked out one by one, for they have no place that is really and completely their own. Their only protection is in the lee of the corpses on the parikarma and the dead are riddled so often with bullets that they literally fall apart.

Then, in the frenzy of the fighting, Fareed feels a tremor run through the earth beneath his belly and an instant after hears a loud, shattering explosion. He turns instinctively towards the Akal Takht and sees the building shake. A moment after huge flames leap out of it into the sky. A series of loud booms follow, shells, he understands, fired from tanks he cannot see. The Akal Takht, all five tiers of it sandbagged and bricked, sways and totters, ready to come down. The soldiers rush at it with their guns at the ready, waiting for the flames and falling masonry to flush out the boys.

*

In the quadrangle below, the corpses are already starting to rot. Every time the Sikhs have lost, it has been because their leaders have let them down. Santji knows that he will never let down the Sikhs, ever. They will fight to the last man, to their last bullet. Not just the soldiers, their generals too. To the last man. It is the return to the great, the joyful, the resplendent. To the days of Ranjit Singh; to the great Guru Gobind Singh himself. The Sikhs are alive again, risen from the ashes that have been smeared across their foreheads by the debauched maharajahs, the treacherous generals, of their history. Their pure blood shall anoint the Harmandar once again.

When the man himself is gone, his words keep Karnail going still. Santji is gone, Shahbeg is gone, he has to be the general now. With the entire building in flames around them, he collects the weapons, the ammunition, the money, and has it all thrown into a deep well behind the Akal Takht. It is a last rite for Bhindranwale.

'It's better than waiting like cooped chickens for the butcher...' he says to the boys, but it is clear that each must suit himself.

At noon, Fareed sees them break and rush out of the Akal Takht in a group, flinging off their guns. Jumping into the Sarovar they make a desperate bid for the Harmandar at its centre, but all are killed in the water.

*

Sikand had started the night thinking of himself as not exactly young but youthful in a sense, as one who has yet a host of intriguing thresholds to trip across. In that dark night he tunnels through so many of them, confused mazes, indistinguishable one from the other, that daylight finds him possessed of the single truth that he is an old man.

His knees creak as he crawls from under the table; for a moment it is as if he will pass the few years left to him as a hopeless hunchback. The cessation of the chronic rat-a-tat of bullets, and of the tremendous boom of shells, leaves him in a daze. He stands in the centre of the room clutching a torch that has long since flickered its last.

The rat stirs too, and the plaster leg rolls over on its side. He is beyond fearing it now. At some time in the night their separate fears have conjoined and they have become companions in misery. His eyes follow its unsteady progress to the door and he stumbles in its wake.

Outside the door Sikand steps into a smoky, odorous day.

On the roof of the Nanak Niwas, Fareed sees him emerge from the fog of cordite like a ghost. Instantly Ameer raises his rifle and Fareed propels himself at it with a yell. The bullet has left the muzzle but, deflected downwards, strikes the ground inches from Sikand's foot. The man doesn't even flinch.

Fareed's arms go around him and he says 'Shaikh', the single word like a statement.

*

It is far from over yet. The soldiers swarm the complex, herding the pilgrims out of the hundreds of rooms in the serais and hostels. Sikand watches them file out of hallways and corridors into the Teja Singh hall, carrying their children who have not eaten or had a sip of water for days.

Out of a group roughly pushed together a man suddenly breaks apart and opens fire. In the pandemonium, women and children run helter-skelter, caught in waves of fire and crossfire.

The soldiers take no risks thereafter, pushing and shoving at the men, separating even ten and twelve-year-old boys from their mothers, making them strip to their underwear and hold their hands locked behind their heads. The police called in to identify the militants find Ameer Singh, a prominent explosives man, huddled in a group of devotees pretending to be one of them. He moves reluctantly, but makes no other protest.

Outside, the langar building is still on fire, sizzling and spitting as the flames engulf the sacks of wheat and rice. Gas cylinders burst with ear-splitting booms and cans of kerosene send fire fountains into the sky.

He recognizes Longowal among the Akali leaders who have been rescued or captured or have surrendered. As they are brought out, the terrified pilgrims flock about them and firing breaks out again from the upper floors into the crowd.

At dusk he is told by an officer that the Madrasis have found Bhindranwale stretched out in death in the basement of the Akal Takht with General Shahbeg, still clutching his walkie-talkie, by his side. The news flies swiftly and a spontaneous cheer arises outside the walls. The Hindu traders around the Temple run into the complex with sweets for the soldiers.

Sikand walks out to the eastern parikarma, into the stench of death. What seems like a tank is still burning feebly on.

Across the Sarovar, the Akal Takht is a gaping wound, like a ghost with its face shot off.

17

What a wasteful luxury all these rooms, one to sleep in, one to eat in, one to read the newspaper in. The stately freedom of a house that has been holding its breath, that has fallen asleep and is now waking, yawning, stretching itself. He comes quite unprepared upon the blue velvet sofa in the guestroom. Like a stuffed peacock it stands in the centre of the room with its legs splayed. Those legs…

'Wha—?' he says.

'How beautiful it looks!' says Raja Ram behind him. 'Excellent job, Sahab, Kirat Singh has done.'

Kirat Singh? The carpenter…

'Wha—?' he says again.

'Yes beautiful,' replies Raja Ram. 'And very little cost too, Sahab. Cheap. Wood is already good, he said. And cloth is available at cutprice from Karol Bagh. Only the foam must be good. First-class. It is like sitting on a cloud. Sit on it Sahab. Sit. See?'

His mother's bed. The bed he'd been born in.

'We thought, who knows if Sahab will come back alive? But, if he does, this is what he always wanted…'

That was before, you fool. Before she died, before all this…

'And Kirat Singh has had no other work, so he did it fast, fast. Three days is all he took. Feel the cloth, Sahab. So shiny, so smooth.'

Sikand runs his fingers over it in involuntary obedience, and then something comes over him; a hot rage, a blind shame. He jumps from the sofa and, as if he were another being, he begins to claw at the velvet, tearing at the nails that bed it down, at the shreds that start to peel off, at the white foam in its heart. Raja Ram stands, as if unable to look upon this, with his hands clapped across his face.

Once he has started, his capacity for destruction overruns him. He looks wildly about for a weapon and finding it—a sharp, pointed, needle-like object—rips at it with manic strength.

The wooden framework will not yield so he throws the letter-opener at Raja Ram's face and pulls at it with both arms. It creaks, the legs scrape the floor, it shakes and begins to give way. At last, with a resounding clatter it collapses; the legs, then the gigantic peacock's tail of the back, pile up, a heap of timber on the floor.

He steps back to view his handiwork, and slams into Ambika.

*

In many ways it has been good for him. 'I had to give up smoking. And am finally what I always wanted to be—a vegetarian!' he says, trying to make her smile.

'What made you do that to the sofa?' she asks.

'Did you see how ugly it was? It deserved what it got.'

'I've never known you to hurt a fly, Sikand.'

'Come on, you can hardly invest that thing with life!' But

the truth is he is embarrassed. The adrenaline still courses through his veins, he feels the pleasure of it like a guilty throb, like illicit sex. What will she do if he were suddenly to lunge for her, crush her in his arms, bruise her face with kisses? He is definitely embarrassed.

'We worried about you all the time.'

'Not Bibs. Though I disappointed him too, you know, by not obliging him with the scoop he thought he was entitled to. He would probably have been happier if I'd been killed, martyred to the cause of journalism. *His* Senior Editor. You can't imagine what a satisfaction it is to dash his hopes.'

She does smile then, not her happy smile, but a gentle quirking of her lips, a sad softening of her eyes, that makes his breath catch. She is almost unbearably beautiful. I must resolve this soon, he tells himself, find a way to take it to its fruition. I have waited far too long already. But it is also too soon. After the Temple, Blue Star. He needs time.

Operation Blue Star is what it was called. Why that and not Operation Pie in the Sky, or Operation Cow Jumps Over the Moon?

The germ of unreality that has invaded him under the table in the Guru Nanak Niwas is spread into a numbing disease. The sort of illness in which the doctor pinches your skin and pricks it with pins and you keep shaking your head because all you can feel is desperation. His body looks strange, he is out of touch with its processes, as with those of his mind that drifts unanchored to meaning.

If a community is a group with shared expectations then he, too, had been a part of that community in the Temple. Together they believed that the Temple was inviolable. The tanks and pillboxes were only bluff and counterbluff, a game, till the Army broke the rules and a chasm opened between expectation and event, shattering all reality. But bullets and blood are not unreal.

Death is too definite. There in front of you smeared like a blotch upon the marble, sprayed like vomit upon the wall.

Yes, he needs time.

*

'You don't grasp at truth, Bibs, you let it flow through you. Like a mild current. Slowly it'll separate the flesh till you can get at the bone.'

Bibs is acting like he is the one who's hurt. First, Sikand has got them into trouble over Shivi. With the police and with the government. Then he's got himself taken prisoner, and not turned it to advantage at all. Then he's written for other papers under obvious pressure, compromised their credibility. And now he doesn't want to have anything to do with Blue Star and its aftermath. When every paper, every magazine, is writing about nothing else. Pulling off scoops like *they* were the ones with the inside story.

'I'm sick of this word of yours, Sikand. This truth. You are intelligent enough to know there's no such thing, that it's all perception. Yet you persist in this stubborn manner. Sometimes I think you just want to get me mad.'

'Believe me, Bibs, that's the last thing I want. Believe me. But look at all the stuff that's coming out. Drugs stashed inside the Temple, women pregnant, prostitutes, condoms. I can't write that sort of shit.'

'So rubbish it! We'll take the big chance,' Bibs is almost leaping across the table at him. 'We'll say it's propaganda; you were there. You know the facts.'

'For God's sake, Bibs, I don't. I was locked up in a cell, an office room. I don't know anything outside that. I know the lies, but I don't know the truth. Oops, I said the word that makes you mad, Bibs. So sorry.'

Bibs is doodling on his pad, circles inside circles, shaded

squares. Suddenly he makes a sharp jab at the paper with the point of the pencil.

'This has really gone on too long, Sikand. For both of us. I suggest we square up and call it quits. Right away.'

Sikand looks up from his pad. He'd been doodling too, birds and planes and shaded guns. He tries to shrug his shoulders, but can't.

'Fine with me, Bibs. Anything you like.'

'I've tried to stick around, be a friend.'

'Where?' Sikand looks around the room, searching. 'Tell me one thing, one piddling little thing, that you did to get me out when I was kidnapped?'

'You weren't kidnapped; you were detained. I've already explained that. And what the hell was I expected to do? Go to the police station and register an FIR? My friend and colleague etc. etc.? They would have raided Bhindranwale and rescued you?'

'You could have made a noise in the magazine, in the papers. The power of the press, remember?'

'While you were writing in all the papers saying what a good egg Bhindranwale was? Come on, chum!'

Sikand has come back to find he's been mentioned in just one issue of *In Sight*. A couple of papers, no lead stories. And he'd been naïve enough to think in the early days that they'd be rooting for him outside, running campaigns, pressuring and clamouring for his release.

'If you'd sent me that article I wanted,' Bibs says, 'what we could have done with it. That was the trigger, don't you see? Instead you sent me sermons and analyses.'

'And survived. Or don't you see that?' But what is the point of it all? He pushes his chair back and holds out his hand. At the door Bibs stops him with, 'We'll do the accounts next week, if that's all right with you, Sikand.'

Wanting to say something, anything, he turns, raises a finger to an imaginary brim. 'Don't call me, I'll call you,' he says, 'Birbal Nath.'

*

He is hoping not to run into Livleen, but the best way to make something happen is to hope it won't.

'Come on, I'll take you out for coffee,' he says putting an arm around her, and is surprised when she hugs him tight and bursts into tears.

He drives past the restaurant, not knowing where they're going. The heat is shimmering off the evening streets and the trees all look tired, gasping for breath. She cries wetly on his shoulder for a long time, and then wipes her face with her dupatta. She is wearing a salwaar-kameez, the sort of thing he thought her wardrobe didn't extend to. Her lipstick is pale to match her clothes and leaves pink smears on his collar. They head out, out, towards the ruins of the fort of Tughlaqabad.

She looks straight ahead and talks about what it means to be a Sikh. For her. He doesn't speak at all, even when she reminds him of the shattered image of the Akal Takht and a shudder snakes through him. It's like destroying a mountain to get at a mouse, she says. A rat. She understands suddenly why the Sikh soldiers are deserting their regiments in all those faraway places, in Bihar, in Maharashtra. She wants to desert too. The mountain is not just a seventeenth-century building, it is the Sikh Faith, she cries. He nods and nods and drives on.

'Did they line up a hundred Sikh boys, children, on the parikarma, and shoot them dead? Did their bodies topple over into the Sarovar? Did they?' she demands.

'No. At least I didn't see them do it. I don't think that's possible.'

'Did they tie people's hands with their turbans and shoot them?'

He is silent. 'Did they?' she says urgently.

'I think, yes, that must be true.'

She grabs his hand on the wheel, and he fights for a moment to save them from going off the road. 'Did you see it?'

He brings the car to the verge and brakes. 'Yes,' he says, his knuckles turgid on the wheel, 'Yes.' His voice had lost its character, he is speaking much too loud. 'But you have to see it. There was no control. They lose it, control. Like animals. Worse. You almost think they're enjoying it. Stop it, stop it, you say and they turn on you like wolves. Just for having spoken. And…Livleen, you don't want to hear it. I don't want to speak of it.'

But she is without mercy, demanding with that dreadful faith in him in her eyes.

'There is only so much you can see,' he begins. 'So much blood, so much killing. And then it becomes like you're watching it on TV, all the blood is ketchup and the dead are just going to walk away when the scene shifts. It isn't like you get inured bit by bit. Something snaps all of a sudden and then it doesn't matter what happens, what bounds are crossed, all is grist to the mill. It doesn't add one mite to your burdens, to your sorrow, to your fright. It's all, frighteningly, horrendously, acceptable. Acceptable!'

His head is on the wheel.

'Until much later. And then all you do is fear this person, this thing inside you, that you never knew existed, and God knows, should not exist, should have been strangled at birth. You put on your shirt and tie and walk around with it inside you. Smile and make conversation. And just when you think you've stifled it, killed it, merciful God, it stands there stark naked in the night.'

Her hand reaches out, moving on his neck. 'I'm sorry. I'm so sorry, Sikand,' she says. 'I wasn't thinking about you at all.'

'Let's go home. There's someone I want you to meet,' he says, starting the engine.

*

'Shaikh,' he calls on walking in. 'It's okay, come on out. Shaikh.'

They are awkward together and he is disappointed. What had he expected: that they'd fall into each other's arms the moment they met just because they were both Sikhs? Be real, he tells himself. 'Shaikh and I were prisoners together,' he says, realizing just in time that it is better to maintain the story, even with her.

She is immediately solicitous. She talks to the boy in Punjabi, calling him 'Tusi', her face with its earnest eyes, the contorted brows, trying so hard.

It makes no difference. Shaikh is sullen, like he's been from the moment that Sikand picked him out of the line-up insisting, 'Colonel, Colonel, you better listen to me about this. We were both prisoners. Prisoners together. If anything happens to him, Colonel, the World Press will know. Prisoners of the Enemy, I tell you. Bhindranwale broke his leg. You better listen to me, he's White. Colonel!'

They were dividing everyone up, into the white, the grey, the black, and the Colonel had a battle on his hands. Children pulled at his fingers, his uniform. One woman grabbed his feet while another thrust a bawling baby into his face. Shooting was still going on in the dark, anonymous explosions that stilled the shouting in one corner and added three-folds to that in another. Sikand, verified by an Intelligence official as 'that press-wallah they had imprisoned'—the only thing the press had done for him—sticking to the Colonel's tails, a recipient of pleas and petitions about thirst, starvation, wounds, death—none of which he or the Colonel could do a thing about.

When the Colonel disentangled himself to hurry to another room in the warren around the hall, Sikand was blocking his path.

'The police will see to all that, don't worry,' he said. And Sikand: 'No that won't do, Colonel. He saved my life. You put him with the others, they'll do anything, anything, to him. Let me speak to your Brigadier. To the General. This won't do… Please.'

The boy, in his underwear, with his hands tied behind his back, said not a word through it all. Shame burned in his face, as if Sikand's stuttering was a personal, an unbearable, abasement.

'I should have died,' he said later as an accusation. That was all.

That is all he seems now to say to Livleen. Looking down at his feet, hostile and mumbling, giving nothing away. He comes from Ludhiana he says.

'Oh, I know Ludhiana,' she says. 'Which is your village?'

'Ludhiana,' he says, only a trifle louder.

'Is Shaikh a pet name? A home name?'

'Yes.'

'It's a nice name.'

'No.'

Don't patronize him, Livleen, Sikand's eyes warn, but she isn't really, just at a loss about how to draw him from his lair. Can't you see how sweet, how simple she really is, Shaikh? How harmless?

But the boy, leaning well away from her warmth, can't see a thing.

She stays for dinner. Fawning and fidgeting, in a hurry to pre-empt the boy's every need. 'No, no, Shaikh. Have this chapatti. It's hot.' 'These potatoes are yum! Won't you have some more?' 'My! How little you eat. Like a sparrow.'

In the end, Sikand is a little irritated with both of them and with himself. Dropping her home, he is silent, distant, and when from force of habit, she leans her head on his shoulder, he pats it absent-mindedly as if from far away.

'You know,' she muses, 'there's something very strange about Shaikh. I can't put my finger on it exactly, but he's…complicated. He looks very simple, innocent like a village boy, and yet at times there's a glimpse of something, something dark and…and sad. Like he knows…everything.'

He feels his irritation mount till it oppresses him like the humidity of the sultry night. 'You know, Livleen,' he says. 'I wasn't entirely truthful about Shaikh. We weren't imprisoned together. He was with them. With Bhindranwale. In fact he was one of the boys who guarded me day and night.'

'You mean?' she says, shifting away to stare at his face.

'Yes Livleen, that is what I mean. Shaikh is a terrorist. A murderer. I don't know how many people he's shot or blown up. How many innocents.'

'You mean,' she says, as if not hearing him, 'that he fought the army in Blue Star?'

The note in her voice, a mix of hope and excitement, makes him falter. 'Yes,' he says, and then: 'It must rain soon. It can't go on like this day after day.'

'Poor Sikand,' she says surprisingly. 'Poor, poor Sikand,' and leans across to wipe the sweat crawling down the side of his neck with a lacy handkerchief. 'It's going to be days. The Met fellows are predicting the monsoon for the first of July.'

In the days pregnant with humidity she is over every other day. On the days between, she calls. A message from Bibs asking for the keys to a drawer in the desk that Sikand has left locked.

'Tell him there's no key. If there is I haven't seen it for seven years.'

'Attaboy! I'll tell him. Is Shaikh there?'

'Of course. Where else could he be? Shaikh!' he calls.

A part of him had wanted this, this great leap of emotion between them, across the chasms of class, of education. He had deliberately introduced Livleen to reconcile Shaikh to a new future, a new life. But now the question of Shaikh, the continental catastrophe of his imagination, is the petty problem of weaning a child off its sulks with a bauble. And he has dangled her iridescence, the soft bubble of her, before the boy, and feels as dirty as a pimp.

Returning early from one of the dreadful interviews that Raghavan at the Intelligence Bureau calls debriefings, Sikand finds the two of them deep in discussion on the balcony.

'There wasn't a wound, Fareed, there wasn't. Not before they did this to the Golden Temple. Not for me. Not for so many Sikhs I know.'

'There was,' says the boy. 'Only hidden, like internal bleeding.'

'Okay what? Tell me, I want to understand, Fareed.'

Sikand breaks in with the brightness of a guilty eavesdropper. 'Fareed? Who's Fareed?' he says.

'That's my full name,' says the boy with a tentative smile. 'Shaikh Fareed.'

*

If he'd let truth flow like a mild current inside him it would separate the flesh from the bone, Sikand had said to Bibs. But the current isn't mild. And he is not the passive observer that he longs to be, and suspects, in nightly waves of terror, will never be again. A wild current in a tumultuous medium can only mangle the flesh.

It is to Ambika's father, the old Brigadier, that he turns. In the evenings when the heat relaxes its hold they sit outside under the trees. A pedestal fan purrs beside them, its breeze dispersing the humidity and gently lifting the mango leaves above their heads, as the old man reminisces, linking memories freely, giving no quarter to chronology, so that in the same narrative he meanders through Gandhi and the Sino-Indian war. Sikand does not speak, just lets the warm wash of the old man's ramblings flow about him like the waters of some curative spring.

'The partition was unexpected. We thought Gandhi and Nehru will never let it happen. My mother and my wife tied up all their jewellery in a cloth but my father said they will kill us just for this handkerchief, and they had to leave it behind, buried in the backyard. My mother cried about it on every occasion. When Ambika got married, she cried. I would have given it all to you, she said. Ambika remembers it till today. Some years ago, she went to Pakistan for a conference and tried to find our house. A big building has come up, some bank or something. Otherwise Ambika would have found the jewellery, she says, even if she had to drive a bulldozer through somebody's backyard.' The old man chuckles and Sikand is as delighted as him at the image of Ambika on a bulldozer leaving a trail of destruction behind her in Lahore.

He is better with each day. As he starts to reject Sikand's helping hand except for the two steps down from the veranda and the final easing into his chair, acknowledging even these moments with a formal 'Thank You, Sikand', Sikand without even realizing it, falls again into the habit of calling him Brigadier. And as he wanders through the past with the Brigadier treating it not with nostalgia for the irrevocable but as something close at hand to delve into, Sikand recognizes how he invests even his pain with the pride of ownership, and with dignity, for its role in the truth of his life.

'Isn't he so much better?' Ambika asks. 'The doctor is so surprised. It's so infuriating when they treat old age as a disease, and act like the effort isn't worth it for a man who's eighty. I said, Doctor Parashar, do you know what is the average life-expectancy for a male in Japan? In America? Just because it's sixty-eight in this country doesn't give you the right to go ho-hum about a human life. They never created it, did they?' Ambika with her trick of turning a rhetorical question on its head, demanding an answer with unnerving intensity in her eyes.

It would have distanced him, she had always made him feel so incompetent before. But now he feels closer to her than ever before.

And it is almost natural to tell her everything about the predicament of Shaikh Fareed.

'Why can't he go back to his family, to his village?' she asks.

'They probably think he's dead. Ghosts are unwelcome, he says.'

'So? I'm sure they'll eventually be overjoyed to find he's alive.'

'Punjab is infested with army, Ambika. He'll be picked up the moment he sets foot there. As it is, I'm awake half the night worrying that the Intelligence Bureau, that Raghavan, the police, someone's going to find out, knock on the door. It isn't good for either of us, believe me.'

'And outside Punjab, he has only you?'

'He has relatives, a brother, in the States. That's all I've been able to figure out. He's not terribly communicative.'

'From your point of view, I'd say you better find a solution. And quick,' she says. 'One alternative is to make a clean breast, tell the whole story to the IB, or whoever, and let them take him in. Perhaps that would be best for him too, in the long run.'

Sikand considers this. It is something he's been thinking of himself for days. But then what had made him pull the boy back from certain death in the Teja Singh Samundari Hall, deciding his future with the arrogance of Fate?

'No,' he says with finality. He *has* to justify that taking over of a life, and now another, with Livleen thrown into the balance. What had given him these demonic visions in the first place?

'Do you remember what you said, Ambika, about all the young men in Punjab being left with no choices? What he needs is a new life. Away from all this; from his series of botched beginnings. He must go to the US. Will you help him? Please?'

18

Sikand has been his prisoner and now Fareed is his. It is Sikand who dictates whether he can step out into the garden or even show himself on the balcony, Sikand who will decide whom he can talk to and for how long, Sikand whose hands hold the reins of his future, to plan and dispose of as he wills. For himself, Fareed is content to float like a stick on the waves of Sikand's decisions.

At one moment he accepted death and it seems from that moment an essential part of his life has ceased to exist. He wakes and eats and sleeps and wanders aimlessly from room to balcony in his pajamas. The place he likes to be best is in the kitchen with Raja Ram, whose fund of silly anecdotes of his village in eastern UP can be tapped just by saying, 'And so, Raja Ramji?' The vegetables burn, the onions blacken, sometimes the milk boils over as Raja Ram narrates his tales of barren cows who can tell the future and one-eyed money-lenders who breed cobras to help recover their loans.

Sometimes Sikand draws him out and thrusts the morning papers under his nose.

'Read this,' he says tapping at an article on the Golden Temple or Blue Star that he has outlined in angry red. Fareed reads aloud following the words slowly with his finger, but when Sikand shouts, 'Lies! Propaganda!' at some line, he stops, bewildered by the pointless agitation. 'There will be assassinations, murders. There will be riots,' Sikand rues and Fareed nods politely but is little concerned.

One day Sikand abruptly decides that the danger of Fareed being arrested at sight has passed.

'Do you want to see India Gate?' he asks, jumping up to search for his car keys on the desk. Fareed would rather watch colour TV with Raja Ram, but feeling vaguely responsible for Sikand's frequent bad moods, he rises.

'You'll have to change out of those pajamas,' Sikand says, and calls after him when he's on the stairs, 'Put on shoes, please, not those stupid slippers.'

A gust of wind has brought a momentary shower and the evening is a little cooler. Fareed rolls down the window to feel the rush of air on his face. Outside men and women stroll together down vast tree-studded lawns, some hand in hand, like in a Hindi movie. In the parallel canals that shoot straight as railway lines towards the distant pink palaces, he sees naked children topple and bob while fountains spray everything with rainbow rain. Ice cream carts, balloons, and a camel for the children to ride on weave about India Gate. And there in the centre under the great arch is the helmet on the reversed rifle that he has seen so often on television—the monument to the unknown soldier. Babaji would bow his head at the sight, and the teardrop in his bad eye would make it look like he was crying.

It is strange to see all this and not feel a thing.

It is getting dark when they drive around the circle of Connaught Place. The names run through his mind: Delhi, Bombay, Calcutta, Connaught Place. Lights bounce off shiny new cars, the shop signs blaze. All night they burn, Raja Ram says, in the streets, and in the windows of the shops. And there are the women—the statues in the windows, like real, white women in bras and panties, just the way they'd been described. Why then does he feel so like an old man, with the taste of fever in his mouth?

'What would you rather do?' Sikand's voice has an irritated edge.

'Who me? I—nothing.'

'Look, Shaikh, you told me I should have left you there in the Temple. Do you still think that?'

Fareed nods automatically.

Suddenly Sikand wrenches the wheel and the car screams into a turn. Headlights rush at them to diverge at the last moment. Their tires screech and stop and start again throwing Fareed back into his seat and then forward into the dashboard. He raises his head with the sour taste of blood on his tongue to see them hurtling down flowing streets, lights streaming before them, behind them, before them, till Fareed is hissing a high-pitched whistle of surprise. They come to a sudden stop before a white gate. The car shudders like an animal and Sikand's eyes blaze into his own.

'Did that wake you up?' he says.

In the dark lawn there are white chairs under a tree where the smell of some sweet creeper steals up on the warm breeze, and he feels Sikand's rage slip away into the silence.

'It must rain soon,' he says with a little cough. 'In these old houses you still hear the koel before it rains.'

Fareed looks around at a white house surrounded by deep, dark, verandas. On Sikand's walls there are photographs like these, white houses and arches and the light and dark playing tricks.

'How old is this house?' he asks.

'1900, I'd say. They were given it as evacuee property, when the family came from Pakistan. In return for what they had to leave behind. They've done a lot of work on it, but from outside it's pretty much the same. Colonial architecture—Lutyens' Delhi, it's called, after the architect who designed it.'

'The same as Connaught Place and the Parliament House and those other buildings?'

He has pleased Sikand who launches happily into history and architecture and all the other things he knows so much about, while Fareed's eyes wander around the house. On a balcony, dim with foliage-shaded light, someone stands smoking a cigarette.

He watches the glow die and realizes with a little start of surprise that it is a woman.

She comes downstairs and turns on a light in the veranda, stopping Sikand in mid-sentence.

'I'm sorry, I just came from a wedding,' she says, walking out to them in a blue sari and jewellery like on a princess. Sikand kisses her on the cheek, and repeats her name at the beginning and end of every sentence like some Sufi. Ambika.

She speaks too fast and too long for Fareed to understand what she says, and under the cloak of the dark he stares at her unashamedly, open-mouthed in wonder. Her small head moves like a bird's and her earrings sparkle and flash as she talks. Nothing she says can possibly be untrue for she doesn't search for words, she doesn't hesitate, she just flows. Fareed is fascinated and frightened. Women like this do not exist, not even in the movies.

A sudden silence falls and he is aware of both of them looking at him. 'Quite right. Yes. Absolutely,' he says, ready to agree to anything in his confusion. Sikand rises and says, 'I'll just go and look in on the Brigadier then.'

She turns in her chair, when he's gone. 'Tell me about your family, Fareed. Is it okay if I call you that?'

The stilted Punjabi unnerves him. 'My family lives, resides, they reside, in Punjab,' he replies taking care with his English.

'Good,' she returns in English, running on like an express train, 'Sikand says you don't want to see them. Maybe you think they'll condemn you as a terrorist. That's wrong. The first thing you have to do is stop thinking that. No family does that. They can't stop caring for you. That's why they're called family, you understand?'

He is miserable, hardly understanding her, but nodding after every sentence.

'If I have to help you get that passport, you have to be straight with me, right?' Right, he nods. 'I mean, though I hardly care what you did, I can't begin till I know that you care. About what you did. And that you want a break; a clean break. I mean, I must know that's what you want.' In utter confusion he nods and nods.

'You have to say it,' she says firmly.

'Good. Right. Correct,' he says in desperation.

'I must be straight too,' she says. 'It's not true that I don't care what you did. I never take on a case when I know the client's not innocent. I just don't do things like that. But in your case I'm going to make an exception.'

He lowers his head.

'And I need you to go to Punjab, to your village and get me papers, your birth certificate, school certificate, character references.'

'Punjab belongs to the army...' he starts. Then making up his mind he breaks out in Punjabi. 'The military has won Punjab. They have won it. Now there's no place for those who lost.'

'I don't think that's true. There must be a place for ordinary people.'

'Ordinary people means women and children, and men so old they can barely walk.'

'That's saying all the young men are like you. Militants, terrorists?'

'Maybe there are others. Those who had a choice. But I don't know where they could be. Hiding out like myself, I'd guess.'

'And you had no choice?'

'No.'

'Fareed, there's always a choice. One way may be harder, but there's always a choice.'

'I took the harder way then.'

'I don't...' but she stops in mid-sentence. 'It must have been hard,' she murmurs.

*

In rare moments Ambika thinks she is too serious. Such moments of realization have the effect of bringing on a display of facetious behaviour that surprises even close friends. So it is, when rising urgently as if she has to rush to the bathroom, she stops and sways in the centre of the room and breaks into a sudden shimmy that makes all of her, her hair, her hips, her long thin arms flow like she were an iridescent bundle of inky snakes that the music blaring from the quadruple speakers was giving birth to. No partner could match her, and the space around her clears. With closed eyes, a half-smile playing on her wet lips, and the rhythm of the music like something primal rippling through her, she is awesome as some bewitched worshipper under a jungle moon.

Sikand wishes the music would go on and on to the end of time. But it ends and she stops, looking a little surprised to find herself where she is. Placing a gentle hand on her elbow he leads her out onto the veranda where, before the dark witness of potted palms, he says,

'Marry me, Ambika.'

'Oh, wow!' she replies, leaning out into the night from the balustrade, shaking her head to clear her mind.

At least she doesn't turn him down outright. She cares for him, she says, but at just this point she has too much going on in her life to figure out exactly how much. He comes out with both hope and pride intact.

On contact with air, his stifled love blooms crazily out of proportion. His toothpaste smells of her. The silk of his tie is her smooth shoulder under his stroking fingertips. And once when he runs to shut the window against a sudden squall, the large drops splatter on the sill and he leans right out, twisting his face to the sky to let her shower right down upon him.

I must not force her, he thinks, and stays away. Abstinence is the sweetest sorrow. Then he has to go and is filled with hope and terror. She isn't there. The Brigadier gloomy with the rains, brightens as they talk of chess and Alsatian dogs. She arrives, looking smart and very severe in her black and white lawyer's clothes. He is a pressure-sensitive instrument, fluttering with her every movement, as the Brigadier talks on about a voyage on a troop ship to Aden. Outside, it starts to rain again.

*

Ambika playing Agony Aunt to her ex-husband over the phone, listens with the sympathy she feels is the least she owes in memoriam to their four years as man and wife. Last month he has lost over a lakh on the stock market, and his second marriage is worse than his first. To top it all, his nephew, his own brother's son, has sold him a dud car. Imagine. Twiddling with the tachometer and his own Uncle.

'Pawan, things will get better, honey,' she consoles, thinking she has recovered herself since the divorce, but he is only more lost.

'No they won't, Ambika. I've just got chronic bad luck.'

'There's no such thing, and you know it,' she says. 'It's only temporary. I promise.'

In the next room is the problem of Sikand. Beside her job and People's Power, Ambika's occupation is her father. What would happen to him, if so much she cares for would have to be pushed against the wall to make room for another husband? The Brigadier is administered without an iota of sentiment: his food, medicines, fresh air, sleep, all strictly regulated according to a campaign strategy, the aim of which is to keep him alive. When he develops strange symptoms, like his wanderlust of a few months ago, the harshness of her regime increases in proportion to the helplessness he makes her feel, but when all is going well, like now, she is a benevolent despot. If only Sikand wasn't so perfect to her father, such a comfort to have around, so liable to be hurt. Men make excellent friends, but as lovers or husbands they quickly lose their shine. She knows.

If only she hadn't known him for so long, didn't like him so much.

And so she leaves him hanging, averting her eyes when he looks her way. Hating herself, and him for not saying bluntly, give me an answer, yes or no. Then at least she'd know what it is she'll say.

*

Time has scythed across Fareed's world but it has stood still for the Peepal and the pond. The microphone at the gurudwara comes on with a buzz of static and the Bhaiji clears his throat a second after Fareed expects the sound. The evening prayer, soft at first, gathers strength, speeding across the water in the deep voice that has marked sundown in Moranwale for so many years.

He had waited for her here, the night she had not come. Khushwant's face, dimmed by time, but still with the look of surprise that played across its features like a breeze, flits across the dark water till he shatters it with a stone. As the ripples chase each other to the shore, he turns and walks towards his father's house.

The moon is old and he keeps to the shadows, lingering under the trees in the orchard by Jeeta's wall for a long while to watch the house.

The big blue door is bolted shut. He goes around to the cattle shed to find another closed door. Then remembering how the rickety doors can be prised apart, he pushes with his shoulder and enters sideways through the narrow crack. Inside there are no animals, which stalls him for a second, until a single lowing query from the courtyard reminds him they are often left outside on clear nights.

He stands at the door of the vacant shed for a long time,

looking out into the courtyard. I don't want to be a ghost, he'd said to Sikand, but huddled out of reach of the moonlight in the doorway he sets his senses free to search the house like spirits. His ears are straining for the little sounds that come from the kitchen, when the object of the search herself comes stooping out into the outer courtyard carrying a bucket. As she bends to pour its contents into the drain, she stumbles and stretches out a hand to the wall to steady herself. Before he knows, he has stepped out to help and she, seeing him, is saying 'Hey Waheguru!' and the bucket is setting up a tremendous clatter as he reaches her, just in time to catch her as she falls.

She has fainted right off. Let her down gently and go, out into the darkness once again. She will wake and think he was a dream. But her eyelids are purple, and thick like onion leaves. He lifts her in his arms, and carries her through the arch into the inner courtyard.

*

The old old man is gone.

'We cremated him without tears,' his mother says. 'He is happier where he's gone.'

Babaji's walking stick, smooth as old clay, his brass pitcher with its square of beaded net to keep the water pure, they retain nothing of him. Dishan rides the cycle that he had used in better days, a man's cycle that obliges her to raise an awkward leg, and when his mother pours a glass of milk from Babaji's pitcher, her eye slips indifferently over it.

He steals quick sideways glances at familiar things, terrified that he will catch his bedclothes, his dusty books, his room, in the act of edging away, of suddenly snapping their thread with his life. He is defined by these things: the fluffy pillow is Dishan's, the hard one his. It alarms him that it can perversely cut him loose forever.

'Your father said, forget Fareed, he's dead. Think we never had a son,' his mother tells him. 'I said how can I? I took Dishan along and we looked for you in Amritsar, all over the Golden Temple.'

'Why? When?'

'In the winter when Babaji was still alive.'

He remembers the cold stone of the parikarma. Once he had followed a woman the length of it because she wore a brown shawl like his mother's, forgetting it was the kind of shawl that every village woman wears.

'After Blue Star he would not let us go again. If he was alive, he said, he is sixteen annas dead now. But day before yesterday, after all these months, he takes his scooter out and says, I'm going to see about the boy. At least I should cremate him properly.'

In his brother's letters from America he searches for Randhir in vain. Khalistan already exists, says one. Don't mourn for Fareed. If he's dead, I am the brother of a shaheed, a martyr who belongs to Khalistan like Bhagat Singh belonged to Hindustan. If he's alive he is the captain of an army every Sikh would be a proud soldier of.

Such things…as if in place of blood, ink flowed in his veins.

It has occurred to Fareed that he had been deceived.

But Randhir is more of a dupe, for he thinks blood flows like smooth lettering on a page, whereas Fareed knows that a bullet wound in the thigh can kill a man in twenty minutes.

Still, that night he dreams of America, where the cars are easy as wind-up toys and peaches and cherries fatten on trees. A woman, a warm sea of blondeness, smiles and says, 'I want the same as you.'

*

In the street it is the same story. The broken wall of Jeeta's house, Khushwant's courtyard, now open to the street. Not a solid edge on which to slide his hand. How quickly mud and mortar become loyal only to themselves, he thinks, and deception seems to stare at him from everywhere.

They have been destined to meet under the Peepal, Shera and him. After Dishan spotted Shera at the gurudwara, Fareed was a shadow there for two evenings, searching in vain. And now when he has wandered to the old pond with no aim, there he is, holding out his arms, saying, 'Brother.'

'Elder brother!' Fareed says hugging him tight. The upturned moustache, the loose black beard curling—how much like me he looks, he thinks.

'I must have killed twenty men. More than that.' Shera's voice is matter of fact. 'How many did you kill?'

'I don't know. I never counted.'

'You mean you lost count,' he says, laughing.

The Dukh Niwaran Gurudwara at Patiala had been Shera's headquarters. Strange how they'd never met in those days.

'Those days will be back,' Shera says. 'This is temporary.'

'A temporary setback,' agrees Fareed. Words of Lal Guru days. Battles lost and wars won.

The Akal Takht is being rebuilt under army protection by Santa Singh.

'The mule of the Sarkar,' says Shera, looking significantly at Fareed. His eyes seem rimmed with kohl. 'How long?'

Fareed nods slowly, fingering his beard. Santa Singh is finished. So also the government-built Akal Takht.

'But he's of little consequence, a mosquito,' Shera says dropping his voice. 'Indira Gandhi!' he murmurs in Fareed's ear.

Fareed feels his skin quiver like a buffalo's. It isn't done with him yet.

A bullock cart creaks down the road. It could only be the two brothers, ageing bachelors both, who till the barren land by the cremation ground for hardly anyone else uses a cart nowadays.

Fareed edges backwards into the shadows of the tree, but Shera walks right out, hailing them with a raised arm.

'How goes it Sukhe? Banso?'

Startled, each responds. Then the cart swings lazily by with both faces averted from the Peepal.

'See, they're scared,' Shera declares. 'Why are you hiding like an owlet? No one's going to talk, not here. We could even organize something, after a while. I have friends. And weapons too, not far. So don't be fearful. *Hnnh!* Hold your chest out! Here let me see it.' And he punches two hard punches into the chest that Fareed holds out.

'That wasn't as hard as the last time,' Fareed says, coming to a decision. Shera may have killed thirty, fifty, but the way he talks of it is a lie.

'You haven't forgotten that? Those were other days.' Shera says.

'It was nothing, but I will never forget it. Never, you understand.'

Shera turns moodily away. A brittle edgy note lines the silence, and he walks away from it to the water. A pebble goes skimming over the surface of the pond, saying Remember? Remember? with each leap and dip.

They both look up into the tree. Its white limbs are phosphorescent against the darkening sky, but Fareed cannot place the branch he walked out on that summer afternoon. One looks too easy, another impossible. And Shera, refusing entirely to be drawn, says with a shrug, 'Really? Is that what happened? How can you remember after so long?' What had seemed a feat of immense courage is lost forever.

'Did you ever hear of Khushwant?' he asks Dishan on arriving home. Khushwant had hung above them at the pond, shedding a flickering light like one of those flares on parachutes that never seem to descend. Several times Fareed had tried to say her name, but his throat had been unable to raise the sounds.

His sister plays with the fringes of a pillow-case. She hardly looks directly at anyone nowadays. 'Why don't you look at me, Dishan?' he says, 'I'm not some strange guest. We haven't changed so much.'

She shakes her head rapidly but never raises her eyes from her fingers that nervously smoothen each fringe as if her life depends on finishing the task by daybreak.

19

Fareed wakes with a desire to break into song. In the early hours of the morning a happy dream has come to him, and although he can't remember what he dreamt, the aftertaste lingers. Outside his window, he hears the peacocks cry: *keooo, keooo*, and soon the sky darkens, then crackles, and mighty drops of rain set the leaves of the tali tree rattling in the courtyard. Under the racket he sings out, loud enough to burst his lungs.

Downstairs, Dishan running to bring in the washing is enveloped in a billowing sheet, and Fareed, going out to help her, is useless from laughing so hard at the struggles that get her more entangled still.

'Bagarh Billa,' she cries. 'Chimuni', he replies—words that have peppered every childhood fight. And their mother, with a pinched face ready to scold, is suddenly wreathed in smiles.

Happily, his father chooses this day to return. As Fareed pushes the old man's scooter into the cattle shed, and the women run in and out with towels, clothes and glasses of steaming tea, the common purpose unites them for a while into a seamless family all full of monsoon goodwill that takes them without mishap into the evening and the descent of darkness.

'A Sikh's duty!' the old man reads from one of Randhir's letters. 'The little pup! Sitting well out of harm's way, and writing big words. "A Sikh's duty". Blood for us and Scotch whisky for him! *Hnnh!*' His spit sails out of the veranda into the puddles in the courtyard, punctuating his words, 'Ullu da Patha! Haraam zada!'

Fareed, feeling no urge to rise in defence of Randhir, holds out his glass and notes with approval the hefty shot the old man pours out for him. As the rain gathers strength outside, he leans back in his chair, and half closing his eyes against the dazzle of the veranda bulb, takes a large gulp. The liquid speeds like hot lava down his throat.

His father holds up his glass and squints through the tan liquid at the light bulb. 'You should have let us know,' he says.

'Why? Why put you all at risk? I thought it was safer to be dead.'

His mother mumbles, 'Waheguru, Waheguru,' but more as a reflex: the mention of death no longer worries anyone. 'You should not have gone looking for me,' Fareed says.

'I wanted to see for myself. What they had done to the gurudwaras. Before Blue Star we heard you were at the Harmandar, but after Blue Star...'

'I should have died,' says Fareed. 'I thought I would. A militant's life is short. Eighteen months they used to say.'

'And you were at it for only nine.'

'Yes, half my life, you can say. But it wasn't easy to live out the other half. When Blue Star came, I thought this is my answer.'

'Listen to the boy speak,' the old man says. 'How is death an answer? If that's all that comes out, then your question itself is wrong, Sardarji.'

'What other questions were there, you tell me,' asks Fareed. 'I didn't make the story. Bhindranwale, the Sarkar, the Akalis. They were there without me.'

'But you chose to enter the story. You chose your own path,' says his father.

'What other paths were there, tell me?'

'Why ask me? Did you ask me before running away?'

In the silence that follows, the old man raises his glass again to the light and studies the bulb through the liquor with the air of carrying out a scientific experiment.

Fareed takes two or three quick gulps and, reckless now with the drink inside him, says, 'I went in and I came out. A different person. Now I can't see ahead. I can go in again, come out again, another different person. More changed. The original me, the me I was meant to be, I'll never know, will I, who that was?'

'Why do you speak like you're unique, boy?' His father's voice is harsh. 'As if you came into this world with this original person already stuffed inside you? And the way all shining for you, laid out like some Mughal Garden? Some Chashmashahi? Are you Lord Curzon's favourite son?'

'I never said, did I say that? I just said it all this had not happened to me I would be someone else.'

'All that happens to you is the way. That *is* the way, you understand, Sardar Sahab? You can bash your head on walls, be a Majnu, crying Why? Why? But all that happens to you, that is the way.'

'You're contradicting yourself. First you say the question is wrong, and now you say all that happens is...'

'Hold on, hold on. Don't talk like a parrot...'

His mother's hands flutter. 'Should I bring the food?' she says getting up.

'Shut Up!' shouts the old man. 'Now you listen to me, boy. You didn't do anyone a favour, see, by being born. We are all born, we live, we die. And the rest of the world carries on. That's the way it's been since Baba Adam. You think anyone cares Bhindranwale is dead? A handful will mourn him, and then carry on with their lives.'

'I can't see where this is getting us,' says Fareed rising to go in, but his father's hand shoots out like a claw.

'I will tell you,' he says. 'Your job is to listen, understand?'

'To what?' Fareed resists the pressure of the hand pushing him back into his chair. 'To your drunken talk? Is that it? What qualifies you to speak? Are you some Aflatun? Some sant? What have you ever done?'

His father's eyes, bloodshot as ever, pop out at him.

'Tomorrow morning,' his mother says, 'Talk about it in the morning.'

But there is this heat inside Fareed. He knows for sure that the person inside him is different from his father, his mother, Randhir, different from them all. This person has come out on the other side, somehow saved in spite of everything. And just now, nobody, nothing else, matters.

'What have I done? I'll tell you,' the old man is shouting, responding in the only way he has ever known. 'I have brought bastards into this world. Snakelings. Who turn around and babble: What are your qualifications? What have you done? You will ask me that? After I have fed and clothed and sheltered you...'

'I never asked to be born,' Fareed shouts back.

'Neither did I. Not to nurture mice, to answer for every push, every little graze that life gives them.'

Had he asked that? Had he held his father responsible in any way? He tries to think of what he has said, but everything is confused now, bubbling inside him.

'Then leave me alone,' he says trying to jerk off the old man's grip. 'You didn't want us. But we're here. We will find our way. Without you. In spite of you.'

He is unprepared for the lunge that slaps the glass out of his hand and topples him to the floor. In quick succession the table, the chair, the bottle, glasses, everything crashes around them and the weight of the old man is on his chest. A hard blow jams into the side of his head, darkening everything for a second. He tries to roll out sideways, but is pinned. Like a sharp dagger, something, a piece of broken glass, pierces his side. Then one of his arms is free and moving, too slowly it seems, to connect. The gush of blood that spurts from the old man's nose surprises him with its suddenness. Large drops of it splatter his eyes.

Suddenly he goes limp, still. His father rises clumsily off him, and gropes for the towel that always hangs on the back of his chair. 'Get up,' he growls with the towel on his nose, but Fareed lies prone for a long time with the salt from his father's blood scraping the insides of his eyelids.

Dinner is eaten in silence. Only his father sniffs loudly off and on and Dishan's slippers make wet sucking sounds as she ferries rotis for them across the puddles in the courtyard.

Fareed has never eaten so many.

*

In Delhi Sikand rides up in a carpeted lift to the offices of the Bureau, housed in converted hotel rooms. He has caught sight of himself briefly in the huge mirror that covers one entire wall of the lift and now he keeps his back firmly towards it. Once he had grown a straggly salt and pepper beard that his mother hated, just to avoid the daily intercourse with himself in the shaving mirror.

Outside, a man is waiting to escort him down the corridor to Raghavan's office. He has known Raghavan not well, but long, and the fact that after such a long acquaintance the man should suspect him is interesting in its way. At times Sikand is tempted to play with it a little, solemnly delivering statements of double and triple import, pausing heavily before answering simple questions.

But he is in earnest when he says, 'I am certain that the life of the Prime Minister is in danger.'

Raghavan, typically, lets the words lose their immediacy

while he takes off his watch, lays it on his table, aligns his glass of water with his tray of paper clips: he has a repertoire of these little actions to show that he's low-keyed.

'I see,' he says at last. 'And who is your source?'

'No source. It's what's staring me in the face. The violence in Punjab has not lessened. If anything it's worse. More killings everyday, the Bhakra Canal breached yet again. Another plane hijacked. You can see it the same as me. Bhindranwale's last stand was not in vain. Blue Star was a grave mistake. Now the extremists have legitimacy. And not in the eyes of the Sikhs alone, let me tell you.'

'I see,' says Raghavan. He takes out a startlingly white handkerchief from the pocket of his safari jacket and polishes his glasses. 'Press people are entitled to criticism of Government's policy in a democracy. But assassination is outside this sort of expression, is it not? Why do you speak specifically of it? This sounds to me like special knowledge.'

'Please understand me, Raghavan. You have all the details. I have told you everything about the Golden Temple again and again. I'm sure you people have checked it out.'

'We have checked, yes.'

This reply, delivered disquietingly on the ball, stalls Sikand's progress. He flounders as he resumes: 'I'm anticipating, apprehending rather. Nothing more. Some such threat. On the basis of my experience of the people...'

'I thought you said you were certain.' Behind the bland eyes, the glimmer of a dangerously fine-tuned intelligence makes Sikand feel suddenly vulnerable.

History is a river whose course can only properly be charted from the shore. Having had to plunge in himself, Sikand has been severely disoriented until the change of angle on Ambika. The sudden recognition of a love that has hung for so long as a fuzzy fragment in his semi-consciousness, has jumpstarted him out of the ennui that has engulfed him since the Temple, giving him afresh a vision in his analysis. A vision he has the toughest time explaining to Raghavan, who can only pursue with the tenacity of an old terrier, the hunch that Sikand has a dangerous, a committed, source.

'I have told you once before,' Raghavan says, 'about my theory of self-interest.'

'Oh yes. Yes. But feel free to remind me.' Sikand has done a story once on Raghavan's theory of self-interest, shedding a favourable light on the acumen of our shadowy intelligence agencies. Raghavan was not mentioned by name, but Sikand remembers his call after the article appeared.

'You have revealed professional secrets,' he'd said in mock admonishment. 'But in a most professional way. I congratulate you.'

Self-interest, Raghavan believes, determines whether a man tells the truth or lies. Interrogation is simply a matter of asking a few questions, but investigation is going single-mindedly in search of the suspect's self-interest. The man, lulled by the little pressure he has had to undergo, unaware of the deeper search, often gives up the crucial knowledge almost absent-mindedly. Then the data, his answers in the interrogation, is matched against the findings of the search and a beautiful pattern emerges. Unearthing this pattern has got Raghavan so far in his career and is destined to take him further.

If Sikand is a liar, it is hardly the moral position that interests Raghavan. What makes him lie, that is what he would be after. He has been foolhardy, Sikand realizes, in coming to Raghavan with his predictions.

*

In the night the village is surrounded. 'All the men! All the men outside,' they are calling from the rooftops. The pigeons rise in alarm, flapping against the bars, waking him.

'Fareed!' he hears his father shout from below, and searches in the dark for his turban. Downstairs, there is confusion if he should hide or go outside. His mother runs into the pucca andar and he hears her fiddling with the lock of her dowry sandook. That is the first place they'd look, he thinks, but, carried away, runs after her into the room and then out again. His father says nothing, but turns his back walking to the outer courtyard. Fareed follows.

They walk out of the blue door together. Outside the gurudwara the loudspeaker crackles. 'This is the Army. The Indian Army.'

'Is that so?' his father calls, with perfect timing. 'We thought it was the Chinese!'

The village men, coming out in ones and twos into the street, snigger.

'All males! All males come out. Walk in line, one by one, to the school ground. All males. To the School Ground.'

A ragged procession of torches and lanterns forms up outside the gurudwara gate. Loud 'Sat Sri Akals' are exchanged. A young voice raps, 'To the school! To the school!' and other voices pick up his lead banging imaginary drums and blowing imaginary bugles.

The voice over the mike changes its mind. 'Males over five years. Only males over five years,' it says. Two men, carrying infants in their arms, break off towards their houses to deposit their burdens.

'Good you didn't bring along the fellow that's yet to be born, Preeto,' a voice shouts from the back. And another, encouraged by loud laughter down the line, titters, 'Or the one who's still just a hump in your pajama!'

Preeto, married but four years, already has two children and another on the way. 'Family Planning Matric failed,' he is called.

Spotlit with jungle lights fixed on jeeps and army trucks, the school compound is like a fair ground. Men are being searched at several points and their lanterns and torches confiscated. Inside the cordon of soldiers, they mill around calling to friends and relatives.

A hand pats Fareed all the way up the inside of his pajama leg, while his eyes roam the ground looking for Shera. His father, behind him, is removed from the line and led towards the veranda of the school building with the older men. Other groups are herded roughly to the fringes till just five of them stand in the centre of the ground in the yellow glare of a powerful jungle-light. No Shera.

Boota, who works their fields during the harvest, is first; shirtless and barefooted. An officer walks up to him, followed by a soldier with a clipboard.

'What do you do?' the officer asks.

The whole line watches the tip of Boota's pink tongue flick in and out of his mouth. 'Fields,' he says finally.

'Agriculture,' the officer explains over his shoulder and the soldier writes it down.

'Where do you live?'

'Moranwale,' says Boota immediately.

'Leave it,' says the officer to the soldier.

Preeto, next in line, was three years Fareed's senior in school till he dropped out to marry and have all his kids. Always frowning, even when he smiles, as if the sun were in his eyes, he screws up his face now with earnestness. For some reason the officer takes the frown as an affront. 'Who're you?' he barks.

And before Preeto can reply, a soldier drives the butt of his rifle into his gut with a 'Come to attention!'

Instantly, the atmosphere changes. The whole line comes to attention. Only Lala, next to Fareed, shuffles his slippers in the dust and mumbles into his beard. With a quick stabbing move a soldier punches him in the solar plexus and he doubles up with a whistling sound. There is a commotion from the school veranda as Lala's father, the Sarpanch of the village, breaks out onto the ground and, caught halfway, is bundled off with his protests.

These men, the army, are different. A policeman would have slapped Lala's face or cursed. Fareed is afraid.

'What do you do?' the officer asks coming to him.

'I'm a student.' He keeps his gaze at a steady hundred yards. His father is watching from somewhere.

'College? But all the colleges are closed. Does anyone know him?' The officer lobs the question into the air, and immediately the old man shouts, 'Yes, I do,' from the veranda. 'He is my son,' he says on being brought forward.

'What does your son do, Sardarji?'

'Nothing,' his father replies, admirably calm. 'He was a student till the colleges closed. There is little for him to do now. He helps with the fields, sometimes. Not much.'

'He looks like an Amritdhari to me,' says the officer. The old man is silent. 'What do you say, Sardarji?'

'I don't know what an Amritdhari looks like, Kaptan Sahib. My son has always looked like this.'

Fareed knows the response is unsatisfactory from the way the officer purses his lips, yet in his father's place he couldn't have done any better. What did Amritdharis, the boys baptized with sweet water by Bhindranwale, look like? Did they have horns on their heads?

If the soldiers have been ordered to round up Amritdharis, their task is truly difficult for a sip of sugared water leaves no trace. They may as well go from house to house and pick up everyone. Everyone between the ages of twelve and thirty, say, or whatever figure is convenient. The sifting under lights in the night, the questioning, this is just a show. And the rumour they have been hearing all along that the young men are being rounded up from all the villages is true.

They even take along Boota.

*

Continuous threats are the main weapon. Of cutting off their testicles, of chilli powder up their anuses, of electric shocks. Locking them up under the National Security Act so they'll never see daylight again. A tool like the brush used by housepainters, the bristles replaced with rubber flaps, is used, but in a desultory fashion. Only one fellow puts his shoulder to it and he leaves Fareed's soles so sore he has to be carried out of the kitchen that serves as the Captain's office.

He lies on the floor looking up at the damp-stained ceiling festooned here and there with ageing tinsel: the barrack hall has seen better days as a dormitory for wedding guests. Other trucks arrive, one from a village as far away as Khuara near Sangrur. Released into the hall the young men mill aimlessly about till the soldier with the clipboard appears, when they lump around him eager to be counted. Numbers are what the army seems to care about most of all, numbers and the neat documentation of them. The clipboard goes everywhere.

I wouldn't do it this way at all, Fareed thinks. I would keep everyone apart, question them one by one. And not to make them confess they were Amritdharis!

But then again, I wouldn't have picked them up like this in the first place. Cluelessly. I would set my men on gathering information, and then put them on pointed searches. Moranwale has been searched without unearthing Shera. How can you search a whole village that you do not know like your own? And what do soldiers know of searching? I wouldn't use the army at all, only the police.

It gives him a warm feeling, this analysis, as if he is smart enough to challenge the wisdom of the highest in the land. His throbbing feet are forgotten.

How many people knew for certain that he, Fareed, was at the Golden Temple? Too many by far. I would search out those people. Find the weak links, break them. The same old police informers would do, controlled by fear, enmity, greed. I would nose them out and unleash them in the villages. I would move fast, while everyone was still on the run, not give them time to settle down, to regroup. I would move fast and quiet. Not drive around from village to village with loudspeakers and lights raising dust like on an election campaign. Nor would I make the ordinary villager my enemy, for he must give me information. I wouldn't swoop down on him in the night, as if to surprise some dark conspiracy he's hatching in the village square.

Lala is the first to be freed. There is a new law that says you have to prove you're not a terrorist, he tells Fareed by way of farewell. He still believes in laws. Next to go is Boota, then Preeto. It will be my turn soon, he thinks, realizing he has not felt he belongs so completely anywhere as he has felt in this hall with its broken window panes, he has not been so happy with his thoughts in a long while.

But then the hours go by, boys who came after him are let off, and he is still there. He tears his turban into three pieces, one to bandage each foot and a small piece to tie around his hair, and limps up to the boarded windows on the veranda side. Positioning himself at a chink in the boards, he watches the comings and goings in the veranda. At nightfall he catches a brief glimpse of Shera being led to the Captain's office. Wondering where they'd found him, he waits for them to finish with him and bring him to the hall. It won't take long to find out if he's an Amritdhari. At midnight he's still waiting and worrying if they're finally zeroing in. If they break Shera, then what about himself?

'You were at the Golden Temple in Blue Star,' the Captain barks.

Fareed, wide awake though he's been shaken out of sleep, says without a break, 'That's not true.'

'We have a witness. Someone who was there.'

'He must be mistaken.' Who was it? A part of him wants it all to be over. Let him be recognized, placed, finished.

Beant Singh, the Bhaiji he had guarded in the basement of the Golden Temple is brought in. But in his eyes Fareed meets not the flicker of a recognition. Just the placid face of a man of God.

'Well? Do you recognize him?' the officer asks.

'No,' the Bhaiji shakes his head.

'Now that's something I wouldn't have tried at all. Not like that,' Fareed thinks as, completely drained himself, he runs a sympathetic glance over the Captain's sleep-starved features.

20

Once a moment is captured in the camera it is powerless. It becomes a specimen like the thousands of unlived moments that Sikand has, stuck behind Perspex covers, imprisoned behind glass, caged to walls. The photographs can be studied, even, with an effort of the imagination, felt. But harmlessly. For all purposes, they are fangless.

He can bear to look at his mother's photograph in the hall downstairs. Like a painter he studies the planes that catch the light, the hollows in the shadows. And something strange begins to happen. The features soften imperceptibly, as if someone was shining a light from behind the photograph. The tentative smile creeps to the eyes, goes deeper as his transfixed gaze follows, till with awe he realizes he's looking right into her soul. So vast a country of space: the lights grand burnouts; the shadows bulking clouds of gloom. He is lost, standing like a boy, not knowing which way to turn.

Tossing in his bed, there's no running away from himself. He catches desperately at the thought of Ambika, but his garment snags briefly at that nail and is freed. I am all alone he says. All alone, he weeps.

In the morning with his hormones all aquiver with sleeplessness he calls Ambika, but she has left already for her chambers. Too overwrought to drive, he sends Raja Ram out for a taxi.

The courtroom is a vertical space under a lofty dome; someone's life's drama is being reduced to paper by a patient judge and his recorder who strikes at the keys of his typewriter with a practised enthusiasm. Ambika is small and thin against the teakwood of the judge's desk. She is speaking but her words are like air, rising and falling with no perceptible effect. The other fellow, is he the defence or the prosecution? A fat fellow with an air of staleness about him keeps interrupting her, but she, brave little girl, carries on regardless. The judge listens with half an ear and starts dictating before she's finished. Sikand tries to concentrate; surely something important is going on here for a birdlike man on the sagging bench beside him is scribbling intently into a little black diary, but waves of tenderness for her flow through him like nausea, debilitating his senses.

The fat man, Sikand decides he's the prosecutor, raises his voice. She tries to speak but his voice drowns hers; 'per the accused, y'onour…with nefarious intent y'onour.'

'LET HER SPEAK.' Sikand is standing up in his seat and all in the courtroom are staring at him. The recorder's fingers like an eagle about to land, and her face twisted, recognizing him through her surprise. He wishes to march down the aisle, up to the desk, he sees himself already with the prosecutor's sweat-stained collar between his fingers, but first there is the difficulty of getting out sideways from between the benches. He stumbles over some legs, human or wooden is immaterial, for they are enough to send him, grabbing at the back of a seat in mid-motion, into a noisy heap on the floor. The quick change of angle, or the dust from colonial days rising out of the coir matting, produces an acute vertigo, a hum that spirals to a crescendo.

Give up, he commands, and floats into oblivion.

Ambika, who has never been so embarrassed in her life, has the opportunity to disown him. He is just some crazy; courtrooms are not strangers to his kind. But as the peons and policemen lift him, she hesitates, then trails behind them, leaving her carefully balanced day quite in disarray.

*

Priding himself on a certain disinterestedness in the fate of the magazine under the sole control and direction of Bibs, Sikand is nevertheless pleased to learn it isn't doing well. The sales figures are dropping and with that the advertising that has been Bibs's greatest achievement. How long can you run what is an instrument to inform the public after all, by taking a line found in every other instrument: the line of least resistance? At such times almost any contrary fact or opinion will command credibility. But the magazine under Bibs has no such insight. It too trots out the Sarkari Sikhs and enumerates the increasing incidents of violence as evidence that Blue Star was inevitable, when they are crying to be used to show it was useless.

It is true that public opinion is against the Sikhs, generally, now since so many of them have publicly condemned Blue Star, returning Government awards, resigning from seats in the legislature or from Government services. But it is also true that creating an opinion and then pandering to it unashamedly, besides being positively dangerous to the Sikhs, and ultimately

Sikand believes, to the Nation, is the surest way to dwindling sales. Most especially when everyone else is doing the same.

All this Sikand expresses to Livleen, his professional manner at no time succeeding in concealing the delight he takes in Bibs's tribulations.

'He wants you back, Sikand, only he's not going to ask you himself,' she says. 'We all want you back.' She puts her arm through the crook of his and lays her head on his shoulder. Her affection has not diminished, but now the indulgent element dominates the saucy, and Sikand rues the subtle thrill that is gone forever.

'How can I forgive him for doing damn all when I was kidnapped? And even less than that for Shivi.'

'Well, Shivi's out. Only yesterday. That's what I actually came to tell you.'

Not that Bibs is responsible for it. Some sweet old lady has filed a writ in the Supreme Court, and in panic the Punjab Government has released a host of forgotten detainees rotting in jails all over the state.

'How come I didn't know? There was nothing in the papers.'

'All very hush, hush. They can't afford to say there were so many people they were keeping just like that, simply because no one had asked for them. They look good as figures: so many terrorists arrested after the Ropar carnage, so many held after the murder of the university professor, so many killed in an encounter. I suspect they keep taking them out of the larder, trotting them out, maybe even the same guys again and again, unless they've had to disappear in an encounter or an escape, of course.'

'I don't see this in the magazine. Not even in your stories, Livleen.'

'Ah, Sikand, you always thrust where it hurts the most.'

At least she comes over like this off and on, she hasn't forgotten him.

'When is Fareed to be back? It really isn't safe in Punjab, you know.'

And she always asks after Fareed.

'Where is Shivi? I feel I must go to him,' he asks in turn. How can she care so much for Fareed, and not at all for Shivi? Her colleague, whom she has known for so long? He was much more of a victim than Fareed—at least he never killed anybody.

'In Chandigarh, I guess. I know they've released him, that's for sure. They sent Bibs a message. Somebody did.'

Quite cold, he suddenly feels towards her. And mean. Here she is about to be served Raja Ram's Sabz Biryani at his table.

'And what is Bibs doing about it, may I ask? And you, and that whole den of, the…the caboodle! in the office?'

'Nobody's talked about it. Bibs could give him back his job, I dare say. Though I don't think he'd trust him now. He said Shivi had been playing some sort of a double game, carrying information from the police to the Temple and vice versa. Mucking about, he said, where he wasn't meant to be. That's why Bibs wasn't willing to lift a finger; he considered it unforgivable disloyalty to *In Sight*, to the profession…'

'Bibs as a defender of professional ethics. Doesn't it make your sides split? Or have you too acquired the armour that holds them together?'

'I hate it when you talk like that, Sikand. In fact, Bibs said, we all did, that Shivi was responsible for what happened to you. Just because he wanted to play a character out of John Le Carré, you were held prisoner.'

'Poor me. I must be grateful for your sympathy. It turned out to be quite a boon, what? A fine, double-edged excuse. Oh we can't do anything for Shivi because he got Sikand into this mess, and we can't do anything for Sikand because it was Shivi who got him into this mess!'

'It wasn't like that,' she protests, but without conviction.

At lunch they both move the food around their plates. The biryani has been a spectacular failure and Raja Ram shuffles around in wounded humility. But Sikand is constitutionally incapable of being angry with her for long, especially when she is like that, with enormous eyes downcast, her lashes, like some dark curtain shadowing the honey cheeks. Stumbling around for a subject to break the silence, he can only find what will interest her immediately, and it is Fareed. Fareed who has been sent to manage the essential papers needed for him to leave the country.

'We're trying hard. He's got a brother in the US, that's the best thing. We've managed the sponsorship papers, and a visa, at least a tourist visa, should be possible. But the passport that's the toughest thing.'

'Who's we?' Already starting to show signs of the return of her healthy appetite, she reaches for the raita.

'We—me and Ambika.'

'Ambika and I,' she says, laying her elbows on the table. 'And are you two an item?' Her eyes dance.

'Whatever does that mean?' Sikand asks, dancing back.

'I mean this great big WE you keep using, yes you do, don't try to deny it. Be real. Have you finally got it together? Have you?'

'What do you mean? Finally. Item. Really, child.' He looks sorry for her. After all I've taught her!

'Everyone knows you've been carrying a torch for her all your life,' she says, licking her fingers.

For a second he is tongue-tied. All my life? Of course. She is so right! He beams at her, drinking her in in a sudden inhalation of happiness. Then quite composed he says, 'I've been carrying a torch all my life for *you*, my sweet anemone. And I am wounded grievously because all you care about is Fareed.'

It is her turn. A crimson flare floods her face; he watched in fascination till the very lobes of her ears hang like scarlet pendants. He is charmed by the discovery that a girl so urbane should have fallen in love with someone so gauche, so unformed. It is fascinating and, yes, it is frightening.

'He certainly looks a lot better than I do,' he says with a self-deprecating laugh.

'You know that's not what it is,' she says. Then in a different tone she bursts out, 'I can see beyond the cosmetic, thank god. That's what surprises you, doesn't it? I couldn't before, but now I can. Even beyond the unpleasant cosmetic. Manners, education, that sort of thing. When there's strength, true strength inside, these things fall away. He doesn't know what to do with his strength that's true. In fact he hardly knows of its existence. But this innocence is a part of it. Don't you see it?' Her brown eyes blaze at him in a furious plea to understand. She is beyond embarrassment, and the trite words he starts to speak to damp her passion die on his lips.

His silence can only encourage her. 'It's strange how milk-toasty all the other guys look, Siddharth and Vikram, Bibs, he's gone a little sweet on me too you know, after you left. Bloodless, so mannered, so…so cosmetic! I keep thinking they should see Fareed, they should just see him. Really see him, if you know what I mean. He's so much in the air, in the sky, up there. And yet his roots are down there, deep inside the earth. You know what, Sikand, you know what I imagine in him?' Her eyes shine. 'It is the history of the Sikhs. Their struggle. Their passion. Their great courage and innocence. Their wide, embracing generosity. Not small things. Who's going to win, who's going to lose, who's going to get a medal in this miserable, self-seeking world. Life and death, that's the canvas. And honest sweat, good red blood, that's the paint!'

He shivers in the intensity of her look. Thought takes a while to swim back. And as he reaches out and takes her hand, he feels the halting and hurrying of her pulse and is quite able to believe it is her soul fluttering to break out and soar like some white bird.

A bitter-sweetness oozes through him. What a fine, fortunate thing it will be for Fareed to have her. How his sharp edges, encased in the soft, crinkly tissue of her, will be kept from harming the world and himself. The more he thinks about it, the more the relationship presents itself as nearer and nearer to the ideal.

He can make it come about. His imagination stirs, the philanthropy of the action exerts its passing allure, and with enthusiasm he starts to scheme and plot.

'How would you like to live in America?' he asks. In that melting-pot lies their greatest chance of success.

'Sikand!' she laughs. 'A matchmaker! That's a role I never expected to see you in. But, you know, how well it suits you!'

*

Sikand's first burst of sympathy for the obviously injured Shivi is brushed off: 'A sprained neck. A present for my wife. She thinks I look around too much.' The speech is slightly slurred. Sikand's imagination conjures up electricity, probing fingers, chattering teeth, but 'Antibiotics,' says Shivi. 'For the neck. Blisters all over my mouth.'

Sikand can't quite believe him, and they sit in stiffening silence before a glazed window, watching three boys play tennis ball cricket on a bald patch of lawn. Shivi's wife, the once slender little Pammi, now gone decidedly round, bustles in with tea and biscuits, and both husband and wife enclasp him in a circle of hospitality. As much a slave of manners as them, Sikand is diverted, lulled by the rituals required of him in return. So that when Shivi says, 'I have no problems with anything, Sikand. With any one. Let's leave it like that,' Sikand has already started to nod amiably. Recovering, he splutters:

'What do you mean? I have problems, dammit. I was locked up too. Or didn't you hear?'

Shivi hangs his head quite impossibly in his orthopaedic collar.

'I did,' he says. 'The police told me, again and again.' He embarks on a stumbling monologue: 'Nothing I could do, see, but tell them everything. If they let me off, then you…Sikand. You would also be let off. But Blue Star, and they forgot me. Just forgot.' His hand closes on Sikand's in a feverish clasp. 'No one came; no one spoke to me. Nothing. I was useless. Useless.'

From outside comes a little cheer as a boy running backwards on impossibly short legs takes a catch, and holds it.

*

In the super-deluxe bus back to Delhi Sikand takes refuge for a while in a sort of paralyzed fascination at the driver's wish to hurtle into death with his fifty-four passengers. But one can get used to anything, and soon he is back to the visit just concluded. Shivi never blamed anyone but himself. Gun-running, power-brokering, crossing and double-crossing; he confessed he was involved in too much he wouldn't care to know the consequences of.

'I only got what I deserved, Sikand. I have no problems now.' Having paid his dues, he was content to lie back in his chair before the window and watch kindergarten cricket.

Sikand however is not so easily placated. For one, he can't avoid blaming himself. Come up to any situation without taking sides, he'd taught Shivi, Livleen, all the cub reporters who'd ever worked with him. 'Leave your personal opinions under the doormat,' he'd said, and Shivi, doing just that, had gone in up to his elbows on both sides. And when he'd pleaded to be extricated, Sikand had flapped ineffectually around Bibs, and doled out to Shivi a dose of morale boosting.

Something has to be done. By the time the bus draws into Delhi Sikand has decided to write about it in every possible daily. If no one will print him, he will establish a forum of his own.

*

Testing the rigidity of public opinion against his slightly atrophied writing muscle, Sikand sends the first article, entitled 'A Journalist's Duty', to an obscure newspaper, the only kind that can afford to experiment. Nevertheless, it raises an immediate reaction.

'I say,' Bibs calls, 'There's a touch of vintage Sikand there. Wasted, I'm afraid. I must be one of the six people who've seen it. And one of the three who've actually read it. Actually.'

Sikand, more pleased than he cares to show, says, 'It isn't the time to make a splash, I thought. Just a ripple.'

'Well I'm glad to see you getting over your block, or whatever it was. You must come around, we have unfinished business.' Nice and light.

Very different from Raghavan who, dropping in without warning or excuse, proceeds to rearrange the crystal ashtray and telephone on Sikand's drawing room table to make room for his files, and without preliminaries, launches into 'A Journalist's Duty', reading it aloud in a declamatory voice. It sounds awful. The words are tentative, almost arthritic, and the prose has absolutely no rhythm. Sikand has always made it a point to read aloud everything he writes, but this time he's been remiss and it shows.

'So?' Raghavan says.

'I know. It's sloppy. But your reading too…you stress all the wrong places.'

Raghavan's features quiver with indecision. For a second Sikand is sure he is going to rise in defence against the criticism, but then Raghavan's long training seems to win and he demands, 'Why have you written this?'

'Because writing is what I do for a profession.'

Raghavan's look of exasperation shows his initiative is lost. He can do little after that except point out flaws in Sikand's reasoning, all of which Sikand is able to dismiss with apologetic shrugs. But clever words and actions are illusory victories, and Sikand is careful with every word of his next article, which he titles 'Terrorism and the State.' This time he reads every word out loud before sending it in.

On Raghavan's recommendation, all Sikhs have been posted out from the security detail of the Prime Minister. While he plods on, confident that he will discover Sikand's self-interest and get thereby to the concrete plot if any for the assassination, he is not one to take chances. Further, he discloses this precaution to Sikand, so that Sikand may know that he is taken as highly credible. Such are Raghavan's methods.

'Terrorism and the State' does not make it into print for Raghavan has discovered the self-interest of the editor of the obscure newspaper. Sikand goes to the editor and then to Raghavan himself. He threatens he is going to expose the covert censorship by starting his own journal. He reads aloud to Raghavan, with the proper intonation, the flagship editorial he has provisionally entitled, 'Will History Weep?'

Raghavan waits for him to finish, takes off his watch, lays it before him on the table, straightens its strap, and slowly rubs the mark it has left on his wrist. 'Why didn't you tell me you identified a fellow prisoner to the army in the Golden Temple?' he asks mildly.

'Well, I…did you ask me?' Sikand replies.

'Who was the man? Where is he?' he demands, suddenly raising his voice.

'Which man? How am I to know? I was shouting at the

Colonel all the time. Let this one off, this one's injured, this one's dying. I don't think Raghavan you can get a picture of what was happening there, and I'm not even going to try to draw it for you again.'

'You haven't told me everything you know. Names and faces. Who were your fellow prisoners?'

'There were dozens. It interests me, Raghavan, that you suspect me. After all these years…why don't you ask the Colonel, or whoever gave you that piece of information?'

'Unfortunately I can't. The army's shut up about Blue Star. All I have are the initial statements.'

'I wish I could help you. Believe me. But I have little remembrance of names and faces. I forgot a lot.'

'The terrorists who were guarding you one of them was called Shaikh was he not?'

'Yes. And another one was Karnail. He was the main one, really close to Bhindranwale.'

'An interesting name. "Shaikh". Odd for an alias. You must know of course that there is an old Sufi saint called Shaikh Fareed whose verses are in the Sikh Granth.'

'So there is,' says Sikand.

'Interesting,' Raghavan picks up his paperweight and weighs it from hand to hand. Then he pulls an open file towards him. 'I have an interrogation report here somewhere of a suspected terrorist called Fareed, picked up by the army from, let me see… Moranwale in Ludhiana district.' He shuffles through the papers. 'He has been identified by Dilsher Singh, an informer from his own village, as an escapee from Blue Star. But he could be wrong. These informers you know, mostly terrorists themselves, notorious for settling scores with misinformation. Yes, it says here, he has been positively identified *not* to be Shaikh by a hostage, a Granthi, Beant Singh. Well. For a moment there, it did look like an interesting lead, didn't it?'

Sikand decides he isn't going to do anything about it in a hurry. He has to watch out for Raghavan. Then he quietly finds out that Amreek Singh Gill, the SP who had taken Shivi and him out for dinner in Amritsar is now an SSP in Ludhiana and calls to congratulate him on his well-deserved promotion.

'There is a lawyer friend of mine, a lady, who is filing a writ of habeas corpus. Some chap called Fareed Singh who's missing since the army picked him up from Moranwale in Ludhiana district. I was wondering if you could get her some information.'

'I never do anything for a lawyer, Sikand Sahab. But for you I can do it,' says the SSP, and is as good as his word.

21

It is the last morning of October and the steam hangs over the fields. Soon the mustard will spread yellow as pollen over the countryside and the grass will freeze at dawn. At dusk the smoke suspended in the street will smell of warm winter foods, sarson da saag, khichri, jaun di kheer. And afterwards, bed on a full stomach will be a warm tent in paradise.

Fareed in his new lemon turban, with his shiny suitcase and his plastic folder of official papers is leaving it all behind.

The window seat is a mixed blessing. He rejoices at the fields of green, young wheat, rich with promise, and is distressed with the expanding patches of barren brown.

'The time of plenty is gone,' his father said. 'Who has the time or money now to tend the crops? Go, go to America, boy. Abandon this bitch of a land!'

A large gap between the glass and metal of the battered bus lets in a cold blast. The old woman who shares his seat, wraps her brown shawl around herself tighter and tighter, and offers encouragement each time he takes on fresh battle with the window clasps. She is going to Delhi too. Her daughter is having a second baby. There is one boy already, four years old. Her daughter's husband is a bank officer in the Punjab and Sind Bank in Connaught Place. Second only to the manager.

At Kharar they are stopped for the routine military check. Fareed has a paper signed by the thanedar but he is made to open his suitcase and take off his turban. As the bus crosses into Haryana there is another check. This time he is separated from the other passengers and made to open his suitcase on a table under a tree on the roadside. The only other turbaned Sikh passenger is let off when they find out he's the bus conductor. After the suitcase, Fareed's birth and school certificates, his character references, the sponsorship letter from Randhir, the whole collection that he has taken such pains over, are taken out one by one and scrutinized.

'I am going to my brother in America,' Fareed explains, 'He lives in a place called Yuba City.' But the policemen, silent and severe, give their single-minded attention to the documents. One narrows his eyes and compares Fareed's face with his picture.

'I was younger then,' Fareed says.

The other passengers are drifting back to the bus from behind the eucalyptus trees, buttoning their flies. The driver blows two sharp raps on his horn. The policeman lets him go with some reluctance, and as he squeezes past the grandmother-to-be, she gathers herself in with a sympathetic smile.

'Don't worry,' he says gaily. 'One gets used to it.'

*

At 9:30 a.m. that morning in Delhi when Prime Minister Indira Gandhi walks from her home to the neighbouring bungalow where a camera team awaits her, she is shot nineteen times. The two security guards who empty their magazines into her are Sikhs, part of the detail that Raghavan had got removed, posted back on the Prime Minister's express orders.

'Don't go anywhere,' Raghavan calls. 'I will want to talk to you sometime today.'

'Whatever for?' asks Sikand. 'Is she…?'

'She's alive. She's been taken to the All India Institute.'

'Look here, I'm not going to sit around waiting for you. Give me a place and a time and I'll be there. I'm not running away.'

'All right. I'll stop by at seven tonight. Please be there.'

There is nothing on TV or on All India Radio. Sikand calls Livleen.

'They shot the guards,' she says. 'Immediately afterwards. Now it'll be like Kennedy. We'll never know who all were involved. You know, I saw her being rushed to AIIMS. I was at the hospital crossing, and her white Ambassador car went through the red light. She was propped up between her daughter-in-law and someone else in the backseat. I recognized her and got the scooter rickshaw driver to follow, but they stopped me at the Emergency gate. Still, I was one of the first to find out. I even spoke to her driver. He said there was no time to find her ambulance. They had to rush her in the car.'

'Thank god she's still alive.'

'How ever can she be? With fifty bullets inside her?'

'Nineteen,' says Sikand. 'We'll just have to wait and see.'

'Should I call you if anything comes on the ticker?'

'No, don't worry. I think I'll just walk down to the hospital myself. That's the best way of knowing what's happening.'

Despite the silence of the official media, word of mouth has prevailed, and Sikand finds a sizeable crowd outside the All India Institute of Medical Sciences. As the afternoon advances it spreads onto the roads, blocking the approaches to the hospital, flowing like water over the islands and verges of the Ring Road and inundating the markets and residential colonies that lie along it. Fathers hoist their children onto their shoulders against the crush and vendors weave in and out holding up ice creams and balloons to them.

'She's been shot in the foot,' someone says. The word buzzes like a Chinese whisper from mouth to ear: 'The foot, the foot.'

'Straight through the heart,' says another voice and the machine pumps, 'The heart, the heart!'

Sikand pushes his way onto a traffic island to watch the white Ambassador cars of Ministers and Congress bigwigs arrive. Their sirens scythe a momentary passage then squeal to a stop as the VIP mania of the crowd engulfs them. Two security men are set upon for shoving people off with too much enthusiasm.

The character of the crowd begins to change. Five o'clock, and organised lumps have crystallized out of the amorphous mass of the afternoon. Sikand gravitates with them towards the Ring Road and to the buses bringing the peak hour crowds home from work.

At first the Sikh passengers are pulled out and shooed away, with occasional curses to spur them on their way. But a young fellow with a red turban is stubborn and shrugs off the hands from his shoulders, shouting, 'Don't touch me. Don't touch me.' Immediately a group of five set upon him with slaps and blows. Sikand presses back into the crowd of onlookers extricating himself with difficulty. Realizing it is time to go home, he turns towards the by-lanes of the government flats that line the road. Looking back, he sees a Samaritan intervene and hustle the youth off the road into the lane behind him. For a hundred yards the boy walks up with his red turban trailing behind him and then stops to retie it. The group on the road sees him stop and, with savage hoots, gives chase. Just as they reach the boy, a pregnant woman waddles down the steps of the flat opposite and yells, 'Hey! What's going on?'

Instantly deflated, the men turn back towards the road,

where a fresh string of buses awaits them, and the youth, after having tied his turban to his satisfaction, strolls up the lane with immense dignity. Following, Sikand repeats to himself the woman's words, 'Hey! What's going on? What's going on?' as if they contain some magic power.

*

After innumerable delays the bus pulls into Karnal late in the afternoon. Fareed receives his first inkling of what has happened at Delhi that morning at the fruit-stall as he buys a bunch of bananas for the old lady who shares his seat.

'Oh god!' she says when he tells her, 'what's to happen now?'

A man at the back has a transistor and holds it up with its aerial thrust out of the window. There is soft, slow music and a lot of static but no news.

Before Panipat, a felled eucalyptus trunk brings the bus to a halt and half a dozen village boys with lathis clatter up the steps. Fareed feels the old woman move by his side. 'Get down!' she whispers urgently, and then her shawl is over his head, draping his turban and face, shutting out the world. He hears the driver's voice rise in alarm, for they have taken hold of the Sikh conductor and are trying to drag him out of the bus. The passengers rise in their seats to protest and the driver guns the engine. Then the bus is off the road, bumping and leaning, churning up the berm, shedding the boys like flies. Fareed, extricating himself out of the shawl is in time to see the last fall backwards like a stuntman, and the conductor buttoning up his torn shirt, shaking his head as if trying to clear it of a fog.

A few kilometres on, there is another group of villagers milling over the highway. The driver shouts an alert, the old woman's shawl flies across Fareed's head, and they gird themselves for the speeding and the yawing, as metal and rubber scream and the bus shivers with ominous thuds when its undercarriage meets the ground. When they finally regain the road a spontaneous cheer splits the silence.

The tension in the bus has built an unspoken bond between the passengers. The bus is a ship tossing through a storm with everyone tied to its fate. Each time the driver shouts his alert, the passengers hold on to their seats and each time he regains the road, they cheer madly. This driver is tremendous, Fareed says to the old woman, and from the back someone shouts, 'Balle, balle!' as the bus swings, sending yet another lathi-armed group skittering off the road.

Outside Sonepat the conductor dismounts and disappears into the fields. Darkness and Delhi approach. The silent tension returns. Fareed is folded down into his seat wrapped like a mummy inside the shawl. Just outside Delhi a half-constructed gurudwara looms up to their left and the bus slows. 'This is as far as we go with the Sikh boy,' the driver says.

Fareed runs with his suitcase and his folder into the skeleton of the scaffolded building, realizing too late that he is still clutching the old woman's shawl. The bus changes gears on the road outside and his ears strain to its groan till it is lost to the distance.

A man approaches from behind the building. 'What do you want?' he asks.

'Only a place to spend the night.' Fareed says. 'I am coming from Punjab, and the bus driver said it wasn't safe for a Sikh in Delhi.'

'That it isn't. They killed Indira Gandhi this morning.'

'Is she dead then?'

'Absolutely.' The man turns and Fareed follows. 'You can stay here but I doubt if anyone will get much sleep tonight. We have to watch out for the gurudwara. It is good that many Sardars, truck drivers and travellers, are forced to stop here tonight. Like you.'

He takes Fareed to a rough shed behind the main hall where about twenty Sikhs of varying ages are sitting on their haunches in a circle. One of them startles him by rising and saying, 'Is that you, Fareeda?'

'Shera? I never thought to find you here.' But he's happy there's someone he knows. 'I saw you at the marriage hall that day. In the army camp.'

'Don't know what you're talking about. I've been away all this time at Jaito with my grandparents. I only heard of the army raids when I came back. It must have been someone else.'

A truck-driver called Mukhtiar speaks up: 'Come and join us. We are discussing how to defend the gurudwara in case of an attack. Some of us will get up on the roof, and the rest will stay here on the ground. Where would you like to be?'

Fareed looks up at the roof. 'Perhaps some of us could climb right up to the dome,' he says.

*

The big unfinished dome of the gurudwara bulbs out like a half-eaten onion against the sky. At its base is a wide ornamental ledge which, with the cage of scaffolding pipes surrounding it, makes a safe, comfortable seat. It is possible to sit there for hours, even to fall asleep if one cares to. Fareed, with the cold marble pressing into his back, folds the old woman's shawl tightly about himself. Around him the half-circle of defenders roost like pigeons looking out across the road into the sprawl of slums from where the attack on the gurudwara is expected to come.

At break of dawn, it comes. Urging each other on with shouts and curses, men and boys well out of the slum to spread across the road. *'Now!'* goes up the cry around the dome and a hail of broken bricks and clods of cement rain out onto the gaggle of torches and lanterns and sticks pressing at the steel gate of the gurudwara. Few make it across the gate, but more ammunition is quickly lined up on the ledge from inside the dome and now the air buzzes with bricks and stones.

Through the dusty haze, Fareed follows one of his bricks sail true through the air to hit a man with a lantern. The man collapses instantly. Again he takes careful aim, but the attack is already losing force as small groups break off and head across the road. When just a handful are left a loud cheer goes up from the ground floor and is picked up around the dome, 'Bole Sonihal, Sat Sri Akal!' and the blast of it seems to knock them right back into their hovels.

The sun climbs higher. In the distance the city wears a dark mantle of haze. A truck, a bus, two cars go headlong down the road as if to meet some deadline. Down in the slum, knots of men are moving about the narrow lanes collecting sticks and iron rods, their frenzy making a strange contrast to their women gliding silent as shadows in and out of their yards with pots and buckets and brooms, and their children lined up like little ants, solemnly defecating into the drain.

To their left they look down into another jumble of shacks and shanties where slit-eyed men and women wearing long gowns go busily about their daily business.

'It will be a tight fix,' Fareed says, 'if these Chinese were to attack us also.'

'They're not Chinese!' Mukhtiar, the truck-driver, laughs. 'They're Tibetans. Exiles, like us. You call them Chinese and they'll attack alright.'

From the Tibetan settlement, a fetid smell wafts up.

'Can you smell the chhang?' Mukhtiar asks. 'That's Tibetan rice wine.'

Suddenly everyone is voraciously hungry. Climbing down, they stop to marvel at the wall of broken marble tiles that has been hastily put up along the front of the flat gurudwara roof by the second level of defenders. On the ground there is another reassuring sight. All through the night Sikh truck drivers have been herding their trucks into the ground adjoining the gurudwara and running inside for safety, and now an impressive number of drivers, cleaners, helpers are milling about carrying sawed off girders and all manner of truck tools and machinery as weapons.

Behind the main hall a langar is being improvised to feed the defence force. Two large brick stoves have been constructed among the foundation trenches of the out-houses and, fuelled by door-frames and planks and a dash of smoking diesel, they are now ablaze.

The Granthi haggles with two bald Tibetans for their sacks of flour and dal.

'We have carried these for you down the riverbed at great risk to ourselves, Sardarji. Still I am willing to give you all ten kilos of flour for just one hundred rupee note,' says one.

'Ten kilos! This is not ten kilos. Why I can lift it with one hand,' whines the Granthi. 'You are taking advantage of my plight, Lama Sahib. And we're neighbours!' He shakes his head in disbelief at such inhumanity, but the Lama too shakes his head and reaches for his sack. Just as he begins to hoist it onto his shoulder, Shera breaks away and grabbing a piece of flaming wood from the stove slams it across the bent back of the Tibetan with a mighty roar.

For a moment everyone freezes as the Lama crumples to the floor, his brown robe rising and settling about him. The flour explodes into the air, then rains down on him.

With not a glance at his fallen comrade, the second Tibetan takes to his heels and immediately Shera is in hot pursuit. Noise and confusion prevail but Shera is beyond heeding their shouts. Fareed, taking the only way, launches himself into the air and wrestles Shera to the ground. As they struggle in the dust, the others run after the fleeing man and, soothing him with assurances and apologies, bring him back from the crucial gate. Most of the flour has been lost but now the Tibetans have to be paid whatever they ask, for it would be suicide to set them against the gurudwara too.

*

Back on the ledge they see the mob start to thicken on the road. A solitary truck blunders up, its double toned horn rising to an urgent wail. But the crowd does not part and as the driver brakes he is roughly pulled down into the crowd. They see his turban fly off and the coil of hair on his head unwinding before he is swallowed by the mob and set to with sticks and punches. Then someone runs to his truck and back and the crowd opens out.

'Diesel,' Mukhtiar shouts. 'They're splashing him with diesel!'

Everyone knows the logic of the next step, yet when the flames leap from the broken heap on the ground they are like marble pigeons on the ledge, staring stony-eyed at a crowd that shimmers and breaks as if in some ritual dance around a tribal fire. Fareed reaches out to steady himself and feels the sinews of Mukhtiar's arm jump under his hand, but the long silence remains like they have become strangers to each other, even to themselves.

Till 'Bastards!' Shera shouts out. In disgrace over losing his head with the Tibetan, stiff and sullen, he climbs down from the dome alone. In a few minutes he returns holding aloft a glass bottle of diesel stopped with a dirty twist of cloth.

'Maltycock,' he announces laying it on the ledge. One by one, making innumerable trips, he brings up and carefully lays out a series of glass bottles, till finally someone asks what they are for.

'Maltycocks,' he explains with relish, 'are Russian bombs.'

Now they wait eagerly for the mob as it drifts up the road and back, its numbers swelling with each minute. The abandoned truck is set afire and then they are at the steel gate making it shiver and clang out loud. As it does not give way, their fury mounts and young and old throw themselves at it. One man climbs over the shoulders and heads of the crowd and teeters on the wall. 'Sikhra. Sikhra Bastards!' he shouts, drunkenly waving a dagger at the gurudwara.

They, who have always been called Sardarji, react with a turmoil of stones, he makes such a fine target above the crowd. Brainless, Fareed thinks. Mobs have no brains. Shuffling and stumbling, both pulling and pushing at the gate at the same time. He would simply have made them put their shoulders to it and, acting as one, heave it off its hinges. Once the gate was breached the men on the ground, the Granthi and the others, would simply be flattened. How can such insects overpower us, he thinks.

But now someone has actually stolen his idea and is shouting above the tumult, 'Lift it up. Put your shoulders to it, boys. Lift it off its hinges!'

The first Maltycock explodes short of the gate in a whoosh of flame.

'Watch the gate,' Mukhtiar shouts, as Fareed swings. His bottle, dripping flames in a neat arc, lands where he'd placed it, among the insects. They scurry backwards over each other like larvae, born blind, flattening the fallen. One, with flames darting from him, jumps straight into the glistening drain.

'Bombs, bombs!' they shout scurrying for their holes, and like a battle-cry come the words from below: 'Waheguru ji da Khalsa'—to meet the victorious response from above: 'Waheguru ji di Fateh!'

For the rest of the afternoon small groups of boys come out now and again to throw stones at the gate from the opposite side of the road, but no attempt is made to mount another attack. Sure that they are plotting in their jhuggies, waiting for the darkness to attack in larger numbers, Mukhtiar keeps them busy making Maltycocks and collecting bricks and stones.

From the city comes a distant rumble like thunder. The black smoke has smudged out its buildings and its towers. Now and then a high-pitched scream will pierce the skin and someone will ask, 'When will it end?' and someone will reply, 'No worry. The army will be out tonight.'

Fareed's lips curl at the irony; the army, the Great Deliverer. It will never end, he wants to say, but his lips are dry as paper, his swollen tongue cleaves to the roof of his mouth, and he cannot speak a word to save his life.

The sun dips towards the slums, its rays slanting off the Yamuna behind them, setting afire the thorn and brush along its banks. Straining through the orange glow for the first sign of attack, their eyes pick out a movement on the road. A solitary cycle, with a pennant flapping above its handlebars. Slowly the cyclist pedals to a stop at the gate. 'Open up,' he shouts in Punjabi, and they all climb down to see.

Fauja Singh Nihang, in his big blue turban ringed with its guard of steel, pats the seat of his cycle on dismounting and pushes it at Fareed. Leading it away, wondering if he is to feed and water it, Fareed hears the Nihang call, 'Leave it outside the gate, son. Nothing's going to happen to it.'

He has cycled down the five kilometres from gurudwara Sis Ganj, Fauja Singh says, after they have repulsed two attacks on it in the afternoon.

'But why?' they marvel.

'Just to see,' he says, 'how it's going here.'

The man must be sixty years old but he shoots a tonic through their arteries. When the attack comes at last and the mob breaks through the gate, he scorns their precious Maltycocks, and with a bloodcurdling war-cry rushes out alone with the blue pennant on his spear rippling madly above his head and his long blue kurta swirling about his knees. They can do little else but follow in haste, their confusion growing as they smash into the attackers, and blowing up into hoops of victory as they chase them in their hundreds, pleading, 'Sardarji, Sardarji,' into the very veins of their slum.

22

For Ambika it is now a journey that should never have been made.

Of course she made it for him, her father. A niche had lain empty for so long on the Ghats at Benaras, waiting for him to complete the chain unbroken from the time of his ancestors. And last evening, as they'd stood on the sand with the funeral pyres dotting the evening, he had been luminous with fulfilment.

But then the nightmare began. At an obscure railway station not far from Delhi, she had woken, aware that the train had not moved for far too long. At this rate she would certainly miss her first hearing at the High Court. She had climbed down from her berth to look out of the window into the darkness and then had sat on her father's berth, towards his feet so as not to stir him. A useless precaution, for the next second a hammering fit enough to break down the door of the compartment had made him start into wakefulness, clutching the air and calling her name.

The neighbouring compartments rattled too and from outside came the sounds of shattering glass and loud voices as if sudden bedlam had gripped the train.

'What do you want?' she screamed over the noise, at their door.

'Open up. Take out the Sardars.'

'There are no Sardars here. Go away. Please. There's a sick old man. No Sardars. Please!'

They had heard in Benaras about the assassination, and the late-city edition of a newspaper she had bought on the platform said it was Mrs. Gandhi's Sikh bodyguards who had shot her. But so absorbed had she been in the task of getting her father back home that something like this had hardly passed through her mind.

The door shook violently again; it was impossible to think with the racket. Sliding it partially open she started, 'What the…?' But they had wrenched the handle out of her hand and in a trice the little space in the coupe was overrun with men, sticks, rods. They looked under the bunk and were gone but she had remained for a long time stuck against the corner, as if those few square inches were all that were left for her.

'Don't shut the door, they'll only be back again,' her father had said with deathly calmness from his berth.

On the platform a crowd, scores of men, were beating up two Sikhs dragged out of the train. Down the corridor, they were trying to break down the door of the bathroom, shouting to the Sardar they knew was in there, to come out. The other passengers, out in the corridor like her with their faces to the window, were obliged every few minutes to press themselves against the wall as groups of men with sticks and rods ran up and down the narrow passage.

One passenger, a man in his thirties, was struck with a cycle chain across the back of his head for not being quick enough.

'I'm a doctor. I'm a doctor,' he mumbled, lurching backwards into his compartment with the blood streaming from him.

Outside the bathroom, a boy with thick spectacles was pleading with the crowd. 'It's my mother. She's in there. My mother's in the bathroom.'

'It's not allowed to go to the bathroom at the station.' Someone pushed him.

Despite the nausea that rose in her at the thought of being

there, in that cramped rectangle of space, she was pushing through and saying in a high-pitched whinny that was not her voice: 'There's a lady in there. This boy's mother. Why are you trying to shame her?'

'Let her say something then. Let us hear her voice.' The man had a red rag tied bandana style across his forehead.

'Mother,' the young boy put his mouth to the door, 'Please speak. Say something.' There was a silence. Then a breathless squeak, 'What am I to say? I am very scared,' came from inside.

The situation stood poised. There were degrees of doubt and satisfaction on their faces. But outside the hubbub increased: a new victim had been found. 'Let's go,' shouted the red bandana and they thumped out of the door.

'Who's in there?' Ambika asked the boy. His eyes looked eloquently at her through their thick glass panes.

'You better get him out. Quick. Someone else is bound to come along.'

The clatter of another train arriving, slowly shrieking to a halt. The mob regrouping to receive it. On the platform lay four bodies, four abandoned ragdolls. She just had to look, slow and long, in a vicious, deliberate way, creating the stuff of future nightmares. As she watched, one of them, a Sikh with an army uniform shirt half-buttoned over his pajamas, twitched a finger.

She ran out, then back into the coupe for a shawl, forgot what she'd come back for, and heard her father mumble something about Lahore. He was trying to sit up, and she had to stop to help him. His hand gripped her like a talon.

'Under the pillow,' he said urgently. 'My gun.'

She freed herself and left him. 'The kartoos,' he was saying, 'the cartridges!'

A policeman with a rifle chained to his belt. She runs up and is saying unintelligible words pointing to the military man. An arm is moving. Even he can see it from that distance. He shakes his head, says he's only authorized to look after railway property. Someone may steal an engine while you're not looking, she says, but he does not understand. She runs into an office. A man is speaking on the phone. She waits politely. What had she come to say? Her shawl, that's what she forgot. Why are they stopping all the trains? The mobs, he shrugs, they're all over the tracks. Trains are lined up all the way to Delhi. She feels quite unhinged. A man is alive, there on the platform, come with me, I'll…his hand, his arm, is moving. The mobs, he says, Behenji, he says, then picks up the phone. Puts it down. No reply from the police station, he says. A policeman is there, on the platform, he has a gun. Oh he, he says, he's for protection, railway protection. Behenji, your train is leaving. See?

Her train was moving, and none of the ragdolls were moving now. She ran as if the mob were chasing her.

The door of the bathroom was open, swinging on its hinges with the motion of the train. The basin flowed over with thick black hair. She leaned over the hole in the floor, trying to retch, but the nausea sat like a stone in her gut, refusing to be ousted.

She rocked her way back to the compartment and wondered what her father was doing, lying on the floor. All the sheets, the pillow and the blankets too, such a mess on the floor. Stepping carefully, she pulled them up, and made the bed again, smoothing out the creases. 'Come on, Papa,' she said, sliding her arms through his armpits, getting no help from him. It was only then that it occurred to her. Quickly down on her knees, she put her ear to his mouth, then a hand to his pulse. Nothing.

Just the rattle of the wheels on the track, in such a desperate hurry to get to Delhi.

It was a journey that should never have been made. She had thought she was doing it for him, but it had been for herself. Just herself. If he hadn't gone to Benaras, she couldn't have borne it; after him the regret of it would have poisoned all her life. She had done it for herself. All her life she had pitched against his few remaining years.

She sinks beside him to the floor, with her head in her hands.

Under the berth, something moves. A young man, his hair strange, like ragged twigs, slides awkwardly out from under the seat and sits, with hands folded in his lap, mute in mourning beside her. She is beyond surprise. He makes a helping gesture and together they lift her father off the floor onto the bed she had made. Then they perch in silence on the edge of the berth feeling the dead man move gently against their backs with the motion of the train.

'I was in the bathroom,' he says, 'they were breaking down the door, and I was cutting my hair, shaving. I've never done it before.' Stray tufts of beard still cling to his face; she has to look away or weep. 'When they left, I ran out, here the door was open. The old man was sitting up. Then they came back again. I was under the bed. And he just slid off the berth to the floor. With all the bedclothes, and himself. Like he was hiding me. He said something to them. I think he said he's sick. Then the train moved, and you came.'

Wisps of thought float in and out of her mind. She is alone now. The police. The mobs. The boy with the spectacles?

'A passenger, I met him on the train.'

That was a comfort, she didn't know why. Only that she must cling to that.

'Here, let me do a better job with your hair,' she says, 'before we get to Delhi.'

*

The noon sun has deprived the vandalized street objects of their shadows. At the mouth of the bridge Sikand notes a scooter burning on its side, the flames overpowered by the glare of the white sunlight, only a black spume of smoke rising like a signal into the sky. The taxi-driver swerves, then veers again to avoid hitting a monkey, which for some unearthly reason has abandoned the shady forest around the zoo to cross this desert of tarmac. After they pass, Sikand swivels in his seat to see what the monkey will make of the burning scooter, but apart from giving the flames a wide berth, it takes no notice.

It is a tight squeeze, their team of concerned citizens: Livleen, a newspaperman, a photographer for a foreign magazine, a lady doctor friend of Livleen's, Sikand and the driver. Formed over endless phone calls.

The gurudwara down the street was on fire, houses were being looted, a man was carrying away, all on his own, a fridge on his back. A crowd led by a Congress party goon was going around with voting lists identifying Sikh homes. In another area it was the ration card lists. The fair-price shop was giving them away with free kerosene, to anyone who asked.

All over the city the pattern was the same, first the attacks on businesses and religious places, then vehicles, taxis and trucks, then crowds descending on isolated homes, the hot murderous pursuit of some victim down the street, then the killings. If one part of the city discovered an innovation, it was transmitted to another, quickly, over invisible wires.

On the other side of the river they are suddenly into the thick of it. Jay, the photographer, is clicking away, changing lenses, zooming and panning. Shooting a man on fire at the edge of the street. Crying 'Stop. Thehro. Roko,' to the taxi driver.

Gone quite crazy, he jumps out of the slowing cab and scoots down the street behind a running mob. Sikand wants to forget all about him but Livleen is like a frenzied hen, urging, shouting at the reluctant driver to follow. Just in time, for the crowd, in no awe of white skin, has Jay by the neck, and it takes all their persuasion to rescue him. His camera, with its double speed motor and its Takumar zoom, cannot be saved.

'You either live through a moment or you photograph it,' Sikand says through his teeth, but Jay undeterred, reaches for Sikand's camera.

Trilokpuri Block 32. The doors of the houses have been torn off their hinges. The lady doctor covers her face with her hands but Livleen…Livleen, dry eyed, iron jawed, will not turn away. And Sikand finds it harder to look at her than at the series of bonfires. Twenty-four, the newspaperman counts. With the television showing nothing but the calm dead face of the Prime Minister and rows of gloomy people filing past, the size of the scoop this twenty-four will be! He is already placing his story. 'This must be the only milk booth in the area,' he says.

The milk booth! Alerted, Sikand looks about. That's what he had come looking for months ago when he hadn't found Kirat Singh, the carpenter. He lived down a street in Trilokpuri, down the street from the milk booth he hadn't found. All around him, in the desolate, vacant houses, like sockets in skulls, he can see the carpenter's trade: a saw, a plane, a rickety bench, and what is that thing called, an adze? Out of the twenty-four, which one is Kirat Singh?

The life of the mind has one advantage that Sikand has always rested his case on. At all times it allows an honourable withdrawal into the sort of dispassionate contemplation that makes sense out of senselessness. But Kirat Singh, Labhana Sikh, would not have understood the assassins of Indira Gandhi in a conversation, even if they had talked down to him in their simplest Punjabi. All that they shared was a turban, a moustache, a beard. That was it. There are forms and forms of senselessness, and in these days, the advantage of the life of the mind that Sikand had rested his case on is tested to its limits, and snaps.

Trying to make sense of the bizarre: the taxi driver, who couldn't have run over a monkey, saying, man to man, 'This'll show them. They really asked for it, didn't they?'

He has to run his taxi, it's an economic thing, the decimation of the competition. Poverty leaves little room for fine distinctions. It is a consoling notion, an ism that could be intellectualized. But Trilokpuri, where the poorest who could offer little to loot were garlanded with burning rubber tyres, wantonly—against that unending horror the mind fails to comprehend a response.

He calls a police officer who says nothing is happening in Trilokpuri, the wireless sets are silent, the city is peaceful.

'There are people crowded on the roofs of buses driving past your Police Headquarters. Look out of the window. See them. Isn't there supposed to be a curfew?' he says.

'They're all going to pay their respects to the Prime Minister. We can't prevent that, can we?'

'The buses are going the other way across the Yamuna.'

'Then they're coming back from Teen Murti after the darshan. We can't prevent that, can we?'

He tries to see it as if it were already over, from another of his time-honoured vantage points. The communal fissure, now fully established, will be a great help to the ruling party in the forthcoming elections, he analyzes. Someone said that the mobs had been let loose for a definite number of hours, that they would be leashed when the time was up. But with every hour the fuel: alcohol, kerosene and rumour, seemed in more abundant supply. His neighbours from down the road came to ask him to join the night vigil. 'Don't drink the water they said, it's been poisoned by the Sikhs.' And Raja Ram tells him about the trains that are arriving from Punjab chock-full of Hindu dead, women and babies. How can he pretend it is over? There is no place to run away to.

Unthinking action is the only course, he decides. Leach the mind; contemplation is suicide. With trembling fingers, he rolls a sheet of paper into his typewriter and fills the room with the urgent patter of its keys. Against that background he is safe. He is describing everything that has happened, all that he has seen or heard or been told. The sound of hair being pulled out of a scalp; the smell of burning flesh. He is fixing the material, before time in its mercy will glaze the contours. He is simply reporting.

On the fourth sheet of A4, it runs out. His mind, squeezed of every drop, has suddenly the power to threaten him with an idea.

History is not a river, it is a sea. Perpetually lapping at the shore, retreating, advancing, leaving it ever the same. Our Nadir Shahs, our Hitlers, they are not our past, they are us.

Under our skins we are the same. This flow of moments, this life, has been useless.

He curls up on the floor, and in the gathering darkness of the evening, gives in to his despair.

*

On the third day, Shera says he is going to make a break for it after dark. He has friends at the Bangla Sahib Gurudwara, who can look after them till the danger is over. Fareed agrees to chance it with him.

They make it to the interstate bus stop without incident. The roads are deserted; a solitary rickshaw man, whom they approach for directions is more scared of them than they are of him. Their confidence grows, the city seems under control. But they can still be picked up for violating curfew, so they keep off the main roads, winding their way into the lanes of Kashmiri Gate. It is a mistake, for neither knows the city, and in the lanes there is no curfew: where can the people who live on the streets go? As they circle around in the mesh of streets, they see not a single turban. Increasingly sensitive to the eyes watching them from the corners, from recesses below staircases and balconies, faster and faster they walk, till in response to a collection of small sounds behind them, they break into a headlong run. Immediately, there are cries behind them, people calling, the sound of running feet.

The alley that they run into is blocked by a rickety gate topped with barbed wire. '*Khoon ka badla Khoon...*', it is the same cry for blood, the battle cry of the slum-dwellers, and it comes from so close behind them that, as one body, they push at the gate till a gap appears, and slip through. Inside, though they are silent as the breeze, a sentry steps suddenly out of the shadows of a creeper and points a gun at them.

'Halt!' he shouts in military fashion, 'Who are you?'

When they turn towards him with their hands in the air, he takes several quick steps backwards, and seeing he is so jumpy Fareed speaks in a low, measured tone: 'We have come from Majnu da tilla, Brother. On our way to Bangla Saab. We have lost our way.'

'Where is your pass? You can't come in here without a pass. This is government establishment.' He waves his gun like he is in a movie.

'Brother,' Fareed says, 'there are killers on the street looking for us.'

Outside, on both sides of the rectangular plot they hear voices, raised in confusion.

'Have the two Sardars come in there?' someone shouts over the wall.

The sentry manages to look left and right without taking his eyes off them.

Fareed stares hard at him. 'If they come in here, we'll get you before they get us,' he says taking a step forward. The man gulps twice, but is silent.

'There's no one here,' Shera shouts back in Hindi. They hear the men wandering about, calling to each other, petering off.

'We're not going to harm you,' Fareed says amiably. 'You can put your gun down.'

But the man keeps it pointed at them like it's a talisman against bad spirits. It takes a while before their helplessness gets through to him, and then he does put it down, but still within grab's distance of his hand.

Five signs the Guru has dictated for a Sikh: the kanga, kes, kada, kutcha, kirpan. Of these Fareed has kept just two: the steel bangle, the kada, and the hair, the kes. The rest are symbols, he'd decided. The comb kanga for hygiene, the long drawers of the kutcha for something relevant only if you didn't wear trousers over them, and the kirpan, the sword…why, that was an attitude. Even the two he's kept he hasn't been fanatical about. His kada was often forgotten on the bathroom ledge and his hair has been cut twice in his childhood for reasons of hygiene. Before Bhindranwale, he had often shaped his fledgling beard and moustache with scissors. Without guilt. Yet, when the sentry says that the only way they could get to Bangla Sahib is by cutting their hair, something rebels within him. And as Shera takes the scissors to his hair, he averts his eyes when the heavy locks start to hit the newspaper on the floor.

'The Guru will forgive,' Shera says with a sorry laugh, but Fareed can only shake his head.

If I get out of this alive he thinks, I'll cut my hair. But not now, not here.

Never.

'If one of you still has hair, you'll both be unsafe,' the sentry points out, at which Shera, making a good job with a razor on his cheek, looks over at him and seeing him still determined, says, 'We'll have to split then, you know.'

Fareed shrugs. But they don't part at the opening in the back wall that the sentry leads them to. In silence they cross a square of barren land where hunks of rusted machinery seem to grow out of the ground and at its edge, within sight of the wide road that stretches away into the dark, they stop and, incongruously, impossibly, quarrel.

'Always thought you were too great, didn't you?' Shera says. 'Better than everyone else? So proud today for having kept your hair. Much good it's going to do you when they lop off your head for it.' In a chopping motion he lets his hand brush Fareed's head.

'*Oi!* Don't touch my turban Shere! It's my own head. None of your business what I choose to give it for.'

'Then you're stupider than I thought. A stupid Sardar. Risking your neck for a moment of useless glory. Like on the Peepal tree.'

'It's good of you to remember that at least. I thought you'd clean forgotten. But don't think I've forgotten the beating you gave me at the same Peepal. It's on the scoreboard.' Fareed's narrowed eyes bore into Shera. This is no time for retribution, but he cannot help himself. 'I haven't forgotten Khushwant either. You wanted to marry her. But she turned you down, didn't she?'

'Marry her?' Shera snorts. 'A slut like her? I had my way with her, don't worry. So did others. Many others. Only poor you, you got left with your flag dangling in the air.' And like he's won a decisive victory, he turns and steps rapidly onto the road. With an angry roar, Fareed follows, not knowing what he is going to do, but Shera is running fast, shouting, 'Stay away from me. We've split. Go your own stupid way. Go!' Faster and faster he runs, shouting louder and louder, 'Help, Help. Help!'

Hurtling after him with the single thought of catching him, tasting already the satisfaction of showering his shaven monkey face with blows, Fareed becomes only gradually aware of what Shera is trying to do. Stunned, he stops short. The madness of chasing down the road a clean-shaven man hollering for help! Already a window is flung open, someone is calling from a doorway. He sees Shera stop, and out of breath himself, feels his vulnerability now as a physical chill. He stumbles into a lane, straight into two men running his way. There is a quick flash of a knife that seems to bounce off him and he is struggling to wrest it from the hand that holds it, dimly aware that the second man is running on towards the road crying, 'Sardar! Sardar!'

In the darkness, muffled echoes, running feet, and a string of barking dogs somewhere. He is wrestling with a phantom in a whirlpool of sound. Their feet scrape the ground; their breaths mingle. He has sudden control of the knife, feels it meet the resistance of flesh, thrusts, then twists, then thrusts again. The phantom falls onto him with the weight of a man, a wail dying on its lips. It smells of liquor and soursweet sweat.

Men turn into the lane, their torch beams meeting and parting, crossing each other. The dead man stops them. Over the confusion Shera's voice rules. 'Spread out, spread out,' he says. 'He couldn't have gone far.'

Fareed, thirty feet away, cramped among the ash and cinders under a press-wallah's table, waits with the old woman's shawl wrapped around him. The men cling together in a knot, reluctant to leave the body. Then, as Shera's voice harangues them still, a sudden cry goes up, 'Sardar, Sardar.'

And Shera is running past him with the mob in pursuit. Someone must have shone a torch into his face with its patches of white where his turban and beard have so recently been.

They catch him, and Fareed crouches lower still, trying to shut out the world and Shera's cries. Very quickly it is over. Lighting up, the men starting to flee in various directions, the flames leap out from the still form. It rises suddenly into a sitting posture with its arms in the air, stopping them in their tracks, but then sinks back down at rest, and they run.

23

All Ambika had asked of her father was to live. According to a method, obedient to a regime of medicine, nutrition, sunshine. What a sense of accomplishment when fed and bathed and dressed, he would be settled under the tree with a blanket around his knees and his newspaper on his lap. She remembers it with a stab of pain. Because he couldn't button up his own shirt, he had become a mental and emotional child as well, and his amiable forgiveness of her for this presumption torments her now.

Had he fallen off the berth or launched himself off to save the Sardar boy? In the cavernous house, suddenly silent after the departure of condoling friends and relatives, this is a question she needs to be answered. Sikand leans out to take her hand, but it is Fareed who answers, 'Of course he didn't fall. He told the mob he was sick, didn't he? If he'd fallen, why would he say that? It would be obvious, wouldn't it? I'm sure that had a purpose. So they wouldn't come in or move him aside to find the man hidden under the berth.'

His certainty is a little thing, but how she needs the fledgling mantra that hides in little things. He is right, she says, so right. We have grown grey, Sikand and I, too saturated with fineness, too fine-tuned to the blurred shadows that sharp edges throw. We need the boy to see black and white.

Meanwhile, it is not time, it is not yet time. Sikand is still seeking the right moment. In a sea of misery, we will find our island. She was supposed to consider him, to let him know. But he will not press her. Now is not the time. So he holds her hand, pats it with soft, lifeless pats. The vitality that he has assumed in some blithe moment she would always bestow on him, flickers. Now even she has no power to light the spark in him. We have grown grey, he thinks, Ambika and I...

Fareed's papers, his suitcase left at the gurudwara, must be recovered.

'I will go with him,' Ambika jumps up.

'No wait,' Sikand says. 'Wait a few days.'

Will this city ever again feel safe? He had driven in rescue after Fareed's phone call down heavily patrolled streets, for the army had at last been called out during that night. But even after it has gone back to the barracks, after the curfew has been lifted, when someone says, 'The city is back to normal,' he wonders if it isn't like saying after the tremors have passed into the depths whence they had arisen, that a city flattened by an earthquake is normal.

He tries to revive his little project with Livleen, idiosyncratic as it seems. They look so good together, he tells himself, watching from his typewriter desk as Fareed and Livleen talk softly on the balcony. They have much to talk about, but she looks so sad, and Fareed seems not to take her in at all.

Livleen has come from her work in the relief camps, where she spends most of her time filling in application forms for the riot victims, multiple copies that will secure Rs. this much for a house burnt, Rs. that much for a husband. Her black diary is packed with lengthy accounts of the violence in her small, antlike handwriting and bulges with loose papers, letters and eyewitness statements in all languages. Her record of black deeds, she calls it; it helps the victims share their trauma. But that is not all, for she and her group are also steadily making lists of the people responsible—names, descriptions, anything that they can come by.

Her pen is out, and pushing back her hair in irritation, adjusting herself like a secretary, she is already scribbling into her diary.

'I tell you I don't know anyone,' says Fareed. 'They were crowds, mobs wanting blood. If they had been people with names and faces, you think I would have run?'

'Just describe them, the faces. Their language, what they said, anything. Don't worry about who they were.' She waits with poised pen.

'Why don't you understand? I didn't see anyone. I only felt them, smelt them. We were actors in a drama together and I was too bloody busy playing my part to see what anyone else was doing. And for that drama, I do not have the words.'

'Try to find the words, Fareed, please. I will help you. It is a story that must be told...'

'To whom? To whom, Livleen? I am not a story. What happened is me, those moments have become my blood and bone, like the food I've eaten, the milk I've drunk. Your story, it is me. Take my photograph and be done with it. See your story there, if you have the eyes.'

She is giving up, turning despairingly to Sikand who sits, crouched over the typewriter desk, cut off from them by the geometry of space, but enclosed with them in its geography. He cannot help her, nor can he stop the words that are tumbling out of the boy.

'If you want to help them, all these victims in the camps, get them things they need, food, clothing, money. And then leave them alone. Filling up your diary is not what they went through hell for, Livleen. Hell is private. Hell is dark and solitary. You can't go in there with them.'

'But justice? How can this have happened, and no one suffers? Who is going to get justice for them?'

'Justice will not return to anyone what is lost. The police, the courts, they should have been there when people were burnt alive in the streets. Now justice is only a sop for people like you, like Sikand. Not for them.'

Sikand comes out to the balcony. 'Justice is a substitute for revenge, Fareed. If the courts don't give it the victims will have to take it themselves. So the cycle of blood for blood could well go on.'

His words silence the boy, but he is weary of them himself. Each word seems to have its own blurred shadow, shadows that throw greyer shadows, till the whole is imbued with unfathomable grey.

*

It is a crisp November day when Ambika and Fareed at last drive to the gurudwara for Fareed's luggage.

He is in a fever of communication. 'In my village two men, brothers called, don't laugh, Santa and Banta. They have their fields next to the cremation ground, that's why no one will marry them.'

'Why? Surely their wives would live at home, not in their fields by the cremation grounds.' She is half serious, not knowing how to handle his frivolity.

'It isn't, how you call it, auspicious. Yes, not auspicious,' he replies solemnly.

In spite of herself, she giggles.

'One night,' he continues, 'when the wheat was ripening and they were sleeping guard in the fields, two string cots side by side on a moonless night, two spirits came from the cremation ground next door and sat on their chests. One spirit on each chest, one on Santa's, one on Banta's, you understand? Each thinks it's his brother. Santa? Yes. Are you sitting on my chest? No, Banta…Silence. Then: Banta? Yes. Are you sitting on my chest? No, Santa. So then they both realized that it was spirits sitting on their chests, and started to fight them. I have an axe under my pillow, one said, and the other, I have a sickle, and the spirits were scared and were trying to run away. But both the brothers held on fast, would not let go. When we go back to the village in the morning and tell the people our story, how will they believe us? So both the spirits must give something of themselves to show to the villagers in the morning. When the spirits realized that was the only way, one gave a hair of its beard and another a piece of its fingernail, and the brothers, satisfied, went back to sleep.'

They are at the gurudwara, and her 'Then what happened?' is left in the air. He gets out of the car and is lost to view behind the semi-constructed building.

She leans back into the warmth of the seat and, with eyes half closed, loses herself in the rainbow dance of the sunlight trapped in her lashes. The sound of metal ringing against stone floats down to her, lazy, unhurried, but when she looks up to see the workers against the dome, their movements seem fast and full.

He is back. The Bhaiji has gone out and Fareed's luggage is locked up in his room. It is pointless to drive back, better to wait, and she remembers a park from her University days that may still be unspoilt.

She prefers the bench and he the grass so he's stretched out at her feet.

'What happened then, to Santa and to Banta?'

'*Hmm,* well Santa and Banta came back next morning and made a great hue and cry in the village about how they'd scared the spirits away. But of course, no one would believe them. No one at all. So they opened out their fists, they'd kept them tightly clenched all night, and said See! But there was nothing there. All the villagers laughed at them, for everyone knows that people who sleep by cremation grounds can go quite mad. Not that it bothered Santa and Banta. Spirits are invisible they said, and here's one invisible hair of a beard, and here's one invisible piece of fingernail!'

'Tell me more,' she says.

'It's finished.'

'Another story, then.'

'I don't know any stories,' he says looking solemnly up at her.

'These are the truths of my village. How can I tell you more if you will call them stories?'

'Okay, tell me truths then. I am ravenous for truths.'

*

And at the end of this long, late season, comes want.

In Amritsar, early in this *annus horribilis*, Shivi had warned, 'I know the Sikhs, Sikand. We are a lot of Don Quixote Singhs. Looking for dragons to slay.'

Bhindranwale discovered the Nirankaris, but they were mere windmills. A few tilted their way but most saw them for what they were: edifices to harness the prevailing winds.

Yet History, Sikand knows, will find its agents: fools and seers alike are grist. And here at last, made flesh from wisps of myth, from fire and blood and shared memories of fear and pain, were dragons.

The real thing.

But now there is no one who wants to listen to Sikand. And in his failure, he sees the history that he makes as mere fancy, the servant of a fractured memory. No one wants to read what he has to say. He must dip for the necessities of life, into what his mother had insisted on referring to as her 'Capital'. He will never be free of her now.

*

Ambika too discovers want.

During the days she runs about with Fareed's papers. He follows in her wake, bemused by the drone of courts and offices, taking fright at the slightest indifference.

In the evenings, rich with the promise of winter, she dresses high and drives with him to rediscover the fairgrounds of the city. On a grassy patch she stumbles and his hands reach to steady her, his touch searing her as she arches into him, leaving as it were a scorched stain against her back and thighs.

And in the night her face is forever changed, the contours running like watercolour. Alone in her bed, she stretches out her parched body, welcoming the want.

But, 'Why now? Why?" she thinks, 'Why this boy?'

Fareed is troubled by dreams of Ambika…

Her lawyer's black coat billows behind her as she flies over mountains. A babu with oily hair slavers all over the floor as he tries to touch her feet. Another night she unwinds ever so slowly a tiara, the kind Miss India wears, out of her hair. And one night on the pillow, as he raises his head on his elbow to look down at her, her face in its cloud of hair seems forever changed. The world, which has been holding its breath outside their window, starts once again to lap at the door. 'Shoot!' he says to the firing squad that suddenly appears, without making so much as a move to cover his nakedness.

*

'Why didn't you ever marry?' he asks Sikand at breakfast.

'There didn't seem much need. Until…'

'Until now?'

'Oh no. One gets too old for it, by and by. It's time for you to marry, not me.'

'Not me, either. I couldn't burden some poor woman with me.'

'You know Fareed,' Sikand says, picking up his fork and knife, 'I think Livleen, she really likes you.'

'Forget it, that's not possible. What would a Jat like me do with someone like Livleen?'

'Why do you think she's trying to go to the States too? And you won't remain a Jat forever. Not when you're out there.'

Fareed drops his fork and starts to eat his omelette with his fingers. 'What's wrong with being a Jat? *Hnnh*?' he says between bites. 'What the bhhen di is wrong with it?'

'Nothing. Nothing at all. Why get excited? You know I didn't mean it like that.'

That is what Sikand always does. Use words and then back out.

'If Livleen can like a Jat like me, then why not Ambika, *hnnh*?' says Fareed. He smiles grimly as Sikand's fork and knife clatter on to his plate.

Fork *and* knife, the bastard!

*

The black mood remains with Fareed for days. On the bus to the passport office he shouts at the conductor, 'Why are you staring at me? Haven't you seen a Sardar before?'

The driver offloads him, and he walks around in circles, not asking for directions, till he spots another Sardar to show him the way. Once there, he waits for five minutes, and when no one attends him, he walks out in disgust.

He sticks his fingers in his ears when Livleen screams: 'Two per cent, two per cent.' That's what all the papers say is the percentage of the Sikhs to the rest of the country.

'In America you won't even be that,' he smirks at her.

'I'd rather be zero per cent than be told that all my life!'

'You are,' he says, without knowing why.

At the US Embassy he is tongue-tied before the Visa Counsellor and his visa is refused. For three days Ambika battles, and when at last she hands him his passport open at the page with the US visa, he holds it to his nose to smell the new gummy smell of it and then falls on his knees before her. When she tries to help him rise, he takes her small hand and covers it with tears.

It is a turning point. He lies awake the whole night to avoid his dreams.

At India Gate, glowing like mother of pearl against a pink

sky, he buys all the gas balloons from an old woman who wears a coarse brown shawl of the kind they wear in his village. Ambika clutches them all the way to the fountains.

'A woman in my village made a rag doll,' he says. 'She put on its head all the guilt that was tormenting her, and threw it into the well. Within a year their well went dry.'

When it's time to go home Ambika opens her fingers and they watch the white dots of the balloons against the sky till they are lost to sight.

No rag dolls for me. I can't dry up my well; I've only just begun. With every breath I create myself. With every word I represent myself. With every act I realize myself.

When all the preparations are done and it is time to buy his ticket, Fareed stops Sikand in his tracks. 'I'm not going to America. I've decided to return to my village.'

'You know it will never work. One side or the other will get to you. You'll begin all over again.'

'No, Sikand,' Fareed shakes his head. 'I have caught the thing. The malign-benign. I realized it was inside me all the time.'

On one crazed night in a street of barking dogs I caught it. I stabbed it to death. I felt its dead weight on me for one last time and then I pushed it off me forever. Or maybe, maybe it happened some other way, maybe that was another dream.

'What are you going to do then?'

'I'm going to put the green back into my land again.'

*

'But the girl is no more,' Sikand could have said, if the granthi's words weren't with him still: *'Do you think it would be wise for me to tell him?'*

No it is not wise. He would find out soon enough that new beginnings inter the old.

So Livleen flies alone to the land of opportunity where it

doesn't matter if she is no more, she says, than a decimal point. At the airport she hands Sikand her black diary. 'That's history, if you ever want to use it.'

Next, Sikand sees off Fareed at the bus terminus, and returning, imagines himself unblinkered.

He can predict again.

The Sikhs will throw off the malign-benign. The plain of La Mancha shall be green again. It is a time for healing.

But a bright new hoarding is being put up on the roadside for the forthcoming election. 'Do you trust your taxi-driver?' it says. Elect the Congress Party, which alone will save you from the Sikhs, it means.

Let us kill the goose for now. Healing is for later.

He stumbles into the guest-room where stacked against the wall are the pieces of the bed, the sofa that Kirat Singh had built. Going down on his knees he starts to put it together again. Those elephantine legs, that Taj Mahal back. He is no carpenter but he will discover the process.

After all, it's only a reversal of the act of destroying it.

Bit by bit, with eyes shut in concentration, he starts to play it back in slow motion.